Han bent forward to scoop up the pot, and the Barabel female let out a roar. "Cheater! He's got a skifter! No one can be so lucky!"

Han sat back and looked at her, outraged. He had cheated at sabacc plenty of times, using skifters—cards that would assume different values when their edges were tapped—but this time he had won fair and square. Shaking his head vehemently, he said, "I wasn't cheating. You were just outplayed, sister!" When Han reached for the last of the card-chips, the Barabel roared again. One armored, sharp-taloned hand came sweeping down in a mighty blow that smashed the table in two, sending board, credits, and card-chips flying. Snarling, she advanced on Han. "I'm going to bite your head off, cheater!"

Han took one look at her gaping maw, realized that she was big enough to make good on her threat, and went for his blaster. His right hand dropped down to his thigh with blurring speed, then the well-worn grip was there, nestled against his palm.

His hand, still moving with extraordinary speed, started back up as he began his draw—

—only to stop short when the blaster hung up in the holster!

Han had barely a second to realize that the blaster's front sight, mounted on the end of the barrel, was caught at the bottom of his holster. He tugged, trying to free his weapon.

The Barabel leaped for him. Han jumped back, but not far enough. . . .

The sensational *Star Wars* series published by
Bantam Books and available from all good bookshops

The *Empire* Trilogy by Timothy Zahn
Heir to the Empire • Dark Force Rising
The Last Command

The *Jedi Academy* Trilogy by Kevin J. Anderson
Jedi Search • Dark Apprentice
Champions of the Force

The Truce at Bakura
by Kathy Tyers

The Courtship of Princess Leia
by Dave Wolverton

The *Corellian* Trilogy by Roger MacBride Allen
Ambush at Corellia • Assault at Selonia
Showdown at Centerpoint

The *Cantina* Trilogy edited by Kevin J. Anderson
Tales from the Mos Eisley Cantina
Tales from Jabba's Palace • Tales of the Bounty Hunters

The Crystal Star
by Vonda McIntyre

The *X-Wing* Series by Michael Stackpole
Rogue Squadron • Wedge's Gamble
The Krytos Trap • The Bacta War

The *Black Fleet Crisis* Trilogy by Michael P. Kube-McDowell
Before the Storm • Shield of Lies
Tyrant's Test

Children of the Jedi
by Barbara Hambly

Darksaber
by Kevin J. Anderson

Shadows of the Empire
by Steve Perry

The *Han Solo* Trilogy by A. C. Crispin
The Paradise Snare • The Hutt Gambit
Rebel Dawn

and in hardcover

The Illustrated Star Wars Universe
by Kevin J. Anderson & Ralph McQuarrie

The New Rebellion
by Kristine Kathryn Rusch

Planet of Twilight
by Barbara Hambly

STAR WARS®

THE HUTT GAMBIT

A. C. Crispin

BANTAM BOOKS

TORONTO · NEW YORK · LONDON · SYDNEY · AUCKLAND

THE HUTT GAMBIT
A BANTAM BOOK : 0 553 50547 5

First publication in Great Britain

PRINTING HISTORY
Bantam edition published 1997

Set in New Caledonia by Berryville Graphics

Bantam Books are published by Transworld Publishers Ltd,
61–63 Uxbridge Road, London W5 5SA,
in Australia by Transworld Publishers (Australia) Pty Ltd,
15–25 Helles Avenue, Moorebank, NSW 2170,
and in New Zealand by Transworld Publishers (NZ) Ltd,
3 William Pickering Drive, Albany, Auckland.

Reproduced, printed and bound in Great Britain by
Cox & Wyman Ltd, Reading, Berkshire.

This book is dedicated to my good friend and fellow writer, Kevin J. Anderson, with thanks for all the help and encouragement.

ACKNOWLEDGMENTS

As I noted in my previous *Star Wars* novel, *The Paradise Snare*, being invited to write in the *Star Wars* universe is rather like being adopted into a big family. Writers and fans share information, anecdotes, and stories of how much fun they've had in the *Star Wars* universe over the years.

I feel privileged to be the first writer to produce a book using the expanded information and visuals provided by the new special editions of *Star Wars*, *The Empire Strikes Back*, and *Return of the Jedi*. It was very helpful seeing the newly restored films with their added footage—especially the scene where Jabba moves under his own steam.

With the caveat that all mistakes herein are my own, I'd like to thank the following people for their help:

First and foremost, my friend Steve Osmanski, who helped me with military, strategic, and technical information throughout, patiently answering my hundreds of questions, reviewing the battle scenes numerous times.

My friend Mary Frey, Steve's wife, for allowing me to "borrow" her husband for hours on end as we planned battles and went over strategies.

Tim O'Brien, expert on every aspect of the Imperial military, who answered questions and gave patient advice.

(Steve and Tim O'Brien designed the battle plan for the Battle of Nar Shaddaa, and I am forever indebted to both of them for their expertise in *Star Wars* battlegaming.)

Bill, Peter, and Paul, of West End Games, who answered my endless questions about the *Star Wars* universe and its denizens.

Michael Capobianco, closet *Star Wars* fan, who used his experience as SFWA President to help me plot all the Hutt intrigues. Michael also kept my antique computers functioning.

Pat LoBrutto and Tom Dupree, my editors on this book. Thank you, gentlemen, for all the help, and for being patient and understanding. Thanks also to Evelyn Cainto, who keeps things running smoothly in the Bantam *Star Wars* department.

Nancy Wiesenfeld, top-notch copy editor.

Sue Rostoni of Lucasfilm for her painstaking review of the book.

My fellow *Star Wars* authors, who provided help, advice, and generously "lent" their characters so I could use them in this book: Vonda N. McIntyre, Michael A. Stackpole, Kristine Kathryn Rusch, and Kevin J. Anderson.

You, the *Star Wars* fans, for taking such an interest in this project from the very beginning.

And, as always, George Lucas, for starting it all, twenty years ago.

May the Force be with you!

THE HUTT GAMBIT

Chapter One:

New Friends, Old Enemies

Han Solo, former Imperial officer, sat despondently at a sticky table in a dingy bar on Devaron, sipping an inferior Alderaanian ale and wishing he were alone. Not that he minded the other denizens of the bar—horned Devish males and furry Devish females, plus a smattering of nonhumans from other worlds. Han was used to aliens; he'd grown up with them aboard *Trader's Luck,* a large trading ship that wandered the spacelanes of the galaxy. By the time he was ten, Han had been able to speak and understand half a dozen nonhuman languages.

No, it wasn't the aliens around him. It was the alien *beside* him. Han took a swig of his ale, grimaced at the sour taste, then glanced sidelong at the cause of all his troubles.

The huge, hairy being gazed back at him with concerned blue eyes. Han sighed heavily. *If only he'd go home!* But the Wookiee—Chew-something—utterly refused to go home to Kashyyyk, despite Han's repeated urging. The alien claimed he owed something called a "life debt" to former Imperial Lieutenant Han Solo.

Life debt . . . great. Just what I need, Han thought bitterly. *A big furry nursemaid trailing after me, giving me advice, fussing over me if I drink too much, telling me he's gonna take care of me. Great. Just great.*

Han scowled into his ale, and the pale, watery brew reflected his countenance back at him, distorting his features until he appeared nearly as alien as the Wookiee. What *was* his name? Chew-something. The Wookiee had told him, but Han wasn't good at pronouncing Wookiee, even though he understood it perfectly.

Besides, he didn't *want* to learn this particular Wookiee's name. If he learned his name, he'd likely never get rid of his hairy shadow.

Han rubbed a hand over his face blearily, feeling several days' stubble. Ever since he'd been kicked out of the service, he kept forgetting to shave. When he'd been a cadet, then a junior lieutenant, then a full lieutenant, he'd been meticulous with his grooming, the way an officer and a gentleman should be . . . but now . . . what difference did it make?

Han raised his glass in a slightly unsteady hand and gulped the sour ale. He put the empty tankard down, and glanced around the bar for the server. *Need another drink. One more, and I'll feel much better. Just one more . . .*

The Wookiee moaned quietly. Han's scowl deepened. "Keep your opinions to yourself, hairball," he snarled. "I'll know when I've had enough. Th' las' thing I need is a Wookiee playin' nursemaid for me."

The Wookiee—Chewbacca, that was it—growled softly,

his blue eyes shadowed with concern. Han's lip curled. "I'm perfectly capable of lookin' after myself, and don't you forget it. Just 'cause I saved your furry butt from being vaporized doesn't mean you owe me a thing. I tol' you before—I owed a Wookiee, long ago. Owed her my life, coupla times over. So I saved you, 'cause I owed her."

Chewbacca made a sound halfway between a moan and a snarl. Han shook his head. "No, that means you don't owe me a thing, don't you get it? I owed her, but I couldn't repay her. So I helped you out, which makes us even . . . square. So will you *please* take those credits I gave you, and go back to Kashyyyk? You ain't doin' me any favors staying here, hairball. I need you like I need a blaster burn on my butt."

Affronted, Chewbacca drew himself up to his full Wookiee height. He growled low in his throat.

"Yeah, I know I tossed away my career and my livin' that day on Coruscant when I stopped Commander Nyklas from shootin' you. I *hate* slavery, and watchin' Nyklas use a force whip ain't a particularly appetizing sight. I know Wookiees, you see. When I was growin' up, a Wookiee was my best friend. I knew you were gonna turn on Nyklas before you did it—just like I knew Nyklas would go for his blaster. I couldn't just stand there and watch him blast you. But don't go tryin' to make me out as some kinda hero, Chewie. I don't need a partner, and I don't *want* a friend. My name says it all, pal. Solo."

Han jerked a thumb at his chest. "Solo. In my language, that means me, alone, by myself. Get it? That's the way it is, and that's the way I like it. So . . . no offense, Chewie, but why don't you just *scram*. As in, *go away. Permanently.*"

Chewie stared at Han for a long moment, then he snorted disdainfully, turned, and strode out of the bar.

Han wondered disinterestedly if he'd actually managed

to convince the big hairy oaf to leave for good. If he had, that was reason for celebration. For another drink . . .

As he glanced around the bar, he saw that over in the corner several patrons were gathering around a table. A sabacc game was forming. Han wondered whether he ought to try to get in on it. Mentally he reviewed the contents of his credit pouch, and decided that might not be a bad idea. He usually had very good luck at sabacc, and every credit counted, these days.

These days . . .

Han sighed. How long had it been since that fateful day when he'd been sent to assist Commander Nyklas with the crew of Wookiee laborers assigned to complete a new wing on the Imperial Hall of Heroes? He counted, grimacing as he realized that he'd lost days on end in there . . . days probably spent in a dark haze of ale and bitter recrimination. In two days it would be two months.

Han's mouth tightened and he ran an unsteady hand through his unruly brown hair. For the past five years he'd kept it cut short in approved military fashion, but now it was growing out, getting almost shaggy. He had a sudden, sharp mental image of himself as he'd been then—immaculately groomed, insignia polished, boots shining—and glanced down at himself.

What a contrast between then and now. He was wearing a stained, grayish shirt that had once been white, a stained, gray neo-leather jacket he'd purchased secondhand, and dark blue military-style trousers with his Corellian bloodstripe running down the outside seam. Only the boots were the same. They were custom-fitted when each cadet was commissioned, so the Empire hadn't wanted them back. Han had been commissioned just a little over eight months ago, and no junior lieutenant had ever been prouder of his rank—or of those shining boots.

The boots were scuffed now, and worn. Han's lip curled

as he regarded them. Scuffed and worn by life, all the spit
and polish gone . . . that about described *him* these days,
too.

In a moment of painful honesty, Han admitted that he
probably wouldn't have been able to stay in the Imperial
Navy even if he hadn't gotten himself cashiered for rescu-
ing and freeing Chewbacca. He'd started his career with
high hopes, but disillusionment had quickly set in. The
prejudice against nonhumans had been hard to take for
someone raised the way Han had been, but he'd bitten his
tongue and remained silent. But the endless, silly bureaucratic regs, the blind stupidity of so many of the officers—
Han had already begun to wonder how long he'd be able to
take it.

But he'd never figured on a dishonorable discharge, loss
of pension and back pay, and—worst of all—being blacklisted as a pilot. They hadn't taken his license, but Han had
quickly discovered that no legitimate company would hire
him. He'd tramped the permacrete of Coruscant for weeks,
in between alcoholic binges, looking for work—and found
all respectable doors closed to him.

Then, one night, as he'd tavern-hopped in a section of
the planet-wide city near the alien ghetto, a huge, furred
shadow had flowed out of the deeper shadows of an alley
and confronted Han.

For long moments Han's ale-fogged brain hadn't even
recognized the Wookiee as the one he'd saved. It was only
when Chewbacca began speaking, thanking Han for saving
his life and freeing him from slavery, that Han had realized
who he was. Chewie had been quite direct—his people
didn't mince words. He, Chewbacca, had sworn a life debt
to Han Solo. Where Han went, from that day forward, he
would go, too.

And he had.

When Han had finally gotten them passage off Coruscant, piloting a ship with a load of contraband to Tralus (the cargo had been magnetically sealed into the hold—Han hadn't had the equipment or the energy to break in and find out exactly what it was he was smuggling), Chewbacca had gone with him. On the week-long voyage, Han began teaching the Wookiee the rudiments of piloting. Space travel was boring, and at least that gave him something to do besides brood over lost futures . . .

Once on Tralus, he turned over his ship and cargo, then went looking for another assignment. He wound up at Truthful Toryl's Used Spaceship Lot, asking the Duros for work. Toryl was an old acquaintance, and he knew Han was a reliable and expert pilot.

The Empire was tightening its grip all the time, taking away the rights of its worlds as well as its citizens. Duro had a shipbuilding industry nearly equal to that of Corellia, but they had recently been prohibited by Imperial directive from placing weapons systems in their ships. Han's clandestine cargo proved to be a shipment of components useful in outfitting ships with weapons.

By the time they reached Duro, Chewie was becoming a fair copilot and gunner. Han hoped that teaching the Wookiee these skills would make it easier to get rid of him on some world. If he knew the Wookiee could hire on as a skilled pilot or copilot, he wouldn't hesitate to dump him in some port and then lift ship—or so Han told himself.

Once on Duro, Han drank up some of the profits from his mission, while waiting to be contacted for another piloting job. His patience was rewarded one day when a Sullustan approached him and offered him good pay to take a ship from Duro, avoiding any Imperial ports of call, a third of the way across the galaxy to Kothlis, a Bothan colony world.

Of course the sleek, swift little craft was "hot"—stolen from some wealthy owner's landing pad. Han had to remind himself that he was no longer in the business of keeping the law—he was in the business of breaking it.

So he set his jaw and piloted the stolen vessel to her new home on Kothlis. Then he went looking for another assignment, and eventually found one. On the surface, this job seemed legit. Han was to ferry a large nalargon from Kothlis to Devaron.

Han had never heard of a nalargon before, which wasn't surprising, as his exposure to music had been limited. A nalargon proved to be a very large instrument that was operated by a keyboard and foot pedals. Pipes and subharmonic resonance generators produced sound on many wave bands. The instruments were in demand for the jizz craze that was sweeping the galaxy.

Accordingly, the huge instrument was brought aboard the ship Han had been assigned, bolted to the deck, then left sealed in the cargo compartment.

Han investigated the instrument once he and Chewie were safely in hyperspace. He tapped it, poked and nudged it, turned it on, then tried pressing the keys and pedals. No sound, except the sound he made trying to make it work.

But his tappings proved it wasn't hollow. Han sat back on his heels, gazing at the huge instrument. The thing was obviously a dummy—a shell, with something inside. What?

Han knew from his stint in the Imperial Navy that Devaron was a world in turmoil. Not long ago a group of rebels had risen against the Imperial governor, demanding independence from the Empire. Han's lip curled disdainfully. Stupid fools, thinking they had a chance against the Empire. Seven hundred of the rebels had been captured when the ancient holy city of Montellian Serat had been overrun by Imperial troops a few months ago. They'd been summarily executed without trial, killed without mercy. The remaining rebels were still hiding out in the hills, holding out, attacking commando fashion, but Han knew it was only a matter of time before they, too, would be ground beneath Palpatine's heel, their world rigidly controlled by the Empire, as so many other worlds had been.

Eyeing the nalargon, Han made some mental calculations based on the instrument being hollow. Yeah . . . a short-bore mobile laser cannon would just about fit inside that shell. The weapon could be mounted on the back of a landskimmer, and was capable of blowing small targets—a building, or a short-range Imperial fighter—into very small pieces.

It could also be blast rifles, of course. Ten or fifteen would fit inside there, if they were cleverly packed.

Whatever was inside the nalargon, Han had a bad feeling about the assignment he'd taken on. He resolved to land the ship, then walk away from it and not go back. He had fake landing codes, provided by the Bothans. He'd use them, and then get away as quickly as he could . . .

He'd landed yesterday, and for all Han knew, the ship was still sitting on the field with the nalargon in her cargo hold. But he had a hunch that the rebels on Devaron hadn't wasted any time . . .

Han shook his head a little blearily, half wishing he hadn't had that last ale. The sour taste was still in his mouth, and his head buzzed. Han looked from side to side, testingly, and the room stayed still. Good. He wasn't too drunk to play sabacc and win. *Let's get on with it, Solo. Every little credit helps* . . .

The smuggler rose to his feet and strolled quite steadily across the room to the table. "Greetings, gentles," he said, in Basic. "Got room for another player?"

The dealer, a Devaronian male, turned his head with its waxed, polished horns to regard Han questioningly. He must have decided that the newcomer looked okay, because he shrugged and gestured at the vacant seat. "Welcome, Pilot. As long as your credits hold out, so does your welcome." He grinned, showing sharp, feral teeth.

Han nodded, then slid into the seat.

He'd first learned to play sabacc when he was about fourteen. Han anted credits into the high-stakes pot, the "sabacc pot," then picked up the two cards he'd been dealt and scanned them, all the while covertly studying his opponents. When the bet for the "hand pot" came round to him, he tossed the requisite number of credit disks into that pot, too.

Han had the six of staves and the Queen of Air and Darkness, but at any moment the dealer could push a button, and all the card-values would change. Han eyed his opponents: a tiny Sullustan, a furry Devaronian female, the Devaronian male dealer, and a huge female Barabel, a reptiloid being from Barab One. This was the first time Han had seen a Barabel up close, and she was an impressive sight. Over two meters tall, covered with tough black scales that would repel even a stun blast, the Barabel had a mouthful of daggerlike teeth and a clublike tail that reportedly made them nasty customers in a fight. This one, who had introduced herself as Shallamar, seemed peaceful enough, though. She picked up the newest card-chip she'd been dealt and studied her hand intently through narrowed slit-pupiled eyes.

The object of sabacc was to get cards to equal, but not exceed, the number twenty-three—either positive or negative. In case of a tie, positive totals beat negatives.

At the moment the cards in Han's hand had a numerical value of positive four. The Queen of Air and Darkness had a value of minus two. Han could throw that card into the interference field, which would "freeze" its value, then hope to get the Idiot and a card with the face value of three. Since the Idiot had a value of zero, this would give him an "Idiot's Array," which would beat even a pure sabacc . . . that is, cards whose value added up to either positive or negative twenty-three.

As Han hesitated, gazing at his Queen, the card-chips rippled and altered. His Queen was now the Master of sabers. The six of sabers had become the eight of flasks. His total was . . . positive twenty-two. He waited while the other players examined their card-chips. The Barabel, the female Devaronian, and the dealer threw in their hands disgustedly—they'd "bombed out" by exceeding twenty-three.

The Sullustan raised the bet, which Han matched and raised. "I call," the little alien said, laying down his card-chips with a flourish. "Twenty," he announced.

Han grinned and put down his own. "Twenty-two," he announced casually, laying down his own hand. "Afraid that hand pot's mine, pal."

The other players grumbled a bit as he scooped up their money. The Barabel female hissed and gave him a look that could have melted titanium, but said nothing.

The Sullustan took the next hand, and the Devaronian dealer the one that followed. Han eyed the growing sabacc pot, and decided to try to go for the bigger payoff.

They continued to play for several more hands. Han won the hand pot again, but nobody had gotten the sabacc pot. Han tossed the three of coins and the Idiot into the interference field, and his luck held—the very next change of cards left him holding the two of flasks.

"Idiot's Array . . ." Han said casually, tossing the two down next to the other two cards in the interference field. "The sabacc pot is mine, ladies and gentlemen . . ."

He bent forward to scoop up the pot, and the Barabel female let out a roar. "Cheater! He's got a skifter, he must have! No one can be so lucky!"

Han sat back and stared at her, outraged. He had cheated at sabacc plenty of times, using skifters—cards that would assume different values when their edges were tapped—and in other ways. But this time he'd won fair and square!

"You can take your accusations and stick 'em in your ear!" the Corellian burst out indignantly. Of course the Barabel didn't have any visible ears, but his meaning wasn't lost on her. Dropping his right hand down to his thigh, he silently unsnapped the strap on the top of his holster. Shaking his head vehemently, he added, "I wasn't cheating! You were just outplayed, sister!"

Left-handed, Han reached across the table, grabbed a fistful of credits, and stuffed them into his pocket. Nobody moved or spoke, so he reached for the remaining handful. In a blur of reddish fur, the Devaronian female's hand shot out, grabbed his wrist, and pinned it to the table. "Maybe Shallamar is right," she said, in strongly accented Basic. "We should search him to make sure."

Han glared at her. "Take your hands off me," he said very quietly. "Or I'll make you really sorry."

Something in his eyes and voice must have impressed her, because she let go of him and stepped back.

"Coward!" Shallamar snarled at the Devaronian. "He's just a puny human!"

The Devaronian shook her head and backed away, indicating that she wanted no further part in the conflict.

Han smiled smugly as he reached for the last of the card-chips. Seeing that smile, the Barabel roared again. One armored, sharp-taloned hand came sweeping down in a mighty blow that smashed the table in two, sending board, credits, and card-chips flying. Snarling, she advanced on Han. "No! I'm going to bite your head off, cheater! We'll see how good you are *then*!"

Han took one look at her gaping maw, realizing that she was big enough to make good on her threat, and went for his blaster. His right hand dropped to his thigh with blurring speed, then the well-worn grip was there, nestled against his palm.

His hand, still moving with extraordinary speed, started back up as he began his draw—

—only to stop short when the blaster hung up in the holster!

Han had barely a second to realize that the blaster's front sight, mounted on the end of the barrel, was caught at the bottom of his holster. He tugged, trying to free his weapon.

The Barabel leaped for him. Han jumped back, but not far enough. Shallamar's huge, sharp talons grabbed the front of his jacket, slashing the tough material as though it were tissue. Still yanking at his trapped blaster, Han was hauled toward the Barabel's wide-open mouth so fast his vision blurred. He let out a choked gasp as a blast of hot, reeking reptiloid breath engulfed him.

Suddenly Han glimpsed a blur of brownish tan at the corner of his vision, just as a huge roar nearly deafened him. A long, furred arm snaked around Shallamar's neck, jerking her back, away from Han.

"Chewie!" Han yelled. He'd never been so glad to see someone in his life.

The Barabel roared back at the Wookiee, dropping the Corellian as she swung around to grapple with her attacker.

"Hold her for a second, Chewie!" Han yelled, yanking at the bottom of his holster as he twisted the grip of his blaster. At last! He pulled it up and sighted at the Barabel as she wrestled with the Wookiee, but he couldn't get a clear shot.

The two huge beings, snarling and hissing, rampaged across the room, knocking over tables and chairs. The other sabacc players and denizens of the bar scattered before the fray, screaming advice and curses in multiple languages.

The Sullustan sabacc player dropped his hand to his own

blaster, but when he saw that Han was now armed, he turned and flung himself behind the bar.

Shallamar and Chewbacca swayed back and forth, locked in a grim parody of a loving embrace, each testing the other's strength, trying to get each other off balance. "Chewie, c'mon!" Han yelled. "Let's get outta here!"

Chewbacca and Shallamar whirled in a blur of brown fur and black scales, then Shallamar lowered her head and snapped at the Wookiee's arm. Her needle-sharp teeth sheared off a chunk of fur and meat. The Wookiee roared in agony and, with a burst of strength, grabbed the Barabel's arm and slung her around with dizzying speed, so fast that her feet slid out from under her. As she went down, Chewie also grabbed her tail, swinging her so hard she was airborne.

With a final howl of triumph, Chewbacca released his grip and sent the huge reptiloid flying across the room, while sentients scattered to avoid her trajectory. Shallamar landed on her back amid a ruin of chairs, tables, and sabacc card-chips.

Stun won't work, don't want to kill—a jumble of thoughts raced through Han's mind as he thumbed the setting on the blaster, aimed, and fired at the dazed Shallamar, hitting her at half force just below one huge knee joint. She hissed in pain and sagged back, black scales smoking and steaming.

"Chewie, c'mon!" Han yelled, snapping off a stun shot at the sabacc dealer, who was aiming a blaster at the Wookiee. The Devaronian went down without a sound. Chewie, dripping blood, was right behind Han as they raced for the exit, knocking over chairs and tables.

The tavern's owner, a Devaronian female, blocked his way, screaming curses and threats, but Han slapped her aside with the barrel of his blaster and kept running. He slammed the door with his shoulder, then bounced off. Locked!

Swearing in six nonhuman languages, Han thumbed the indicator on his weapon up to its highest power, and blasted the door. The proprietor howled in protest, but the Corellian and the Wookiee were already gone.

Han and Chewbacca pelted down the squalid alley, then swung out onto the street with its rustic-looking buildings made of blue native wood and stuccoed permacrete. A chilly breeze made the Corellian shiver. It was early spring here on Devaron's south polar continent.

Han quickly holstered his blaster as he dropped his pace to a fast walk. "How's the arm, pal?"

Chewie groaned, ending in a snarl. Han glanced down at the damage. "Well, it was your choice to come back," he pointed out. "Not that I'm sorry you did, mind you. I . . . I want to say . . . uh . . . thanks for saving my rear."

The Wookiee made an interrogatory sound. Han shrugged. "Well, sure, I guess . . ." he mumbled. "I've never had a partner before, but . . . yeah, why not? It can get kinda boring on long space flights without someone to talk to, I guess."

Chewie rumbled with satisfaction, despite his pain. "Don't push your luck," Han said dryly. "Listen, we got to get that arm seen to. There's a med droid's clinic across the street. Let's go."

An hour later the two were back on the street. Chewie's arm, after a bacta treatment, was sheathed in a protective bandage, but the med droid had assured them that Wookiees were quick healers.

The Wookiee had just finished commenting that he was hungry, when Han heard a soft call from the shelter of a nearby doorway. "Pilot Solo . . ."

Han stopped in his tracks and looked over to find a Duros male beckoning to him. He glanced from side to side, but the Devaronian street scene was quiet and peaceful. This section near the town square was reserved for pedestrian traffic. "Yeah?" he replied, in a low voice.

The blue-skinned Duros motioned for Han to follow him into a nearby alley. The Corellian walked to the mouth, turned the corner, then stood with his back against the wall, hand on the grip of his blaster. "Okay, this is as far as I go without knowing what you want."

The Duro's mournful expression lengthened even farther. "You are not a trusting sentient, Pilot Solo. I was referred to you by a mutual friend, Truthful Toryl. He said you are an excellent pilot."

Han relaxed slightly, but didn't take his hand off his gun. "I'm good, all right," he said. "If Truthful Toryl sent you . . . prove it."

The Duros gazed straight at him with calm, moonstone-colored eyes. "He said I was to tell you that the *Talisman* you brought him is no more."

Han relaxed and took his hand off his weapon. "Okay, you've convinced me he sent you," he said. "State your business."

"I need a ship delivered to Nar Hekka, in the Hutt system," the Duros said. "I am willing to pay well . . . but, Pilot Solo, you must *not* allow Imperials to board her should you run into any patrols."

Han sighed. More intrigues. But the Duros's offer interested him. He'd been planning all along to eventually make his way to Nar Shaddaa, the "Smuggler's Moon" that orbited Nal Hutta. Now would be as good a time as any. From Nar Hekka, he could easily catch a ship to Nal Hutta or Nar Shaddaa.

"Tell me more," he said.

"Only if you can raise ship within two hours," the Duros said. "If not, tell me, and I will look elsewhere for a pilot."

Han considered for a moment. "Well . . . I could maybe change my plans . . . for the right price."

The Duros named a figure, then added, "And the same sum upon delivery."

Han snorted, then shook his head, though inwardly he was surprised at how high the initial bid was. "C'mon, Chewie," he said, "we've got places to go, people to see."

Too quickly, the Duros named another, higher sum.

This guy must really be desperate, Han thought as he pretended to hesitate for a beat. He shook his head. "I dunno . . . it's not worth my butt if the Imperials are lookin' for this ship of yours. What's she carrying?"

The Duros's expression did not change. "That I cannot tell you. But I will tell you that if you deliver the ship and its contents safely to Tagta the Hutt, he will be pleased, and pleasing a Hutt Lord is generally considered to be a good thing for one's financial well-being. Tagta is Jiliac the Hutt's highest-ranking subordinate on Nar Hekka."

Han's ears pricked up. Jiliac the Hutt was a very high-ranking Hutt Lord indeed. Maybe this Tagta would give him a recommendation to the boss . . .

"Hmmmmmmmmm . . ." Han scratched his head, then named a sum. "And all in advance," he added.

The Duros's pale blue skin seemed to grow even paler, but then he nodded. "Very well as to the sum, but half up front. You will receive the rest from Tagta, Pilot Solo."

Han considered, then nodded. "Okay, you've got yourself a deal. Chewie"—he turned to address the Wookiee, who was hovering nearby, listening intently—"go on back to that lockbox where we left our stuff and get it, will you, while I conclude my business with our friend here?"

The Wookiee rumbled a soft assent.

"Thanks. I'll meet you on the north side of the town square in an hour, okay?"

Chewbacca nodded and moved off down the street.

Han walked closer to the Duros, and said, "Okay, you've got yourself a pilot. We'll raise ship within two hours. Fill me in on the rest of it. Where do I find this Tagta the Hutt?"

Within minutes Han had all the details. The Duros handed over a sheaf of credit vouchers, gave him the ship's security code, and the location of the vessel. Then the blue-skinned alien melted away into the dimness of the alley.

Han had a couple of minutes to kill, so he grabbed a quick bite at the cafe next door. He had to argue with the Devish female chef to get her to *cook* his meat. But it was worth it. The food drowned the last of the ale-induced muzziness. Clearheaded, his energy renewed, Han felt considerably cheered.

On his way to the town square, he stopped off at a secondhand shop that catered to spacers of all species. There he bought a beat-up black lizard-hide jacket to replace the one the Barabel had shredded. Respectably clothed again, he started up the street toward his rendezvous with Chewbacca.

Han knew something was up long before he reached the town square. The sound of a huge crowd was unmistakable. They seemed to be shouting in unison. The skin at the back of Han's neck prickled suddenly as he realized that there was something *familiar* about those words. They weren't in Basic, but he'd heard those simple, repetitious phrases before.

But where?

I've got a bad feeling about this . . . he thought, turning the corner and seeing the crowd. They were chanting. Chanting, swaying, rocking with religious fervor. Mostly Devaronians, of course, but there were a smattering of humans and other sentients. Han's gaze raked the crowd, following it to the front. A hastily erected dais stood there, and atop it, leading the revival, stood a figure out of Han's past.

Oh, no! he thought. *This is a Ylesian revival, and that missionary is Veratil! I can't let him see me!*

Five years ago, Han had spent almost six months on the steaming, fungus-infested world of Ylesia. He'd been working as a pilot before taking the examinations to get into the Academy, practicing and honing his piloting skills. Ylesia was a world at the edge of Hutt space, where a race of beings called the t'landa Til—distant cousins of the Hutts—offered "pilgrims" supposed religious sanctuary.

The t'landa Til sent missionaries to many worlds to preach about the One and the All. Han had known that for years, but he'd never been unlucky enough to run into a Ylesian revival before now.

For a wild moment the Corellian wanted to draw his blaster, shoot Veratil down, and yell to the assembled crowd of potential pilgrims, "Go home! It's all a big fake! They just want you so they can enslave you, you fools! Get out of here!"

But how could he make them believe him? To most sentients in the galaxy, Ylesia was perceived as a place of religious retreat, where the faithful gathered, and those wishing to hide from their pasts could find sanctuary.

The fact that the Ylesian "sanctuary" would turn out to be a trap was known only to the lucky few—like Han—who'd managed to escape. No doubt Veratil had a transport standing by to load the pilgrims on board. Unfortunate sentients who followed him would have no idea that their voyage to Ylesia would lead only to slavery in the spice factories, then, when they grew too weak or sick to work, they'd face death in the spice mines of Kessel. Ylesia was a golden dream for the faithful, but the reality was a world of bondage and unending toil.

Teroenza, Veratil's boss, was the High Priest of Ylesia.

Before fleeing the colony, Han had robbed the t'landa Til leader of the most valuable pieces in a rare and extensive collection. He'd left Teroenza wounded, but alive.

Han had escaped Ylesia in Teroenza's personal yacht, the *Talisman*. Soon after his getaway, Han discovered that the t'landa Til and their Hutt overlords had placed a fat bounty on the head of "Vykk Draygo"—Han's alias. Han had to change his identity, even his retinal patterns, to escape detection and capture.

Now, seeing Veratil, Han ducked his head and turned away, wishing he had a hood he could pull up to hide his face. If the Sacredot saw him and recognized him, Han knew that he was in for it.

The chanting surrounding him intensified. Han began to sweat, despite the chill of the Devaronian weather, because he knew what was coming.

Across the town square, he saw a tall, furred shape standing on the edge of the crowd, watching the ceremony curiously. *Chewie! Can't let him get drawn into this! The Exultation is going to come in just a couple of minutes!*

Han plunged into the crowd, keeping his head ducked, fighting his way through the throng as he would have clawed his way through a heavy surf. He was breathing hard and his elbows and ribs ached by the time he reached the Wookiee. "Chewie!" he yelled, grabbing the big sentient by the arm. "Let's get outta here! This is gonna turn into a mob scene any second now!"

The Wookiee whined inquiringly. "Never *mind* how I know!" Han yelled above the chanting. "I just know! Trust me!"

Chewbacca nodded and turned away, using his huge size to part the crowd before him. Han started to follow him, then something caught the corner of his eye, and he turned his head. A gleam . . . a gleam of reddish gold on a stray curl.

Han caught just a glimpse of her, but his whole mind and body jolted to a stop as though he'd slammed into a stone wall while running at top speed.

Bria? Bria!

He caught only that one brief glimpse of a pale, perfect profile and a stray reddish-blond curl, but it was enough. She was standing there, wearing a black cloak and hood, in this crowd.

Memories came surging back, so strong that they scared him . . .

Bria, a pale ghost of a slave in the spice factories of Ylesia. Bria, scared but determined as they robbed Teroenza of his treasures. Bria, sitting beside him on a golden sand beach on Togoria, her mouth soft and red and just begging to be kissed. Bria, lying in his arms late at night . . .

Bria, who had left him behind, saying she needed to fight her addiction to the t'landa Til's Exultation by herself . . .

Han had spent the past five years convincing himself that he'd forgotten her. After four years in the Imperial Academy, plus nearly a year of commissioned service, he'd been convinced that he no longer cared. But now, in a single searing blaze of insight, Han Solo knew he'd been lying to himself.

Without hesitating, he turned and plunged back into the crowd, heading for the woman in the black cloak. He was halfway there when the Exultation hit the crowd, and the throng of sentients collapsed onto the cobblestones of the town square as though they'd been stun-blasted.

Han had forgotten how strong the Exultation was. Waves of intense pleasure rolled through his mind as well as his body. No wonder the Ylesian pilgrims thought the t'landa Til were Divinely Gifted! Even knowing, as Han did, that the Exultation was caused by an empathic transmission coupled with a subsonic vibration that caused a wave of pleasure that acted on the brains of most bipedal sentients, Han had to brace himself to resist it.

He knew without seeing it that the pouch beneath Veratil's "chin" had swelled, and that the Sacredot was "humming" those vibrations as he concentrated on warm, positive emotions. To anyone unprepared for the force of the Exultation, the effect was as intoxicating as any pleasure drug. The ability to produce the Exultation was one that all t'landa Til males shared—it was actually a sex-linked biological ability they possessed that, in their natural habitat, was used to attract t'landa Til females.

All around Han the crowd had fallen prone, and most of the sentients were writhing in pleasure. The sight sickened Han. He'd shaken off the effects of the Exultation now, and he concentrated on not stepping on bodies as he plunged toward the woman in the black cloak and hood. He could no longer see her face or that betraying tendril of hair.

His fingers remembered the soft silkiness of that hair . . . he used to play with Bria's curls, watching them capture the light, bringing the reddish gold to vibrant life . . .

The woman in the black cloak and hood disappeared behind a stone bench as the crowd heaved in a wave of ecstasy from the Exultation. Han swallowed hard. Bria had left him because she was addicted to the Exultation. Was that where she'd been for the past five years? A willing slave on Ylesia, bound to her t'landa Til masters because she needed her daily dose of pleasure? Funny . . . he'd thought Bria had more strength than that . . .

Han reached the stone bench, then stopped, staring around him. The woman in the black cloak was nowhere in sight. *Where'd she go? Bria!* Han thought, staring around him wildly. From all sides he could hear the gasps and moans of the crowd filling the air.

He jumped up on the bench, straining his eyes, trying to pick up any trace of the woman in the black cloak. Han only realized what a terrible mistake he'd made when he found himself staring across the crowd, straight into the eyes of Veratil.

The huge, four-legged creature with the tiny arms and the broad, single-horned head was staring back at him, his small, reddish eyes wide with surprise.

The Corellian had no doubt that Veratil had just recognized him as "Vykk Draygo," the man who'd wrecked the glitterstim factory, stolen Teroenza's treasure, and caused the death of the Ylesian Hutt overlord, Zavval.

All around Han the moans of pleasure suddenly altered into cries of dismay and loss—Veratil's attention had been diverted, and the Exultation had come to an abrupt, jarring halt.

Some of the throng wailed aloud, others jerked convulsively. Still others dragged themselves to their feet with cries of distress and anger. Han ducked his head and bolted forward, determined to lose himself in the crowd. And then, ahead of him, he caught a glimpse of black.

Bria!

Forgetting Veratil, forgetting the danger he was in, Han plunged forward, slamming into would-be pilgrims, tripping over feet, elbowing his fellow sentients aside.

"Bria!" he yelled. "Stop!"

Putting on a burst of speed, Han reached the edge of the crowd. The woman was running now, but Han was moving at top speed and he caught her in a dozen swift strides.

Reaching out, he managed to grab the black fabric, yank her to a halt, then he grabbed her elbow and spun her around to face him—

—only to find that the woman he'd chased was a total stranger.

How could he have mistaken her for Bria? This woman wasn't homely, she was even pretty in a rather worn way

. . . but Bria—Bria had been one of the loveliest women Han had ever seen. This woman's hair was dark blond, not gold with warm reddish highlights.

Bria had been tall. This woman was short.

She was also angry. "What do you think you're doing?" she demanded in Basic. "Leave me alone or I'll summon security!"

"I . . . I'm sorry . . ." Han mumbled, stepped back, holding up both hands in as nonthreatening a manner as he could manage. "I thought you were someone else."

"Well, I feel sorry for *her*," the woman said huffily. "With an ill-mannered, scruffy lout like *you* in her life!"

"Look . . ." Han continued to back away, hands up. "I said I was sorry, sister. I'm going, okay?"

"I think you'd better," she said pointedly. "That priest has summoned security, I think."

Han looked over his shoulder, cursed, then took to his heels, heading away from the crowd. He could see Chewbacca waiting for him, and waved to the Wookiee.

He lengthened his stride, and a glance back at his pursuers reassured him that he was losing them.

Been drinking too much . . . he decided as he ran. *That's gotta be it. I'm gonna be more careful from now on* . . . *a lot more careful* . . .

"Did Han get away?" Bria Tharen asked her friend as Lanah Malo walked into the room, carrying Bria's black cloak under her arm. Bria was seated on the single human-styled chair in the cheap room they'd rented for their short stay on Devaron.

"I think so," Lanah Malo replied, tossing the cloak to her friend, then picking up her travel bag and dumping it on the bed. "The last I saw, he and that big Wookiee he was traveling with jumped into a public skimmer. Security was still on foot. My guess is, he made it."

"He's probably off-world by now," Bria said softly, wistfully. Rising, she walked over to the window, then stood for a moment gazing up into Devaron's coral-tinted sky. Tears gathered in her blue-green eyes. *I never thought I'd ever see him again. I never thought it would hurt so much* . . .

The pain she felt completely eclipsed the triumph she should have been experiencing. Today she'd faced the Exultation and successfully resisted it. After years of fighting her addiction to it, now she finally knew for certain that she was a free woman. She'd looked forward to this day for a long time—but any joy she felt was drowned in her grief at seeing Han again, and knowing she couldn't be with him.

"Couldn't you have talked to him?" the shorter woman asked, almost echoing Bria's own thoughts. Bria turned from the window and watched her friend and comrade-in-arms pulling on her battered, khaki-colored jacket. Quickly Lanah stuffed the last of her personal belongings into the small travel bag. "What harm could it do?" she asked, giving Bria a sharp, quizzical glance.

Bria shivered, then pulled the cloak around her shoulders. It was chilly, now that the sun was low on the horizon. "No," she said in a low voice. "I couldn't talk to him."

"Why not?" Lanah asked. "Don't you trust him?"

Moving as methodically and carefully as a droid, Bria checked the charge in the blaster she wore strapped to her thigh—low-down the way Han had taught her, five years ago when they'd been partners, companions . . . lovers. "Yes," she said, after a moment. "I trust him. I trust him with anything that's mine. But what we're trying to accomplish—that's not mine. That's all of us. Betrayal at this point could mean the end of the entire movement. I couldn't risk it."

Lanah nodded. "Solo showing up when he did sure

messed up our plans," she said. "No telling when we'll get a clear shot at Veratil again. My guess is that he'll hightail it back to Ylesia to tell Teroenza he spotted your ex-boy-friend."

Bria nodded tiredly as she ran her hands through her hair. *Han loved to do that,* she thought with a sudden surge of memory so vivid that it felt like a blow. *Oh, Han . . .*

Lanah Malo gave her an assessing glance that was half sympathetic, half cynical. "You can fall apart later, Bria. Right now we've got to catch the transport back to Corellia. The Commander's going to expect a full report. Even if we failed to take out Veratil, we still succeeded in making contact with the Devaronian group . . . so the trip wasn't a total waste."

"I'm not going to fall apart," Bria said dully, holstering her blaster without looking at it—the way Han had taught her. "I got over Han long ago."

"Sure you did," Lanah agreed, not unkindly, as the two women picked up their bags and headed for the door. "Sure you did . . ."

Chapter Two:
The Smuggler's Road

Han Solo shuffled into the tiny control room of the Durosian ship, cradling a mug of stim-tea. He glanced at the viewscreen, which showed the comforting starline patterns of hyperspace, then blinked blearily over at the big Wookiee who lounged in the copilot's seat. "I overslept," he said accusingly. "You didn't call me."

Chewbacca made a short comment. "Well, yeah, I probably did need the rest," Han admitted. "But you're the one who got wounded. How's the arm?"

The Wookiee reassured Han that it was healing just fine. The Corellian glanced at the wound, and nodded, then he sank into the pilot's seat. "Good. Let me tell you, pal, it's fortunate that you showed up when you did, yesterday.

That Barabel wasn't messing around. Things could have gotten sticky."

Chewie pointed out, truthfully, that things *had* gotten sticky. Han shrugged. "You're right. And that reminds me of something." Getting up from his seat, he went over to the toolbox that was standard issue on every ship, and came back with a tiny lasertorch and a microfile. Taking his blaster out of the holster, he carefully sliced off the sight at the end of the barrel, then began smoothing the spot.

Chewbacca wondered aloud what Han was doing. "Fixing my weapon so it won't ever hang up in my holster again," the Corellian explained. "That was a bad couple of seconds in that tavern, there, when I couldn't draw. I'm a good shot—losing the sight won't affect my aim."

Chewie watched as Han worked. After a moment the human spoke again. "Bad enough that I couldn't draw. If it had been a blaster shoot-out, instead of a slugfest, I don't think either of us would have made it out of there alive. But I guess it could have been worse. We were actually in more danger at that Ylesian revival. If Veratil's security people had grabbed us . . . believe me, pal, those t'landa Til don't mess around. If they'd caught us, we'd be in deep humbaba manure, my friend."

Chewie made an interrogatory sound. "Yeah, I guess I do owe you an explanation about that," Han said with a sigh. "Y'see, about five years ago I needed experience piloting big ships, 'cause I was hoping to get into the Academy. So I took a job piloting for the t'landa Til on Ylesia. Ever hear of it before?"

Chewie whined, low in his throat. "You got it. The pilgrim colony. 'Cept that it ain't, pal. It's nothin' but a big scam, a major trap. The Hutts control the place. Pilgrims travel there hoping to join with the cosmic All, or some such, but they turn 'em into slaves and make them work in the spice factories. Most of the poor fools don't last long.

They had three colonies on Ylesia when I was there, but I heard they've expanded to five or six, now."

Chewbacca shook his head sadly.

Han grimaced as he sighted down the barrel of his blaster. "Somebody ought to go in there and shut those creeps down, Chewie. I've been a thief, a smuggler, a con man, a gambler, and some other things I ain't particularly proud of, pal . . . but slavery—I can't *stand* it. Or slavers, either. Scum of the universe. For two credits, I'd blast 'em all into oblivion . . ."

Chewbacca, naturally, voiced vehement support for Han's opinion. The Corellian grinned crookedly as he ran his thumb over the now-smooth barrel tip. Satisfied, he replaced the weapon in his holster. "Yeah, well, I kinda forgot who I was talkin' to. But anyhow, it's a long story. The end result was, I decided I had to get outta there, so I stole a bunch of stuff from the High Priest. He had a great collection of art objects, jeweled weapons, stuff like that. Only trouble was, Teroenza and his Hutt boss, Zavval, showed up at a real inopportune time. The shooting started, and Zavval died."

Chewbacca made an interrogatory sound.

Han sighed. "No, I didn't shoot him. But you could sorta say it was my fault that he bought it."

Chewie commented that from what he knew of Hutts, the fewer the better. "Yeah, I've thought that myself," Han said. "But we may wind up workin' for a Hutt, so you'd better keep your opinion to yourself, pal." He sipped his stim-tea and looked out at the racing star patterns for a long second, lost in memories. "So, anyhow, I got away. But I wish Veratil hadn't gotten a look at me yesterday. I got a bad feelin' about that. The t'landa Til can be pretty nasty . . ."

Chewie asked a question. Han looked down and cleared his throat. "Why'd I go back into the crowd and give Veratil

the chance to see me? Well, pal . . . there was this
girl . . ."

The Wookiee grunted a phrase. Translated, it meant,
"Why am I not surprised?"

"Well, this one was . . . special," Han said, feeling
rather defensive. "Bria Tharen. Yesterday, in that crowd, I
thought . . ." He shrugged, his eyes shadowed. "I thought
I saw her. I coulda sworn that was her, standing there in
the crowd. Five years ago, we were . . . friends. *Close*
friends."

Chewbacca nodded. After only a month with Han Solo,
the Wookiee was perfectly aware that human females almost invariably found the Corellian attractive.

Han shrugged again. "But my eyes were playing tricks
on me. When I finally caught up to her, she wasn't Bria. It
was really aw—" He cleared his throat self-consciously.
"Uh, that is . . . I was sort of disappointed. I really hoped
I'd found her again." He took another gulp of the cooling
tea. "I dreamed about Bria last night," he muttered, almost
to himself. "I was wearing my uniform, and she was smiling
at me . . ."

Chewbacca made a sympathetic sound. Han looked up
at the Wookiee. "But, hey, Bria's part of the past. I gotta
look ahead. What about you, pal? You got a girlfriend?"

The Wookiee hesitated. Han grinned knowingly. "Someone special? Or someone you'd *like* to be special?"

Chewie fiddled with the STABILIZER CONTROL button.
"Careful, don't push that," Han said. "Okay, you don't have
to tell me. But hey . . . I told *you*. If we're gonna be
partners, doesn't that mean we oughta trust each other?"

His hairy companion mulled that over for a moment.
Finally he nodded, and began talking, slowly at first, then
with increasing confidence. There *was* a young Wookiee
female, Mallatobuck, that Chewie found attractive. She had
come around several times to help care for elderly mem-

bers of Chewie's arboreal "community" on Kashyyyk, and had helped Chewbacca care for his father, Attichitcuk, an aged and rather irascible Wookiee.

"So, you like her," Han said. "Does she like you?"

Chewbacca wasn't sure. They'd never spent much time alone together. But there was a warmth in her blue eyes that he remembered . . .

"So, how long has it been since you've seen her?" Han persisted.

Chewie thought for a moment, then growled a reply.

"Fifty years!" Han yelped. He knew Wookiees lived many times longer than humans, but still . . .

He took another swallow. "Hey, pal . . . I hate to tell you. Mallatobuck might be married with six little Wooks by now. You sure ask a lot, wanting a girl to wait for you *that* long."

Chewbacca agreed that perhaps he should return to Kashyyyk and reestablish contact as soon as possible.

"Tell you what," Han said. "When we've gotten our own ship, bought and paid for, Kashyyyk will be our first stop, okay?"

The big Wookiee roared an enthusiastic agreement.

Han glanced over at him, and found himself thinking that it *was* nice to have someone to talk to during voyages. Space travel, once you made the jump to hyperspace, could be pretty dull.

"I saw that package you brought aboard," he said, changing the subject. "What did you buy?"

Chewbacca fetched the bundle, and returned to the co-pilot's seat. He opened the parcel. Inside was a jumble of various lengths of metal and wood, plus a handgrip and a powerful-looking spring attachment.

Han eyed the assortment, puzzled. "What's that?"

The Wookiee grunted a reply. "It's going to be a bow-caster," Han repeated. "Well, good luck puttin' it together.

That spring is so strong that no human would be able to draw a weapon like that."

Chewie agreed and, taking out the toolbox, began putting his new bowcaster together.

"You a good shot?" Han asked.

Chewbacca modestly allowed that among his people he was considered quite a marksman. "Good," Han said. "We're headin' for Nar Shaddaa, so we'll need to cover each other's back. It's a moon that orbits the Hutt planet, Nal Hutta. You ever hear of it?"

Chewie hadn't.

"Well, I've never been there, but from what I've heard, it can be a little rough. Even the Empire doesn't mess with Nar Shaddaa. If you're hot, or you want to make some kinda deal that the authorities would frown on—you go to Nar Shaddaa. It's that kinda place."

Han began checking the controls, making sure everything was shipshape. Not much longer before they emerged into realspace, not far from Nar Hekka. Chewbacca watched him with bright blue eyes, then asked a quiet question.

Han glanced up. "I *did* try to find Bria," he admitted after a long moment. "At first I was mad at her, for leaving me, but hey . . . she was going through a lot. A couple of years ago, while I was on leave from the Academy, I looked up her dad, Renn Tharen. He said he hadn't heard from her in a year. He had no idea where she was." Han sighed. "I liked her dad. The rest of her family was a pain in the butt, but I liked Renn. He helped me out when I was in a spot. Most of my first six months' paychecks when I was commissioned went to pay him back some money he'd loaned me. He was—"

The ship's hyperspace alarm sounded. "Coming out of hyperspace," Han said, his hands flying over the controls.

"Next stop, Nar Hekka. We've got to find us a Hutt Lord named Tagta, pal."

After landing the Duros's ship at the spaceport the alien had specified, Han and Chewbacca gathered up their scanty belongings and left it behind, under no illusions that it would be there when they got back. Together, they boarded a public tube-speeder that would take them into the city where Tagta the Hutt held court.

Han had been to Nal Hutta, and found it an unpleasant world . . . damp, slimy, and smelly—rather like the Hutts themselves. He'd braced himself to endure more of the same on Nar Hekka, but he was pleasantly surprised. The planet was a cold world that orbited a dim red star on the edge of the Y'Toub system, but Hutt credits and colonies of various galactic species had transformed it into a technological wonder. Beneath enormous hothouse domes, the skies shone blue with a faint tinge of violet. Although the planet had little indigenous plant life, vegetation from many worlds had been transplanted and carefully cultivated. There were numerous parks, botanical gardens, and arboretums. Everywhere Han and Chewie looked, beds of flowering plants boasted large, lovely blooms of differing hues.

Once in the city, Han and the big Wookiee walked along enjoying the sights. Artificial convection currents wafted soft breezes that caressed their faces. Being "outside" on a balmy day was a wonderful change of pace from being cooped up in a cramped spaceship, Han said, and Chewbacca agreed with a throaty growl.

All too soon, it seemed, they approached an imposing white stone edifice that they'd been told marked the home and business center of Tagta the Hutt. Even though Tagta worked for Jiliac, he was still a prominent and wealthy Hutt Lord in his own right.

They walked up the ramp (Hutt designs did not utilize stairs, for obvious reasons) and then paused outside the huge doorway, large enough to admit even a corpulent Hutt on an anti-grav sled. The majordomo was a diminutive Sullustan female. Her jowls quivered as Han introduced himself and requested an audience with Lord Tagta.

The Sullustan left, ostensibly to check out their bonafides, and returned a few minutes later. "Lord Tagta will see you. He asks me to ask you whether you have eaten? He is partaking of the noonday meal."

Han *was* hungry, and he suspected Chewie was, too, but the thought of eating with a Hutt was not appetizing. Hutt body odor was strong enough to turn a sensitive human's stomach. "We just finished," Han lied. "But we thank Lord Tagta very much for his graciousness in inquiring."

After several more minutes, the two smugglers, escorted by three liveried Gamorrean guards, were ushered into the Hutt's private dining chamber. The room boasted high, vaulted ceilings that reminded Han of cathedrals he'd seen. A large, floor-to-ceiling window allowed reddish sunlight to flood in, making the white walls appear faintly rosy. Their host was reclining (Hutt anatomy didn't permit sitting, after all) before a table, sampling various "dishes."

Han took one glance at the wriggling, squirming fare that comprised the noontime repast, and averted his eyes. He didn't allow his squeamishness to show, however, as he and Chewbacca approached the Hutt Lord.

Han had learned Huttese while on Ylesia, and understood it well. He couldn't speak it, though, because the language depended on subharmonics for subtle nuances in meaning, and the human throat was not constructed to produce those sounds. He wondered whether he and the Hutt

Lord would need an interpreter droid. He glanced around, but didn't see one.

Tagta was reclining on a hovering anti-grav sled, but Han got the impression that the Hutt could move around if he wished. Some Hutts, he knew, grew so corpulent that they could no longer glide about under their own power, but Tagta didn't seem either that old or that fat.

Still, watching the Hutt delicately select yet another wriggler from a glass aquarium filled with viscous fluid and stuff it into his mouth, Han figured that Tagta would probably make it to the "fully corpulent" stage of Hutt life. Green drool gathered at the corners of Tagta's mouth as he rolled the live treat around in his mouth before, finally, swallowing it.

Han forced himself not to look away.

Finally, after several more minutes of gluttony, Tagta's hunger seemed to be abating. He looked up at his visitors and said, in Huttese, "Does either of you comprehend the spoken communication of the only truly civilized beings?"

Knowing that Tagta meant Huttese, Han nodded and said, in Basic, "Yes, Lord Tagta, I understand it. I cannot speak it well, though."

The Hutt waved a plump little hand and blinked his bulbous eyes in surprise. "That is much to your credit, then, Captain Solo. I understand your primitive Basic, so we will not require an interpreter to converse." He waved at the Wookiee. "And your companion?"

"My friend and first mate does not speak the language of your exalted people, Lord Tagta," Han said. He hated having to stick flattery into each sentence, but he was highly motivated to stay on this Hutt's good side. When dealing with Hutts, that was generally the best policy—and Han didn't forget that he wanted this particular Hutt to do him a favor.

"Very well, Captain Solo," Tagta said. "Have you brought my ship, as you were hired to do?"

"Yes I have, Your Excellency," Han replied. "It is docked in berth number thirty-eight, Starport Complex Q-7." Nar Hekka boasted a huge starport, since it was the main crossroads of trade into and out of the Hutt systems.

"Excellent, Captain," Tagta said. "You have done well." He waved a dismissal. "You have our leave to go."

Han didn't budge. "Uh, Lord Tagta, I am still owed half my payment."

Tagta reared back slightly in surprise. "What? You came expecting payment from *me*?"

Han took a deep breath. One part of him wanted to just beat a quick retreat. Angering a powerful Hutt Lord probably wasn't worth it. But he held his ground, forcing himself to remain outwardly calm. He had a feeling he was being tested. "Yes, Your Excellency, I was promised the second half of the payment when I successfully delivered the ship to Nar Hekka—having managed to avoid any Imperial vessels that might be interested in the ship . . . or its cargo. I was told that you would furnish the other half of my payment when I saw you."

Tagta huffed indignantly. "How dare you imply that I would make such a ridiculous bargain? Leave me immediately, human!"

Han was getting mad now. Crossing his arms on his chest, he planted his feet and shook his head. "No way, Your Excellency. I know what I was promised. Pay up."

"You dare to demand payment of *me*?"

"When it comes to credits, I dare quite a lot of things," Han said imperturbably.

"Hrrrrrmmmmmmph!" Tagta was full of disdain. "This is your last chance, Corellian," he warned. "Leave, or I will summon my guards!"

"You think me and Chewie can't handle a bunch of Gamorreans?" Han said scornfully. "Think again!"

Tagta gazed at the Corellian balefully, but did not summon the guards.

"Listen, Your Excellency, you want me to tell every other pilot I meet that Tagta the Hutt welshes on his debts?" Han added with a curl of his lip. "You'll have a tough time gettin' anyone to work for you, when *I'm* finished."

The Hutt Lord rumbled deep in his chest, a sort of "hrrrrrmmmmmmmmmpppppphhhhhhh!" sound that made Han's mouth go dry. Had he pushed his luck too far?

Seconds ticked by in Han's head as he waited, forcing himself to remain immobile and silent.

Then Tagta actually chuckled, a deep but unmistakable sound. "Captain Solo, you are a brave sentient indeed! I admire courage!" He fumbled amid the welter of items scattered among the squirming foodstuffs, and tossed Han a pouch. "There, I believe the amount is correct."

The old villain! Han thought, half admiringly. *He had it ready all the time! He WAS just testing me . . .*

With the realization came a surge of confidence. Han bowed. "Please accept our thanks, Lord Tagta. And I wish to ask a favor, Your Excellency . . ."

"A favor?" the Hutt boomed, blinking his bulbous eyes rapidly. "You are indeed a bold sentient! What is this favor?"

"I understand that you know Lord Jiliac, sir?"

The huge, slit-pupiled eyes blinked again. "Yes, I do business with Jiliac. We belong to the same clan. What of it?"

"Well, I hear that there's work for good pilots to be had on Nar Shaddaa. And that Lord Jiliac owns or controls a lot of the Smuggler's Moon. I'm a good pilot, sir, I really am. If you could, I'd appreciate a recommendation to Lord Jiliac. Chewie and I would like to work for him."

"Ahhhhh . . ." The deep voice boomed in the massive chest. "I see. What shall I tell my clan lord? Shall I tell him that you are brazen and greedy, Captain Solo?"

Han grinned, suddenly daring. He was learning that Hutts had a sense of humor—twisted, but definitely a sense of humor. "If you think it would help, Lord Tagta."

"Ho-HO!" the Hutt leader boomed a mighty shout of laughter. "Well, let me tell you, Captain Solo, there are not many humans with the intelligence to claim those qualities as virtues. But among my people—they are, indeed, sterling attributes."

"As you say, sir," murmured Han, not quite sure what to reply to this.

The Hutt Lord bellowed, "Scribe!" in Huttese, and a bipedal droid came scuttling from behind the drapes in the cavernous room. "Yes, Your Impressiveness?"

Tagta waved a hand at the droid and gave it an order in Huttese so rapid that Han had trouble following it. Something about "seals" and "messages."

Moments later the droid reappeared with a small, palm-sized holocube. After handing it to the Hutt, it stood back respectfully. Tagta took the little holocube, perused the message it contained, and grunted with satisfaction. Then, quite deliberately, the Hutt licked one side of it, leaving a green smear.

After holding the cube for a moment, Tagta activated the side of it, and a clear film slid down to cover the greenish smear. "Here, Captain Solo," the Hutt said, handing Han the holocube. "By this Lord Jiliac will know that I sent you. He is indeed in need of good pilots. Work hard for him, and you will be rewarded. We Hutts are known for our generosity and beneficence to lower life-forms who serve us ably."

Han took the cube rather gingerly, but it was no longer wet. He looked at the greenish smear, realizing that Jiliac would be able to do a sensor analysis and verify that the holocube had indeed come from his relative. *Clever, even if it is disgusting,* he thought.

He bowed deeply, and nudged Chewbacca, who also bowed. "Thank you, Your Excellency!"

Then, clutching his holocube, Han left the Hutt overlord behind. As they were walking down the ramp outside the Hutt mansion, Han insisted on divvying up the credits from the voyage. "Just in case one of us gets robbed," he explained, to quiet Chewbacca's protests. "That way one of us is sure to have some money."

Once back out on the street, Han suggested that they get some food before heading to the shuttleport to catch the next ship for Nar Shaddaa. Stopping by a flower-seller's booth, Han asked the proprietor, a spindly humanoid with long, wiry whiskers and tufted ears, whether there was a good restaurant in the vicinity. The sentient directed him to the Starfarer Diner, a few blocks away.

They were halfway there, strolling casually and chatting, when Han suddenly stopped in midsentence and swung around, alarmed—and not even sure why. Out of the corner of his eye he caught a glimpse of a pale-skinned humanoid with two long fleshy tails instead of hair. The Twi'lek was just stepping out of a doorway behind him. There was a drawn blaster in his hand. As Han turned, the Twi'lek shouted, in accented but understandable Basic, "Halt, both of you, or I shoot you now!"

Han knew instinctively that if he obeyed the command to stop, he'd wind up dead, sooner or later. He didn't hesitate for even a second. With an earsplitting yell, the Corellian threw himself to the side, hit the ground, rolled, and came up on one knee, blaster in hand.

The Twi'lek's weapon spat a blue-green burst. Han dodged.

Stun blast!

Han aimed, fired, and the reddish beam struck his attacker mid-torso. He went down, dead or incapacitated. The Corellian made sure the Twi'lek wasn't getting up anytime soon, then he turned to look for Chewbacca. The Wookiee was leaning heavily against a parked speeder, dazed. He'd evidently been grazed by the stun beam. Han ran over to him, his heart pounding from the rush of adrenaline. "Did he get you bad, pal?"

With a muffled growl, Chewbacca assured his partner that he'd be fine. Han peered up into the Wookiee's furry face, saw that his eyes were clear, the pupils even. Only then did he draw a long breath of relief. He hadn't realized until that moment that he was getting used to having the big hairy lug around. If anything had happened to Chewie . . .

Going over to the Twi'lek, Han knelt down. One glance at the huge blaster wound that had turned the Twi'lek's chest to blackened slag was enough to tell him the being was dead. Han experienced a quick pang—he'd killed before, but he didn't like doing it.

Gritting his teeth, he forced himself to search the dead sentient. There was a vibroblade strapped to the inside of a sleeve, another on the calf. On the inside of the other wrist the Twi'lek wore a "wrist vac," a device that when triggered would send small, deadly blades flying into an opponent's vitals.

Shoved into his belt, covered by his tunic, was a sleep-inducer. A short-range weapon, but very effective. The Twi'lek could have simply walked up behind Han, stuck the sleep-inducer in his back, then pulled the trigger to send the Corellian off to dreamland.

Han stared at the weapon, his mouth dry. *A bounty hunter. Great. Why am I not surprised? This must be Teroenza's doing. He's found out I'm alive, and he wants me . . .*

If not for instinct and fast reflexes, Han knew, at this very moment he'd be out cold and on his way back to Ylesia to face a terrible vengeance . . .

He heard Chewbacca make an anxious sound, glanced up, only to find that the encounter had drawn a crowd.

Abandoning the Twi'lek where he lay, Han stood up, blaster still ostentatiously held in his right hand. The crowd backed away, muttering. The Corellian moved sideways with a dancer's grace, never turning his back on the crowd, until he and Chewbacca were side by side. He knew someone must've summoned planetary security, but he also knew that since the Twi'lek was a bounty hunter, he was more or less outside planetary law. A bounty hunter was presumed able to take care of himself. If the intended prey fought back . . . well, tough luck.

Moving slowly, step by step, Han and the Wookiee backed away from the crowd until they reached the closest alley. Then, moving like a single entity with one mind, they leaped sideways, and ran.

No one followed them.

Teroenza, High Priest and unofficial master of the steamy world of Ylesia, a world that produced drugs and slaves in impressive amounts, lounged in his sling-seat in his sumptuous apartments while his Zisian majordomo, Ganar Tos, massaged his massive shoulders.

The t'landa Til were enormous creatures, standing nearly as tall as a human male on their four tree-trunklike legs. With their barrel-shaped bodies, tiny arms, and huge heads that somewhat resembled those of their distant cousins, the Hutts—except for the enormous horn protruding from the middle of their faces—the t'landa Til considered themselves the handsomest sentients in the galaxy. The vast majority of other sentients would not have agreed with their assessment.

Teroenza raised one of his small, almost dainty forearms, and used his fingers to smooth a soothing oil into his leathery skin. He rubbed gently around his bulbous eyes. The sun on Ylesia was frequently sheathed in clouds, but it had enough strength to cause his skin to dry out unless he took care of it. Frequent mud baths helped, as did this expensive emollient. He began rubbing the oil into his horn, remembering the last time he'd been home, on Nal Hutta. He'd attracted a mate, Tilenna, and they'd spent hours together, rubbing each other with oils . . .

The High Priest sighed. Doing his duty to his homeworld and the clan of Hutts his family served called for sacrifices. One of them was that only male priests were needed on Ylesia, to provide the Exultation, so no female t'landa Til were here. No mates, no potential mates . . .

"Harder, Ganar Tos," Teroenza murmured, in his own language. "I have been working too hard these days. Too much work, too much stress. I must learn to slow down, relax more . . ."

Teroenza glanced longingly at the huge door in his apartments that led next door, to his treasure collection. The High Priest was an avid collector of the rare, the unusual, the beautiful. He bought and "acquired" rarities and art objects from all over the galaxy. His collection was his one pleasure on this steamy, backwater world that was populated mostly by slaves and inferiors.

It had taken him nearly four years to restore the collection after that vile, despicable excuse for a sentient, Vykk Draygo, had ransacked the place and stolen many of the rarest and most valuable pieces. Several days ago Teroenza had discovered that "Vykk Draygo" was still alive. A check of the Devaronian Port Authority records had shown that the Corellian scoundrel's *real* name was "Han Solo."

Remembering the terrible night when his collection had been violated, Teroenza's small hands clenched involuntarily into fists, and his head lowered with the longing to impale a victim on his horn. Ganar Tos's fingers dug into suddenly taut clumps of muscle, causing the t'landa Til to wince and curse in his own language. Solo had fired blasters in the treasure room, causing irreparable damage to some of Teroenza's finest pieces. The white jade fountain had been repaired by the best sculptor in the galaxy, but it would never be the same . . .

Teroenza was distracted from his memories when the front door to his apartments opened, and Kibbick the Hutt undulated in. The young Hutt was far from being old or corpulent enough to require an anti-grav sled—he got around fine under his own power, propelling himself forward in a series of glides by contracting his powerful lower body and tail muscles.

Teroenza knew he should rise from his lounge-sling, and greet his nominal master with deference, but he didn't. Kibbick was a young Hutt, barely past the age of full Hutt accountability, and he didn't want to be here on Ylesia. He was the nephew of the dead Zavval, Teroenza's former Hutt overseer. Zavval's sibling, the powerful Hutt clan leader, Lord Aruk, was his uncle.

The High Priest raised a hand and nodded politely enough, though. He certainly didn't want to alienate Kibbick. "Greetings, Your Excellency. How are you today?"

The young Hutt glided up to the High Priest and then stopped. He was still young enough to be a uniform light tan in color, lacking the greenish pigmentation on the spine and down the tail that older, nonmobile Hutts frequently acquired. Since he was not fat, as Hutts went, Kibbick's eyes were not hidden in leathery folds of skin, but instead protruded slightly, giving him a rather pop-eyed, inquisitive air. Teroenza had good reason to know, however, that that wide-eyed, curious stare was misleading.

"The nala-tree frogs you promised me," Kibbick began in Huttese. Lacking the huge chest of older Hutts, his words were deep, but not particularly resonant. "The shipment hasn't arrived, Teroenza! I was particularly looking forward to a repast of nala-tree frogs tonight." He gave a theatrical sigh. "There is so little to look forward to on this benighted world! Can you see about it, Teroenza?"

The High Priest made soothing gestures with his tiny hands. "Of course, Your Excellency. You shall have your nala-tree frogs, never fear. I do not relish them myself, but I know that Zavval did. I shall order an expedition of guards to collect some today."

Kibbick relaxed visibly. "That's much better," he said. "Oh, and, Teroenza, I require a new bath slave. The old one hurt her back when she was lifting my tail to oil it, and I ordered her back to the factories. Her whimpering was getting on my nerves . . . and I have very delicate nerves, as you know."

"Yes, I'm aware of that," Teroenza said soothingly. Inwardly the High Priest gritted his bite-plates. *I have to remember that Kibbick, although a whining nuisance, allows me complete autonomy. If I must have a Hutt overlord, he is the best choice . . .* "I shall see to it right away."

Privately, Teroenza knew that he could run the Ylesian spice and slave operation with no Hutt involvement. In the year following Zavval's "untimely" death at the hands of Han Solo, this had become clear to the High Priest. But the Besadii criminal enterprise, the kajidic, was ruled by a powerful old Hutt named Aruk, who clung to tradition. If a Besadii undertaking was to prosper, a Hutt from their own kin, the Besadii clan, must be in charge.

Thus, Teroenza found himself saddled with Kibbick. He repressed a sigh. It would not be wise to let his impatience show. "Will there be anything else, Your Excellency?" he asked, forcing himself to assume a servile, almost obsequious demeanor.

Kibbick thought hard for a moment. "Yes, come to think of it. I spoke with Uncle Aruk this morning, and he was checking last week's accounts. He wanted to know what is this five-thousand-credit bounty you've placed on this human, Han Solo?"

Teroenza rubbed his small, delicate hands together. "Inform Lord Aruk that only a few days ago I discovered that Vykk Draygo, Zavval's murderer, whom we had presumed to be dead for the past five years, has resurfaced! His real name is Han Solo, and he was drummed out of the Imperial Navy just two months ago." Teroenza's protuberant eyes were suddenly moist and glittering with anticipation. "By offering a sizable bounty and specifying 'no disintegrations,' that will ensure that they'll bring this Hutt-slaying monster back here to Ylesia, so he may pay for his crimes."

"I see," Kibbick said. "I shall explain that to Aruk, but I don't believe he'll go along with paying the extra credits for a 'no disintegrations' bounty. That's not necessary, under the circumstances, really. Simple proof that it's indeed Solo's body—genetic material, for example—would suffice, wouldn't it?"

Teroenza lurched up out of his lounge-sling with an awkward, fierce movement. He began to pace his spacious, sumptuous apartment, his long, whippy tail slashing the air. "You fail to understand the nature of Solo's crime, Your Excellency! If only you had been here, to see what Solo did to your uncle! His death agonies were horrible! His moans! His spasms of agony! And all because of that wretched little human!"

The High Priest took a deep breath, realizing he was shaking with anger. "An example must be made, an example that will be remembered down through the ages by anyone of an inferior species who even *contemplates* harming a Hutt! Solo must die, die in agony, die screaming for mercy!"

Teroenza halted in the middle of his room, panting with fury, little hands balled into fists. "Ask Ganar Tos!" he cried passionately, knowing he was making a spectacle of himself in front of Kibbick, but unable to stop. "Ask him about Solo's audacity, his arrogance! He deserves to die, doesn't he?"

The High Priest's voice scaled up toward hysteria. The old Zisian majordomo bowed humbly, but his eyes were also glittering in their rheumy sockets. "My master, you speak the truth. Han Solo deserves only death, as painful and long-lasting a death as you can contrive. He has injured many sentients, including myself. He stole my mate, my bride, my beautiful Bria! I look forward to the day that a bounty hunter drags him into your presence, alive and awaiting your pleasure! I shall dance for joy while he screams!"

Kibbick was reared back, upright, staring at the vehemence his companions had displayed with some consternation. "I . . . see . . ." he said, finally. "I shall do my best to convince Uncle Aruk."

Teroenza nodded, and for once, his gratitude was not feigned. "Convince him, please," he said, his voice low and harsh with feeling. "I have worked hard for the Besadii clan and their kajidic for almost a decade now. You know, only too well, about the privations of living on this world, Your

Excellency. I ask little . . . but Han Solo—Han Solo, I must have. He will die at my hands, for a long, long time."

Kibbick inclined his massive head. "I'll explain it to Aruk," he promised. "Han Solo will be yours, High Priest . . ."

Chapter Three:

Nar Shaddaa

Before Han bought passage for himself and Chewbacca to Nar Shaddaa, he spent some time in a seamy section of the Nar Hekka spaceport, busily muddying their trail. A few judicious conversations in a couple of sleazy taverns gave him the name of the best ID forger on the planet.

The forger proved to be a Tsyklen from Tsyk, a round, hairless being with taut, pale skin. She was admirably suited for her chosen profession, having large eyes that provided exceptional vision, and seven fingers so slender and delicate that they resembled tentacles. With two opposing thumbs per hand, she could actually manipulate two holo-scribers at once! Han watched in fascination as she produced an ID naming him as Garris Kyll, and Chewbacca as Arrikabukk.

Han had no idea whether Teroenza knew anything about Chewie, but he was taking no chances.

With the forged IDs in their possession, and their store of credits considerably lighter, the two boarded the *Stellar Princess* for Nar Shaddaa.

The trip was an uneventful one, though Han couldn't shake his hyper-alertness. Being a hunted man again was something he hadn't wanted to deal with this soon in his new career as a smuggler. The trip took a little more than a standard day, even though Nar Hekka lay barely beyond the edge of the Y'Toub system, because the trip had to be accomplished at sublight speeds. The *Princess* was an old vessel, and its antique navicomputer wasn't up to calculating hyperspace jumps so close to the gravity wells produced by Y'Toub's star and six planets. Gravity wells, as any pilot knew, made plotting hyperspace jump calculations tricky.

That night, asleep in his narrow bunk aboard the transport, Han dreamed he was a cadet again, back in the Academy on Carida. In his dream, he was hurrying to finish polishing his boots, then he was assembling in formation on the parade ground, his uniform impeccable, every hair in place, boots shining until he could see his face in them.

He stood there, shoulder to shoulder with the other cadets, just as he had in real life, looking up at the nighttime sky, seeing the Academy's small mascot moon shining amid the stars. He was looking up at it, as he'd once done in reality, when suddenly, in eerie silence, it blew apart in a fireball that lit up the night sky. A great cry of amazement and consternation went up from the assembled ranks of cadets. Han stared into the yellow-white fireball, seeing an expanding donut ring of incandescent gas that was accompanied by chunks of debris flung before it. The cataclysm looked like a miniature exploding star . . .

As Cadet Han stared into the fireball, with the sudden unpredictability of dreams, he was somewhere else—facing a military tribunal of high-ranking Imperial officers. One of them, Admiral Ozzel, was reading aloud in flat, monotonous tones, while a young lieutenant methodically ripped every bit of military rank and insignia off Han's dress uniform, leaving him standing in a tattered tunic that hung on him in rags. Coldly expressionless, the young lieutenant solemnly drew Han's ceremonial officer's saber and snapped it over his knee (the blade had already been weakened by a laser score, so it would break easily).

Then the lieutenant, still as blank-faced as a droid (though Tedris Bjalin had graduated a year ahead of Han and they'd been good friends), coldly slapped Han across the face, a stinging blow that was meant to express derision and scorn. Finally, as a last ritual gesture of ultimate contempt for one in disgrace, Tedris spat, and the glob of his spittle landed on Han's boot. Han stared down at the shining surface, seeing the silver-white thread of saliva crawling toward his toes, marring the shining surface of his right boot . . .

At the time it had actually happened, Han had been vaguely grateful that Tedris hadn't actually spat in his face, as was his right if he'd elected to do so. The Corellian had endured it all without expression, steeling himself to show no reaction, but this time, in his dream, he screamed a hot protest—"NO!" and lunged at Tedris—

—and awoke, sweating and shaking, in his bunk.

Sitting up, he ran unsteady hands through his hair, telling himself it was only a dream—that the humiliation was done, over, that he never had to go through that again.

Never again.

Han sighed. He'd worked so hard to get into the Academy, so hard to stay there. Despite the lacks in his pre-Academy education (and there had been many) Han Solo had worked to better himself, to be the very best cadet he could. And he'd succeeded. Han's mouth tightened as he remembered commencement day. He'd graduated from the Academy with honors, and that had been one of the best days of his life.

Han shook his head. *Doesn't do any good to live in the past, Solo* . . . he reminded himself. All of those people— Tedris, Captain Meis, Admiral Ozzel (and what an old fool *he* was!)—all of his fellow officers were out of his life. Han Solo was a dead man to them, dead and gone. He'd never see Tedris again . . .

Han swallowed, and it hurt. When he'd entered the Academy he'd had such dreams, such hopes for a bright and shining future. He'd wanted to leave the old life of crime behind him, to become respectable. All his life he'd nurtured secret dreams of himself as an Imperial officer, esteemed and admired by all. Han knew he was smart, and he'd worked hard to make good grades, to fill in the gaps in his education. He'd had visions of himself one day in the uniform of an Imperial admiral, commanding a fleet, or, if he'd transferred to commanding a wing of TIE fighters, a general.

General Solo . . . Han sighed. It had a nice ring, but it was time to wake up and face facts. His chance at respectability was gone, ended when he'd refused to let Chewbacca be blasted in cold blood. He didn't regret his choice, either. During his years in the Academy and in the Imperial forces, he'd seen close-up and firsthand the growing callousness, the cruelty of the Imperial officers and those who served under them.

Nonhumans were their favorite target, but the atrocities were spreading to include humans, these days. The Emperor seemed to be moving from being a relatively benign dictator to becoming a ruthless tyrant, determined to crush the worlds he ruled into complete subservience.

Han doubted he'd have lasted much longer in the Imperial Navy anyway. At some point some officer would have ordered him to take part in one of the "demonstrations" designed to intimidate a dissenting world into submission, and Han would have told him what to do with himself. He knew that he could never have participated in some of the Imperial-ordered massacres he'd heard about—like the one on Devaron. Seven hundred people dead, mowed down without mercy.

Han could kill, had done it coolly and without flinching, against armed opponents. But shooting unarmed prisoners? Han shook his head. No. Never. He was better off as a civilian, as a smuggler or thief.

He began dressing. First his dark blue military-style trousers, with the broken red Corellian bloodstripe running down the outside seams. When he'd been discharged from the service, Han had half expected them to deprive him of his bloodstripe, as they'd done with his other decorations and insignia, but they'd left it. Han guessed that was because the bloodstripe wasn't an Imperial award. It was usually earned through military service, and was a mark of unusual heroism, but it was awarded by the Corellian government to a Corellian.

That had been a tough few days, all right, Han thought, remembering exactly how he'd earned the decoration. His right thumb rubbed the bloodstripe as he pulled his right boot on. The bloodstripe was designed so it could be removed and reaffixed to each new pair of trousers. Han had discovered that most non-Corellians had no idea what a mark of distinction it was—many just thought it was pure decoration.

Which suited Han just fine. He wore it, since it was his only remaining military decoration, but he never discussed where and how he'd earned it.

Some things it was better not to dwell on.

He finished getting dressed, pulling on a pale gray shirt

and a darker gray vest. He hurried, knowing they must be approaching Nar Shaddaa by now.

His small travel knapsack slung over his shoulder, Han went out into the corridor and moved toward the observation lounge. This transport hauled both passengers and cargo, so it had few amenities, but it did have a large viewport. Watching the stars was something that amused and soothed most beings, and almost every transport ship had one.

When Han reached the lounge, he discovered Chewbacca was there already, staring out at the stars. Han went over to the viewport and stood beside him, looking at their destination.

They were racing toward a large planet, bigger than Corellia, that boasted brown deserts, sickly green vegetation, and slate-blue oceans. Han recognized it at once. He'd been there before, five years ago. He nudged Chewie. "Nal Hutta," he told his companion. "Means 'Glorious Jewel' in Huttese, but trust me, pal, it ain't pretty. Bunch of swamps and bogs, and the whole place stinks like a sewer in the middle of a garbage dump." The Corellian wrinkled his nose at the memory.

As the partners watched, the *Stellar Princess* swung past the Hutt homeworld, using the planet's gravity to cut velocity. Chewie whined a question. "Nope, I've never been to Nar Shaddaa," Han replied. "When I was here five years ago, I never even got a close look at it." They could see the edge of the big moon now, as it crept over the horizon. Chewie made an inquiring sound. "Yeah, the planet and its moon are tidally locked, so they always keep the same hemispheres facing each other," Han replied. "Synchronous orbit."

As the *Princess* glided around the big world, Han saw that space on this side of the planet was studded with floating debris. As they drew closer, the debris proved to be derelict spaceships of all shapes and sizes. Han's Imperial training allowed him to ID many of them, but there were some that even he'd never seen.

The Smuggler's Moon was a big moon, one of the biggest Han had ever encountered. It was surrounded by the derelict spaceships, and they were numerous enough that the *Princess* had to change course several times to avoid them. Many of them were burned-out hulks, or shells with great holes blasted in their hulls.

From the amount of space-scarring on their sides, it was plain to Han that many of them had been there for decades, even centuries. Han wondered why there were so many, but then he caught a faint glimmer of planet-light off an ephemeral field that enclosed the waiting moon. A moment later a piece of space junk blazed up in a bright explosion.

"Hey, Chewie . . . that explains these hulks," Han said, pointing. "See that glimmer surrounding Nar Shaddaa? The place is shielded. These ships came calling, and if they didn't want to let 'em land, they just refused to drop shields, then used ion guns to blast 'em. Guess they must've had their share of pirates and raiders, huh?"

Chewbacca made a low noise that sounded like "Hrrrrrnnnn . . ." and meant "Right."

The faint haze caused by the moon's shield made it difficult to see specifics about their approaching destination. But Han could tell that the landscape was almost completely covered with structures. Communication spires stuck up in spikes from the welter of buildings. *Like a rundown version of Coruscant,* Han thought, remembering the world that was one vast city—a world so encased in layers upon layers of buildings that the natural landscape was almost completely covered except at the poles.

As Han stared out at the fabled Smuggler's Moon, he found himself remembering his dream again. In the dream he'd been looking up at another, very different moon. He frowned. Funny thing—that stuff about the mascot moon, that had actually *happened*. Han had stood in ranks with the other cadets and watched the little moon explode violently in Carida's nighttime sky.

Perhaps his subconscious had sent him that dream to remind him of something important that he'd forgotten. Han hoisted his knapsack higher on his shoulder. "Mako," he mumbled.

Chewbacca gave him an inquiring glance. Han shrugged. "I was just thinkin' that maybe we should look up Mako."

Chewie cocked his head and mhrrrnnnnned a question.

"Mako Spince. I knew him when he was an upperclassman cadet. Mako and me go back a long ways," Han explained.

Mako Spince was an old friend, and last Han had heard, he'd had ties to Nar Shaddaa. They said he even lived here at times. It wouldn't hurt to look up Mako, see if he could help his old buddy Han find work . . .

Mako Spince was ten years older than Han, and they couldn't have had more opposite childhoods. Han had been a child of the streets until the cruel, sadistic Garris Shrike had taken him in and introduced him to a life of crime. Mako was the son of an important Imperial Senator. He'd been brought up with every advantage—but he'd lacked Han's determination. Mako's main interest while at the Imperial Academy had been in having fun.

Mako had been an upperclassman, two years ahead of Han. Despite their disparate backgrounds, the two had become good friends, racing swoops, hosting clandestine wild parties, playing practical jokes on stodgy instructors. Mako was always the instigator in their mischief. Han had been the cautious one, never forgetting how hard he'd had to work to get into the Academy. The younger cadet was care-

ful never to get caught—but Mako, confident that his father's connections would protect him from consequences,
had dared anything and everything in his pursuit of the
perfect joke, the most daring escapade.

Destroying the Academy's mascot moon had been his
biggest—and last—prank as an Imperial cadet.

Han had known at the time that something was up,
something big. Mako had tried to induce him to come
along when he'd planned the break-in to the physics lab.
But Han had had a test to study for, so he'd refused. If he'd
known what Mako was planning, he'd have tried to talk his
friend out of it.

That night, while Han plotted orbits and worked on his
"Economics of Hyperspace Troop Movement" presentation, Mako broke into Professor Cal-Meg's physics lab. He
stole a gram of antimatter, then a small, one-man shuttle
and a spacesuit from the Academy shuttle hangar, and took
off.

Landing on the small planetoid that was Carida's nearest
of three satellites, Mako planted the antimatter capsule in
the middle of the huge Academy Seal that had been laser-
carved into the satellite decades ago, back when Carida was
still a training planet for the troops of the now-vanished
Republic. Mako triggered the antimatter explosion from a
safe distance in space, intending to blast the seal right off
the face of the little moon.

But Mako had underestimated the power of the antimatter he'd stolen. The entire satellite blew up in a cataclysmic
display that Han and the other cadets witnessed from the
planet's surface.

Mako was immediately one of the prime suspects. He'd
pulled so many pranks in his time, caused so much may-
hem, that the officers began checking on him almost before
the debris from the shattered satellite had either plunged

planetward or drifted into alignment, forming a disjointed ring around Carida.

Han was also a suspect, but fortunately for him, a friend had come over to see him for some astrophysics coaching right at the time of the break-in. Han's alibi was airtight.

But Mako's wasn't.

At the hearing, the prosecution had alleged that Mako was a terrorist who'd infiltrated the Academy. Han himself had volunteered to give testimony under truth drugs in order to clear his friend of *that* charge—and they'd had to accept his word that Mako had acted alone, intending only to play a prank. So Mako was spared the charge of terrorism. In the end, they'd just expelled the senior cadet.

Mako's father had come through one last time, and given Mako the credits to set himself up in business. Little did the Senator suspect that his only son would spend the money on a ship, and contraband to stock it with. Then Mako had disappeared, but Han knew that Mako Spince wasn't the sort to just quietly fade into the background. Not Mako. Where there was excitement to be had, and credits to be accrued, that's where you'd find Mako Spince.

Han was betting that someone on Nar Shaddaa would know where his friend was.

Han watched as the *Princess* drifted closer and closer to the large moon. Nar Shaddaa was actually the size of a small planet, almost a third the size of Nal Hutta. It was hard to make out details through the shield, but he could see lights flashing.

As the *Princess* neared the Smuggler's Moon, a section of the haze that marked the shield suddenly disappeared, and Han knew they'd dropped a shield to admit their ship. The transport went past the shield, and moments later they entered atmosphere.

Now Han could see the source of the flashing lights— huge holosigns that advertised goods and services. As they came closer, he was able to read one. "Sentients—Get It Here! Anything goes! If you have the credits, we have who—or what—you want!"

Just a real classy place, Han thought sarcastically. He'd seen signs for pleasure-houses before, but never anything this blatant.

As the *Princess* dropped "down" toward a large clear space atop a massive pile of permacrete, Han realized this must be their intended landing site. He looked about for a seat to strap himself in, but realized that none of the other passengers seemed concerned. They just grabbed a hand-hold affixed to the inside hull and hung on. Han shrugged, glanced at Chewbacca, and they did likewise. The Corellian discovered that it was much more difficult enduring a tricky landing as a passenger than it was as a pilot. When you were piloting, you were too busy to think about the possible danger.

A moment later there was a slight jar, and they were down.

Han and Chewbacca followed the other passengers toward the airlock, and found a line ahead of them, waiting to disembark. Han couldn't help noticing how hardened and seedy the other passengers appeared. Tough, space-scarred males, with a scattering of even tougher-appearing females. Sapients of assorted species, but no families, and no one was old.

That Barabel would fit right in, he thought, conscious of the comforting weight of his blaster against his thigh.

The airlock door slid open, and the passengers began filing down the ramp, onto the landing pad. Han took a deep breath of the local air, then wrinkled his nose in disgust. Beside him, Chewie whined softly.

"I *know* it stinks," Han said, out of the side of his mouth. "Get used to it, pal. We're gonna be here awhile."

Chewbacca's sigh was eloquent, and required no translation.

Han didn't want to seem like too much of a newcomer, so he tried hard not to stare as they walked down the ramp. Finally, he was able to get a good look at his surroundings.

At first glance, Nar Shaddaa reminded him of Coruscant—there was no open land to be seen at all. Only buildings, towers, spires, pedestrian glidewalks, shuttle landing pads, all of it blending into an unending vista of sentient-created construction. It resembled a permacrete forest studded with garish advertising holosigns.

But as he and Chewie walked slowly across the landing pad, Han quickly realized that even though they were on the topmost levels of the moon, this place differed greatly from the topmost levels of Imperial Center, as it was officially referred to these days.

Coruscant's topmost levels were clean, tastefully lighted marvels of soaring, graceful architecture. Only when one traveled down, hundreds of levels down, to the deeper levels of the planet-wide city, did Coruscant appear dingy and seedy.

The topmost level of Nar Shaddaa looked like the deepest levels of Coruscant. *If this is a top level,* Han thought, catching a glimpse of a dizzying plunge down into an artificial canyon between two massive, graffiti-emblazoned buildings, *I hate to think what it must be like down there* . . .

Han had been down to the bottommost level of Coruscant—once. It wasn't an experience he wanted to repeat.

Glancing surreptitiously around at the cityscape of Nar Shaddaa, Han made a mental note to NEVER visit the bottom levels of the Smuggler's Moon.

Overhead, the sky was a strange color, as though they were looking at a normal blue sky through a dark brownish filter. Nal Hutta hung there, as huge and bloated as the sluglike sentients that called it home. It took up at least ten degrees of the sky. Han realized that Nar Shaddaa must have two nights. One would be the normal long night, when one side of the moon was turned away from the sun. The other relatively short "night" would occur when the sun was eclipsed by the enormous bulk of Nal Hutta. Totality would probably last a couple of hours, Han thought, running a rough calculation in his head.

Chewie groaned and whined. "You're right, pal," Han said. "At least on Coruscant they planted trees and ornamental shrubs. I don't think anything could grow on this slag heap. Not even a lubellian fungus."

The two headed for a ramp that led down off the landing pad. The ramp wound round and round, and was not well lighted. Although they'd landed in daylight, the towering spires and structures that flanked the building with the landing-pad roof blocked out most of the sunlight as they descended. The enclosed ramp quickly grew dark and shadowy. The rest of the travelers had long since departed, and they were alone in the echoing silence of the high-walled, roofed ramp. Wan glowlights provided dim illumination. Han kept his back to the wall, thinking uneasily that this would be a real good place for an ambush.

His hand dropped to the butt of his blaster—

—just as a blue-green splat of energy from a stun beam came out of nowhere!

Han's reflexes had always been quick, and weeks of living on the run had honed them to a sharp edge. Before the beam splashed against the wall, he threw himself out of the way, landing flat. He rolled across the permacrete, sideways and down. When he came up, his blaster was ready in his hand.

Han caught a quick glimpse of his assailant—a stocky male humanoid, with a lot of hair on his face. A Bothan, probably. A bounty hunter, almost certainly. The Corellian snapped off a shot but missed, blowing a hole in the permacrete wall. He crouched beside the opposite wall, watching for the bounty hunter to reappear.

Chewbacca howled. Han looked across the ramp at his partner, who was crouched against the curve of the wall, safe for the moment. He made an urgent "stay still!" sign with his hand. Chewbacca glared at him, and hefted his bowcaster emphatically.

What's he trying to tell me? Han wondered. Chewie roared, and to anyone who didn't understand Wookiee, the sound he produced would have seemed nothing more than a howl of rage. But Han understood. He nodded at Chewie, then dived down-ramp, firing blindly as he went. Two shots sizzled into the wall, and chips of permacrete flew.

The stun beam screamed past him again, and Han took a deep breath, then yelled with anguish, doubling over and dropping his blaster.

He hit the permacrete and lay there, as if stunned. *This had better work . . .*

Steps approached, quick and decisive—

—and then came the *whang* of the bowcaster being fired. A loud, explosive *whump* and a short, choked-off scream followed.

Han rolled over and leaped to his feet, just in time to see his assailant slump to his knees, anguish imprinted on every hairy feature. A Bothan, sure enough. His hands were clutching a smoking hole in his chest.

A Bothan bounty hunter. Han recognized the type, if not the individual.

As he watched, the Bothan pitched over on his face. He thrashed, gurgled, gave one final twitch, then lay still.

Han looked over at his partner and nodded. "Good shooting, Chewie. Thanks."

Walking over to the dead Bothan, Han used the toe of his boot to turn him over onto his back. The hairy features had gone slack in death. Han eyed the wound. "That doesn't look anything like a blaster shot. Can't be all that many Wookiees here on Nar Shaddaa, so I think we need to disguise how this guy met his end."

Drawing his blaster, Han aimed, turned his head, then discharged it full force into the Bothan's chest. When he looked back, the Bothan barely *had* a chest, and all signs of Chewie's distinctive weapon were erased.

Han searched the bounty hunter, finding a few credits in his pockets, and a WANTED flimsy giving a description of one "Han Solo" plus the information that the quarry was thought to be heading for Nar Shaddaa. The bounty posted for Han was seventy-five hundred credits. Live capture only, no disintegrations.

Han scanned it, then stuffed it into his pocket. "Looks like things might get real exciting, Chewie," he said. "We'd better stay sharp."

"Hrrrrrrnnnn . . ."

Han wondered what to do about the Bothan. Should they try to destroy the body? Should they just leave him here, as a warning? Or should they find someplace to dump him where it would take him a while to be discovered?

After some consideration, Han decided to just leave the Bothan. If the sight of one dead bounty hunter might deter another, so much the better. He and Chewbacca set off down the last part of the ramp together. Han half expected the bounty hunter to have a partner, but no one bothered them.

Minutes later they emerged onto a street in Nar Shaddaa. Han stepped onto a lurching glidewalk and let it carry him along, while he looked around.

Nar Shaddaa resembled a tri-dee maze puzzle constructed by a lunatic. Spidery walkways and precipitous ramps joined building to building. Architectural styles and designs from dozens of worlds jostled shoulder to shoulder.

Domes, spires, arches, hulking squat rectangles, parabolas
. . . the jumble of shapes made his head spin. Durasteel
and permacrete and glassine and other building materials
Han couldn't even begin to identify were encrusted with
filth and graffiti. Some of the scrawled names and images
were stories high.

Many of the larger structures had obviously been built
decades ago, when Nar Shaddaa was a respectable spaceport, a pleasure moon where wealthy sentients came to
play. Great buildings that had once been fine hotels were
now gutted and reduced to multilevel hovels, housing the
living detritus of a dozen or more worlds. The streets and
alleys were subject to a constant bombardment of toxic and
noxious wastes spewed down from higher up. The air was
as bad as one of Nal Hutta's bogs—or worse.

The scent of food from multiple worlds warred with the
stench of leaking sewers, mingling with the sharp odors of
intoxicating spices and other drugs. The sharp reek of ship
exhaust was ever-present, as were the ships themselves,
roaring and gliding and swooping overhead, landing and
taking off in an endless bizarre ballet.

Some of the hotels and casinos were still in business—
most likely those owned by the Hutt Lords, Han guessed.
Sentients from dozens of worlds crowded the streets, avoiding eye contact, ever-alert, always poised to seek out and
profit from another sentient's mistake or moment of weakness. Nearly everyone Han saw went armed, with the exception of the droids.

Han was hungry, but he didn't recognize any of the
wares the street vendors were selling. "They say there's a
Corellian section," he muttered to Chewie. "That's probably where we should head." He didn't want to admit that
he was lost, for fear of attracting thieves or worse, but a few
minutes later Han saw a banner hanging from an awning
(most booths and building fronts possessed awnings—they

helped shield the inhabitants from noxious spatters falling from above) that read in six languages and Basic: INFORMATION BROKER.

Han stepped off the glidewalk and headed toward the booth, with Chewie trailing behind. The "Information Broker" proved to be an ancient Twi'lek woman, so old that her ropy head-tails were shriveled and knotty with age. She eyed Han sharply, then spoke in her own language. "What you wish to know, Pilot?"

Han took out a half-credit coin, and laid it on the edge of the booth, ostentatiously keeping his forefinger on it. "Two things," he said, in his own language, knowing she must speak Basic. "Directions on how to get to the Corellian section, by the safest and most direct route"—he paused as she keyed some information onto the ancient datapad before her, and then when she looked up again— "and . . . where can I find a smuggler named Mako Spince?"

The old Twi'lek grinned, showing stained and broken teeth. "For the first," she cried, "take this." She shoved a flimsy into his hand. Han squinted at it, saw that it was a section of a map. One blinking red dot indicated, "You Are Here." Directions to the Corellian sector of Nar Shaddaa were clearly indicated.

Han nodded. "Okay. What about Mako?"

She gave him an amused glance. "Go there, Corellian sector, Pilot. Ask in bars, brothels, gambling dens. You not find Mako, no. But *he* then find *you,* Pilot."

Han grinned reluctantly. "Yeah, that sounds like Mako. Okay, I guess you earned it." He lifted his forefinger off the credit piece, and she caused it to disappear so fast it was like a magic act.

She was watching him, her little orange-red eyes bright in her wrinkled countenance. "Pilot handsome," she said, giving her best approximation of a coy smile. The effect, with her teeth, was hideous. "Oodonnaa old, but lots of life yet. Pilot interested?" The tip of one head-tail lifted off her shriveled shoulder and twitched invitingly at the Corellian.

Han's eyes widened. *Minions of Xendor, she's propositioning me!* The tip of her head-tail made a beckoning motion. Han backed away, shaking his head, feeling his cheeks grow warm. "Uh, no thanks, madam," he said stiffly. "I'm honored, but, uh . . . I've taken a . . . vow. Of abstinence. Yeah. A vow."

She seemed more amused at his discomfiture than angered by his refusal as she waved farewell. Han about-faced and marched away. Beside him, Chewbacca gave an unmistakable Wookiee guffaw. "Yuck it up," Han snapped. "See if I stick my neck out for *you* again."

Chewie just laughed harder.

Two hours later they reached the Corellian sector. The old Twi'lek's map and directions proved accurate, but street signs were often missing, or had been turned around by pranksters. Han was relieved to walk into the Corellian sector and see architecture that was plainly patterned on that of his native world. Scents wafting from the sidewalk cafes tantalized him, familiar and reassuring. "Let's get something to eat," Han said, waving Chewie to one of the bistros that looked marginally cleaner than the others. Chairs and tables that had once been white were ranged beneath one of the omnipresent awnings, a green and red one, this time.

Han ordered traladon goulash, and was pleased to find that it was good, almost like eating back home. He dug into his plate with relish, while Chewbacca attacked a large salad and a plate of bloody-rare traladon ribs.

When Han had finished, he leaned back in his seat, sipping a local ale and trying to decide if he liked the taste. When the serving droid appeared to display his bill, Han asked, "Mako Spince. Does he ever come here? Medium height, broad shoulders, short dark hair, graying at the temples?"

The droid's head swiveled side to side. "No, sir, I have not seen the person you describe."

"Tell your boss I was askin' about him, okay?" Han said. He finished the last of his ale, then he and Chewbacca headed down the street toward the most garish of the bars. Short night was rapidly falling now, as Y'Toub was eclipsed behind the bulk of Nal Hutta. The real night was still many hours away, and would last more than forty standard hours. As the artificial lights came up, Han wondered if he'd ever get used to such long nights. It probably didn't matter, since the moon that was a city never really slept.

At The Smuggler's Rest, Han asked again for Mako Spince, and naturally, nobody had ever heard of him. They did the same thing at The Lucky Star, the tattered remains of what had once been an elegant casino, and then at two or three more bars. Han was getting used to the word "no." He sighed and trudged onward.

The Smuggler's Hideaway.

The Corellian Cafe.

The Golden Orb.

The Exotic Exhibit (LIVE Dancers! LIVE Shows!).

The Comet Casino.

The Drunken Drummer.

By now Han's feet were beginning to hurt from pounding the permacrete, going up and down ramps. Places on Nar Shaddaa were often frustrating to reach unless one had wings, or a jet pak. You could stand on a balcony and look over at your destination, only ten meters away, and yet have to walk for fifteen minutes, up and down rampways, to reach it.

Some of the buildings had ropes or wires strung between them, but Han wasn't desperate or foolhardy enough to trust himself to swing hand over hand across a twenty- or forty- or hundred-story abyss.

The walkways between buildings were frequently in poor repair, and after an assessing look, Han often decided to take the long way around. Some of them might have held him, but he doubted they'd stand up to the Wookiee's weight.

He was beginning to wonder whether they should just give up their search and try to find a flophouse that would be a safe place to grab a few hours' sleep. Thinking back, Han realized that it had been nearly twelve hours since he'd awakened on the *Princess*.

He turned his head as they walked by the mouth of a smelly alley to suggest this to Chewbacca when a hand reached out of the alley and grabbed him by the throat. Half a second later, Han was dragged up against a hard humanoid body. He felt the muzzle of a blaster press his temple.

"Not one step," a deep, congenial voice said over his shoulder, addressing Chewbacca, "or I'll scramble his brains till they run out his ears."

The Wookiee halted, snarling, showing teeth, but obviously unwilling to attack in the face of that threat.

Han *knew* that voice. He gasped, but couldn't get any breath to speak with. The iron hand tightened on his throat. "Mako!" he tried to say.

"Maa—" was all he managed to get out.

"Don't cry to your mama to me, kid," the voice said. "Now who in the Name of Xendor are you, and why were you askin' about me?"

Han gulped, gagged, but still couldn't speak.

Chewbacca growled, then pointed at Mako's quivering captive. "Haaaaannnn," the Wookiee said, twisting his mouth around the human name with great difficulty. "Haaaannnn . . ."

"Huh?" the voice said, sounding stunned. "Han?"

Abruptly Han was released, then swung around. As he gasped, hands to his throat, his captor, who was indeed Mako Spince, grabbed him in a hug so enthusiastic that it deprived him of breath yet again. "Han! Kid, it's great to see you! How ARE you, you old sonofagun?" A hard fist thumped the younger Corellian between the shoulder blades.

Han gasped and wheezed, only to lose his breath again. Mako helpfully slapped him on the back, which didn't improve matters.

"Mako . . ." he managed, finally. "It's been a long time. You've changed."

"So have you," his friend said.

They stood there studying each other. Mako's hair was long enough to brush his shoulders now, and there were more gray threads amid the black. He wore a fierce, bristling mustache, and had gained some weight, mostly in his shoulders. A narrow scar ran down the line of his jaw. Han decided he was glad Mako was on his side. He didn't look like anyone Han wanted to have as an enemy. He wore a scarred jumpsuit of spacer's leather, hide so thin and flexible, and yet so tough, that it was said it could maintain internal pressure even in vacuum.

The two friends stared at each other, sizing each other up, then both burst out with questions. They stopped, laughing. "One at a time!" Mako said.

"Okay," Han said. "You go first . . ."

Minutes later, they were all seated in a tavern, drinking, talking, and spouting questions. Han told Mako his story, and found that his old friend wasn't surprised to learn that he'd left the service. "I knew you'd never be able to go along with the slaving, Han," Mako said. "I remember how it used to set your teeth on edge to even *see* an Imperial slaving detail. Made you crazy, boy. I knew the first time they tried to get you to boss slaves, that would be the end of your brilliant career."

Han looked sheepish as he raised his second tankard of Alderaanian ale to his lips. "You know me too well," he admitted. "But what could I do, Mako? Nyklas was gonna kill Chewie!"

Mako's ice-blue eyes were smiling with unaccustomed warmth. "Nothing else you *could* have done, kid," he said.

"So, Mako, how've you been doing?" Han asked. "How's the business?"

"Booming, Han," Mako said. "The Empire's restrictions are makin' us all rich, runnin' contraband of all kinds these days. Spice, yeah, that's still big. But we do nearly as well these days smuggling arms, weapons components, power paks, all that kind of thing. Luxuries like perfume and Askajian fabric, too. Lemme tell ya, Han, old Palpatine wouldn't rest nearly as easy nights if he knew how *dissatisfied* with his rule some worlds are getting."

"So there's work here?" Han asked eagerly. "Work for pilots? You know I'm good, Mako."

Mako signaled the server droid for another round of drinks. "Kid, you're one of the best, and I'll let everyone know that," Mako said, slapping Han on the shoulder. "Badure didn't name you 'Slick' for nothin'! Tell you what, want to work for me to get your feet wet? I could use a good copilot, and while you're ridin' with me, I can show you some of the best runs. I'll introduce you to all the other runners, too. Some of 'em are bound to need help."

Han hesitated. "Could Chewie here come along?"

Mako shrugged and took a huge swig of ale. "Can he shoot? I can always use a good gunner."

"Yeah," Han said, finishing his own tankard with more confidence than he felt. Chewie was a dead shot with his bowcaster, but he'd only been training as a gunner for a month or so. "He can shoot."

"It's all set, then," Mako said. "Listen, kid, you found yourself a landing zone yet?"

"A landing zone," in smuggler's lingo, meant a room or flat. Han shook his head and felt the room lurch slightly. "I was hoping you could recommend a decent place," he said. "Not too expensive."

"Sure I can!" Mako said, slurring ever so slightly. "But why don' you two come stay with me for a day or so, till we c'n get you set up."

"Well . . ." Han glanced over at Chewie, "sure, we'd love to, wouldn' we, ol' buddy?"

"Hrrrrrrrnnnnnnnnn!"

Mako insisted on paying for the drinks, then the three left, heading for Mako's digs. The two humans were rather the worse for the ale they'd consumed, but Mako assured them it wasn't far. They headed a few levels down, where the buildings were grimier and seamier. "Don' be fooled," Mako said, waving a hand at their surroundings. "I've got plenty of room, 'n my place is fixed up decent. But living down here, you're not as much a target for thieves and burglars as the folks livin' topside." He jerked a thumb upward.

Han eyed their surroundings, and concluded that back in his days as a burglar he'd have given this area a clean miss. It was unprepossessing. Drunks weaved along the permacrete, and the glidewalks down on this level were permanently broken. Beggars and pickpockets eyed them, but didn't approach the trio. Han figured that was because Chewbacca was wearing his fiercest "Don't mess with me or I'll rip your arm off " look.

But suddenly, what Han had assumed was a heap of old, grimy rags stirred. From within the rags a skeletal human hand appeared, and Han caught just a glimpse of a beaky-nosed, nearly toothless face. An ancient crone, whose eyes shone bright with . . . what? Drugs? Madness?

Oh, no! Not again! What is it with all the old women on Nar Shaddaa? Can't wait to get their hands on young pilots?

Han drew back, but the liquor had slowed his reflexes, and he wasn't quick enough. A second talonlike hand shot out of the heap of tatters and grabbed his wrist. "Tell your fortunes, good sirs? Tell your fortunes, masters?" The voice was shrill and squeaky, and Han couldn't place the accent. "The descendant of Vima Sunrider has foreseen the future, good sirs! For a credit she will tell you what lies ahead."

"Lemme go!" Han tried to yank his hand free from the filthy claw, but the ancient woman's grip was surprisingly strong. He fumbled for a credit coin, just to make her let go of him. He didn't want to have to stun the crone—at her age a stun blast might kill her. "Here! Take th' credit and lemme go!" He dropped the money in her lap.

"Vima no beggar!" the old woman insisted indignantly. "She earns her credit! Foresees the future, yesssss she does! Vima knows, yessssss . . ."

Han stopped and sighed, rolling his eyes. At least she wasn't propositioning him. "Go ahead, then," he snapped.

"Ah, young captain . . ." she half crooned, prying open his fist and staring at his palm, then up at his face. "So young . . . so much lies before you. A long road, first the smuggler's road, then the way of the warrior. Glory you will have, yessssss. But first you must face terrible danger. Betrayal, yesssss . . . betrayal from those you trust. Betrayal . . ." Her eyes fixed for a second on Mako, and the older man and Han exchanged exasperated glances.

"So I'm gonna be betrayed," Han said impatiently. "Will I get rich? Thass all I care about."

"Ahhhhhhh . . ." she cackled shrilly. "My young captain, yessssss . . . wealth will come to you, but only after you no longer care about it."

Han burst out laughing. "That'll be th' day! Grandma, gettin' rich is ALL I care about!"

"Yesssss, that is true. Much will you do for money. But more will you do for love."

"Great," Han snarled, trying again to yank free. "Thass it, I've had 'nuff of this garbage," he growled, and with a hard flex of his wrist, he broke her grip. "Thanks for nothing . . . nutty old witch. Don't ever bother me again."

Turning unsteadily on his heel, Han stalked away, scowling, with Chewbacca and Mako in his wake. He could hear Mako snickering, and Chewie was still chuckling. Han scowled. The crazy old thing had made a fool of him!

The permacrete beneath his feet seemed to lurch slightly, and all Han could think about was how good it was going to feel to stretch out on Mako's couch, or floor, and grab some sleep.

Behind him, he could hear the old woman cackling softly, crooning nonsense to herself.

Han hardly remembered climbing the rampway to Mako's flat, and he didn't remember falling onto the couch at all. He was instantly asleep, and this time, he didn't dream.

When he awakened the next morning, he'd forgotten all about the old woman and her "foretelling."

Aruk the Hutt was doing what he loved most in all the universe . . . totaling his profits. The powerful Hutt Lord, head of the Besadii clan and its kajidic, bent over his datapad, his stubby fingers busy as he instructed the machine to calculate a percentage of profits based on a twenty percent yearly growth in product, projected three years into the future.

The resulting graph and accompanying figures made him laugh softly, a booming "Heh, heh, heh . . ." in the solitude of his huge office. No other living thing was present, only Aruk's favorite scribe, who stood poised in the corner, metallically gleaming, waiting until its master summoned it from its artificial repose.

Aruk read the graph again, and blinked his bulbous eyes. He was an old Hutt, approaching his ninth century, and he'd reached the corpulent stage that most Hutts achieved past middle age. It was now such an effort for him to get around under his own power that he seldom bothered anymore. Even the warnings of his personal physician about impending circulatory problems failed to make him exercise these days. Instead, he relied on his anti-gravity repulsor sled. With it, he could go anywhere. Aruk's sled was top quality, the best money could buy. After all, why should the head of the Besadii kajidic deny himself anything?

But Aruk was not one of those sybaritic Hutts who relished the pleasures of the flesh. True, he was a gourmet, and often a gourmand, but he didn't maintain entire palaces filled with slaves to cater to his slightest—or most perverse—whim, the way some Hutts did.

Aruk had heard that Jiliac's nephew, Jabba, kept several female dancing humanoids—humanoids, of all things!—on leashes near him at all times. Aruk considered such indulgences distasteful and extravagant. The Desilijic clan had always had a weakness for fleshly pleasures. Jiliac's taste was better than Jabba's, but he enjoyed hedonistic excess just as much as his nephew.

And that is why we will prevail, Aruk thought. *The Besadii clan is willing to endure a bit of privation, if necessary, to gain our ends . . .*

Aruk knew it wouldn't be easy, though. Jiliac and Jabba were clever and ruthless, and their clan was as wealthy as his own. For years the two richest and most powerful Hutt clans had contended with each other for the most lucrative ventures. Neither clan had eschewed methods such as assassination, kidnapping, and terrorism to gain their ends.

Aruk knew that Jabba and Jiliac would do almost anything to bring Besadii down. But the path to ultimate power was money, and Aruk was pleased with how many credits the Ylesian project was bringing Besadii every year.

Soon, Aruk thought, *we will have so many credits that we will be able to wipe them off the face of Nal Hutta, eliminate them as we would any blight on crops or pestilence in our people. Soon, the Besadii will rule Nal Hutta unopposed . . .*

Aruk, and his dead sibling, Zavval, had been the ones who'd thought of setting up colonies on Ylesia, and using religious pilgrims as slave labor to turn raw spice into the finished product. The only thing they'd feared was a slave uprising, and it had been Aruk who'd come up with the idea of the One, the All, and the Exultation to tie it all together.

Most Hutts knew of the t'landa Til ability to project warm, pleasurable emotions and sensations into the minds of most humanoid species. But it had taken Aruk's quick thinking, his cleverness, to come up with the idea of the Exultation as a mind-numbing "reward" for a day's hard labor in the spice factories.

Once he'd realized how the t'landa Til ability could be utilized, it had been a simple matter for Aruk to make up some doctrine, compose a few hymns, and write several chants and litanies. And that was all it took to produce a "religion" that credulous fools belonging to inferior species could embrace.

Production in the factories was excellent—had been excellent all along. Only once, five years ago, had the Ylesian enterprise not turned a tidy profit. That was the year that wretched Corellian, Han Solo, had destroyed the glitterstim factory. And destroyed Zavval, too, though the financial loss was the one Aruk regretted the most. He did not think himself unduly harsh or unsympathetic for caring so little that his sibling had died. No, he was reacting as any true Hutt would.

Aruk studied one item on the Ylesian colony's project budget. The sum of seventy-five hundred credits to be handed over to the person or persons responsible for Han's live capture. "No disintegrations" was the primary guideline. "Live capture and delivery."

Seventy-five hundred credits. A twenty-five-hundred-credit raise since the bounty was first posted. Apparently Solo was proving . . . difficult. Well, this new bounty was certainly large enough to tempt many hunters, though Aruk had seen larger ones. Still, for a man so young, it was a large bounty.

Was it really necessary to pay extra for the "live capture" option? Aruk had supervised many torture sessions, coolly and efficiently, but unlike many of his people, he took no pleasure in tormenting sentients to gain his own ends. If the Corellian Solo were to be brought before him, Aruk would not bother to torture him before ordering his death.

But Teroenza was a different story. The t'landa Til were vengeful people, and it was obvious to Aruk that the High Priest of Ylesia would not rest until he could personally supervise the long and exceedingly painful death of Han Solo. Moment by moment, scream by scream, groan by groan, Solo would die in the most exquisite agony, while Teroenza savored every second of it.

But did Aruk want to pay extra, just so Teroenza could be satisfied? Aruk considered. Lines of concentration formed above his bulbous, slit-pupiled eyes. After a moment he released his breath in a short, decisive "houf." Very well, he would authorize the payment of the bounty. Let Teroenza look forward to his fun. The anticipation made the High Priest happy, and happy underlings were productive underlings.

Aruk was a bit concerned about Teroenza, actually. The t'landa Til was definitely running the Ylesian operation, no matter how much he and that idiot Kibbick tried to disguise that fact. Aruk frowned. Ylesia was a Hutt operation. It wasn't proper for anyone other than a Hutt to give the orders there. And yet . . . Kibbick was the only high-ranking Hutt in the Besadii clan who was available at the moment to take the Ylesian posting. And Kibbick, there was no denying it, was a fool.

If only I dared send Durga, Aruk thought. *He has the will and the intelligence to rule Ylesia properly, to remind Teroenza of just who his masters are . . .*

Durga was Aruk's only offspring. He was still a very young Hutt, barely past the age of legal responsibility and true self-awareness; only a hundred standard years old. But he was smart, ten times more intelligent and clever than Kibbick.

When Durga was born, all the other Hutts urged Aruk to roll over on the helpless newborn, smothering him, because of the dark birthmark that spread like a foul liquid from his forehead down over one eye and cheek. They said that such a marred countenance would make the youngster socially unacceptable, and speculated that he would be feebleminded all his life. Ancient tales mentioned that such birthmarks were supposed to be omens of disaster, and the elder Hutts predicted all sorts of terrible things should Durga be allowed to survive.

But Aruk had looked down at his tiny, squirming offspring and sensed that his child would grow up to be a worthy Hutt, intelligent, cunning, and, when necessary, ruthless. So he had taken young Durga up into his arms and solemnly pronounced that here was his offspring and heir, and warned the nay-sayers to be silent.

Aruk had seen to it that Durga was well educated, and had everything a growing Hutt could want. The young Hutt responded to his parent's interest, and the bond between the two had become very close.

Staring down at the graphs showing the Ylesian finances, Aruk made a mental note to share his findings with Durga later that day. He was grooming his offspring to take on the leadership of the clan after his own passing.

These figures are so encouraging, Aruk thought, *that we should put some of this profit into founding yet another colony on Ylesia. Seven colonies can produce much more processed spice than six. And we can increase our missionary force by recruiting more t'landa Til males and sending them out to lure in more "pilgrims."*

Aruk's greatest dream was to someday expand their spice-processing and slaving operation to a second world in the Ylesian system. He knew he probably wouldn't live to see two worlds producing at full capacity, but Durga definitely would.

There was only one problem, and that was Desilijic. Aruk knew that Jiliac and Jabba watched every move he and his high-ranking clan members made, and they were ready to pounce at the slightest sign of weakness. They were ruthless, the Desilijic, and they were jealous of the Besadii clan and their success on Ylesia. Aruk knew only too well how much Jabba and Jiliac would give to destroy them all and take over the Ylesian operation.

Still, it was but a sign of the Besadii clan's extraordinary success and accomplishment that they be so envied. Hutt life was full of move and countermove. That was the way of it, and frankly, Aruk thrived on the intrigue, the danger. He wouldn't have changed things if he could have.

With a sigh of contentment, Aruk the Hutt turned off his datapad and stretched, rubbing his bulbous eyes. Ahhhhh . . . a good afternoon's work. Time for dinner, and a chance to spend time with his offspring. How pleasant that he had such good news to impart!

Guiding his repulsor sled with minuscule touches from his thick fingers, Aruk glided from the room, in search of food and companionship . . .

Chapter Four:

Upping the Ante

Five months and six bounty hunters later, Han and Chewbacca had settled down into life on Nar Shaddaa. Han found them a little apartment in the Corellian sector, a megablock or so from Mako's place, and only one level below it. The little flat was set up like a small suite, with two tiny bedrooms with foldout beds, a minuscule kitchen/living area, and refresher unit. But they didn't spend much time at home. As soon as Mako had introduced Han to his associates, the young Corellian found steady work. Good pilots were always valued on Nar Shaddaa.

During his first month, Han filled in as a shift pilot on the Nar Shaddaa to Nal Hutta shuttle, ferrying Hutts and their underlings back and forth from the Smuggler's Moon to the Hutt homeworld. Han had hoped to meet either Jabba or Jiliac that way, but the two top Hutt Lords of the Desilijic clan had their own private shuttles and didn't need to take public ones. Han hung on to the referral Tagta had given him, but decided he'd better learn his way around before he applied for jobs piloting for the Hutts. They were tough masters to please.

Just about the time Han's temporary job ended, the young Corellian went out with Mako on several runs, hauling loads of spice from the Twi'lek homeworld, Ryloth, to a staging area on Roon. There Han met up with an old acquaintance of Mako's, a craggy-faced, aging smuggler named Zeen Afit. Zeen was heading off to Smuggler's Run with a shipment of food, and when he mentioned that he'd like company, Han and Chewbacca offered to ride along.

Smuggler's Run was a hideout for sentients on the lam who were even "hotter" than the denizens of Nar Shaddaa. Smuggler's Run was a series of hideouts—actually, artificial environments whittled out of several large asteroids located in the middle of a huge asteroid field. The main one was a smelly hole bored into a large asteroid that was known as Skip 1.

Zeen Afit showed Han the way into the Run, through the treacherous, constantly changing asteroid field, though he wouldn't let him pilot his clunky old freighter, the *Corona*. "Next time, kid," he promised, in his breathless, wheezy voice, as his fingers flew over the controls. "I promise you. This time, just watch old Uncle Zeen and enjoy the ride."

Han gulped as *Corona* narrowly missed colliding with a jagged, hurtling rock that would have reduced them and their ship to molecules. "If I'm still alive when the next time comes," he pointed out, involuntarily ducking as another asteroid nearly grazed their viewscreen. "Blast it, Zeen, slow down! Are you crazy?"

"Only way to fly an asteroid field is fast and by the seat of your pants, kid," Zeen Afit said, never taking his eyes from his instruments. "If you try and tiptoe in, chances are you'll get smashed before you can wipe your nose. I always just fly right in, keepin' my eyes open, and I'm still here."

When they reached the fabled Smuggler's Run, Han and Chewbacca warily followed Zeen Afit into Skip 1, to meet "the gang," as he called his friends. Han was introduced to a sallow, thin man with scars on his face named Jarril, and another, older man with a receding hairline who incongruously went by the name "Kid DXo'ln."

Skip 1 was a regular warren of rooms, dining halls, gambling dens, bars, and drug hideaways. Han was frankly nervous, as he realized that here, even more than on Nar Shaddaa, there was no law. None.

He could die here, and no one but Chewie (presuming the Wookiee was still alive himself, an unlikely assumption) would ever know or care. Han was careful not to let any of his nervousness show. He had grown up with lawless people, had seen plenty of degenerate spirits by the time he was ten. He'd just never encountered quite so many bloodthirsty, desperate lost beings in one place before.

As he and Zeen headed for the bar, Han noticed the runnel of greenish-yellow gooey liquid oozing along a channel cut into the middle of the stone floor. Chewbacca snuffled, then growled in protest. "Yeah, that really stinks," Han said, his nostrils twitching. "What the heck is that stuff, Zeen? It's on the walls, too . . ."

"Oh, it's just the ooze we gotta put up with, kid," the smuggler told him. "Stinks, don't it? Every so often we get to thinkin' we ought to find out where it comes from and dam it up. It's some kinda proto-organic compound, they say, mixed with sulfur."

Han's nose wrinkled. The ooze smelled like rancid meat mixed with rotting vegetation, laden with a liberal dose of sulfur. He'd smelled worse, but not recently.

As they stepped over the ooze channel and headed over to the bar, Han's attention was caught and held by a beautiful woman with long black hair who definitely stood out in the mix of unsavory smuggler types. She wore a short skirt that showed off magnificent legs, and a top that was little more than a cropped shirt tied tightly to show off her bosom and midriff. Han stared at her, thinking that she was one of the most striking women he'd ever seen. Suddenly he realized she was looking back at him. Han quickly essayed his most charming smile.

She walked toward them. Han's pulse skipped a beat, but then he realized she was regarding him with a marked lack of enthusiasm, as though he were a side of traladon meat that had gone green around the edges. Han's smile stiffened on his lips. *Guess the attraction isn't mutual* . . .

"Han, I'd like you to meet a friend of mine," Zeen said, indicating the woman. "Sinewy Ana Blue, one of the top smugglers around. She also runs a wicked sabacc table. Blue, meet Han Solo, a new kid I brought along for the ride. And this is his pal, Chewie."

Han nodded cordially. "Pleasure to meet you—"

Noting his hesitation over what to call her, she smiled, revealing a shining blue crystal tooth in the front of her mouth. "Call me Blue," she said, in a voice that couldn't help being sultry. "Han Solo, you said? And"—she turned to Han's companion—"Chewie?"

"Chewbacca," Han supplied.

"Pleased to meet you, Chewbacca," she said. "Have you met Wynni yet?"

Chewie cocked his head and whined a soft question.

Sinewy Ana Blue smiled at him. "You'll know her when you meet her," she promised cryptically.

"So," Han said, "may I buy you a drink . . . Blue?"

She glanced at him, seemed to consider, then smiled faintly. "No, I don't think so," she said. "You're cute, but not my type, Solo. I like them a bit more . . . seasoned."

Zeen snickered. "She's particular, our Blue," he said, noting Han's chagrin at the open rebuff. "You young, single types don't offer enough . . . sport. She likes the lure of the chase, especially when it's part of the thrill that comes from stealin' what don't belong to you."

Sinewy Ana Blue gave Zeen a long, up and down stare. "You like to live dangerously these days, don't you?" she drawled. Then she turned back to Han. "Do you play sabacc, Han Solo?"

Han nodded. "I've tried it," he said cautiously.

She gave him a slow, alluring smile. "Come around, then. I'd love to have some fresh blood in my game."

With a final nod to Chewbacca, she turned and walked away. Han watched her go with an admiring headshake. "Minions of Xendor . . . that is one fine-looking woman," he muttered.

"Pure sabacc," Zeen agreed. "Prime grade ore."

"And she only goes after married guys?"

"Let's just say she prefers the thrill of the hunt," Zeen said. "Anyone that's too available, too eager to get caught, isn't challenging enough prey."

"You make her sound like a Devaronian fur-spider," Han said, watching Sinewy Ana Blue's eminently watchable backside vanish amid the crowd of talking, laughing, drinking smugglers.

"Not too far off, kid," Zeen said with a chuckle and a wink. "Our Blue is one of a kind. She—"

He broke off and whirled as a loud roar reverberated through the bar. Han spun on his heel to find a Wookiee standing in the doorway. She was big for a Wookiee female, as tall and muscular as Chewie. Her blue eyes were fixed

unblinkingly upon Han's companion, who was busily looking anywhere but at the newcomer.

"Who's that?" Han asked Zeen.

"Wynni," the senior smuggler replied with a wink and a
leer.

Han and Chewbacca watched as the Wookiee came over
to them. She growled a throaty greeting at Chewie, totally
ignoring his human companion. Then she reached out one
hairy paw and ran it admiringly down Chewbacca's long
arm.

Han turned to Zeen. "I think she likes him," he said
dryly, in Basic.

"Looks like," Zeen agreed. "I think your buddy there is
bein' offered what you weren't, pal. 'Cept he don't look any
too happy about it."

The craggy-faced smuggler was correct. Chewbacca
looked around wildly as the female Wookiee pressed up
close to him, growling suggestively.

Catching Han's eye, Chewie shook his head in a slight
but emphatic movement. Han took pity on his friend.
"Hey, Chewie," he said loudly, "we gotta go."

Wynni turned around and snarled at him. Clearly, she
didn't like having her seduction attempt interfered with.
Han looked at her and shrugged. "Sorry," he said. "We've
got somewhere we have to be. A previous engagement."

Wynni plainly didn't believe him. She growled low in her
throat.

Han realized that they were drawing a crowd. Kid
DXo'ln, Zeen's balding friend, stepped forward. "It ain't
polite to accuse people of lyin', Wynni," he told the
Wookiee. "Han here is tellin' the truth. I just signed him
and his Wookiee pal on to ride as copilot and gunner to
Kessel aboard the *Starfire*. Matter of fact, my droids should
be finished loadin' our cargo by now, Solo. Let's go."

Han smiled sweetly at Wynni and shrugged, with a

"What can you do?" expression. Chewbacca didn't bother trying to hide how glad he was to get away from the predatory female.

As they headed up the corridor toward Skip 1's landing bay, Han gave Kid a grateful smile. "Thanks," he said. "For a while it looked like I wasn't going to be able to get Chewie out of there without making her mad."

Kid DXo'ln grinned. "Yeah, and upsettin' a lovestruck Wookiee ain't exactly a smart thing to do. So, what do you want to do now? You actually up for going on to Kessel with me?"

"Sure," Han said. "I've always wanted to go to Kessel. Are you going on the Run after you off-load your cargo there?"

"I don't know," Kid replied. "Maybe, if there's a cargo waitin' for me to pick up. But there's bound to be somebody you can catch up with who'll take you on the Run."

Han had heard of the Kessel Run, that ultimate test of a smuggler pilot's expertise. Traveling the Kessel Run allowed a pilot to shortcut across a large, uninhabited area of space that would otherwise have taken a vessel two days or more to skirt. But the direct route from Kessel back to the standard trade routes lay perilously close to the Maw, a massive collection of black holes that distorted both space and time. Many a ship had been lost to the Maw, lost with all hands.

Once they were safely aboard the *Starfire,* Kid waved a hand at the controls. "I hear you're pretty good, Solo. Want to try takin' her through the field?"

Han nodded, his mouth suddenly dry. Remembering Zeen's advice, he forced himself to head confidently into the field, instead of holding back. He remembered stories told by the pilots who'd been aboard *Trader's Luck* that indicated Zeen had been right—most asteroid fields could be navigated by someone with steely nerves and quick reflexes. Holding his breath, Han sent the beat-up little freighter skittering from side to side, not slacking off on their speed.

Kid sat back in the pilot's seat and just watched. Only once did he interfere, and that was to increase the ship's acceleration a notch, to avoid a smaller asteroid that was orbiting a larger one. The bigger asteroid had hidden its small companion. The *Starfire* zipped by so close that the deflector shields activated and the ship shuddered in protest. But they avoided the impact.

Han bit his lip when the chunk of rock, half the size of the ship, tumbled away behind him. "Sorry, Kid. I should've seen it."

"No way you could've seen it, Solo," the older man said. "I just been flying into and out of the Run for so many years that I practically got all these rocks memorized. I knew that one had a baby taggin' behind, 'cause I've seen it before."

When they finally emerged into clear space, Han felt as though he'd been piloting for a day instead of half an hour. He wanted to slump back into his seat, but a glance at Kid DXo'ln showed Kid, head tilted back, eyes closed, apparently asleep.

Han looked at Chewie, shrugged, and said, "Take over a second while I plot us a course to Kessel, pal."

Minutes later Han retrieved the final coordinates from the navicomputer, and then finalized his course. He looked over at Kid DXo'ln. One watery blue eye opened. "Punch it, Solo," the raspy voice told him.

Han grinned. "Sure."

Moments later the bright pinpoints of realspace elongated before them, and the *Starfire* shot down a seeming tunnel of starlines. Han realized he was grinning like a kid. It had been a long time since he'd done any real piloting that wasn't just drills.

When he'd been in the Navy, he'd served shifts as a helmsman on the big Imperial ships, but his favorite duty had been flying TIE fighters. Small, nimble, and deadly, they required pinpoint control to maneuver and fire, but they had no shielding at all, which made them very vulnerable. Few TIE pilots lived to grow old.

When the *Starfire* emerged into realspace, Han took one look at the Maw and drew a quick breath. Kid DXo'ln, who had finally awakened from his nap, stretched and grinned. "Impressive, ain't it, Solo?"

"I'll say," Han muttered.

The Maw stretched before them, a collection of black holes that were sucking the life from the nearby stars. Long streamers of gas threaded their way into the monstrous whirlpools of gas and dust that marked the location of the black holes. The holes themselves were invisible, of course. The reason they were called "black" holes was that their gravity was so strong that nothing, not even light, could escape their pull.

But the gas and dust marked their location. There were quite a few of them. So far as Han knew, the Maw was unique in the galaxy.

"Kessel's right on the edge, Solo," Kid said. "Here, I'll show you the coordinates on the screen."

Han studied readouts on the lumpy, misshapen little planet that orbited a small, fierce, blue-white star. Kessel was orbited by its small, solitary moon. "The planet isn't even spherical," he muttered. "It doesn't mass enough to hold onto an atmosphere."

"Yeah, I know. You gotta wear a breath mask there, but they keep a couple of atmosphere-generating plants runnin', so we won't have to put on vacuum gear," Kid told him.

Han frowned down at the readouts. "I didn't know Kessel had a moon."

"Yeah, there's rumors that the Imps have been scouting it, that they might actually build something there. Crazy, if you ask me."

"There are Imperial ships around here?" Kid's revelation worried Han. Chewie was still an escaped slave, after all. They'd just love to recapture him.

"Yeah, I ran into a guy who works for Imp security as a snitch, and he told me the Imps are considering putting some kind of big hush-hush installation right smack in the middle of the Maw," Kid said thoughtfully.

Han stared at the whirling vortices of dust and gas that marked the black holes and shook his head. "A base? In *there?* They're crazy, all right!"

Kid shrugged. "There's more space than you'd guess between those black holes. Some smugglers say that you can actually shorten your Kessel Run by skimming close to the Maw."

Han frowned as he studied his readouts. "You mean make the Run in less time."

Kid chuckled, a creaky sound. "Well, that, too. But they say that both time and space get warped, distorted so close to the Maw. So you can not only make your run faster, but actually shave off part of the distance."

"What's the record?" Han asked curiously.

"Dunno," Kid DXo'ln said. "I think it's down below ten hours these days, but I never been crazy enough to try for it. Take my advice, and don't play games with the Maw, Solo."

Han tended to think Kid's advice was good. Skimming the Maw seemed like the act of an idiot—a suicidal idiot.

Han set the *Starfire* down on Kessel, and the three smugglers donned breath masks and got out. There was a small cantina that served as a recreation area where pilots and crews could get something to eat and drink while waiting for the loading droids to fill their cargo bays.

Kid DXo'ln stayed behind to oversee the loading, leaving Han and Chewie to grab a quick bite. Ten minutes later Han was halfway through a hasty meal and a glass of Polanis ale. Privately, he wondered what to do now. Kid DXo'ln had made it clear that he was bound for parts he preferred to remain unknown—at least to Han—when the *Starfire* was finished loading. The older man had commented that he was sure Han could catch a ride back to Smuggler's Run, or back to Nar Shaddaa, probably via the Kessel Run, from here.

Kessel boasted no facilities for overnight guests. Han glanced around when the cantina door opened, and then his eyes widened as he beheld a familiar face.

"Roa!" he exclaimed, waving at the older man who'd just entered and was removing his breathing mask. "Hey, Roa! C'mon over and I'll buy you a drink!"

Roa—if he had another name, Han had never heard it— was a big, stocky man with graying hair and a charming smile. He had a roguish twinkle in his blue eyes, and a sense of humor that made him friends easily. It seemed that everyone on Nar Shaddaa knew Roa, and he knew them.

Roa and Mako were old friends, and Roa had been one of the first pals Mako had introduced Han to when he'd arrived on Nar Shaddaa.

Roa had been in the smuggling business for more than twenty years, which made him the grand old man of the trade. He enjoyed playing the role of "shepherd" to some of the younger smugglers, and was generous about sharing what he'd learned during his career.

Unlike many of the smugglers, who were little better than pirates, Roa had his own private "code" that he taught the young smugglers who rode shotgun with him on his old but meticulously maintained speedy freighter, the *Wayfarer*. Roa had taught Han, as he'd taught so many others:

never ignore a call for help . . . never take from those who are poorer than yourself . . . never play sabacc unless you're prepared to lose, always be prepared to make a quick getaway . . . never pilot a ship under the influence.

Roa's Rules, the smugglers called them.

Now, seeing his young friend, Roa's friendly, open face broke into a wide grin. "Han, what're you doing here?"

Han gestured to the seat beside him. "It's a long story, Roa. Mostly we wound up here because a female Wookiee took too much of a liking to Chewie, here."

Roa chuckled as he threw a leg across the bar stool. "Chewbacca, don't tell me you got to meet Wynni!"

Chewie moaned aloud, rolling his blue eyes expressively. Roa guffawed. "Oh, c'mon, Chewie, how bad could it be, entertaining an amorous lady Wookiee?"

Chewbacca snorted, then launched into a vivid explanation of how strenuous—and, at times, hazardous—Wookiee romance could be. Han could understand him, of course, but it was obvious that Roa was barely getting the gist of it.

The older smuggler's eyebrows went up, then he shook his head when Chewie finished. "All right, sounds like you did the right thing by beating a hasty retreat, Chewbacca! Remind me never to attract Wynni's attention."

Han grinned. "Me neither," he said, then sobered. "Problem is, we're stranded here now. Kid DXo'ln brought us, but he's heading out of here on some private business, and he doesn't need a crew. So I'm lookin' for a ride back to Nar Shaddaa. Any chance we can catch one with you, Roa?"

The older man smiled. "Sure, Han. Only trouble is, we're not going directly back. I've got a load of spice to take on to Myrkr. How does Nar Shaddaa by way of the Kessel Run strike you?"

Han's eyes lit up. "That would be great! I can't really get the top piloting assignments until I've got a Run or two under my belt. Roa . . . any chance you'd let me pilot, and coach me through it?"

The older man grinned. "Depends, Solo."

"On what?"

"How many drinks you buy me."

Han chuckled, and waved to the bar droid for fresh ammunition. "Tell me about the Run," he said. "I think I'm ready."

As Roa explained it, the Kessel Run took ships traveling in realspace from the Kessel sector past and around the Maw, then through a rough, uninhabited sector of space known as "the Pit." The Pit wasn't as hard to navigate as the Maw, but more ships had actually been lost there than near the Maw, because after successfully making it past the black-hole cluster, pilots tended to be tired, their reflexes slowed. And just when they needed to rest, the Pit was waiting for them.

The Pit contained a scattered asteroid field that wasn't nearly as concentrated as the one surrounding Smuggler's Run, but it was encased inside a wispy arm of a nebula. The gas and dust from the nebula tended to make most ships' sensors imprecise, and the pilot's line-of-sight was seriously compromised. Zigging in and out of the gauzy tendrils of the nebula was a confusing, chancy business, and there was always the chance that when a pilot zigged to avoid one asteroid, he'd zag right into another.

Roa explained all of this to Han, then took him back to the *Wayfarer* and showed him a complete schematic of their course from the navicomputer. Han studied it all intently, then nodded. "Okay. I think I can handle it, Roa."

The *Wayfarer's* captain gave him a long, measuring glance, then nodded. "Okay, son. Go ahead. Take us out."

Han nodded, then his world narrowed into the viewscreen, his coordinates, his controls, and his hands and eyes. He felt almost like a bio droid, someone who could link his nervous system into the ship. It was as though Han had become the ship—as though they were one entity.

Flying past the center of the Maw, Han was acutely conscious that the slightest mistake on his part could result in disaster for the *Wayfarer.* He felt sweat break out on his forehead as he manipulated the controls, avoiding gravitational eddies and anomalies. Beside him, in the copilot's seat, he could sense Roa's tension, though the stocky older man made no sound. Behind him, Chewbacca whined softly, a thin thread of sound in the otherwise silent control cabin.

The Maw was all around them now as they skirted the dangerous black-hole clusters. Han knew that it would be possible to make the Run by looping wide around this entire perilous sector, but the cost—in fuel, in time, and in the extra distance that had to be traveled—made negotiating the obstacle course of the Maw worthwhile.

Barely.

So far, Roa had not spoken as Han took the *Wayfarer* along the twisting, tricky course that was the shortest safe way through the Maw. Han figured that must mean he was doing all right. He tried to take a deep breath as they sped past a whorl of bluish gas and dust, but it was as though a durasteel band was tightening around his chest.

When Roa spoke softly in the silent cabin, the sound made Han jump. "Past the halfway point. Good job, lad. Watch this one coming up. It's a bit tricky."

Han nodded, and felt a greasy drop of sweat slide past his eyebrow. He flipped *Wayfarer* up on her side as they hurtled past the whirlpool of cosmic dust that had once been a star.

Nearly an hour later, when Han felt as though he hadn't drawn a deep breath for the whole trip, they were out of the Maw and entering the Pit.

An asteroid whizzed by. Han throttled back a bit as he

tried to watch every direction at once, wishing for eyes in the back of his head like a Moloskian.

Roa's voice was sharp. "Hard to port!"

Han caught barely a glimpse of the onrushing asteroid, the size of a mountain. His sweaty hand found the control to implement Roa's order—and slipped!

Panic erupted in Han's chest as he clamped slick fingers onto the controls, overcompensating and causing them to nearly skid into the path of yet another asteroid!

Chewbacca howled, and Roa cursed. Han managed to miss the chunk of rock by the skin of his teeth.

"Sorry," he said tightly. "Fingers slipped."

Without another word, Roa reached into a storage bin and pulled something out. "Here. My present for making it past the Maw. I'll take over while you put 'em on."

Han grabbed the pair of pilot's gloves with their nonslip finger pads and tugged them on, snapping them securely into place. He flexed his fingers. "Thanks, Roa."

"Don't mention it," the older smuggler said. "I always wear 'em, and I suggest you do, too."

Han nodded. "I will."

Several hours later, when Han had finished his first Kessel Run, and they were relaxing in the relative safety of hyperspace, Roa leaned back in the copilot's seat. "So," he said, "I have to say, I've never seen anyone fly the Run any smoother on his first try, Han. You're a natural, son."

Han grinned at his friend. "You're a good coach."

Chewbacca commented sourly that he wouldn't have objected to a bit *more* coaching from Roa—Han had frightened him so badly it was a wonder his hair hadn't fallen out.

Han turned around and glared at his furry friend. "Hey, just keep it up, and I'll give Wynni our home address the next time I see her."

Chewie subsided into glaring silence.

"So, what are you going to do now, Han?" Roa asked. "Not every smuggler can brag that he's flown the Kessel Run, and you made it in excellent time. What's your next move?"

Han had been thinking about that. "I want a ship of our own for me and Chewie," he told Roa. "First I'll have to lease one, of course, but then maybe someday I'll find one I can buy. But I'll need a pile of credits, Roa. So when I get back to Nar Shaddaa, I'm going where the credits are."

Roa's eyebrows went up. "The Hutts," he said.

Han checked his stabilizers. "Yeah, the Hutts."

Roa shook his head, frowning. "Working for the Hutts has its dangers, Han. Hutts make risky employers. Displease them, and you can end up swimming through vacuum without a suit."

Han nodded. "Yeah," he agreed bleakly. "I've worked for them before. But to make the big money, you've got to be willing to take those risks . . ."

Two weeks and yet another bounty hunter later, Han and Chewbacca walked up to the largest building in the Hutt section of Nar Shaddaa. Once a luxury hotel, The Jewel was now headquarters to the Desilijic kajidic.

When The Jewel had been a hotel, the management had boasted that it could provide quarters for over half the known sentient races in the galaxy. Aquatic beings, methane breathers, and beings who could only be comfortable in low gravity—The Jewel had accommodated them all, and more.

As he approached the old building, Han could see that it had been vastly remodeled to suit its new tenants. The giant lobby area was now festooned with glide ramps leading to higher levels. The carpeting had been pulled up, and the stone floors were polished to a brilliant shine to ease a Hutt's passage when gliding along.

Han checked, for the fourth time, that he had Tagta's message cube safely in his pocket. He glanced over at Chewbacca. "You don't have to come in, pal. I can probably handle this interview myself."

Chewie's only response was a firm shake of his head. Han shrugged. "Okay, then, but let me do the talking."

Jiliac's majordomo on Nar Shaddaa proved to be a human woman, a striking redhead who was approaching middle years. She wore a simple green gown, modest in cut. Han was impressed by her dignity and presence as she introduced herself. "I am Dielo, Lord Jiliac's assistant. You said that you had a letter of recommendation, sir?"

Han nodded, feeling rather shabby by comparison, even though he'd worn his best pants, shirt, and jacket. Inside he felt defensive, but he'd learned long ago never to show discomfort or nerves. So his insouciant smile never wavered, and not the slightest crack showed in his air of casual bravado. "Yes, I do."

"May I see it?"

"Sure, long as you don't leave with it." Han produced the small holocube, handed it to her. She glanced quickly at the greenish smear on the side, scanned the message, then nodded. "Very well," she said, handing the holocube back. "Please wait here. I will call you in presently."

Forty-five minutes later, she reappeared and ushered Han into Lord Jiliac's audience chamber.

Han was a little nervous, wondering whether Jiliac the Hutt would recognize him as one of the messengers who, five years ago, had delivered a message to him in his palace on Nal Hutta. The message had come from Jiliac's archrival, Zavval. The Ylesian overlord had challenged Jiliac and threatened him with dire consequences. When he'd heard it, Jiliac had flown into a rage and wrecked a large portion of his audience hall.

Han hoped the Hutt Lord wouldn't recognize him. He'd never told Jiliac his name, after all. Besides, he was no longer nineteen . . . he looked different. His face was thinner, older, and he'd put on weight and muscle from his time in the Academy. Not to mention that in all probability most humans looked pretty much alike—to a Hutt.

Still, Han's mouth was dry as he stepped through the door into the innermost chamber.

Han was surprised to see two Hutts in the room. One was nearly twice the size of the other, which Han knew meant that it was older. Hutts grew throughout their life spans, and some of them reached impressive proportions indeed. The average Hutt underwent several growth spurts after reaching adulthood. Han had heard that some of them could more than double in size in a matter of a few years.

Han squinted at the Hutts. He was pretty sure that Jiliac was the larger of the two.

The room was huge and ornate; this audience chamber had evidently been the hotel's main ballroom. Mirrors lined the walls, and Han caught sight of himself on both sides.

When Han finally stood before the two Hutts, he bowed deeply. Dielo waved a hand at him and spoke in passable Huttese. "Lord Jiliac, this is the Corellian pilot your cousin Lord Tagta recommended to you. His name is Han Solo. The Wookiee is named Chewbacca."

Han bowed again. "Lord Jiliac," he said, in Basic, "it is a privilege to meet you, Your Excellency. Your cousin Lord Tagta says that you are always in need of good pilots."

"Pilot Solo"—Jiliac turned bulbous eyes layered in fat upon Han, and peered down at him with faint curiosity—"do you speak and understand Huttese?"

"I understand it, Your Excellency. I do not speak it well enough to convey the beauty of the language, therefore it is not proper for me to attempt to utter it," Han said earnestly.

Fortunately, Hutts were easy to flatter, and this one bought it. "Ah, a human that understands the beauty of our language," Jiliac said, turning to the smaller Hutt. "Truly an insightful and sensitive member of his species."

"That isn't saying much," the other Hutt replied with a deep chuckle. "I wonder if Captain Solo can pilot as well as he dissembles?"

Han glanced over at the younger, smaller Hutt. Sharp intelligence shone in his narrow-pupiled eyes. He was about Han's height, and only about four or five meters long. Jiliac noticed Han looking at his companion.

"Captain Solo, this is my nephew, Jabba. He has become indispensable to me in running the Desilijic kajidic."

Han bowed to the younger Hutt. "Greetings, Your Excellency."

"Greetings, Captain Solo," Jabba replied with a gracious wave of his small hand. "Your reputation precedes you."

Jiliac held out his own hand. "Enough chitchat. The holocube, Captain?"

"Certainly, Your Excellency." Han produced it, handed it to Jiliac.

The Hutt Lord examined the holocube for several minutes, then passed a small scanning device over the green smear. Finally satisfied, he looked at Han. "You come highly recommended, Captain. We can always use expert pilots."

Han nodded. "I'd like to work for you and your nephew, Your Excellency."

"Very well, then you are hired, Captain. But what about your companion here?" Jiliac indicated Chewbacca.

"We're a team, Your Excellency. Chewie is my copilot."

"Indeed?" said Jabba. "He looks more like a bodyguard to me."

Han could feel Chewie stiffen next to him, and he felt, more than heard, the soft rumble of anger emanating from his furred chest. "Chewie's a good pilot," Han insisted.

"These are perilous times for honest business persons," Jiliac pointed out. "Is one of you trained in weapons systems?"

"I'm the gunner, Your Excellency," Han said. "Chewie is a pretty fair shot, I admit, but I'm better."

"Ah!" Jabba sounded delighted. "Finally, a human who does not deluge us with his silly notion of 'modesty.' "

"Glad you approve," Han said dryly.

"Kessel," Jiliac said thoughtfully. "Our sources say you have been to Kessel."

Han nodded. "Yes, Your Excellency. And I did the Run in nearly record time, my first time through."

"Excellent!" boomed Jabba, who had a voice nearly as deep as his far larger uncle. He chuckled, a low "ho-ho-ho" sound. "Then you are willing to tackle the Kessel Run while hauling cargo for us?"

"Depends on the cargo, Your Excellency," Han said.

"We have no way to determine, at this time, what the cargo will be," Jiliac said. "Obviously, you will leave Kessel carrying a cargo of spice, probably glitterstim, for Kessel is where that spice is mined. But as to what you will be carrying when you land on Kessel, that is bound to vary a great deal. Food, luxuries, a shipment of slaves, or—"

"No slaves," Han interrupted curtly. He had to make this clear. If they dumped him over it, he'd keep on looking for work. "I'll haul most anything for you, Your Excellency. But not slaves."

Both Hutts stared at Han, obviously taken aback by his temerity. Finally Jabba spoke.

"Why not, Captain Solo?"

"Personal reasons, Your Excellency," Han said. "I've seen slavery up close—and I didn't like it."

"Oho!" Jabba chuckled again. "Our brave captain has scruples . . . morals, even, perhaps!"

Han refused to be baited. He just stood his ground.

Jiliac made a curt gesture to Han to stay where he was, then he and the younger Hutt wriggled toward each other. Watching them move, Han couldn't decide whether they reminded him more of a snake or a slug. They undulated along, using muscular contractions to move.

The two Hutts put their heads together and conferred. After a couple of minutes, they broke apart and turned back to Han and Chewie. "Very well, Captain Solo," Jiliac boomed, "we will not assign you to transport slaves."

"Thank you, Your Excellency," Han said, feeling a wash of relief.

"Slaving is not a large part of our business," Jabba said, with a touch of scorn in his voice. "We leave most of that trade to the Besadii kajidic that operates out of Ylesia."

"Have you ever heard of Ylesia, Captain Solo?" Jiliac asked.

Han tensed, but kept it from showing. "Yes, I've heard of it, Your Excellency."

"Our main shipment these days is ryll, Captain," Jabba said. "We have just discovered a new source to trade with on Ryloth, the Twi'lek world. Have you been there?"

"Yes, Your Excellency, I have. I know the spacelanes in that area."

"Good," Jabba said. He studied Han closely with his huge, rarely blinking eyes. "Tell me, Captain, have you ever piloted a space yacht?"

Han had to stifle an ironic grin. The reason all these bounty hunters were after him was that in addition to swiping the cream of Teroenza's treasure, he'd stolen Zavval and Teroenza's personal space yacht.

"Yes, Your Excellency," Han said. "I have."

Jabba regarded Han thoughtfully. "I shall keep that in mind."

Jiliac made a dismissive gesture. "We shall be in touch, Captain. At the moment, you have our leave to depart."

Han bowed to the Hutts, and as he did so, he surreptitiously gave his Wookiee friend a poke. Chewbacca growled softly, but he, too, bobbed his upper body forward.

Han left the audience, feeling sweat trickling down between his shoulder blades. Slowly, carefully, he let out a deep sigh of relief.

This had better be worth it . . .

During the next three months, Han worked for Roa on and off, but he also flew many missions for the Hutts. He developed a reputation for being able to coax top speeds out of even inferior vessels, and for being willing to do whatever it took to get his smuggled cargo through to its destination.

He flew the Kessel Run so many times he lost count.

There were times when the Hutts didn't need him for days or weeks at a time, and he took assignments from Mako, Roa, or other employers. But Jiliac and Jabba provided him with fairly steady work, and most of his income.

Both Jiliac and Jabba had personal space yachts. Han discovered that each of them had sizable holdings on other worlds than Nal Hutta—matter of fact, Jiliac was the de facto ruler of Dilbana, and Jabba was the top crime lord on a backwater world called Tatooine.

One day Han and Chewie were called upon to pilot Jabba's personal yacht, the *Star Jewel*, to Tatooine. Han would've rather hauled spice, frankly. Jabba was temperamental and used to getting his own way, and made a demanding, irascible passenger. Han was glad that the Hutt had brought several of his personal servants along to tend to him, so that all he, Han, had to do was pilot the ship.

Foremost among Jabba's entourage was a Twi'lek valet named Lobb Gerido. Jabba treated Gerido terribly, ordering him around, snapping at him, and insulting him. Han was just glad that he didn't have to put up with that sort of thing. Jabba's entourage also included several humanoid dancing girls, a nalargon player nicknamed "Whizz-Bang" and Jabba's and Jiliac's chef from their residence on Nar Shaddaa, an Ishi Tib named Totoplat.

The purpose of Jabba's voyage was to transport a "pet" he'd recently acquired to his palace on Tatooine. The thing was a nightmare—slashing claws, a huge suckerlike mouth, and an insatiable appetite. Han discovered it was called an Oskan blood eater. Han's stomach turned over the one time he watched its keeper feed it. The entire hold area stank from the creature's occupation. It was a messy eater, and its effluvia was enough to gag a Corellian corpse-grub.

The yacht was a big ship, a Ubrikkian cruiser. It was fast, powered by a pair of Ubrikkian N2 ion engines, with auxiliary power provided by three smaller Kuat T-c40 ion engines. It was also well shielded and heavily armed with six turbolasers. In its docking bay was space for six Z-95 Headhunter fighters, as well as two small landing shuttles.

This trip, as happened frequently, Star Jewel was down to two Headhunters, with two pilots to crew them. The little fighters were tough, but they had no hyperdrive, and Jabba was known to order them deployed as a rear guard while he took off into hyperspace. Jabba was tough on Headhunters and their pilots.

Tatooine was a remote world, back of beyond, and Han had to make several hyperspace jumps to reach it. His next-to-last jump put him into a little-traveled spacelane, but it was the most direct route to Tatooine.

That's where the pirate ships were waiting for them.

Four Drell teardrop-shaped vessels, sleek and shining, small but deadly. Han had faced their like before, when he'd been piloting for the Ylesians. The moment he saw them his mental alarm bells went off. *Pirates!?! They could be! Better to be safe than sorry* . . .

"Chewie, shields on maximum!" Han snapped, sending the yacht into an evasive maneuvering pattern while his copilot adjusted their deflectors to maximum strength. Han flipped on the comm unit. "Attention! Gunnery crew, stand ready! We may be seeing some action!" He switched frequencies. "Headhunter pilots, report to your snubs! This is not a drill!"

Even as the words left his mouth, the closest ship spat a salvo of quad laser fire at them. *I was right!* Han mentally congratulated himself. Thanks to his caution, the Drell ship's fire went wide.

The ships were only a third the size of Jabba's massive space yacht, but their quad laser cannons spat deadly bursts at the bigger ship as they rushed in at top speed. They were so small they were going to be difficult to hit. Han banked the *Star Jewel* around and yelled, "Gunnery crew . . . fire at will!"

Even as the crews manning the yacht's six heavy turbolasers began returning fire, Han switched to another comm frequency. "Attention, passengers and crew—we are under attack! Prepare for evasive maneuvers. Activate your restraint systems."

Beside him Chewie was performing his job ably, leaving the piloting mostly to Han, but busy balancing and distributing power to their shields, monitoring the ship's status, checking on how much power they could channel to the weapons. The Hutt yacht's turbolasers, mounted discreetly beneath the ridge of the yacht's superstructure, actually tapped directly into the ship's power core, thus giving them far more destructive capability than any opponent would expect.

Han dodged an incoming Drell ship, saw the turbolasers fire a vicious burst at the oncoming vessel, but at the last moment it dodged the fire. *Blasted little ships are too fast!*

His comm unit crackled. "Headhunters here. Ready for launch."

Chewie opened the cargo-bay doors, and dropped one shield amidships so the two fighters could launch.

Han activated the comm. "Pilots . . . launch on my order! Three . . . two . . . one . . . NOW!"

Jabba was hollering over the comm, demanding an explanation. Han could hear wails and curses from the Twi'lek and the dancing girls. Totoplat, the cook, was fussing that Jabba's dinner was *ruined,* just *ruined!*

With a muttered curse, Han spared half a second to close the comm channel from the passenger section. When he looked back up, he paled.

"Incoming amidships, Chewie!" he yelled, knowing this time he couldn't evade fast enough. The *Star Jewel* shuddered violently, then shuddered again. Han realized the first ship had swung around and was now firing on their stern! He cursed when he saw that his rear deflectors were nearly gone. "Chewie! I'm coming about! Compensate for that shield!"

Activating the comm, Han shouted, "I'm coming about, hard to port! You guys get that blasted pirate off my rear!"

The Wookiee snarled as he worked frantically on the shields. Han sent the *Star Jewel* into a hard port turn, then a second later he felt the faint jolts as the gunners fired.

Another miss!

Han cursed and activated the comm. "Listen up, you guys! I want portside gunner one to target the following coordinates, and fire on my order!"

Glancing at his sensors, Han located the position of the

first Drell ship, saw that it had swung far out, then turned and was coming back for another run. Han checked his X-Y coordinate grids and made a rapid calculation. He spat out a string of coordinates.

"Coordinates acknowledged, sir!" the portside gunnery chief said.

"Gunner two, target the following coordinates and fire your burst five seconds after gunner one! Got that?" Han reeled off another string of coordinates.

"We copy, Captain!"

"Gunner three, target the following coordinates and fire your weapon five seconds after gunner one." Again, Han gave the prescribed coordinates.

"Yes, Captain! Ready!"

"Okay . . . gunner one . . . prepare to fire!"

What Han was attempting was a military technique called a limited barrage pattern. It was designed to make a ship dodge a burst of fire, only to run right into another blast. Tricky, but if they could get the timing right . . .

Han counted seconds in his head as he angled his stern slightly toward the Drell, offering the most tempting target he could. *Three . . . two . . . one!*

"Portside gunner one—fire!"

The deadly beam shot out, but as Han had figured, the agile Drell vessel evaded the blast.

Four . . . three . . . two . . . one . . . Han counted, watching the portside viewscreen. "Yes!" he shouted as the evading ship ran straight into the blast from portside gun two!

Incandescent white fire blossomed against the blackness.

"You got him!"

Cheers erupted from the comm unit.

The Headhunters were zeroing in on another of the

Drell ships. Stuttering bursts from their lasers shone red against the star-speckled blackness.

Han could only spare a glance for the snubfighters and their battle. He sent the *Star Jewel* hurtling toward the two remaining Drell ships, then spoke into the comm. "Starboard gunners, prepare to fire continuous bursts on my order. Coordinates are . . ." Glancing at his board, he gave them a string of numbers.

He watched as the two Drell ships came about for another attack run, then began hurtling toward the yacht at full speed. "Starboard gunners, fire at maximum . . . *now!*"

The three powerful turbolasers blasted away into empty space. *Those captains are gonna think I've lost my mind,* Han thought as he counted the bursts from his starboard battery, mentally timing their pounding rhythm. What he was planning required pinpoint timing.

As the Drells reached firing range, Han wrenched his controls, rolling the big ship to port, turning it up on its side.

Seeing that Han hadn't lost his mind after all, the Drell pirates scattered wildly, trying to evade the bursts from the turbolasers that were now aiming directly at them!

One Drell pirate managed to evade, but the other one was trapped in the middle of the full barrage pattern. The blast from starboard gun two caught it dead center.

This time, the *Star Jewel* was close enough to the explosion to lose a starboard deflector when it was repeatedly pummeled by wreckage. Han watched the indicators on his instruments leap as the Hutt yacht sheered through the zone of destruction, then out the other side.

He glanced at the port viewscreen. The other Drell ship was slowly spinning, a huge hole blown in its side. Only one of the Headhunters was visible. The fourth Drell ship, the one that had escaped the barrage pattern, was hightailing it.

Han considered giving chase, but he knew the pirate had too much of a headstart. Instead he turned the yacht and headed back to pick up the remaining Headhunter.

By the time he remembered to flick the comm unit back on, Jabba's threats and imprecations had died away. Han cleared his throat. "We're okay, Your Excellency. Hope I didn't jounce you around too much back there."

"My precious cargo is upset!" Jabba grumbled. "I may have to sacrifice one of my dancers to appease his appetite. Blood eaters are sensitive creatures, Solo!"

"Uh . . . yessir. Sorry about that, sir. But I had to fight. Otherwise we'd have been blown out of space. Those pirates weren't just looking for loot and salvage, Your Excellency. They *knew* we were coming. They were waiting at exactly the right spot to intercept a ship making the last leg of a trip to Tatooine."

"Really?" Jabba's petulant tones suddenly hardened. Now the crime lord was all business. "What do you think they were attempting to do, Captain?"

"Disable or destroy us, Your Excellency," Han said, opening the landing-bay doors so the one remaining Headhunter could limp in. "I believe they were after you, sir."

"Another assassination attempt . . ." Jabba sounded very thoughtful. Han knew that devious mind was working at lightspeed.

"I think so, sir."

"Interesting," Jabba grunted. "Captain, may I ask where you learned those . . . unorthodox . . . maneuvers?"

"At the Imperial Academy, Your Excellency."

"I see. They proved most useful, I must admit. You are to be doubly commended for foiling this cowardly attempt to murder me, Captain Solo. Remind me of that when we return to Nar Shaddaa."

"You bet," Han promised.

• • •

"Solo knows something," Jabba the Hutt said to his Uncle Jiliac two weeks later as they shared a light repast in the small lounge that adjoined Jiliac's audience chamber on Nar Shaddaa.

Jiliac reached into his elegant combination snackquarium and water pipe—a gift from the long-dead Zavval—and extracted a wriggling morsel. Holding the frantic creature in midair, he regarded it absently. "Really?" he said after a moment's silent consideration. "Knows what?"

Jabba wriggled closer to the snackquarium and, at a wave from his clan lord, reached in for a choice little snack. Green slime gathered at the corners of his mouth as he anticipated the delicious rubbery warmth of the little amphibian sliding down his gullet. Even with this distraction, he was still able to focus on Jiliac's question. Jabba was nothing if not practical.

"I don't know," he said. "I suspect the only way to find out is to ask him."

"Ask him *what*?" demanded Jiliac as Jabba popped the treat into his mouth.

Glunk . . . Jabba swallowed noisily before answering, "Ask him how he knew to react so quickly with those Drell ships. Ship's log showed he was tracking with his weapons systems and taking evasive maneuvers even before they fired on us. How did Solo know those Drell ships meant trouble?"

"We have hired Drell pirates ourselves, in the past," Jiliac reminded him. "The question we must ask is, was this attack one from within our clan, or from outside?" He folded his small hands together on the swell of his bellyfolds. "Make no mistake, nephew. There are those within Desilijic who would wrest the leadership of the kajidic from me . . ."

"True," Jabba agreed. "But I do not think this was an attack from within the kajidic. My informants assure me that the entire clan was pleased with our profit ratio last quarter."

"Then who do you think was behind the attack?" Jiliac asked.

"Besadii," Jabba replied flatly.

Jiliac cursed. "Naturally. They are the only ones who have sufficient funds to hire the Drell pirates. Blast them!" The Hutt Lord's massive tail whipped back and forth on the polished floor. "Nephew, Aruk grows above himself. Ylesian trade is making Besadii so wealthy they are becoming a personal danger, not simply an economic threat. We must act . . . and soon. This threat to Desilijic must not go unpunished."

"Agreed, Uncle," Jabba said, after swallowing another Serendina wriggler. "But what should we do?"

"We need more information," Jiliac decided. "Then we can plan our retaliation." Flicking on the comm unit, he said, "Dielo!"

Immediately the response came back. "I am here, Your Magnificence. What do you wish?"

"Summon Solo to us," Jiliac ordered. "We wish to speak with him."

"Immediately, Lord Jiliac," Dielo replied.

It was several hours before Solo appeared, and Jabba and Jiliac were growing increasingly annoyed at having to wait by the time the Corellian entered the audience chamber. He was accompanied, as always, by his tall, hairy companion.

Both Hutts looked him over in silence for several minutes. Solo shifted a little, and Jabba sensed that he was uneasy, though, for a human, he hid anxiety well.

"Greetings, Solo," Jiliac finally intoned in his deepest, most intimidating voice.

The Corellian Captain bowed. "Greetings, Your Excellency. What can I do for you?"

"We want the truth," Jabba said, not waiting for Jiliac to mince around the subject. Jabba enjoyed being direct, and putting other sentients on the spot. "You can give us the truth."

Jabba's eyesight was sharp, and Hutts could see farther into the infrared than humans could. He watched the blood ebb from Solo's face as he paled, though his expression did not change. The Wookiee shifted uneasily and whined softly.

"Uh, Your Impressiveness . . ." Solo wet his lips. "I'm afraid I don't understand. The truth about what?"

Jabba didn't mince words. "I've reviewed the *Star Jewel*'s log. Captain, how did you know the Drell pirates were waiting to attack us?"

Solo hesitated, then drew a deep breath. "I've run into an ambush from pirates in Drell-built cruisers before," he said. "And I know that you, Jiliac, and you, Jabba, have enemies that are wealthy enough to hire assassins."

Jiliac was staring hard at the young Corellian. "When did you encounter such an ambush, Captain?" he asked slowly.

"Five years ago, Your Excellency."

Jabba leaned forward. "And who were you working for when you encountered them, Solo?"

The Corellian smuggler hesitated, then said quietly, "I was working for Zavval, sir. On Ylesia."

Jiliac's eyes widened. "Yes . . . my memory is stirring. Was it *you* that brought me my snackquarium? I remember the Sullustan, but humans look so much alike . . ."

"Yes, sir, that was me," Han said. Jabba could tell that it cost him something to admit the truth.

"Why didn't you tell us this before?" Jiliac asked, his voice as cold as a Hothan glacier. "What are you hiding, Captain?"

"Nothing!" Solo protested, shaking his head. "Listen, this is the truth, Your Excellency! I wanted to work for you, but I thought you wouldn't like it if you knew I'd worked for Besadii clan—even just piloting spice freighters. So I didn't mention it, that's all!" His brown eyes blazed, and he waved his arms to emphasize his point. "Truth is, I actually worked for Teroenza. I barely knew Zavval. I'm sorry if you thought any different, Your Excellency."

Jiliac gazed down at the Corellian from his dais. "You are correct, Solo. I would not have hired you had I known this."

Silence. Solo had no answer save a shrug.

Jiliac considered for a moment. "Are you still working for them?"

"No, Your Excellency," Solo said. "I'm willing to testify to that under truth drug. Or you can take glitterstim and scan me. I left Ylesia five years ago, and I never want to go back."

Jabba turned to his uncle. "Uncle, it occurs to me that Solo is probably telling the truth. If he were still working for Besadii at present, he hardly would have fought so valiantly to save the *Star Jewel* and me, would he? Instead our brave captain would have heaved my ship to and allowed it to be boarded—and me killed." The smaller Hutt gazed at the Corellian solemnly. "Therefore, unless Besadii is far more subtle and clever than I believe them to be, our captain is telling the truth."

Solo nodded. "I am, Your Excellency! Matter of fact, I got no use for Ylesia and those who run it. You know what I think of slavers and the slave trade—and Besadii's the biggest exporter of slaves in the galaxy."

"True," Jabba said. "Captain Solo, now that my uncle has identified you as one of the messengers from Zavval, my own memory has been refreshed. Very soon after that threat from Zavval, we received reports that there had been an uprising on Ylesia. The glitterstim factory was destroyed, Zavval was killed in an armed attack, and several slaves were rescued. Two ships were stolen."

Jabba watched Solo's face intently for his reaction, but the Corellian smuggler revealed nothing. "Captain," Jiliac said, "we were told that a human . . . one 'Vykk Draygo,' was single-handedly responsible for the conflict on Ylesia. We were also told that Vykk Draygo was reported killed by bounty hunters soon afterward. What do you know of all this?"

Solo shifted, and now Jabba could tell he was struggling to make a decision. Finally, he nodded. "I know a lot about it," he admitted. "I'm 'Vykk Draygo.'"

Jabba and Jiliac exchanged a long look. "Did you kill Zavval?" Jabba said, in his deepest, most intimidating voice.

"Not really . . ." Solo wet his lips. "I just . . . it was an accident, sort of. Hey . . . it wasn't my fault!"

Both Hutts looked at each other again, then burst out into booming roars of laughter. "Ho-ho-HO!" Jabba shouted. "Solo, for a human you are a rare sentient!"

The Corellian seemed taken aback. "You're not mad 'cause I caused a Hutt to die?"

"Zavval threatened me," Jiliac reminded the Corellian. "He and his clan caused Desilijic many problems, and cost us some lives. Hutts prefer to ruin enemies by stripping them of their wealth, Captain, but we are not above assassination as a means to rid ourselves of a problem."

Jabba watched as Solo visibly relaxed. "Oh. Well, humans do that, too, sometimes."

"Really?" Jiliac seemed surprised. "Then perhaps there is hope for your species after all, Captain Solo."

The Corellian smiled wryly. Jabba recognized the expression because he was so used to having humans attend him.

"However," Jabba said, waving a cautionary finger, "it

would not do for it to become generally known that a human killed a Hutt and remained unmolested, Captain. If you ever divulge the truth to anyone else . . . we will have to see that you are silenced. Permanently. Do we understand each other?"

Solo nodded silently, obviously impressed by Jabba's threat.

"So . . ." Jiliac was all business once more. "You worked for Besadii, Captain Solo. What can you tell us about them?"

"Well, I was there about five years ago," Solo cautioned. "But living on Ylesia is something I could hardly forget."

"Who gave you your orders, Solo?" Jabba asked.

"Teroenza," the human replied. "He really runs the place, being High Priest and all."

"Teroenza? Tell us about him," Jabba instructed.

"Well, he's a t'landa Til," the Corellian said. "You know what they are, right?"

Both Hutts indicated that they did. "Well, Teroenza reports to his Hutt overlord, the way he did to Zavval when I was there," Solo said. "But he's the one who makes the decisions, and who oversees the day-to-day administration of the Ylesian colonies. Teroenza's pretty smart, and he's an efficient administrator. I gather profits were pretty good—though I'm sure they had a bad year after I destroyed the glitterstim factory."

At the thought of the destruction of so much valuable property and spice, both Hutts winced. Solo shrugged again. "Yeah, it bothered me, too. But I needed a diversion."

"How did Zavval really die?"

"The ceiling collapsed on him," Solo said. "While we were raiding Teroenza's treasure room we got caught, and—"

Jabba's eyes narrowed. "Treasure room? What treasure?"

"That's what we called it," Solo explained. "Teroenza's a really single-minded collector of rare things—art, antiquities, weapons, musical instruments, furniture, jewelry. You name it, and he's got some. He's built a big room to house his collection down in the bowels of the Administration Building on Ylesia. He lives for his collection, 'cause there's not much to do on Ylesia. It's mostly jungle."

"I see . . ." Jiliac said thoughtfully, with a sideways glance at Jabba. The younger Hutt could tell that his uncle's mind was busily churning out a plot based on the information Solo had just given them.

Jiliac continued to question Solo about the spice factories on Ylesia, how the operation was set up, how many guards there were, etc. Jabba listened with interest. His uncle was an experienced and devious leader of the kajidic. What did he have in mind now?

Finally, Jiliac dismissed the Corellian, and Solo and the Wookiee turned and left the audience chamber.

"So, Uncle," Jabba said, "what are you thinking?"

Jiliac slowly took his hookah out of the bottom of the snackquarium and began puffing on it. Jabba smelled the sweetish odor of marcan herbs, a mild euphoric drug. It was several minutes before the kajidic leader spoke. "Jabba, my nephew, I am thinking that all this enmity between Besadii and Desilijic must cease. Sooner or later one of their attempts against us will succeed, and that would be a tragedy."

"I agree," Jabba said, feeling his hide prickle as he imagined what an assassin's vibroblade would do to him. Or perhaps they'd just dump him into vacuum without a suit . . . he shuddered at the thought. "But what can we do?"

"I believe we should call for an inter-clan meeting, to be

held on neutral ground," Jiliac said slowly, between puffs. "And that we should offer a nonviolence pact to Besadii."

"Will they accept it?" Jabba couldn't see why they should.

"Aruk is no fool. He will at least *appear* to accept it, Nephew."

Jabba knew there had to be more to it than that. "What is behind this request?" he asked slowly. Jabba knew he himself was a clever Hutt, but sometimes Jiliac could be downright devious.

"My agenda for this meeting will include a request for up-to-date profit disclosure on both sides," Jiliac said. "And a request for income equalization."

"Besadii will never agree to that!"

"I know. But it is a valid reason for requesting profit disclosure, and Besadii will recognize that."

"And you think Besadii will share their information with us?"

"I believe they will, Nephew. Aruk will enjoy the chance to flaunt their profit margins before Desilijic."

Jabba nodded. "He will, you are correct."

"I believe that he will take this chance to bring in the leadership of Ylesia in order to validate their figures, so Aruk can boast about their profits."

"Who is the current overseer?"

"Kibbick is in charge of the Ylesian operation."

"But Kibbick is an idiot," Jabba pointed out. He'd met the younger Hutt before, at an inter-kajidic conference.

"True," Jiliac said. "My guess is that the *true* leader of Ylesia will also be summoned to report."

Jabba's eyes widened, then narrowed, at the thought. He chuckled aloud. "I begin to see your drift, Uncle . . ."

Jiliac puffed serenely on his hookah. The corners of his wide, lipless mouth turned up.

Teroenza was relaxing in his sling when the most famous bounty hunter in the Empire arrived to see him. Ganar Tos came hurrying into the t'landa Til's inner sanctum, twisting his warty green hands anxiously. "Sir! Your Excellency! Boba Fett is here, and says you are paying him to come for a personal interview! Is that true, sir?"

"Yesssss . . ." the High Priest of Ylesia said, his breath puffing out in a long hiss as he struggled up out of his sling to stand upon all four pillarlike feet. Anticipation pounded like a drumroll in his two hearts and three stomachs.

The sentient who entered the room wore battered, greenish Mandalorian battle armor. Two braided Wookiee scalps, one black and one white, hung from his right shoulder. His features were completely masked by his helmet. Behind the eye slit, Teroenza thought he could make out the glint of his eyes.

"Greetings, Master Fett!" Teroenza boomed, wondering whether to offer his hand. He had a feeling that if he did, Fett would ignore it, so he didn't. "I would like to thank you for coming so promptly! I trust you had no problems with our treacherous Ylesian air currents and storms on your way through our atmosphere."

"Let's not waste time," Fett said, his voice flat and inhuman as it came through the helmet's speaker. "You mentioned Mandalorian wrist-darts in your collection as my fee for coming here for a personal interview. Take me to see them. Now."

"Oh, certainly, certainly, Master Fett, sir," Teroenza cried. He had a sudden cold certainty that if Fett were to decide for some reason to kill him, there would be little he could do to prevent it. Despite Teroenza's massive bulk, easily five times that of the human, he felt naked and vulnerable in the presence of the notorious bounty hunter.

Quickly he ushered Fett through the door in his private apartment that led into his treasure room. "They're right here," he said, having to forcibly stop himself from talking too quickly, almost babbling. Fett moved beside him, his progress as silent and deadly as a poison dart.

Opening a case, the Ylesian High Priest seized the wristlets. Each contained a spring mechanism that would shoot a profusion of tiny, deadly darts when the wearer moved his fingers in a certain way. "A matched set," Teroenza gabbled. "I was assured they're in perfect working order."

"I'll determine that for myself," Fett said, his voice, as always, flat and emotionless. Sealing the wristlets on, he turned in one smooth, lithe motion, and fired both of them into a thick tapestry that adorned the wall. Teroenza squeaked in protest, but dared not say more.

Only after Fett had collected the darts from the tapestry did he turn to face the High Priest. "Very well. I am paid for my time, Priest. What is it you wish?"

Teroenza pulled himself together. Fett was about to become his employee, after all . . . in a manner of speaking. He summoned as much dignity as he could, despite the racing of his pulses. "There is a smuggler, Han Solo by name. You may have seen WANTED posters for him."

Fett nodded once.

"Solo travels with a Wookiee, they say, these days. He's been reported seen on Nar Shaddaa. They say that nine or ten bounty hunters have tried for him, but he's been too quick for all of them."

Fett nodded again. Teroenza found his silence unnerving, but he continued doggedly, "I want him. Alive, and relatively unharmed. No disintegrations."

"That makes it harder," Fett said. "For seventy-five hundred credits, it's not worth my time."

Teroenza had been afraid of this. Inwardly, he quailed at the thought of what Aruk would have to say about this.

Aruk liked to call himself "frugal." Teroenza thought of him as a cheap old miser. But . . . he *had* to have Solo. Should he try raising the bounty credits himself? He didn't want to sell part of his collection . . .

"Ylesia will increase the bounty on Solo to twenty thousand credits," Teroenza said firmly. He resolved to talk Kibbick and Aruk into approving the increase. He'd manage . . . somehow. After all, it was Aruk's responsibility, as head of Besadii.

Fett remained motionless, then, finally, just when Teroenza thought he'd say no, he nodded again. "All right."

The High Priest had to resist the urge to babble thanks at the bounty hunter. "When do you think you can have him?" Teroenza asked eagerly.

"That's not enough of a bounty to make me put aside my other commitments," Fett said. "You'll have him when I get to him, Priest."

Teroenza fought his disappointment. "But . . ."

"Make it a hundred thousand, and I'll put Solo as my first priority," Fett offered.

A hundred thousand credits! Teroenza's mind reeled. His entire collection wasn't worth much more than that! Aruk would have him drowned in Ylesia's oceans if he promised such a bounty. He shook his head. "No. Just put him on your list. We'll wait."

"And you'll have Solo," Fett promised.

As Teroenza stood watching, Boba Fett turned and walked away. Teroenza strained his excellent hearing, but he could hear nothing. Soundlessly, Fett vanished through the door. The High Priest knew he wouldn't see him again, until the day he brought Han Solo back to Ylesia, to face a terrible fate.

Just wait, Solo, he thought. *You are a dead man. You just don't know it . . . yet.*

Chapter Five:

The Thirteenth Bounty Hunter

T wo months and three bounty hunters later, Han and Chewbacca were well on their way to saving the credits they'd need to lease a ship of their own. Jabba and Jiliac were sticklers when it came to keeping schedules, but they paid well if their orders were followed to the letter.

There were no further attacks on the Hutt yachts. But it was obvious to Han that a confrontation was brewing between Desilijic and Besadii . . . he knew that Jiliac's messengers had made some kind of proposal to Aruk the Hutt's representatives. Aruk had come back with a request for a face-to-face conference. Han gathered that such conferences were highly unusual in Hutt society. He kept his eyes and ears open, wondering if he'd be ordered to fly Jabba and Jiliac to attend the meeting.

Han and Chewie worked long hours, but sometimes days went by between missions. During their off-hours, they hung out with the other smugglers in the Corellian sector, playing sabacc and other games of chance.

Always ready for entertainment, and intrigued by novelty, Han was attracted one day by a huge holosign on one of the ancient, though still maintained, hotel-casinos. Headlining at The Chance Castle was a stage magician who was, by all reports, one of the best illusionists in the galaxy.

Her name was Xaverri. Han checked out the admission price, and when he discovered they could afford it, he suggested to Chewbacca that they attend a magic show that night.

Han didn't believe in magic any more than he believed in religion. But he'd had some experience at sleight of hand in learning pickpocketing and card tricks, and he enjoyed trying to figure out how each trick was done.

Chewbacca proved strangely reluctant to go. He whined and shook his head, telling Han that they should go out with Mako that night, or over to see Roa, who had bought a small, one-man snubfighter that pirates had salvaged, and was working on it. Several times Han and Chewie had given him a hand fixing it up.

Han pointed out that they could help Roa any night, but that Xaverri was only scheduled to appear for a week's run.

Chewie shook his head, silent, but obviously unhappy. Han stared at the Wookiee, wondering just what in the name of blazes was wrong with him. "Hey, pal, what's the matter? This would be fun!"

Chewie just grunted and shook his head, not answering. Han regarded him, puzzled, when suddenly he had a flash of insight. Wookiees were still a primal people. They'd incorporated and adapted advanced technology so it fit into their society, but they weren't naturally technological. Wookiees were a very intelligent species who had learned to pilot spaceships through hyperspace, but they'd never built any of their own. Wookiees who left Kashyyyk— though that was rare now that the Empire had declared Kashyyyk a slave-labor world—did so on ships built by other sentients than themselves.

Wookiee society still contained rites and customs that many citizens of the Empire would consider primitive. Chewie had his own beliefs, and they included a certain amount of what Han regarded as superstition. Wookiee legends contained frightening tales of supernatural beings that prowled, hungered, and thirsted by night, as well as stories of evil magicians and sorcerers who could work their will on others for nefarious purposes.

Han stared at his hairy partner for a long moment. "Hey, Chewie," he said, finally, "you know as well as I do that what they're calling 'magic' in Xaverri's act ain't nothin' but a bunch of simple tricks and nonsense, right?"

Chewbacca hrrrrnnnned, but he didn't sound too positive about it.

Han reached up and ruffled the hair on the top of the Wookiee's head. Dewlanna had often caressed him in just that way. It was the Wookiee equivalent of a comforting pat on the shoulder. "Believe me, Chewie," he continued, "these stage magicians don't actually do real *magic*. Not the kind in Wookiee legends. What this Xaverri does is all sleight of hand, like what I can do with card-chips. Either that or it's done with holo-projections or mirrors or something like that. No real magic. Nothing supernatural."

Chewie whined, but he was beginning to look reassured. "I'll bet you that if you come with me tonight, I can spot how this Xaverri does all of her tricks," Han said. "How 'bout it, pal, is it a deal?"

The Wookiee wanted to know what Han was willing to

bet. The Corellian thought for a moment. "I'll fix breakfast and clean up for a month if I can't figure out how she does 'em," he promised. "And if I do manage to do it, you pay me back for your own ticket, how's that?"

Chewbacca decided that was fair.

The two smugglers got to the performance early enough to get seats close to the stage. They waited restlessly until there came a blare of fanfare, and the holo-curtain vanished, to reveal the stage and its sole occupant.

Xaverri proved to be a voluptuous, attractive woman several years older than Han. She had long, heavy black hair that she wore in an elaborate coiffure. Her eyes flashed silver from the iris-enhancers she wore. The magician wore a costume of violet silk, slashed in strategic places to permit occasional tantalizing glimpses of the golden skin beneath it.

She was an exciting, exotic-looking woman. Han wondered what planet she came from. He'd never seen anyone who looked like her before.

After she was introduced, she went straight into her act. With a minimum of stage patter, she performed increasingly difficult tricks. Both Han and Chewbacca were captivated as they watched her illusions. Several times Han thought he might be able to guess how a trick had been engineered, but he was never able to spot any flaws in her routine. He knew he'd lost his bet with Chewie.

Xaverri performed all the traditional illusions—and then improved on them. She lasered a volunteer from the audience in half, then lasered *herself* in two. She "teleported" not only herself but a small flock of Rodian batwings from one glassine cage to another one across the stage—all in one burst of smoke and flame. Her illusions were stylish and imaginative—and so well done it appeared she really possessed supernatural powers.

When she seemingly released a flock of Kayven whistlers

to attack the audience, even Han flinched, and Chewie had to be restrained from trying to attack the illusionary beasts, so real did they appear.

For the grand finale of her act, Xaverri made the entire wall of the hotel ballroom disappear, replaced with a star-flecked blackness of space. As the audience oohed and ahhhed, suddenly the emptiness of space was filled with a terrifying vision of a rogue dwarf star rushing headlong at them. Even Han couldn't stop himself from crying out and ducking as the enormous illusion dominated the room; Chewie howled in terror and nearly crawled under his seat. It was all Han could do to drag him back upright when the illusion abruptly vanished, and there, replacing it, was a huge image of Xaverri, bowing and smiling.

Han clapped until his hands were sore, yelling and whistling. What a show!

After all the applause had died away, Han made sure that he found his way backstage. He wanted to meet the lovely illusionist, wanted to tell her that she was extraordinarily talented.

Xaverri was the first woman he'd found himself really attracted to in a very long time. Since Bria had left, matter of fact.

After a long wait amid the stage-door crowd, Han saw Xaverri emerge from her dressing room. The silver iris-enhancers were gone, and her eyes were now their natural dark brown. She wore a stylish street outfit instead of the silk costume. Smiling warmly, she scribed her signature and personalized messages to her fans, then thumbprinted them onto tiny holocubes as a memento. She was gracious and pleasant to her admirers.

Han deliberately hung back until everyone except her assistant, a surly Rodian, was gone.

Finally, he stepped forward, smiling his best, most charming smile. "Hi," he said, looking her in the eye.

Xaverri was nearly as tall as he was, and her high-heeled, elaborately decorated boots made them the same height. "Han Solo, Lady Xaverri. And my partner, Chewbacca. I wanted to tell you that I thought that was the most original and exciting magic act I've ever seen."

Xaverri looked him and Chewbacca up and down assessingly, then smiled—a very different sort of smile, cold and cynical. "Greetings, Solo. Let me guess," she said. "You're selling something?"

Han shook his head. *Very perceptive of her. But it's been a long time since I've been a con man. These days I'm just a pilot . . .* "Not at all, lady. I'm just a fan who admires stage magic. Also, I wanted to give Chewie a chance to see you and smell you so he'll know you're as human as I am. I'm afraid you more than impressed him. When you filled the air with those Kayven whistlers, it was like something out of a Wookiee night-flyer legend. He didn't know whether to dig a hole in the floor or fight for his life."

She glanced up at Chewbacca, then, slowly, slowly, her cynical smile faded, to be replaced by the real thing. "Pleased to meet you, Chewbacca. Sorry if I scared you," she said, holding out her hand.

Chewie engulfed her hand in his two hairy paws and spouted Wookiee at her, which she seemed to understand perfectly. He told her that her show had amazed and terrified him, but that now it was over, he found that he'd really enjoyed himself.

"Why, thank you!" she exclaimed. "That's the reaction a magician hopes to get!" Han was almost jealous to see how she and the Wookiee seemed to hit it off. Xaverri responded to Chewie's open admiration with genuine warmth.

Before the moment could be lost, Han stepped forward and invited the illusionist to go out with them for a post-performance snack.

She eyed him, the caution back in her eyes. Han studied her, and suddenly realized that this was a human who had suffered a terrible loss in the past. It had made her cautious, protective. *She'll say no,* he thought, disappointed. But, to his surprise, after a moment's consideration, Xaverri agreed to accompany them.

Han took her to a little bistro in the Corellian sector where the food and drink were good and cheap, and a woman with a lute-pipe alternately strummed and sang softly.

It took a while, but Xaverri slowly relaxed, and even smiled at Han as well as Chewie. After they walked her back to her hotel, the magician took Han's hand in both of hers and gazed at him earnestly. "Solo . . . thank you. I've really enjoyed meeting you and Chewbacca." She looked over at the Wookiee, who gave her a pleased whine. "I find I'm sorry to have to say good-bye, and it's been a long time since I could say that to anyone."

Han smiled at her. "Then don't say good-bye, Xaverri. Say, 'I'll be seeing you,' because it's true."

She took a deep breath. "I don't know if that's a good idea, Solo . . ."

"I do," Han said. "Trust me."

Han was back at the stage door the next night, and the next. He and Xaverri got to know each other, little by cautious little. She was uncommunicative about her past, even more reticent than Han himself. By listening and asking roundabout questions, Han managed to discover a few things about her: she hated the Empire and Imperial officials with a single-minded quiet ferocity that he found disturbing, she was proud of her skills as a magician and couldn't resist a challenge, and . . . she was lonely.

It was a hard life, traveling from planet to planet, playing to cheering crowds, but always winding up alone in some hotel room. Han got the impression that it had been a long time, perhaps years, since Xaverri had spent time with a man. She had many opportunities, but her natural reserve and suspicion made her resist involvements.

For the first time in his life, Han found that *he* was the person who had to open up, to try to get past barriers that made his own considerable emotional defenses seem puny. It was hard to do—several times he was tempted to quit, to give up his pursuit as hopeless.

But Xaverri intrigued and excited him. He wanted to get to know her, and he wanted her to trust him . . . even a little.

The third night he spent time with her, Xaverri gave him a quick kiss at the door to her room, before vanishing inside. Han went home smiling.

When he got ready to go out late the next night, Chewbacca rose to accompany him. Han held up a warning hand to the Wookiee. "Chewie, old buddy, you don't have to come with me tonight."

Chewbacca made a derisive sound. Han would get into trouble without him, he just knew it.

Han smiled, a slow, irresistible smile. "Yep. That's what I'm hopin', pal. I'm goin' alone tonight. See you later. *Much* later—I hope."

Smiling and whistling the beginning notes from Xaverri's opening number, Han left his apartment and headed for The Chance Castle.

When he waited outside the door this night, Xaverri emerged, wearing a simple black and scarlet jumpsuit that set off her hair and skin. She looked pleased to see him, but glanced around, obviously searching for Chewbacca. "Where's Chewie?"

Han took her arm. "He stayed home tonight. Tonight it's just you and me, babe. If that's okay."

She looked at him, trying to look stern, then suddenly

she smiled at him knowingly. "Solo, you're a rogue, you know that?"

He smiled back. "I'm glad you noticed. That means I'm your kind of guy, right?"

She shook her head. "You never know."

They went to one of the Hutt-owned casinos, and thanks to Han's privileged status as Jabba and Jiliac's pilot, they were given special treatment—free drinks, admission to special high-stakes games, plus good seats at the shows.

It was late before they left, and true night still reigned over this section of Nar Shaddaa. Han walked Xaverri back to her hotel. She asked him how he'd become partners with Chewie, and he found himself telling her about his time as an officer in the Imperial Navy.

"And so, after they threw me out," he finished, "I found that I couldn't get honest work as a pilot. I was blacklisted. I didn't know where my next meal was coming from. But even though I got mad and ordered Chewie to go, he wouldn't. Said a life debt is the most serious obligation a Wookiee can have. Even takes precedence over family ties." He glanced at Xaverri. "Does that bother you that I was an Imperial officer? I know you hate the Empire."

She shook her head. "No, it doesn't bother me. You didn't stay in long enough to get corrupted. For that, you should give thanks to whatever gods you believe in."

Han shrugged. "I'm afraid that's a real short list. Not even one entry," he said, keeping it light. "What about you?"

She glanced at him, and her eyes were haunted. "Revenge is my religion, Solo. Revenge against the Empire for what they did to me . . . and mine."

Han reached over and took her hand, gripped it strongly. "Tell me . . . if you can."

She shook her head. "I can't. I've never told anyone. I

will never talk about it. If I did . . . I think it might kill
me. I really do, Solo."

"The Empire . . ." Han was guessing, "they killed your
family?"

She drew a long breath, nodded, lips tightly pressed together. "Husband. Children," she said flatly. "Yes. They
killed them."

"I'm sorry," Han said. "I never knew my family. I'm not
sure I had one. Sometimes, like now, I think that might not
be such a bad thing."

Xaverri shook her head. "I don't know. You may be
right, Solo. All I do know is that I never miss an opportunity to hurt them. My work takes me through the galaxy,
and, believe me, this is the first engagement I've had in a
long time where I haven't spent every free moment figuring
out a way to hurt the Empire."

Han smiled wryly. "That's because there are no Imperials here on Nar Shaddaa." Which wasn't quite true, but it
might as well be. There *was* an Imperial Customs office on
the Smuggler's Moon. The office was staffed by an old man
named Dedro Needalb, who basically worked for the
Hutts. He bore the title of "Imperial Customs Inspector,"
though. He transmitted data about ships and their cargoes
to the local Sector Moff, Sarn Shild, when he felt like it. No
one ever verified whether the data he transmitted were
accurate.

Basically, the Hutts had their own arrangements with
Sarn Shild. They made "political contributions" and "personal gifts" to Shild as "gratitude" for being such a good
Imperial rep. Shild, in turn, left the Hutts and their holdings pretty much alone.

Each prospered from the arrangement. Like a symbiotic
organism, Han thought.

"Exactly," she said. "There's no point in harming old
Dedro Needalb. Hurting him would hurt the Hutts and

Nar Shaddaa, and it might actually benefit the Empire. That's the last thing I want."

"So how do you hurt them?" Han asked, wondering whether she was an assassin. She was an accomplished gymnast and contortionist, and some of her tricks involved weapons such as daggers, sabers, and vibroblades. But he had trouble imagining her in the role of an assassin. Xaverri was smart, very smart. Probably smarter, Han had to concede, than he was. She'd be more likely to use brains rather than weapons in her one-woman vendetta against the Empire.

She gave him an enigmatic smile. "That would be telling."

Han shrugged. "Hey, I got no love for the Empire myself. They're slavers these days, and I *hate* slavery. Maybe I could give you a hand sometime. I'm pretty good in a fight."

Xaverri regarded him thoughtfully. "I'll consider it. I've been thinking about replacing old Glarret soon. He's not quick enough anymore to be a good assistant in the act, and he can't pilot. It's hard on me to do all the piloting myself."

"Well, lady, let me tell you, I'm a first-class pilot," Han said with a grin. "Matter of fact, I'm good at a lot of things."

She rolled her eyes. "And modest, too."

By now they had reached the door to Xaverri's room. The illusionist looked at Han for a long level second. "It's pretty late, Solo."

He didn't move. "Yeah."

She pressed the doorlock with her forefinger and thumb, and it opened silently. Xaverri hesitated for a second, then walked into her room.

Leaving the door open.

Han smiled, and followed her in.

· · ·

Han awoke after a few hours, and decided to leave Xaverri, who was still deeply asleep, to finish her rest. Quietly, he dressed and let himself out of the room, after leaving a message on her comlink that he'd see her later that day.

It was just after sunrise on Nar Shaddaa, though the activity on the Smuggler's Moon had little to do with the unnaturally (to most sentients) long days and nights. Nar Shaddaa was always awake, always active. Han walked toward home through crowded streets, hearing the cries of the street vendors selling their myriad wares.

Han whistled a few bars of an old Corellian folk song as he walked. He felt great. He hadn't realized how lonely he'd been for female companionship. It had been a long time since he'd met a woman he really cared for, and Xaverri obviously found him as attractive as he found her. The memory of her kisses still had the power to stir him.

Han found himself counting the hours until he could see her again, and chuckled to himself, shaking his head. *Get hold of yourself, Solo. You're no moony-eyed kid anymore, you're—*

Without warning, something jabbed him in the right buttock. At first Han thought he'd staggered and bumped his rear against a sharp piece of glassine protruding from the half-ruined building beside him.

Then a rush of strange, tingling warmth engulfed him. His steps faltered, and his vision blurred, then cleared.

What's happening?

Steely fingers clamped on to his arm and dragged him into the alley. Han realized, with horror, that he couldn't fight back. His hands wouldn't obey the commands of his brain.

Drugged? Oh, no!

A flat, inhuman voice spoke to him from just behind his right shoulder. "Stand still, Solo."

Han discovered that he could do nothing else than stand perfectly still. Inwardly he was raging, his anger as hot and explosive as star-plasma, but outwardly his body was completely obedient to that artificially amplified voice.

Who's got me? What does he want?

Han concentrated every muscle, every sinew, every neuron of his being into moving his hands, his arms, his legs. Sweat gathered on his forehead, trickled down into his eyes. But he couldn't so much as twitch a finger.

The hand left his arm, went down to his thigh to unfasten the leather strap that held his blaster secure in its holster. Han could feel the weight against his thigh lighten as his attacker disarmed him. Raging, he tried again to move, but he might as well have tried to push a ship into hyperspace using his own muscle power.

He tried to speak, tried to say, "Who are you?" but that proved beyond him, too. All he could do was to breathe, in and out, blink his eyes, and obey.

If Han had been a Wookiee, he'd have howled, long and loud.

After relieving Han of his blaster, his captor walked around him. Finally, Han got a look at him. *Bounty hunter!* his mind screamed.

Beat-up greenish-gray Mandalorian armor, a helmet that completely hid his features, and armed to the teeth. He even had black and white braided scalps of some kind hanging from his right shoulder. Han wondered what the man's name was. He must be one of the elite—a bounty hunter who only went after "tough" cases.

The Corellian supposed that he ought to be flattered, but it seemed a dubious honor at best.

The bounty hunter went on to pat Han down, looking for more weaponry. He found Han's multitool in his pocket, and confiscated that. The Corellian tried again to move, but he could do absolutely nothing but inhale and exhale. His breathing was loud and harsh in his own ears.

The figure in the Mandalorian armor glanced up at him. "Don't waste your energy, Solo. I jabbed you with a dose of a handy little potion they've come up with on Ryloth. Expensive, but for the bounty they're paying, you're worth it. You won't be able to move, except at my command, for several hours. It varies from subject to subject. By the time you can move under your own power, we'll be aboard my ship and halfway to Ylesia."

Han stared at the bounty hunter, suddenly realizing he'd seen that figure in Mandalorian armor before, a long time ago. Where? He concentrated, but the memory wouldn't surface.

Having finished his search, the bounty hunter straightened. "All right. Turn around."

Han found himself turning.

"Now walk. Turn right at the mouth of the alley."

The Corellian raged helplessly as his body obeyed every command. Right-left, right-left. He was walking, and the bounty hunter was right behind him. Han could catch occasional glimpses of him with his peripheral vision.

They walked down the street of Nar Shaddaa, and for a moment Han hoped that they might encounter one of his friends, even, possibly, Chewie. Surely *someone* would notice what was happening to him!

But although many of the denizens of Nar Shaddaa watched bounty hunter and prize walk past, nobody even spoke to them. Han didn't really blame them. This bounty hunter, whoever he was, was a different sort than the ones he'd dealt with before. This guy was skilled, clever, and extremely dangerous. Anyone who interfered with him would undoubtedly suffer dire consequences.

Right-left, right-left, right-left.

The bounty hunter turned right at the intersection leading to the nearest transport tube. Han knew where they must be heading—the closest public landing platform. The bounty hunter must have a ship waiting there.

Obediently, Han stepped into the transport tube. He tried again to move. Just let him wiggle even a finger or a toe! But it was hopeless. The public transport system consisted of small capsules that would hold four or five individuals, all strung together in a line like beads on a string.

Han's captor did not sit down, but he ordered Han to do so. The Corellian sat there, fuming, imagining all the things he would do to this bounty hunter if only he could move.

The man did not speak. Han could not. It was a short, silent ride.

When they debarked from the tube capsule, Han found himself, as he'd suspected, at one of the public rooftop landing fields. The field was huge, broken only by several airshafts that gave light to the buildings beneath the platform. The airshafts yawned, with no railings to protect a careless walker from plunging to his, her, or its death hundreds or thousands of stories below.

Han had a sudden vivid memory of the night Garris Shrike had chased him across the topmost platforms on Coruscant. He'd barely escaped with his life then. The Corellian had a bad feeling that this time he wasn't going to be so lucky.

Han found himself wondering what fate held in store for him back on Ylesia. Teroenza didn't have a molecule of kindness or mercy in his entire enormous body. He'd see that his prisoner met a slow and agonizing end.

For a moment Han wished he could get control of his body just long enough to make a running dive down one of those airshafts. But no matter how he struggled to move, he could do nothing except obey orders.

Han and his captor strode between the grounded ships, heading Han knew not where.

Right-left, right-left, right-left . . .

The bounty hunter pointed, his arm coming into Han's view. "Head for that ship. The modified Firespray class."

Han could see it now. The bounty hunter wasn't kidding when he said "modified." The patrol and attack ship was very unusual, obviously heavily modified. Unlike other vessels, it landed with its Kuat Engineering Systems F-31 drive engines down against the permacrete. Roughly egg-shaped, when those powerful engines were engaged, the ship would "stand up" on end to fly. Han had never seen anything quite like it, but the vessel reminded him of its owner—powerful and deadly.

For a moment, forgetting his predicament in his interest in the ship, Han found himself wishing he could get a look at the interior—only to catch himself in disgust. He was going to get a look at the interior, all right. He'd spend several days aboard that modified Firespray as it took him to certain torture and inevitable death.

They were walking down the ragged "aisle" between two huge Durosian-built freighters now. In just a few steps, they'd be at the bounty hunter's ship, and that would be it. Han knew better than to imagine he'd be able to somehow overpower this guy, seize control of the Firespray, and save himself.

He wished he could swallow. His throat was so dry it ached.

Right-left, right-left, right-left . . .

This is it, Han thought. *This is really it* . . .

Chapter Six:

Love at First Flight

As Han marched woodenly forward, he caught a blur of motion out of the corner of his eye—a figure stepped out from behind the freighter's massive stabilizer fin. A voice he'd never heard before, low, pleasant, but holding plenty of authority, said, "Freeze, bounty hunter. Move and you've had it."

The hand that had been resting lightly on Han's arm fell away. The Corellian, of course, was unable to stop walking. He marched forward into the sunlit expanse between himself and the modified Firespray, leaving his captor and his unknown benefactor behind him in the shadow of the ship.

Relief washed through him. *I'm saved!* only to be replaced with terror. Now that his eyes had adjusted to the sudden change from shadow to sunlight, he could see there was an airshaft between him and the Firespray. Unable to stop himself, he was going to walk right off the edge!

Then the voice called after him. "Hey, you! Solo! Stop!"

Han felt himself halting, and was again flooded with relief. Fortunately, his body would obey orders from anyone, not just the unknown bounty hunter. "Turn around and come back here!" the voice added.

Joyfully, Han obeyed.

As he walked toward his former captor and his rescuer, he stared into the shadows, but could make out little except that someone stood half behind the bounty hunter, holding the muzzle of a blaster shoved up under the edge of the Mandalorian helmet, so it dug into the man's neck.

As he walked back into the shadow of the freighter's stabilizer fin, and his eyes adjusted from full sunlight, Han finally got a good look at his rescuer.

He was a male, human, approximately Han's age, maybe a couple of years older. Slightly shorter than Han himself, he was slender and fit. He was clean-shaven, with curling black hair, dark eyes, and skin the color of vine-coffeine lightened with traladon milk.

The man was dressed in the height of fashion, a pale gold shirt that laced up the front, accented with black embroidery on the wide collar and cuffs. His narrow black trousers were impeccably pressed. A wide, cummerbund-like embroidered belt accented his narrow waist and flat stomach. He wore black softboots, which explained why he'd been able to ambush the bounty hunter so soundlessly. A short, black cape hung from his shoulders.

As Han approached him, he smiled, an exceptionally charming smile that revealed excellent white teeth. "You may stop now, Solo," he said, halting Han well out of range of his erstwhile captor.

Han stopped, and stood watching as his rescuer's thumb

moved on the firing control of the blaster as he pulled his hand back slightly. Feeling the newcomer's grip slacken, the bounty hunter started to swing around, raising his wrists. The bounty hunter wore Mandalorian wristlets that were undoubtedly loaded with deadly little darts!

Han tried without success to scream a warning, but it was unnecessary. The newcomer was already firing. The stun blast hit the bounty hunter, and at such close range, even his Mandalorian armor couldn't deflect its effects. The bounty hunter went down bonelessly. The edges of his armor clattered on the permacrete as he landed.

Han's rescuer replaced his small but deadly holdout blaster in a concealed holster attached to the ornamental belt. He gestured to Han. "Help me pick him up."

Naturally, Han did as he was told.

Together, he and the newcomer carried the unconscious hunter toward his ship. Han wondered what they were going to do with him. It wouldn't be long before he regained consciousness.

"I wonder how long that stuff will affect you," the rescuer said thoughtfully. "Can you talk, Solo?"

Han felt his lips moving. "Yes," he said. He tried to say more than that simple assent, but he couldn't.

The man glanced over at him. "I get it. You can respond to orders, but no more, right?"

"I guess so," Han found himself replying.

"Nasty stuff he shot you with," the man said. "I've heard of it, but never seen it in action. I'll have to investigate getting some of it. Could come in handy in a pinch."

When they reached the ramp leading to the airlock of the Firespray, they laid the bounty hunter on the permacrete. The newcomer then proceeded to search his pockets and all the concealed places in his armor. "Hello, what have we here?" he exclaimed as his deft fingers encountered several vials in the bounty hunter's belt pocket.

After holding each vial up to the light so he could read the label, Han's rescuer flashed him a roguish grin. "You're in luck, Solo," he said. "This is the stuff he shot into you"—he held up a blue vial—"and here's the antidote." He held up a green vial.

Han waited impatiently as the newcomer loaded the injector with the substance. "I'm having to guess at the dosage," he said. "I'll give you the minimum, and if that doesn't help, I'll try a bit more." He placed the injector against Han's torso and then triggered it.

As soon as his rescuer depressed the trigger, and the substance flooded his body, Han felt himself tingle all over. Moments later he could move and speak.

"Pal, I owe you one," he said, extending his hand to the other. "If it hadn't been for you . . ." He shook his head. "So who are you and why did you rescue me? I've never seen you before in my life."

The other grinned. "Lando Calrissian," he replied. "And as to why I saved you, it's a bit of a story. Let's deal with Boba Fett here, and then we'll talk." His gaze sharpened. "Hey, Solo, you okay?"

Han felt dizzy. He dropped to one knee beside the prone figure of the bounty hunter and shook his head. "Boba . . . Boba Fett? *This* is *Boba Fett*?"

The most famous bounty hunter in the galaxy had been hired to bring him in? Han felt himself tremble in reaction to the news. "Oh, man . . . Lando . . ." he said. "I didn't know . . ."

"Well, you're safe now," Calrissian said cheerfully. "You can get the shakes later, Solo. Right now we have to figure out what we're going to do with Master Fett, here." He thought for a moment, then a slow, unpleasant smile stole across his face. He snapped his fingers. "Got it!"

"What?"

Calrissian was already loading the injector again, this

time with the other vial, the blue one. He shook the bounty hunter, who groaned and stirred. "He's coming around, so here goes nothing," he grunted. Han, who had reappropriated his blaster, kept the bounty hunter covered while Calrissian lifted the front of Fett's helmet, exposing his throat. The bounty hunter suddenly struggled violently. "Freeze!" Han ordered, holding the blaster against his helmet. "This isn't set on stun, Fett," he snarled. "After what you almost did to me, I'd cheerfully disintegrate you."

Boba Fett lay quiet as Calrissian shoved the injector against his neck and triggered it.

Moments later Fett shivered. "Lie still," Calrissian ordered.

The bounty hunter obeyed. Han and Lando grinned at each other . . . slow, nasty grins.

"All right, sit up," Calrissian said.

Boba Fett did as he was told.

"You know what we ought to do," Calrissian said thoughtfully. "If we had any idea of how long this stuff stays in the system, I'd say take him down to one of the local bars for a couple of hours and collect fees from folks who'd pay well to humiliate this guy. He's taken a lot of bounties. He's got to have lots of enemies."

"He said it would last several hours. There's no way to tell exactly," Han pointed out. Personally, he wanted nothing more than to get as far away from Fett and *Slave I* as he could. For a moment he considered ordering Fett to march himself across the permacrete and down an airshaft, but a moment's reflection convinced him that even though it might be the smart thing to do, he just couldn't do it. Killing someone in a blaster fight was one thing, but callously ordering a sentient to kill himself—even when that sentient was a scummy bounty hunter—was quite another.

"True." Calrissian stood up. "Well, I think maybe my

first idea is the best one. Stand up, Boba Fett," he commanded.

The bounty hunter stood up.

"Disarm yourself. Now."

Minutes later Han and Lando regarded a largish pile of assorted weaponry of all different kinds that lay before them on the sunlit permacrete. "Minions of Xendor," Han said, shaking his head, "this guy could have set up shop with just what he had on him. Lookit those Mandalorian wristlets. Bet the darts are poisoned, too."

"One way to find out," said Lando. "Boba Fett, answer me. Are these darts poisoned?"

"Some of them," the bounty hunter replied.

"Which ones?"

"Left wristlet."

"What's on the right wristlet darts?"

"Soporific."

"Nice," Han said, fingering the wristlets carefully. "These oughta be worth quite a bit to a collector. So, now . . . what do we do with him?"

"I think we set his autopilot to blast out of here, and set a course for some far system. Then we order him not to interfere with the course we've set. If this stuff takes hours to wear off, by the time it does, he could be sectors away." Calrissian paused. "He's killed so many people, I'm almost tempted to just shoot him. But I've never killed anyone in cold blood like that." He frowned, almost seeming embarrassed. "I'm not eager to start now, I have to admit."

"Me, too," Han said. "Your plan sounds fine. Let's get him aboard."

Obediently, Boba Fett opened up his ship, and the three of them walked into *Slave I*. Han and Lando strapped Fett into one of the passenger seats. "Are you a pilot?" Han asked.

"No, I'm not," Calrissian admitted. "Matter of fact, that's why I was looking for you. I need to hire a pilot."

"You got one," Han said. "Anything I can do to help you out. Like I said, I owe you, pal."

"We'll talk about that later. Let's get rid of our friend here."

Han quickly set the autopilot to take the ship up, and prerecorded all the necessary responses *Slave I* would need to make to Nar Shaddaa's sector traffic control. Then he chose a course that would take *Slave I* clear across Imperial space in a series of bewildering hyperspace jumps. With any luck, Boba Fett would be unable to regain control until he was tens of thousands of parsecs away.

"We're ready," Han said, finally. "She'll lift in three minutes."

"Okay." Lando turned back to the helpless bounty hunter. "Fett, listen to me, and do exactly what I say. You are to sit in this seat, strapped in, and not go near the controls of your ship until you reach the destination Solo has set for it, or until your obedience drug wears off, whichever comes first. Do you understand?"

"Yes," said Fett.

"Good." Calrissian waved a jaunty good-bye to the bounty hunter and headed for the ramp.

Han stared hard at Boba Fett. "Have a nice trip, bounty hunter. I hope I never see you again. And you can tell Teroenza from me that the next time I come back to Ylesia, he's one dead t'landa Til. You hear me?"

"Yes."

"So long, Fett," Han said. He could hear the engines whine, and the ramp trembled beneath his feet as he ran down it, pressing the CLOSE button as he did so. He had to jump down from the ramp as it rose beneath his feet.

Lando had already scooped up Boba Fett's weaponry, and together, the young men jogged to a safe distance.

They turned back to watch *Slave I* rear up on its end, then take off, its powerful engines flaring.

Only when it had disappeared into the distance did Han finally draw a long, deep breath and then let it out slowly. "Whew. Close call," he said.

"I'll say," Calrissian agreed. "You're lucky I spotted you, Solo."

Han nodded and held out his hand to the other. "Call me Han. I owe you, Calrissian."

"Call me Lando." The other man's irresistible grin flashed. "And . . . don't worry. I'll see you pay up."

"Whatever you want, pal. You don't know what would have happened to me if Boba Fett had succeeded." The Corellian shivered, even in the sun's warmth. "Trust me, you don't *want* to know."

"I can guess," Lando said. "Boba Fett doesn't work cheap. If somebody wanted you that bad, chances are it wasn't just because you welshed on a debt, or anything minor."

Han grinned. "You are an insightful guy, pal." He beckoned to the other, and they began walking back across the landing platform. "Want to get some breakfast? I find I'm really hungry. Nearly meeting a fate worse than death has that effect on me."

"Sure," Lando said. "You buying?"

"You bet."

By the time they were settled at a little cafe Han knew, sipping cups of stim-tea, Han was beginning to feel as though he'd known Lando for years, instead of just an hour. "So, tell me," he said, finishing off the last slice of flatbread, "how did you find me? And why were you lookin' for me?"

"Well, I've actually seen you a time or two before," Lando admitted. "You were pointed out to me in a couple of night spots as a fair sabacc player, a good smuggler, and an excellent pilot."

Han tried, without much success, to look suitably modest. "I don't recall seein' you, Lando, but I didn't have any reason to remember, I guess. So, okay, you knew what I look like. What happened this morning?"

"Well, last night I went by your place to talk to you, and your friend told me that he didn't think you'd be home that night." Lando gave Han a knowing smile. "But he told me you'd probably be staying with a . . . friend . . . at The Chance Castle. So, when I finished the night's work, I dropped by on my way home."

"You work at night? What do you do?" Han asked.

"Gambler," Lando said. "Mostly. Though I've been known to try my hand at various schemes as they come along."

"I see. So you hadn't been to bed yet, but you came by The Castle on the way home."

"It wasn't far out of my way. Most of the big casinos in that section of Nar Shaddaa are within walking distance of each other. Anyway, when I got there, I saw you on the street, ahead of me. I followed you, intending to catch up and introduce myself—"

"Only to see Boba Fett get the drop on me," Han guessed.

"Exactly. I don't much like bounty hunters, so I followed you until I was pretty sure where he was heading. Then I managed to slip around the perimeter of the landing field and get ahead of you. You were walking pretty slowly, you know. I recognized *Slave I,* so I was able to hide between you and the ship, then get the drop on Fett when he walked past."

Han nodded. "And I'm real glad you did, pal." He shook his head. "Listen, don't tell Chewie about this, okay? He's sworn something called a life debt to me, 'cause he thinks he owes me, you see. I had a hard time talkin' him out of coming with me last night. He was sure I'd get myself into trouble . . ."

"Well, you did," Lando said, chuckling.

"I know I did," Han admitted ruefully. "But if Chewie ever finds out about it, he'll never let me out of his sight again. And, hey . . . there are times when a guy would like some privacy, you know?"

Lando shook his head ruefully. "I get your point. Okay, Han, I'll keep your secret." He leaned forward and poured himself another cup of stim-tea. "Is she pretty?"

Han nodded. "I know you'll appreciate what I mean when I say that she's *almost* worth what I went through this morning."

Lando looked impressed. "Maybe you should introduce me, old buddy."

Han shook his head. "I don't think so . . . old buddy. You strike me as a bit of a ladykiller. You'd probably try to charm her away from me."

Lando shrugged and sat back, smiling smugly. "You never know."

Han grinned. "The operative word here is 'try,' Lando. So why were you lookin' for me in the first place? You mentioned needing a pilot?"

"That's right. I was playing sabacc over on Bespin a week or so ago, and one of the players threw in a marker for his ship. High-stakes game, it was."

"And you won the ship," Han guessed.

"That's right. But I've never piloted one. I need to learn—especially now, with a chance that Boba Fett will come looking for me. I'm going to head for greener pastures and fresh sabacc tables for a while, and I thought it would be fun to travel in my own ship. I had to hire a pilot to fly me back here, and it was expensive. So I want you to teach me to fly my ship,"

"Okay," Han said. "I can do that. When do you want to start?"

Lando shrugged. "My adrenaline level is still pretty high after dealing with Fett. I'm not sleepy at all. How about now?"

Han nodded. "Sure."

They took a different tube to a different landing platform. Side by side, Han and Lando walked across the windswept surface of the platform, through ranks of parked vessels, until Lando stopped and pointed.

"There it is. The *Millennium Falcon*."

Han stared across the permacrete at the modified light stock freighter, Corellian made and engineered, model YT-1300 Transport. He'd seen plenty of them before, and had always liked them—Corellians were good engineers as well as good pilots.

But, as Han stared at this particular ship, something strange happened. Without warning, he fell suddenly, irrevocably, irretrievably in love. This ship *called* to him, she *sang* to him a siren song of speed, of maneuverability, of narrow escapes and adventures and successful smuggling runs galore.

That ship is going to be mine, Han thought. *Mine. The* Millennium Falcon *will be mine* . . .

The Corellian suddenly realized he was staring, his mouth agape. Lando was looking at him, his eyes narrowed suspiciously. Hastily Han closed his mouth, and tried his best to purge the sudden yearning, the *wanting* from his mind. He had to play it cool. If Lando knew how much Han wanted the ship, he'd surely jack the price up . . .

"So, what do you think of her?" Lando asked.

Han shook his head. "What a hunk of junk!" he exclaimed, mentally begging the *Falcon*'s pardon. "That game wasn't nearly as high stakes as you're tryin' to make me believe, old buddy."

"Hey, the pilot who flew it back here for me said it's a really fast ship," Lando said, sounding defensive.

"Really?" Han looked doubtful. He shrugged. "Well, you never know till you try her out. Shall we go for a spin?"

"Sure," Lando said.

Minutes later Han sat at the controls of Lando's new acquisition, savoring the *Falcon*'s response as she lifted on her repulsors, then he engaged the sublight drive. He still couldn't believe what he'd seen in her engine room—this ship boasted a military-grade hyperdrive! *Oh, you honey!*

Her sublight speeds were good, too. Han sent the *Falcon* hurtling upward in a steep rush. The resulting surge of power exhilarated him, but he was careful not to show it. "Not bad," he said indifferently. "But I've seen better. Let's see how she maneuvers."

Quickly he took the *Falcon* up out of Nar Shaddaa's atmosphere, then through the opening in the shield, all the while giving the correct responses to traffic control. Once free of the gravity well and past the floating obstacle course of the derelict ships, Han sent the *Falcon* into a dizzying series of spins, rolls, and flips.

"Hey!" Lando protested, gulping audibly. "You got a passenger here, don't forget! You want me to lose my breakfast?"

Han grinned at him. He was tempted to ask Lando how much he wanted for the ship, but he knew it would be more than he could possibly afford. Wild schemes about getting the Hutts to buy the *Falcon* so he could fly it regularly—and then maybe steal it, someday—raced through his mind.

But he didn't want Jabba or Jiliac owning the *Falcon*. They wouldn't appreciate this beauty, this work of art.

Han quickly checked out the weaponry. *Her legs are good, but she could use more muscle . . .* Only one light laser cannon, in a top gun turret. *Not enough,* Han thought.

As though Lando were reading Han's thoughts, the gambler said, "The pilot that brought me here said it might need some more weaponry to be a really good smuggler. What do you think?"

"I think if this were my ship, I'd install another gun turret and some quad lasers, as well as a repeating blaster in the belly, to cover quick getaways," Han said. *Maybe some concussion missiles, too . . .*

"Huh," Lando said. "I'll have to think about that. But it is a fast ship, isn't it?"

Han nodded grudgingly. "Yeah, she's got a pretty good set of legs on her, Lando." He surreptitiously patted the pilot's console. *Oh, you sweetheart . . .*

A few minutes later Lando cleared his throat. "I thought the object of taking it out was that you were going to start teaching *me* to pilot, Han."

"Oh . . . oh, yeah," Han said. "I was just . . . checking her out. So I could teach you all her little quirks and stuff."

"You sound like this thing is alive," Lando said.

"Well, pilots get to think of their ships sort of like that," Han admitted. "They become like a . . . friend. You'll see."

"Don't forget, the *Falcon* is *my* ship," Lando said, with a slight edge in his voice.

"Of course," Han said, carefully casual. "Now, listen here. We're going to start at sublight speeds. That's where most of the maneuvering expertise comes. See that lever? Pull that lever and we'll go into hyperdrive, and that's not something you want to do less you've got a course laid in. So . . . don't touch that lever. Got it?"

Lando leaned forward intently. "Got it . . ."

· · ·

Thousands of light-years away, Teroenza, High Priest of Ylesia, stood in the middle of Colony Three, surveying the damage from a dawn terrorist raid. Nearly a dozen bodies were sprawled around, most of them his own security guards. Blaster marks scored the factory buildings. The door to the mess hall was slagged. A crew was finishing putting out a fire in the Administration Building. The smell of burning fought with the hothouse odor of the wet, steaming jungle.

The High Priest snorted nervously. All this from a slave raid. Not a raid to *gain* slaves, a raid to *rescue* them.

The troops had been human, most of them. Teroenza had seen their images on his communications monitors from his headquarters at Colony One. Two ships had spiraled down through Ylesia's treacherous air currents, but only one had managed to land safely. The other vessel had gotten caught in a wind shear, and was destroyed.

Which was only justice, Teroenza thought grumpily as he surveyed the damage the remaining ship had caused. Meddlers! The group had landed, then armed troops dressed in green and khaki uniforms had leaped out and attacked the Ylesian guards. A firefight had ensued, and more than a dozen guards had been killed.

Then the attackers had stormed the refectory where the pilgrims were having breakfast. They'd entreated them to come with them, saying they were here to rescue them from slavery.

Teroenza made a soft whuffling sound that was his species' equivalent of a chuckle. Stupid raiders! Stupid to think the pilgrims would renounce the Exultation for freedom. Only two pilgrims out of the two hundred in the mess hall had run to join the invaders.

And then—Teroenza's expression darkened—*she* had stepped forward to address the assembled pilgrims. The High Priest had thought her dead long since. He remem-

bered her very well. Pilgrim 921, birth name Bria Tharen.
A Corellian . . . and a traitor.

Bria had argued with the pilgrims, telling them the truth
about the Exultation. She'd told the group that someday
they'd thank her—and then she'd given the order for her
troops to turn stun beams on the crowd. Pilgrims had fallen
in their tracks.

The group of Corellians had gotten away with nearly a
hundred prime slaves. Teroenza cursed softly. Bria Tharen!
He couldn't decide which Corellian he hated more, Bria or
that accursed Han Solo.

Teroenza was worried about this raid. There was money
behind this group. Ships and weapons cost money. They
were well organized and efficient, like a real military cadre.
Who were they?

Teroenza had heard of various rebel groups rising
against the Empire. Could the squadron of soldiers that
attacked Colony Three today have been part of such a
group?

The High Priest experienced a flicker of satisfaction,
though, when he imagined how miserable the rescuers
would be when the stunned pilgrims awakened. The t'landa
Til knew only too well how addicted most humanoids
quickly became when exposed to the Exultation on a daily
basis.

By now the pilgrims must be missing the Exultation a
great deal. They would be screaming and wailing and making threats, begging to return to Ylesia. They might even
commandeer the rebel ship and bring it back here, like
faithful pilgrims. One thing was certain . . . tonight the
Corellian rebels would have their hands full.

The thought made Teroenza smile.

*   *   *

Several days after Boba Fett's attempt to capture him, Han went to see Jabba and Jiliac to tell them that he would be scarce on Nar Shaddaa for a while. He'd decided to take Xaverri up on her offer, and become her assistant during her next tour. He had a feeling Boba Fett wouldn't be easily discouraged, and it wouldn't hurt to get off Nar Shaddaa for the next few months.

But the words died unspoken on his lips. The moment he was ushered into their presence, Jabba hailed him with impatient cries, ordering him to prepare the *Star Jewel* for an immediate trip to Nal Hutta. The emissaries sent from the Desilijic and the Besadii kajidics had convened a meeting of the Hutt kajidics for the next day. Apparently Besadii had been holding up the negotiations, but had suddenly made several important concessions, in the interest of holding the meeting quickly.

"Today?" Han said, thinking that he'd have to cancel his lesson with Lando this afternoon. "That's pretty short notice, isn't it?"

"Yes," Jiliac agreed. "We know of no reason for things to have been speeded up, but something must have happened."

"Okay, I'll take you down this afternoon," Han said. "Just give me an hour or so to get the ship ready, and check out our course."

"And, Captain Solo, you must be prepared to give us your smoothest flight," Jabba cautioned. "No turbulence. My aunt is in a delicate condition, and she must not be jostled."

Han glanced around for another Hutt, but saw only Jiliac. "Your aunt? I beg your pardon, Lord Jabba? There will be three Hutts for me to transport?"

"No, human!" Jabba was impatient. "Jiliac and myself, as always! Don't you have eyes? Didn't you notice her skin texture? Her condition is plain!"

Han looked over at Jiliac, and suddenly realized that the Hutt *did* appear different. Warty excrescences had erupted on the being's face, and purplish patches mingled with the greenish ones on the leathery tan skin. Jiliac also appeared bigger, and rather lethargic. *Oh, wonderful, I get to play nursemaid to a sick Hutt? Great!*

"Uh, Lord Jiliac, are you feeling—" Han began, only to have Jabba round on him with withering scorn.

"Human idiot! Can't you see that Lord Jiliac is now *Lady* Jiliac? She is expecting! In her delicate condition, she really should not make this effort, but we Desilijic are nothing if not faithful to our duty!"

She? Pregnant? Han's mouth dropped open, and Chewie roared softly in surprise.

Han recovered quickly, and bowed to Jiliac. "Your pardon, Lady Jiliac. I am not familiar with your species' . . . uh, er . . . reproductive habits. I meant no offense."

Jiliac blinked at Han sleepily. "No offense taken. My people reproduce as they will, and I decided it was time for me to do so. My child is due in a few months. I will be able to make the trip safely, my nephew Jabba is merely overprotective. But a smooth flight would be advisable."

"Yes, lady," Han said, bowing. "Smooth flight to Nal Hutta. Leaving this afternoon. I'll get right on it."

"Very well, Captain. You are dismissed. We wish to leave as soon as possible."

Han bowed again, and left, with Chewie trailing behind him. As soon as he was out of sight, he shook his head. *Hutts! The more I get to know them, the weirder they are . . .*

A veritable tide of Hutts wriggled and glided toward the large Hutt Grand Council Hall on Nal Hutta. Jabba and Jiliac undulated along, side by side, accompanied by the

Desilijic security guards. Most of the Hutts preferred to move under their own power if they still could. It was permissible to show weakness before humans and other underlings, but in the company of their own kind, Hutts preferred to appear strong and fit. All of Desilijic moved under their own power, and among the Besadii clan, only Aruk was too old and corpulent to manage without his sled.

As the Hutts moved toward the council chambers, they and their guards passed through multiple security and scanning devices. None of the guards was allowed a weapon, and each attendee was scanned, internally as well as externally, to make sure no dangerous substances were being smuggled into the hall. Hutts were not trusting beings, especially in the company of other Hutts—and with good reason. Long ago, every prominent Hutt on Nal Hutta had been eliminated en masse by a single ingenious assassin.

Hutts were determined that nothing like that would ever happen again.

The Grand Council Hall was a huge room, big enough to comfortably hold nearly fifty Hutts. At the moment twenty-seven Hutts were gathered—representatives of all the major clans and kajidics, as well as "neutral" parties from the Hutt government who would be overseeing and administering the conference.

The Hutt homeworld was governed by the Grand Council—an oligarchy composed of one representative appointed by each major Hutt clan. In reality, though, the power of the crime syndicates—the kajidics—was far greater than that of the Grand Council.

Jabba and Jiliac had summoned two other Desilijic members to attend them. Aruk had brought the Besadii contingent, consisting of himself, his offspring Durga, and his nephew Kibbick. Jabba was pleased to note that a t'landa Til trailed in Kibbick's wake. Jiliac was right, Besadii had indeed summoned Teroenza.

After the mass of Hutts had arranged themselves in a circle around the speaker's platform, the conference was brought to order by the Executive Secretary of the Grand Council, a Hutt named Mardoc. After each of the clans had officially identified itself and its contingent, Mardoc spoke again:

"Comrades-in-power, siblings-in-profit, I have convened you today to discuss some very serious developments on the Besadii colony world of Ylesia. I ask Lord Aruk to speak."

Aruk moved his sled closer to the speaker's platform. He waved his small arms at his fellow Hutts for emphasis and began, "Fellow Hutts. Two days ago Colony Three on Ylesia was attacked by well-armed terrorists. Kibbick and our overseer, Teroenza, barely escaped with their lives. Much destruction was done, and the attackers made off with nearly one hundred valuable slaves."

A ripple of consternation ran around the conference room as the assorted Hutts reacted to Aruk's news. Jabba realized that Aruk was staring straight at him and Jiliac. *Gauging our reaction,* he realized. For just a moment, Jabba wondered if Jiliac had decided to play it ultra-subtle, and had arranged the raid, but not told him. After a moment's thought, however, he rejected the notion. His Aunt was so caught up in her recent pregnancy that she had little energy for plotting—especially commando raids. Besides, Jiliac normally eschewed direct assaults, preferring to work against enemies in more subtle ways.

"Hutt brethren, we of the Besadii clan demand that Jiliac, as head of clan Desilijic, personally assure us that this terrible raid, this theft of valuable Besadii property, was not done by Desilijic! Otherwise, this means war between our kajidics!"

A collective gasp echoed through the Grand Hall. Aruk's challenge hung in the air like the smoke from the hookahs some of the Hutt Lords were smoking.

Slowly, Jiliac pulled herself up, appearing almost regal in her new maternal dignity. "Fellow Hutts," she said. "Desilijic is innocent of any taint of aggression in this matter. As a guarantee of this, Desilijic pledges that if any link can be discovered between the raiders and Desilijic, Desilijic will remit to Besadii the sum of one million credits."

Silence for a beat, then Aruk inclined his head in the Hutt equivalent of a bow. "Very well. Never let it be said that Desilijic refused to back its integrity with money. We ask that the Grand Council investigate and give us their findings in one month."

Mardoc agreed, but then yielded the floor to Jiliac when she indicated that she had more to say. "However, I wish that I could say the same for Besadii. Just a few months ago, my nephew here"—she indicated Jabba—"was brutally attacked by hired mercenaries. Only the fact that we cannot definitively state who sent them keeps us from leveling accusations at our rivals! Unlike Besadii, we do not make accusations unless we have *proof*!"

Another hubbub of voices and whispers erupted in the Grand Hall.

Aruk drew himself up to his most impressive height, his rheumy old eyes red-rimmed. "Besadii has done nothing wrong!"

"Do you deny that you sent Drell pirates to assassinate my nephew?"

"Yes!" thundered Aruk.

The resulting barrage of threats, insults, and rhetoric from both sides made it necessary for Mardoc to call for a recess. Jabba watched the Hutts around him, talking in small groups, and began wondering just who it was who had attacked Ylesia. If it wasn't Desilijic, then who?

Did Ylesia have a new rival in the slave trade?

* * *

Durga the Hutt lay stretched beside his parent on his repulsor sled during the afternoon session. He was concerned about Aruk. The conference had been going on for hours, and Aruk had been in the middle of it the whole time. Durga knew that his parent wasn't up to this level of stress. Aruk was a very old Hutt, nearly a thousand years old.

The young Hutt listened intently, aware that his parent would quiz him point by point on the conference. Beside Durga, Kibbick blinked slowly, obviously fighting sleep. Durga looked at his cousin scornfully, Kibbick was an idiot. Didn't he understand that these kinds of meetings, these feints and counterfeints, thrusts and parries and ripostes, constituted the life's fluid of Hutt society? Didn't he understand that power and profit were food and drink and breath to their people?

This was the first Hutt conference to be held in Durga's short lifetime, and he was pleased that his parent had allowed him to attend. Durga knew that because of the birthmark he'd been born with, some of the Besadii kajidic would question whether he was fit to lead Besadii when Aruk died.

Durga knew that he had all the most essential qualities to lead Besadii. He was smart, scheming, devious, and ruthless. All estimable qualities in a Hutt. But he had to demonstrate those qualities to Besadii, before Aruk died, or he'd have trouble succeeding his parent.

If only I could take over Ylesia, instead of Kibbick, Durga thought. He knew that his father had spent a good part of yesterday evening raging at Kibbick for allowing Teroenza to take over the running of Ylesia. Aruk had also sternly advised the t'landa Til that he must know his place, lest he lose his position as High Priest. Teroenza had cowered before the old Hutt Lord, but Durga thought he'd caught a flash of anger from him. He resolved to keep a careful eye on Teroenza.

Kibbick, on the other hand, had simply whined about how unpleasant life was on Ylesia, and how hard he was working. Aruk had let him off with a stern warning. Durga privately thought that Aruk should have relieved him of his post. Idly, he wondered whether assassinating his cousin was a good idea . . .

But he had a feeling that Aruk wouldn't like it. So that meant he couldn't do it while his parent lived.

Not that Durga wished Aruk's death. He was genuinely fond of his parent, as he knew Aruk was fond of him. Durga knew only too well that he owed Aruk his life in every possible way. Most Hutt parents would not have allowed a child with a birthmark to live.

Durga also wanted to make Aruk proud of him. That motivation was even stronger in him than his need to gain power and profit—something that he knew would be seen as practically sacrilegious by other Hutts, so he never revealed it.

Durga watched as Jabba the Hutt wriggled forward to take the floor. The second-in-command of Desilijic was said to be an exemplary Hutt in many ways, but most Hutts found his preoccupation with humanoid females both perverse and inexplicable. Still, Jabba was sharp, Durga had to grant him that, as he listened to him speak.

"Honored Hutt Lords, listen to me! Besadii claims that their recent expansions on Ylesia are just good business, but shall we allow good business for one kajidic to undermine the financial underpinnings of our world? Besadii has grabbed such a large share of the spice trade, and the slave trade, that we must all make them see reason! What does it profit them to fill their own coffers if their policies bring disaster to our world?"

"Disaster?" Aruk's voice boomed out so deep and authoritative that Durga felt a ripple of pride. His parent was as fine a Hutt leader as had ever been born! "Disaster, my friends? We had one hundred and eighty-seven percent profit in the past year! How could this possibly be construed to be anything but something to be praised and honored for? I ask you that, Jabba! How could it?"

"Because some of your profit has come out of the coffers of your fellow Hutts," Jabba pointed out. "It is fine to take from others, from humans and Rodians and Sullustans and from all the other creatures of the galaxy. That is why they are there—so that we Hutts may profit from them. But there is a danger in pulling away too much income from Nal Hutta and your fellow Hutts."

"Oh?" sarcasm tinged Aruk's voice. "And what is that danger, Lord Jabba?"

"Too much conspicuous profit may bring us to the attention of the Emperor or his minions," Jabba pointed out. "Nal Hutta is far from Imperial Center. Out here near the Rim Territories, we are protected to some extent by distance, and protected even more by Moff Sarn Shild, whom we generously support in the style to which he has become accustomed. But if any one Hutt clan makes a point of having tremendous wealth, it may bring *all* of us to the attention of the Emperor. And that, fellow Hutts, is an attention we do not want."

Durga heard the other Hutts murmuring, and had to admit that Jabba had made a good point. When the Empire took a close interest in any one world, it was always unfortunate for that world.

Durga wondered how Jabba and Jiliac had discovered that Besadii was behind the attack of Drell pirates. Too bad they'd missed their chance to rid Nal Hutta of Jabba. Without Jabba, Jiliac would be easier to get out of the way.

Jabba was a crafty Hutt, who was protective of his Aunt. His security forces were better than Jiliac's.

The Hutt Lords were unable to reach a conclusion about Besadii's off-the-scale profits. The discussion rambled on, degenerated into personal insults, then ended with no conclusion.

Aruk took the floor again. He was still concerned about the recent violence. Jiliac acknowledged that she was concerned, too. Durga was surprised that they could agree on anything. Finally, Desilijic and Besadii united to put forward an unprecedented proposal.

"I propose," Aruk said, in summary, "that the Grand Council declare a moratorium on violence between the kajidics for at least the next three standard months! Who will support me in this?"

Jiliac and Jabba voiced their enthusiastic approval, then, one by one, the representatives of the other clans chimed in. Mardoc declared Aruk's proposal adopted.

Durga looked up at his parent and felt another wave of pride. *Aruk is a giant among Hutts!*

Much later that night, as both Hutts prepared to sleep in Jiliac's Nal Hutta mansion, which was located on an island in one of Nal Hutta's more temperate zones, Jiliac turned to Jabba. "Aruk is dangerous. I am more convinced of it than ever."

"Yes, he was quite impressive when he managed to rally the clans," Jabba agreed. "He has . . . charisma. He can be very persuasive."

"It is truly ironic that it was Aruk who wound up proposing my idea about the moratorium," Jiliac said. "But as the meeting progressed, I realized that if I hoped to convince the others of the wisdom of the moratorium, the idea would have to come from Aruk."

Jabba nodded. "He is a forceful orator, Aunt."

"An orator who must be deprived of his voice, or Desilijic will suffer even more," Jiliac said soberly. "A three-month moratorium on inter-kajidic violence will free our minds so that we may look at the problem of Aruk without distractions."

Jabba blinked his bulbous eyes at his aunt as she settled herself comfortably on her padded resting spot. "What are you thinking, Aunt?"

Jiliac was silent for a moment, then said, "I am thinking that this is our chance to strike at Aruk's weak spot."

"His weak spot?"

"Yes, Nephew. Aruk has a weak spot, and it has a name. And that name is . . ."

"Teroenza," Jabba said.

"Correct, Nephew."

When Teroenza boarded Kibbick's space yacht for the trip back to Ylesia, he was in a very bad mood. Aruk had not permitted them to have any kind of a holiday on Nal Hutta, stressing that they must get back to Ylesia to see to the rebuilding after the raid.

Teroenza had been profoundly disappointed. He'd hoped to see his mate, Tilenna, while he was home.

But Aruk had said "no," and said it with such stern disapproval that Teroenza hadn't dared to ask again.

So here he was, stuck with that idiot Kibbick for company. When he could have been sporting with his lovely mate in a delicious, sensual mud wallow.

Disgustedly, Teroenza plodded into his large, well-appointed cabin, and sank into his resting sling. Blast Aruk! The Hutt Lord was getting irrational in his old age—irrational and mean. Meaner, that is, than he'd been before.

The High Priest still smarted from the "financial review"

he'd been forced to sit through. Aruk had questioned every expenditure, carped about every extra credit. He'd gone on and on about how the bounty Teroenza had posted on Solo was completely unnecessary. "Let Boba Fett blast him into atoms!" he'd raged. "Disintegrations are much cheaper! Allowing yourself personal revenge on Solo is simply self-indulgent!"

Grumpily, Teroenza reached out and turned on his comm unit. Words in Huttese formed on the screen, even before he could key in his personal code.

Eyes widening, Teroenza read the following message: "This message will vanish in sixty seconds. Attempting to save it will destroy your comm unit. Memorize the following comcode and reply to it."

A complicated comcode followed.

Intrigued, Teroenza memorized the code. As promised, in sixty seconds, it blinked off, to be replaced by the words "What do you want most? We'd like to know. Perhaps we can help each other."

The message, of course, was unsigned, but Teroenza had a good idea of who had sent it. As he sat watching it blink off, to be replaced by his comm unit's standard greeting and request for ID code, Teroenza realized what this meant.

Would he reply to the message?

Was he a traitor?

What *did* he want most?

Chapter Seven:
Con Games

When Han flew Jabba back to Nar Shaddaa following the big Hutt conference (Jiliac had decided to stay on Nal Hutta for the length of her confinement) he immediately sought out Lando Calrissian.

During his trip to Nal Hutta, Chewbacca had been continuing the young gambler's piloting lessons, and Han was encouraged at his new friend's progress. "You're coming right along, old buddy," he said as Lando, his mouth tight with concentration, executed a perfect landing. The ship settled into the *Millennium Falcon*'s assigned berth with nary a wobble. "Another week, and you'll be ready to solo."

Lando glanced up at Han, his dark eyes very serious. "I think I'm ready now, Han. Fact is, I've *got* to be ready now.

I'm leaving tomorrow. I've heard there's some good gambling and pleasure worlds out in the Oseonian system, and I'm heading out to see for myself. Or maybe I'll hit the Corporate Sector."

"Lando, that's clean out of Imperial space!" Han exclaimed. "You're not ready to navigate this ship that far! Especially flying alone!"

"Want to come with me?" Lando offered.

Han thought about it, and for a moment was tempted. But he'd given his word to Xaverri, and . . . he shook his head. "Can't, Lando. I'm signing on with Xaverri to work for her during this next tour. I promised her, and she's counting on me."

"Not to mention that she's a lot prettier than I am," Lando added dryly.

Han grinned. "Well . . . there *is* that." He sobered. "Just wait a couple more days, Lando. Trust me, pal, you're not ready yet to go that far, especially with no copilot." Inwardly he was thinking, *I'm losing the* Falcon *. . . what if I never see her again?*

"Chewbacca here has been giving me good lessons," the gambler insisted. "He's barely had to touch the controls the last couple of times I've taken us out."

"But—" Han began.

"No buts," Lando said. "I'm living on borrowed time here on Nar Shaddaa, Han—and so are you. Boba Fett isn't one to forgive and forget. I'm making myself scarce for at least six months. When does Xaverri leave?"

"Next week," Han said. "Her engagement was held over another week. By popular demand."

"Have you told Jabba that you're leaving?"

"Yeah, I did. He wasn't happy about it."

Chewie interjected a comment.

"Hey, Jabba was *born* cranky," Han said defensively.

"He's one of the orneriest Hutts I've met—and that's sayin' something."

"Did you tell him why you've got to leave?"

"Yeah, I did. That was the only thing that calmed him down. I think even Jabba might be a little nervous if he knew Boba Fett was gunning for him."

"Well . . . if I were you, I'd get out of here as soon as you can," Lando said. "And until you're off Nar Shaddaa, you'd better watch your back."

Nothing Han said could change Lando's decision. It was with a heavy heart that he stood on the landing platform the next morning and watched the *Falcon* take off. The freighter wobbled slightly as she went soaring into the sky. Han shook his head. "Use your stabilizers!" he said, aloud.

He's not ready, he thought dejectedly. *I'll probably never see the* Falcon—*or Lando—again*.

Bria Tharen sat at her desk at the largest Imperial military base on Corellia, watching the screen of her datapad as she updated the food requisition lists for all troops stationed in the Corellian system. Her reddish-gold hair, which had grown into a long, curly mane during the past five years, was swept up in a smart, businesslike style, and she wore a crisp civilian support staff uniform—black jacket and skirt, with black boots. The unrelieved black set off her pale skin and exquisite bone structure.

Her blue-green eyes narrowed as she studied the screens of data. The Empire was definitely building up strength in this sector. Did that mean the Imperial commanders were anticipating some kind of rebellion here in the Corellian system?

She found herself wondering how long her group could manage to hold off the Empire if it attacked in force. Two days? A week?

In the end, they'd all be slaughtered, she knew that. Their small group of rebels was growing every month, as the people of her world grew restive at being ground beneath Palpatine's relentless heel. But there was no way they were ready yet to take on the Imperial forces.

From a very small beginning, though, they'd made good progress over the past three years. Their movement had started with barely a score of unhappy dissidents gathering for clandestine meetings in cellars, and had grown by leaps and bounds, until they now had cells in most of the major cities on the planet. Bria had no idea how many rebels there were on Corellia, but it had to be several thousand.

The reason she had no idea how many rebels were on Corellia was that it was not necessary for her to know. Even though she was fairly high-ranking in the rebel hierarchy, she was not part of personnel or recruitment. Information about the rebel groups on her world was doled out sparingly. Only one or two commanders knew the whole picture. Individual members were informed strictly on a "need to know" basis. The less they knew, the less they could be forced to reveal under torture.

Bria's current assignment was in intelligence. She didn't particularly like spying, but she was good at it. She preferred her old job, though, that of making contact with rebel groups on other worlds. It was obvious to her that if the rebels were to really oppose the Empire, they'd have to unite.

But, so far, they'd barely begun reaching out to other groups. Communication was monitored, travel was restricted—it was so difficult to maintain links between groups on different planets. As fast as their rebel group devised codes, the Imperials broke them.

Just last month one cell of rebels had been raided during a meeting on the eastern continent. They'd disappeared as completely as though a krayt dragon had opened its mouth and swallowed them whole. Bria thought that she'd much prefer to be gobbled alive by a monster than caught by the Emperor's security forces . . .

Her friend Lanah had been one of those taken. Bria knew she'd never see her again.

Bria was worried that her entire homeworld would wind up as a police state. Corellia had always been an independent world, a proud world that governed itself. So far, the Emperor had not appointed an Imperial governor to usurp all power on Corellia. But that didn't mean he wouldn't someday. The Empire did not allow pride or independence in the worlds it claimed.

One of the reasons for Palpatine's not overtly taking over the Corellian government was that Corellia had such a large human population. The Empire made no secret of the fact that it regarded nonhuman species as inferior, incapable of governing themselves.

Two alien species shared the Corellian system worlds with their human inhabitants, the Selonians and the Drall. If Corellia had been inhabited solely by those nonhuman sentients, they'd have been a much more inviting target for repression—possibly even being declared a slave-labor planet. Look at what had happened to Kashyyyk. The proud Wookiees captured and led away in binders and shackles . . .

Bria's fingers tightened on the edge of her desk. She hated the Empire, but even more than the Empire, she hated slavery. Having been a slave on Ylesia (though at the time she'd called herself a "pilgrim"), Bria was determined to do everything she could to destroy the Empire that allowed slavery, that used and owned beings.

When that task was done, she would devote whatever remained of her life to freeing every slave in the galaxy.

Her lovely mouth turned down at the corners as she thought about the raid six months ago that she'd led on

Ylesia. She and her rebel friends had managed to rescue ninety-seven slaves, mostly Corellians, and bring them back to their homeworlds and their families.

Within the next month, fifty-three of those freed slaves had run away and boarded ships to return to Ylesia.

In a way, Bria couldn't blame them. Living without the Exultation was difficult. It had taken her years to overcome her craving for the feel-good rush of euphoria the t'landa Til priests could project.

But forty-four of the freed slaves are still free, Bria reminded herself fiercely. *And just yesterday Rion told me that one of the women had sent him a message, thanking him for returning her to her husband and children . . .*

Rion was Bria's main link to rebel command now that she'd taken this new position at Imperial headquarters. It was Rion to whom she reported every scrap of information she could glean. He took the information that Bria could gather or construe, then relayed it to the leaders of the Corellian underground rebel group.

Bria hoped that soon she'd have more than bureaucratic lists of supply requisition orders to relay to her group. Ever since she'd taken this job last month, she'd been careful to wear the most flattering hairstyles and makeup, hoping that her looks would bring her to the attention of a high-ranking Imperial officer.

Her efforts were paying off, too. Just yesterday admiral Trefaren had stopped by her desk to ask her if she would accompany him to a reception that was being held by the Corellian government for the high-ranking Imperial officers. Several Sector Moffs were supposed to attend. It would be quite a gala evening, he'd assured her.

Bria had lowered her eyelids coyly, blushed attractively, and breathed a halting, girlish "yes." The Admiral had beamed at her, the deep lines that ran vertically down his sallow cheeks appearing even more like canyons in the desert, and told her he'd pick her up in his chauffeured speeder. Then he'd reached out and touched one of her curls, letting it wind around his finger. "And, my dear," he'd added, "wear something that will set off your beauty. I want the other officers to be jealous of the golden treasure I've discovered."

Bria hadn't had to feign her inarticulate response— which had only charmed him further!—because she'd been too angry to speak clearly. *The old lecher!* she thought disgustedly, resolving not to forget to strap her dainty little vibroblade to her upper thigh . . . just in case.

But usually, men of his age were more talk than action. What they mostly wanted, as the admiral had frankly admitted, was for other men to admire them—and any attractive young woman they'd managed to snare with their power and wealth.

Admiral Trefaren might be our key to learn more about these new Imperial weapons and ships we've heard rumors of, Bria thought.

So, when the evening of the reception came, she'd don a lovely, elegant gown (she'd grown up the daughter of a rich man, and knew how to dress for maximum effect), style her hair, tastefully paint her face, and spend the evening smiling warmly at Admiral Trefaren. She'd dance with him, give him admiring glances, and keep her ears open for every scrap of information.

And, just in case she needed help in fending off his advances, Bria already had a tiny drop of a substance she planned to wear beneath one manicured fingernail. All she had to do was touch the tip of her fingernail to the surface of his drink of choice, toward the end of the evening, and the old vrelt would swiftly become so pleasantly tired, sleepy, and drunk that she'd have no trouble dealing with him.

Bria could use that vibroblade, and use it well, but she

had no intention of doing so. Vibroblades were for amateurs. She was an expert at *not* needing them.

For a moment she missed her battle fatigues, the weight of her blaster strapped to her thigh. She'd much prefer leading another armed raid against the Ylesian Hutts, or the Imperial slavers (who were even worse than the Hutts), than she did the prospect of playing tabaga-and-vrelt all evening with Admiral Trefaren and his Imperial cronies.

She'd turned over her blaster to Rion when she'd taken on this assignment. It wasn't improbable that Admiral Trefaren would have her apartment searched as part of the background check he'd get his minions to perform, to ensure that she was "safe" for him to be seen with. Bria always kept the vibroblade with her, so she wasn't worried about searchers finding it.

At least she knew her IDs would stand up to most security checks. Six years ago she'd learned all about establishing new identities from an expert. Han Solo had taught her much more than just how to fire a blaster effectively.

Her lips curved in a soft smile as she indulged herself in a moment of nostalgia for those days. She and Han had been on the run together, living on the edge, never knowing what would happen next.

Those had been the happiest days of her life, she realized now. It had been worth every tense moment, every jolt of fear, every mad chase, every terrified escape, every blaster bolt she'd had to duck to be with him . . . to be free to love him.

And she loved him still.

Seeing him on Devaron a year ago had brought it all back to her so vividly. After years of denial, Bria had had to admit the truth to herself. Han Solo was the man she loved, would always love.

But they couldn't be together. She'd had to accept that. Han was a con man, a rogue, an outlaw who was out for himself. Bria knew he'd loved her deeply—he'd even asked her to marry him—but Han wasn't the kind of man to forsake everything for a philosophical ideal.

During the months they'd spent together, Bria had sensed that someday he might have the potential to embrace a cause, give himself to a goal. But it would have to be a cause that he'd chosen for himself, in his own time. Bria knew she couldn't expect him to adopt *her* cause.

She wondered what he was doing right now. Was he happy? Was he with somebody? Did he have friends? When she'd seen him on Devaron, he'd been wearing typically scruffy spacefarer's garb—not an Imperial uniform.

But she'd heard he'd graduated from the Academy with honors. What could have happened to end his career?

On one hand, Bria was sorry that the dream he'd pursued so single-mindedly had obviously come to a crashing end, but on the other, she was glad to discover that Han was no longer an Imperial officer. It had tortured her to think that someday they might come face-to-face in battle, or, even worse, that she might give the order to fire on an Imperial ship and cause his death, all unknowing. At least she didn't have to worry about *that* possibility anymore.

I wonder if I'll ever see him again . . . she thought. *Maybe . . . maybe when this is all over, when the Empire is no more . . .*

Bria gave herself a mental shake, and told herself to get back to business. The Empire was firmly entrenched. Rooting it out would require many years, and the sacrifice of countless lives. She couldn't let herself think about what might happen in the dim, distant future. She had to concentrate on the here and now.

Resolutely, she activated her datapad again, and went back to work.

.   .   .

At the same moment as Bria Tharen was wondering about him, Han Solo was *not* thinking about her. He was, however, feeling more wounded by a woman than he had at any time since Bria Tharen had left him.

He sat on the edge of the bed in a hotel room on Velga, a luxury moon where the wealthy came to be entertained and play games of chance, scowling and reading Xaverri's message on his datapad. It said:

Dear Solo,
I can't stand good-byes, so I'm not going to put either of us through one. The tour is over, and I'm off for a short rest before taking to the road again. I thought about asking you to go with me, but I think it's better that I make a clean break now.

The last six months have been wonderful, among the best I can recall. During that time I've grown very fond of you, dear. Too fond. You know me by now . . . I can't afford to get too fond of anyone. That would be danger-ous for both of us. Caring too much about another per-son makes you soft, makes you vulnerable. In my line of business, I can't afford that.

I've paid the hotel bill through tomorrow for you and Chewbacca. You've been two of the best assistants and companions I've ever had. Tell him I'm sorry I couldn't say farewell. There is a bonus for you both in the local branch of the Imperial Bank, account code 651374, keyed to your retinal scan.

I'm going to miss you more than I can say. If you ever need to contact me, you can do so through the Galaxy of Stars booking agency. Maybe someday we can do it all again, when I've gotten my perspective back.

Take care of yourself, Han. And take care of your Wookiee friend. Devotion like that is rare.

> Love,
> Xaverri

Blast! Han thought, not sure whether what he was feeling was anger or profound regret—some mixture of both, he guessed. *Why does this always happen to me?*

For a moment he remembered the anguish that had engulfed him when Bria had left him with just a good-bye note, then he wrenched his mind away from that memory. *That was a long time ago. I'm not a kid anymore . . .*

He realized that he'd have to book commercial flights back to Nar Shaddaa for himself and Chewie. But that wouldn't eat into his savings too much, especially in light of Xaverri's bonus. She paid well, though she had high expectations.

During the past six months, they'd been more like business partners than employee and employer. Every time they'd pulled a successful scam on some puffed-up Imperial officer, or some smug, complacent Imperial bureaucrat, Xaverri had shared the proceeds equally with Han and Chewie.

Han's mouth curved into a reminiscent smile. They'd had some exciting times. With all the experience he'd had conning civilians while part of Garris Shrike's "family," Han had thought he had little to learn about the art of scamming people. But a month with Xaverri had convinced him that compared to her, Garris Shrike had been a clumsy, mendacious amateur.

Xaverri's schemes had ranged from elegantly simple to fiendishly complex. She seldom pulled exactly the same scam twice. Instead she tailored each caper to the mark, frequently using her skills as an illusionist to trick the pompous Imperials she preyed upon.

There had been that time they'd conned the Assistant Secretary to the D'Aelgoth Sector Moff out of most of his life savings—and put him under suspicion of committing treason to the Empire. Han's smile broadened into a grin. The guy was a venal jerk—sooner or later he would've betrayed the Empire anyhow.

Not that all their scams had been successful. Two had fizzled out, and one had blown up in their faces, forcing them to run from the planetary officials until Chewbacca had been able to locate them and pick them up.

Han would never forget that escape—running, dodging, pursued through the countryside by tracer droids and the local version of canoid-hounds. The only way they'd been able to hide their scent was to spend the night up to their necks in a swamp.

He'd also enjoyed his work as Xaverri's stage assistant. It had been fun, helping to create the illusions, finding out how it was really done, and taking a bow before cheering crowds, night after night. Even Chewbacca had gotten to enjoy the public attention, and Xaverri had worked up several tricks that gave Chewie a chance to show off his Wookiee strength.

The hardest thing for Han had been getting used to the skintight, spangled stage costume he'd had to wear. He'd felt horribly self-conscious the first few times he'd gone onstage wearing it. But eventually he'd gotten used to it, and even learned to enjoy the hoots and whistles from some of the female audience members when he'd make his entrance.

Xaverri had teased him about that, especially the time a girl had dashed up onstage and kissed him full on the mouth, making him blush. Han had teased her back about her costumes, which were often daring.

Han sighed. *If only I'd known she was planning this. I could have talked to her . . .* Already he missed her, missed her presence, her smile, her affection. Her warmth, her kisses . . .

She was a special woman, and Han knew now that he'd loved her. Would it have made any difference if he'd told her? He decided that it wouldn't. As her letter said, Xaverri was not someone who *wanted* love. She didn't want to love, or to be loved. Love, she'd discovered, made you too vulnerable.

"Love makes you love life," she'd told him once. "And once you love life, you're in real danger. You want to hold on to it, and that wanting clouds your thinking."

"You want to hold on to which?" Han had asked her. "Love, or life?"

"Both," she said. "Love is the riskiest thing in the universe."

Xaverri had risked herself more than anyone he'd ever known in everything *except* love. If she hadn't been so coolly deliberate, he'd have called her reckless. But she wasn't. Danger meant nothing to her, because she didn't worry about dying. Han had seen her stare death in the face without turning a hair.

One time he'd complimented her on her courage. She'd shaken her head. "No, Solo," she said. "I'm not brave. *You're* brave. You have courage. I just don't care. They aren't the same thing."

He sighed again, then rose from the bed. Xaverri was gone. By now her ship, *The Phantasm,* was long gone from Velga.

Okay, he thought, reaching for his clothes, *show's over. Time to go back to the real world . . .*

At least he and Chewie now had plenty of money to lease their own ship. For the first time in a long while, Han wondered how things were going back on Nar Shaddaa.

When they got back to the Smuggler's Moon, Han was surprised to realize that it felt like coming home. He and

Chewie went to see Mako first. They found him and Roa having a companionable drink together at one of the taverns. Han entered the place, grinned, and waved. "Mako! Roa!"

Both men turned at the hail and grinned broadly. "Han! Chewbacca!"

"Hey, Roa! Hey, Mako," Han said. "How's business?"

"Not bad," Mako said. "Jabba misses you, kid."

"Oh, yeah, I'm sure," Han said with a chuckle. "Did Jiliac have her baby Hutt?"

"Don't know," Roa said. "She ain't been around, though. So maybe not. How're you doin', kid? You've been gone so long, we thought Boba Fett had got you!"

Han grinned back. "Not yet," he said. "He been around much?"

Mako glanced around reflexively, "Well, they said he was here on Nar Shaddaa lookin' for you, several months ago. But nobody's seen him lately."

"Good. Keep me informed," Han said. "So . . . anyone seen Lando?" He tried to seem casual. "He still got that old clunker of his, the *Millennium Falcon*?"

"Oh, yeah, he's still got it," Roa said. "And, Han, you're not gonna believe this. Calrissian made a killing out there in the Oseon system. Picked up a load of life-crystals, and sold 'em for a bundle. Guess what he's into now?"

Han made a ribald guess. Both Roa and Mako cracked up.

Chewie roared an interrogatory.

"He's bought himself a used spaceship lot!" Mako said. "Got it lock, stock, and barrel from a Duros who'd decided to go back to Duro and tend the family farm."

"Well, I'm in the market for a ship to lease," Han said. "Guess I'll pay Lando a visit, see what he's got."

"Better see Jabba first," Mako advised. "He's put the word out that as soon as you came back to send you on."

Han nodded. "Okay. I'll do that. Where can I find Lando's place?"

They gave him the coordinates.

With a cheerful wave, Han headed out of the tavern. He found that it was good to be back. The interval with Xaverri had been pleasant, and profitable, but his real calling was smuggling, and he was eager to get back to it.

Jabba was so pleased to see Han that he actually wriggled down off his dais and undulated toward the Corellian. "Han, my boy! You've returned!"

Han nodded, and decided not to bow. Jabba had obviously missed him. "Hello, Jabba . . . Your Excellency. How's business?"

Jabba sighed theatrically. "Business would be much better if only Besadii would learn that they are not the only rightful destination for the credits in the galaxy. Han . . . I must admit that I have missed you. We lost a ship in the Maw, and it cost Desilijic dearly. We need you, Han."

"Well, this time you're going to have to pay me more, Jabba," Han said resolutely. "Chewie and me are about to lease our own ship. That'll be better for both of us—you won't risk your ships, and I won't have to take less 'cause I'm flyin' your ship."

"Fine, fine," Jabba said. "That is fine, Han."

"But, Jabba, I gotta tell you," Han said. "There's still a bounty on my head. Teroenza's got to have talked Besadii into a pretty big one. Most of these bounty hunters I can deal with, no problem. But if I get any hints that Boba Fett is back on my trail, I ain't hanging around here. I'm gone. I'll operate out of Smuggler's Run. Even Fett isn't dedicated enough to head into the Run."

"Han, lad!" Jabba looked pained. "We need you! Desilijic needs you! You're one of the best!"

Han grinned, liking the feeling of being on more equal

footing with the Hutt Lord. "Hey, Jabba, I'm *the* best," he said. "And I'm gonna be provin' it."

Chewie roared. Jabba waved at the Wookiee. "What did he say?"

"He said, '*We're* the best,'" Han replied. "He's right. Soon everyone is gonna know it."

Han's next stop, as promised, was Lando's used shipyard. He and Chewie went straight to the office, where they found a small, multi-armed droid with a single ruby-red eye in charge. "Where's Lando?" Han demanded.

"My master is not here at the moment, sir," the little droid replied. "May I be of service? I am Vuffi Raa, his assistant."

Han looked at Chewbacca, who rolled his blue eyes.

"I want to speak to Lando," Han said. "Where is he?"

"Out in the shipyard," Vuffi Raa replied. "But . . . sir! Wait! Admittance to the shipyard is not permitted unless Master Calrissian has authorized it! Sir! Come back! Sir!"

Han kept on walking. Chewbacca, however, did stop. As the little droid approached him, arms flailing, he let loose with a snarl that swiftly built to a full-throated roar. Vuffi Raa stopped in his tracks so fast that he nearly fell over backward, then went scuttling off, calling "Master! Master!" in a plaintive voice.

Han found Lando out back, with the *Falcon*. He didn't know which one of them he was gladder to see. The *Falcon* was all in one piece, he was pleased to note.

For once, the gambler wasn't his usual dapper self. Han was surprised to see that he was wearing greasy mechanic's coveralls, and his hands were filthy as he gripped a hydrospanner.

"Lando!" Han shouted.

His friend turned around, and his handsome features lit up. "Han, you old pirate! How long have you been back?"

"Just got home," Han said, shaking Lando's hand. They

grabbed each other, thumping each other on the back, then stood back, grinning. "Hey, Han, it's good to see you, man!"

"You, too!"

Before the end of the day, Han and Chewie had leased their new ship from Lando. It was a small SoroSuub freighter, *Starmite*-class, heavily modified. The ship was about two-thirds the size of the *Millennium Falcon*, and had a blunt, rounded bow, thick, stubby wings, and a rounded, thick body that narrowed back to a flattened tail section. The ship resembled a coarse, unstreamlined tear-drop and, as one of Han's Quarren acquaintances later told him, looked like "something we raise for snacks." Each of the wings ended in a gun turret that held two fixed laser cannons, and the pilot also controlled a set of laser cannons mounted on the bow.

Han christened her the *Bria*.

"Lord Aruk wishes to see you, Your Excellency," Ganar Tos, Teroenza's majordomo, said. "He is waiting in your office."

The High Priest tensed. *I don't think I can take any more of his criticism!* he thought, hoisting himself out of his resting sling resentfully.

Lord Aruk and his offspring Durga had come for a special inspection tour of the Ylesian operation two days ago. Teroenza had been proud to show them the progress they'd made, the new factories, the productive pilgrims, the steadily growing supply of valuable spice that they'd ship off-world. He'd even been able to show them the new cleared plot of land for the new colony—Colony Eight.

But the more Teroenza had shown the Hutt Lord, the more Aruk had nitpicked. The High Priest was beginning to feel a little desperate.

Now, as he lumbered down the hallway of the Administration Building in Colony One, Teroenza's mind was busy composing replies to any of the charges Aruk might fling at him. Production was up. The workers were efficient. They were exploring new exports . . . those nala-tree frogs, for example.

Aruk had developed quite a taste for them during his visit. Kibbick had introduced them to his uncle, insisting that Aruk had to try them. Durga had sampled them also, and had pronounced himself unimpressed, but Aruk had loved the ugly amphibians, and had commanded Teroenza to make sure he received a supply of live ones on every ship shuttling between Ylesia and Nal Hutta.

Teroenza entered his office, trying not to let his nervousness show. "I am here, Your Excellency," he said to Aruk.

The Hutt Lord was accompanied only by his offspring, Durga. He looked up at Teroenza. "We need to have a talk, High Priest," he said gruffly.

Oh, no. This is worse than I feared, Teroenza thought. "Yes, Your Excellency?"

"I am canceling your vacation, High Priest," Aruk said. "I want you to stay here and bring Kibbick up to speed on all Ylesian operations. His level of ignorance is shameful, and it is *your* fault! Teroenza, you have forgotten who are the true lords of Ylesia. You have grown arrogant, and think yourself in command. This is not permissible. You must learn your place, High Priest. When you have learned to serve, to take the subservient role in governing this world, you will be rewarded. Only then can you return to Nal Hutta."

Teroenza remained silent during Aruk's tirade. When the Hutt Lord finally ran down, he found himself wanting to quit, to just walk away from the entire ridiculous operation. Kibbick was an idiot, and no amount of coaching from his overseer was going to make the young Hutt into anything but an idiot!

And he hadn't seen his mate, Tilenna, in a year. What if she decided to mate with someone else because he had been gone so long? How could he expect her to remain faithful under these circumstances?

Resentment boiled up inside the t'landa Til, but with a great effort of will, he managed to conceal his reaction.

"It shall be as you say, Your Excellency," he murmured. "I shall do my best."

"See that you do," Aruk rumbled, in his deepest, most threatening tone. "You are dismissed, High Priest."

Teroenza's hot rage boiled and bubbled as he walked back to his quarters, but by the time he reached them, he was calm again. Strangely, coldly calm. He lowered himself into his resting sling and dismissed his majordomo.

If his thoughts could have been expressed in one word, it would have been: *Enough.*

After a few more minutes of consideration, the High Priest reached for his comlink. The code he'd memorized all those months ago came readily to his fingers as he tapped it out. And then, he keyed in the following message: "I am willing to talk. What do you have to offer?"

With a triumphant, savage stab of his dainty finger, he keyed the message to SEND.

Teroenza leaned back in his resting sling and, for the first time in six months, felt at peace with the universe.

Chapter Eight:
The Shadow of the Empire

The man in the Mandalorian armor walked steadily down the dark, cavernous entrance hall of Jabba the Hutt's palace on Tatooine. Once, years ago, the man had been a Journeyman Protector named "Jaster Mereel." That had been before he killed a man, and paid the price for his crime.

Now he had no name save the one he had adopted for himself—Boba Fett. Over the past ten years, he'd become the best-known and most feared bounty hunter in the Empire. He was not an Imperial bounty hunter, though at times he worked for the Empire. He was not a Guild bounty hunter, though he regularly took Guild commissions and paid dues. No, Boba Fett was an independent bounty hunter. He set his own hours, selected his own commissions, and lived by his own rules.

He paused midway down the stairs leading to Jabba's throne room to survey what lay before him. The huge chamber was dark, cavernous, filled with booming music. Everywhere bodies milled and swayed. Fett's gaze followed the movements of several of Jabba's humanoid dancing girls, admiring their lithe suppleness. The bounty hunter was not one to indulge in sybaritic pleasures of the flesh, however. Boba Fett was far too self-disciplined to seek carnal gratification. The joy of the hunt was his sole pleasure, what he lived for. The credits were an extra, a necessary bonus, a means to accomplish his ends, but it was the hunt that nurtured him, kept him strong and self-reliant and focused.

As Fett descended the steps that led into Jabba's audience chamber, the Hutt Lord's Twi'lek majordomo, Lobb Gerido, bustled toward the bounty hunter, bowing unctuously and babbling greetings in his fractured Basic. Fett ignored him.

Realizing that he would never be allowed to approach Jabba carrying his BlasTech EE-3 rifle, Fett carefully laid it down on the bottom step. He was still armed dangerously enough to have killed Jabba and completely destroyed the audience chamber, and Jabba probably knew that, but the Hutt Lord also knew Boba Fett's reputation for honesty. Jabba had paid him to come here and speak with him, and it would have been a breach of bounty hunter protocol for Fett to accept such a meeting if he'd had an outstanding bounty on Jabba's grotesque head.

Leaving his blast rifle on the stairs, Fett strode straight up to Jabba's dais. The Hutt Lord was reclining above the crowd, so he'd be high enough up to have the best view of all the degenerate festivities. Even from inside the Mandalorian face mask, Boba Fett could whiff the pungent odor of the Hutt. Something between ancient mold and garbage . . .

At a gesture from the Hutt Lord, the band quieted down. Fett stood before Jabba, and inclined his head slightly. He spoke Basic. "You sent for me?"

"I did," boomed Jabba in Huttese. "Do you understand me, bounty hunter?"

Fett inclined his helmeted head in a "yes."

"Very well. Lobb Gerido, clear the room, and then make yourself scarce."

"Yes, Master," the Twi'lek babbled, and then he scuttled about, head-tails flying, shooing all the sycophants and hangers-on out of the audience chamber. Finally, with a last bow, Gerido himself vanished.

Jabba glanced around, took a puff off his hookah pipe, then, when he was sure they were alone, he leaned forward confidingly. "Bounty hunter, I thank you for coming to see me. Your five thousand credits will be deposited before you leave this throne room."

Fett nodded silently.

"I have already spoken to the Guild representative in this sector, and arranged a generous endowment of the Guildhouse," Jabba said. "However, he told me that you are not governed by the Guild, though you sometimes take on Guild commissions."

"That's correct," Fett confirmed. He was becoming intrigued. If Jabba just wanted someone dead, why this elaborate buildup? What was the Bloated One getting at?

Jabba puffed thoughtfully on his water pipe for nearly a minute, cogitating, his bulbous eyes with their slitted pupils blinking. "Do you know why I have summoned you here, bounty hunter?"

"I'm assuming it's because you want to post a bounty, so I'll hunt down and kill someone," Fett said. "That's why people contact me."

"No," Jabba said. He put the hookah aside and stared levelly at Fett, obviously getting to the point. "I want to pay you to *not* kill someone."

The macrobinocular viewplate that was built into Fett's Mandalorian helmet included infrared vision, plus motion and sound sensors. The bounty hunter could literally *see* Jabba tense, and change color. *This is important to him,* Fett realized, surprised. Most Hutts were such phenomenally selfish beings that he'd never heard of one willing to stick his neck out for anyone.

"State your offer," Fett said.

"There is an outstanding bounty of twenty thousand credits on a human who has proven very useful to me. I wish to pay you twenty-five thousand to ignore that bounty until further notice."

Fett had one word for Jabba. "Who?"

"Han Solo. He's a good pilot, the best. He runs our spice on schedule, and the Imperials can never catch him. He's proven extremely valuable to Desilijic. I'll pay you to stop hunting him."

Boba Fett stood there in silence, thinking hard.

For the first time in years, the bounty hunter was in a quandary, torn between his duty, his need for extra credits, and his own personal desires. Jabba's offer was tempting in many ways. Boba Fett's ship, *Slave I,* had recently been damaged in an asteroid field, and Fett needed some rather expensive repairs to get the weapons systems back up to full capability.

On the other hand, he'd been looking forward to bringing Solo in for a long time, ever since he and that gambler friend of his, Calrissian, had captured, drugged, and robbed the bounty hunter. Boba Fett couldn't allow two space bums to get the best of him and live . . .

On the *other* hand, just last week, Lord Aruk of Besadii had contacted Boba Fett in an interstellar holo-communication, and told him that he was no longer willing to pay top credits for Solo. Instead, he wanted a priority live delivery bounty on a Corellian woman, Bria Tharen. He'd raised the amount, too. The bounty on her was fifty thousand credits. And the Hutt Lord had reduced the bounty on Solo to ten thousand credits, disintegration now permitted. Teroenza, Fett gathered, was unaware of this change.

Fifty thousand credits was the biggest bounty currently on Boba Fett's list. He'd immediately begun searching for this woman named Tharen, whom Aruk had described as being a leader in the Corellian rebel movement. The Besadii Lord said she had led a raid to Ylesia to rescue slaves, and she was also suspected of leading several space raids to free slaves bound from Ylesia to the mines of Kessel.

Fett had checked his sources, and traced the woman to Corellia, then to one of the Outer Rim sectors, but then she'd dropped out of sight completely. There was one possible lead linking her to a private yacht bound for Coruscant, but that was an unconfirmed rumor at this point.

But . . . Fett hated the thought of not bringing in Solo to face a humiliating, painful end at the hands of the High Priest, Teroenza. Fett had tortured captives, when necessary, to obtain information. He didn't take pleasure in it—or in their deaths, when that was what the bounty required.

But for Han Solo, he was willing to make an exception . . .

"Well?" Jabba's deep voice boomed, startling Fett out of his reflections. "What do you say, bounty hunter?"

Boba Fett thought fast, and finally arrived at a solution that was, he felt, the best under the circumstances. It allowed him to maintain his integrity as a bounty hunter, while also allowing him to do the practical thing.

"Very well," he said. "I'll take the twenty-five thousand."

Aruk wants me to pursue Tharen as a priority anyway,

he told himself, *so I'll be fulfilling the client's wish. And the bounty on the Tharen woman is fifty thousand, so when I've brought her in, I'll send Jabba back his twenty-five, then hunt and kill Solo. Honor is satisfied, I'll have fulfilled my commissions, and gotten the chance to see Solo die.*

It was a good compromise, Fett decided. Everyone except Teroenza would be pleased—and, officially, Boba Fett wasn't working for the High Priest, he was working for Lord Aruk. It was Aruk's bounty, and the Besadii Lord had made it clear that all he wanted was Solo dead.

Simple and profitable. Fett was satisfied.

"Very well," Jabba boomed, obviously pleased. He made a note on a palm-sized datapad. "A total of thirty thousand credits has just been added to your account."

Fett inclined his head in that not-quite bow. "I'll show myself out," he said.

"No, no," Jabba said hastily. "Lobb will have to open the blast door for you." He pressed a button on his datapad, and the Twi'lek appeared seconds later, head-tails flying. Lobb bowed repeatedly.

"Farewell, Fett," Jabba said. "I shall keep you in mind for any further commissions Desilijic has."

Boba Fett did not reply, only turned and followed the majordomo out, stopping on the way to pick up his blast rifle.

The blazing sands of Tatooine seemed doubly bright after the darkness of Jabba's throne room, but Boba Fett's Mandalorian helmet automatically filtered out the harmful rays, allowing him to see clearly.

Boarding *Slave I*, he took off, checking his departure vector, swooping low over the scorching desert. Fett glanced down at those featureless expanses, those dunes that rippled, almost like the waves of an ocean. He'd rarely been to Tatooine, and he couldn't imagine ever returning. What a desolate place. He knew that there was supposed to be life in the deserts, but here, there was nothing. Just unmarked sand.

But wait . . . what was that?

Fett leaned closer to his viewscreen as *Slave I* swooped over a huge pit that yawned open at the bottom of a depression in the sand. Fett thought he saw something moving within the pit . . . spiky fronds or perhaps tentacles.

Wonder what that thing is? he thought, sending *Slave I* soaring up into the atmosphere. *Guess there is something living in that desert, after all.*

Moments later the stark brownish world was far behind the bounty hunter, so distant it was not even a memory . . .

One week after leasing the *Bria* from Lando, Han Solo was cursing the little freighter, himself, Lando, and the universe in general.

"Chewie, old pal," Han said, during a moment of uncompromising honesty, "I am an idiot for picking this ship. She's nothing but a pain in the ass."

"Hrrrrrrrnnnnnn," rumbled Chewie, in complete agreement.

The *Bria* needed considerable work, they discovered from almost the very beginning. She'd flown fine during their "test spin," but as soon as the lease was finalized, the problems erupted like geysers on the methane moons of Thermon. The first time they took their new acquisition out on a smuggling run, for the first ten minutes the ship worked fine . . . then the aft stabilizer shorted out, and they had to have her towed back to Nar Shaddaa via tractor beam. They fixed the stabilizer, aided by Lando's little tentacled droid, Vuffi Raa (whom, it seemed, was the *Millennium Falcon*'s main pilot these days), and then tried again.

This time the bow stabilizer blew.

Han and Chewie fixed the *Bria* again, cursing and sweating through the repairs, then tried again. And again. Sometimes their little SoroSuub Starmite worked fine; other times they were lucky if they could limp back to Lando's shipyard for repairs.

The *Bria*'s navicomputer developed amnesia and her hyperdrive went on vacation. On her good days, Han was such an expert pilot that he could coax a fair turn of speed out of her, but nearly every time they took her out on a test run, some new problem surfaced in the ship.

Han complained to Lando, who only pointed out that the lease Han had signed said "as is," and that he'd made no guarantees about the ship's spaceworthiness. Also, Lando pointed out—correctly—he was leasing the little Starmite to Han at a very reasonable price.

Han couldn't argue with that, but it didn't help when the *Bria* just quit cold, as she did at least half the time.

Han mentioned his ship woes to Mako, who introduced his friend to yet another of his acquaintants.

"Master starship mechanic, pilot, and repair tech Shug Ninx, meet Han Solo and his partner Chewbacca. They got a ship needs some work."

Shug Ninx was humanoid, but though he looked mostly human, Han could tell immediately that he had some alien blood. He was tall, with spiky brownish-blond hair and pale blue eyes. The skin on the lower half of his face was mottled with pale spots, and his hands only had two fingers plus an extra joint in his opposable thumb. It gave him great dexterity when fiddling with machinery.

Han could tell from the man's wary expression that Shug Ninx had frequently met with suspicion because of his mixed blood. Most of that distaste had probably come from Imperial officials. They regarded anyone who was a "half-breed" as a lower-class citizen.

Han held out his hand, smiling. "Pleased to meet you,

Shug," he said. "Think you can help me get this bucket of bolts up and running?"

"We can sure give it a try," Shug said, visibly relaxing. "Bring her over to my spacebarn today, and we'll check her out."

To reach Shug's facility, Han had to fly the *Bria* down a narrow abyss between the tall, vertical towers of two huge, jumbled building complexes. When Han and Chewie reached the "spacebarn," Shug's huge spacedock and garage, located deep down in the warren that was Nar Shaddaa, he was impressed with the facility. "Wow," he said, looking around at all the ships in various states of assembly, "this place beats any Imp spacedock I ever saw. You've got just about anything you could want here."

Equipment lined the walls, and was kicked into corners. At first glance the place seemed chaotic and cluttered, but as Han was soon to discover, Shug Ninx could immediately locate any piece of equipment in the place.

"Yeah," Shug said proudly, obviously pleased by Han's frank admiration. "I saved for a long time to buy this place."

After Shug had a chance to check out the *Bria,* the half-breed shook his head mournfully. "Han, half your problem with this ship is that she's been modified using non-SoroSuub parts and components! Everyone knows that SoroSuubs don't take kindly to that!"

"Can you help us get her running?" Han asked.

Shug nodded. "Won't be easy, but we'll try."

Over the next few weeks, Han and Chewie helped Shug Ninx fix up their new ship. The two smugglers worked each day until they were exhausted, tinkering and learning the intricacies of starship repair from the master mechanic.

Han was so tired by all of the work, he almost quit going out, but one evening, on impulse, he stopped off for a drink in a local tavern he frequented in the Corellian sector. The

Blue Light served only liquor, and was mostly a dive, but Han kind of liked the dark little place with its holo-posters of Corellian cities and natural wonders on the wall. It was too dark to see them well, of course—especially after a drink or two. But it suited him better than the glitzier joints.

While he was sitting at the bar, sipping an Alderaanian ale, a fracas erupted in the back of the place. Han jumped to his feet at the sound of a woman's curse, then a man's drunken growl. "Hey, baby, that's no way for a lady to talk!"

"I'm no lady," a woman said in a deep, angry voice. Peering into the dimness, Han could make out two struggling figures, hear the sounds of a scuffle, then a slap.

"C'mere, you tramp!" the man said.

The woman swore, then Han heard the meaty sound of a punch. The man yowled, then lunged at her. As he raced toward the back, Han saw the man's feet leave the floor. The woman tossed him, using a single-shoulder throw that was accompanied by a popping sound. The man shrieked, a short, bitten-off scream, then thumped to the floor and lay there, sniveling and whimpering.

When he reached the back of the dimly lit bar, Han found a short, spindly smuggler and thug-for-hire he knew only as "Jump" moaning and writhing at the feet of a tall woman. As Jump's buddy (who had wisely not joined the fracas) helped the thug sit up, Han could see that his arm hung at an odd angle, plainly dislocated. The woman stood over them, hand on the grip of her undrawn blaster, eyes narrowed, not even breathing hard.

As Han approached, she turned on him. "Mind your own business, man!"

Han took a step back before her flashing amber eyes. She was as tall as he was, with skin the color of Lando's, and a wild frizz of black curls standing out from her head like a brelet's mane. She looked tougher than neutronium, and mad clear through.

The Corellian hastily put up both hands in a gesture of peace. "Hey, I'm not one to interfere. Looks to me like the situation's been handled."

"I can take care of myself," she snapped, striding past him on her way toward the front entrance. Her boot heels clicked on the scarred floor. She wore a long, tan-colored skirt, a brown silk blouse, and a half carapace of black armor, festooned with metallic studs. Her blaster rode her hip, and Han could tell by its worn grip that she knew exactly what to do with it.

Intrigued, he jogged up to the front of the Blue Light, then, careful not to stand between her and the front door, Han gestured to a couple of empty bar stools. "So . . . do you have to rush off? Can't I buy you a drink?" he asked.

She studied him for a long moment, her anger fading. In the back, Jump's whimpers faded as the thug was led out the back way by his friends. "Maybe," she said. Sticking out a gauntleted hand, she said, "Salla Zend."

"Han Solo." They shook, then Han threw a leg over the nearest bar stool. "What are you drinking?"

Salla sat down, too. "Mad Mrelf, straight up."

"Right," said Han, carefully not showing any reaction to the strong liquor. He wouldn't have drunk Mad Mrelf on a bet—tales abounded of spacers who had gone on a Mad Mrelf spree, and wound up in Imp labor camps—or worse.

They talked, and Han discovered that Salla was also a smuggler, newly come to Nar Shaddaa. "I've got a ship," she said. "The *Rimrunner*. But it needs some work. I've got some modifications I'd like to make."

"Hey," Han said, "do I know a place for you. My ship's getting some work done, too. The guy's a real wizard. Name of Shug Ninx."

"I'm a pretty good mechanic myself," Salla said. "I'd like to meet your friend."

"I'm going back to work on the *Bria* tomorrow morning," Han said. "If you like, why not meet me tomorrow, and we can go over to Shug's spacebarn together?"

She gave him a measuring glance, then smiled, a slow, amused smile. "I've got a better idea," she said. "You come home with me tonight. Can you cook?"

Han's eyes widened. *Well! Talk about being direct!*

He smiled back at her, his slow, lopsided grin. He could tell that even Salla wasn't immune to its effects—or maybe it was the drink. "Sure," he said. "One of my best friends was a cook."

Salla laughed. "Hey, Solo, give a girl a break and turn off the charm. Want to break my heart?"

"No," Han said, reaching out to touch the back of her hand with one finger, "I want to fix you dinner. Sounds like a great plan to me. You like traladon steaks?"

"Sure," she said lightly. "Rare."

"I'll keep that in mind," Han promised.

When they finished their drinks, they went out into the squalid Nar Shaddaa street. Salla hooked her arm through Han's. "I'm glad I found you. I burn water, so I don't even try cooking anymore. I love the prospect of a home-cooked dinner."

Han smiled at her again, putting every bit of charm he possessed into it. "Dinner it is. Then maybe . . . breakfast?"

She laughed and shook her head. "You are a rogue, aren't you!"

"I try," Han said modestly.

"Well, don't push your luck, honey," she warned, smiling to let him know she wasn't offended. "I can take care of myself."

Remembering how Salla had handled Jump, Han had to

agree. He nodded, and resolved to back off . . . for the moment.

Over the next few weeks, Han and Salla continued to see each other, and their relationship developed and grew closer. By the time they'd been dating for a month, Han *was* fixing her breakfast, and everyone recognized them as a couple.

They had a lot in common, and Han enjoyed the time they spent together. She was an exciting, vibrant woman, smart, sensual, and direct. As Han got to know her better, he discovered she did have a tender side, though it didn't surface often.

Han introduced Salla to Shug, and the two of them hit it off immediately, too, though not romantically. It turned out that Salla was an expert technician, more at home with a lasertorch than most smugglers. She told them she'd been a tech on a corporate transport before she'd managed to acquire *Rimrunner*. Salla occasionally ran spice, but her cargo of choice was weapons. She was an expert gunrunner, fearless and efficient.

Soon Salla was a regular at Shug's spacebarn, where all the smugglers hung out, fixing their ships, swapping stories, and vying with each other to set new performance records. Han found that, sooner or later, most of the human smugglers, and many of the non-humans, wound up at Shug's spacebarn. Many of his pals from Smuggler's Run appeared, even, on one notable occasion, Wynni.

Zeen and Kid, a smuggler and thief named Rik Duel, Sinewy Ana Blue, Roa and Mako . . . all of them had good times at Shug's spacebarn. Shug had only three rules: no intoxicants of any kind, pay promptly for use of tools or his or his techs' services, and clean up after yourself.

Han eventually wound up introducing Salla to Lando, and the two of them hit it off, also. Han could tell they were attracted to each other, but Salla made it clear that Han was her choice . . . for the moment.

One day, when Han was up on the top hull of the *Bria*, working on the main deflector, Chewbacca roared at him, telling him to climb down, someone wanted to see him. Han scuttled down the ladder, to find a youth standing there, a handsome kid with brown hair and brown eyes. He reminded Han a little of himself, when he'd been in his late teens.

The young man held out a hand. "Han Solo? It's an honor to meet you. I'm Jarik. Jarik Solo."

Han's eyes widened as he shook hands. "Solo?" he asked blankly.

"Yeah," the kid answered. "Solo. I think we must be related. I'm Corellian, too."

Since Han knew of only two relatives he could claim (and he didn't choose to claim them—his aunt Tiion was a reclusive paranoid and her son, Han's cousin Thrackan Sal-Solo, was a sadistic creep . . . assuming either of them was still alive), he wasn't sure how to reply to this. "Really?" he said finally. "That's interesting. What branch are you from?"

"Uh, well, I think that my uncle Renn was your father's second cousin," the youth said glibly.

Renn was a common name on Corellia. Han smiled. "Could be," he said. "C'mon over here and let's talk."

He led the youth into Shug's cluttered office and poured them both a cup of stim-tea. Chewie followed them in, and Han introduced the Wookiee properly. Chewie hrrrrrrnn-ned at Jarik, and Han could tell he liked the young man.

"So, why'd you look me up?" Han asked.

"Well, I'd like to learn piloting," the boy replied. "And I hear you're the best. I'll work, if you'll teach me, sir. I promise I'll work hard."

"Well"—Han glanced over at the Wookiee—"we could

use a hand with getting the *Bria* fixed up, I guess. You any good with a hydrospanner?"

"Yessir!" Jarik said. "I sure am."

"We'll see," Han said.

At first he invited the youngster to hang around because he wanted to keep an eye on him. Han didn't believe that the boy was from Corellia. He just didn't *look* right, somehow. He asked Roa, as the senior smuggler, whether he knew anything about a young man named Jarik.

It took a month, but Roa was able to discover that young Jarik was a street kid, born and raised in the depths of Nar Shaddaa. He'd grubbed for every mouthful, every credit, turning his hand to whatever work he could find. His parentage was unknown, probably even to him. He'd always been a denizen of Nar Shaddaa, hanging out in the Corellian sector. It was possible that at least one of his parents was Corellian.

When Han knew for sure that the youth had lied to him, he considered sending the kid packing, but by that time, he'd gotten used to having him around. The youth hung on his every word, tagging along whenever Han would let him. The worshipful attention was flattering. And, after all, Han rationalized, it wasn't as though he himself had never told a lie to get his foot in the door . . .

Jarik proved to be a fast learner. Han taught him to man the *Bria*'s portside gun turret, and he proved to have excellent reflexes and aim. Since pirate activity in Hutt space had been up lately, Han wound up taking the kid on most of their runs. After discussing the matter with Chewbacca, Han decided not to tell the youngster that they knew his name wasn't "Solo." It was Chewie who pointed out that it obviously meant a lot to Jarik to finally have a surname. Wookiees were very family-oriented, and Chewie felt sorry for the boy.

Soon after Han and Salla started their relationship, the

Bria was spaceworthy. Shug's modifications had increased her speed until she was a very respectable little vessel. But she was still, as Jarik put it, "one unpredictable lady."

One run the *Bria* would perform perfectly, but the next . . . there seemed no end to the grief she gave Han, Chewie, and Jarik out in the spacelanes. Han learned a whole new vocabulary of Wookiee swear words while he and Chewie sweated to fix their recalcitrant craft.

Once the sublight motivator burned out as they were skimming past the black-hole clusters of the Maw. *That* was interesting. For a while, Han didn't believe they were ever going to make it back to Nar Shaddaa. If it hadn't been for Chewie's quick repair work and Han's piloting expertise, the freighter would have been sucked into a black hole.

Han found them a new apartment, a bigger one, in a better part of the Corellian section. He was frequently not at home, staying over at Salla's place, so he allowed Jarik to spend the night so Chewbacca would have company.

Life, Han reflected (when he had time to reflect, which wasn't often), was good. It had been at least two months since any bounty hunters had surfaced, and there hadn't been any sightings of Boba Fett. He and Chewie were earning a decent living, and they had a ship of their own. He had friends, and somebody special in his life, somebody who could talk the language of smugglers. Han was as content as he'd ever been . . .

Deep in a remote area of space, between systems, two Hutt ships rendezvoused at a set of highly secret coordinates. Both ships belonged to members of the Desilijic kajidic, though neither ship was piloted by Han Solo. One ship was Jabba's yacht, *Star Jewel*, and the other was Jiliac's yacht, *Dragon Pearl*.

Under the urging of their pilots, who goosed the ships

toward each other with little taps on their maneuvering thrusters, the two ships edged closer and closer, until they were in docking range. An umbilical tube extended from the airlock of *Star Jewel*, until it touched and anchored itself against the airlock of *Dragon Pearl*. The Hutt yachts hung in space, attached to each other by the tube.

Jabba and Jiliac were aboard *Star Jewel*. Comfortably ensconced in the yacht's luxurious salon, Jiliac cradled her young offspring in her arms. As the ship's instruments indicated that the two ships were successfully connected, Jiliac put her tiny, unformed grub of a baby Huttlet down near her pouch-slit, and allowed the little creature to crawl inside. Infant Hutts survived mostly inside their mother's pouch for the first year or so of their young lives.

As the two Hutts waited expectantly, they heard several sets of footsteps coming down the corridor. The door opened, and Teroenza, High Priest of Ylesia, entered.

The huge horned being was almost dwarfed by the enormous sluglike Hutts, but Teroenza didn't seem particularly overawed, Jiliac noted. She gestured graciously to a t'landa Til resting sling she'd had specially installed. "Welcome, Teroenza. Please make yourself at home. I trust you were able to camouflage your absence from your world?"

"My time is limited," Teroenza said. "I set off in a landskimmer this morning, with a Gamorrean pilot, ostensibly to make a personal inspection of the Colony Eight construction. Halfway there, in the deepest jungle, I knocked the guard out, then set the skimmer to crash into a jungle giant. Then I tossed a thermal detonator into the wreckage, and when it was burning well, I tossed the guard in. Your ship was waiting precisely where you guaranteed it would be. Tomorrow it can set me back in that area, and I shall suitably batter and dirty myself, then come staggering out of the jungle in time to meet one of the search parties. Aruk will suspect nothing."

"Well done," Jiliac said. "But, as you note, our time is limited. Let us get right down to business. Aruk has become a . . . nuisance. A nuisance we would like to dispense with."

Teroenza snorted. "No matter how high production is, he is dissatisfied. I have not seen my mate in over a year. He forbids me to take even a short visit home. And he has reduced the bounty on Han Solo, and altered it to a 'kill on sight, disintegrations okay' bounty! He forbade me to raise it, even if I paid with my own credits. Said I was obsessed with Solo! When he did that, I could no longer support him. Contemplating the slow death of that Corellian space tramp has been my only pleasure for months. When I remember how he . . ." the High Priest went on with his litany of grievances against Han Solo.

Jabba and Jiliac looked at each other during Teroenza's tirade. Jiliac knew that Jabba had made some arrangement with Boba Fett so Solo could continue to work for them without fear of bounty hunters. However, that was not information Teroenza ever needed to know.

Seconds later Teroenza ran down. He bowed. "My apologies, Excellencies. As you said . . . to business."

"First, we need to determine a price for your . . . assistance, Teroenza," Jabba pointed out.

The t'landa Til named a sum.

Jabba and Jiliac glanced at each other. Neither spoke.

After a couple of minutes, Teroenza named a second, significantly lower sum. This one, while high, was not unreasonable. Jiliac took a small crustacean from a tray near her resting dais, and contemplated it for several seconds. "Done," she said, then popped the treat into her mouth. "I want no one to suspect murder," she said matter-of-factly. "It must be subtle . . ."

"Subtle . . ." Teroenza murmured, absently stroking

his horn, which already looked as though it had been freshly oiled. "Not an armed attack, then."

"Far from it," Jiliac said. "Besadii security is second only to our own. Our troops would have to blast their way in, and the whole of Nal Hutta would know who started it. No armed attacks."

"An accident?" Jabba wondered aloud. "Perhaps with his river barge? I understand Aruk enjoys his afternoon excursions. He often entertains on the river."

"Possible," Jiliac said. "But such an accident is difficult to control. It might destroy Durga, too, and I do not want Durga killed."

"Why, Aunt? Durga is clever. He could be a possible threat to us," Jabba pointed out.

Before Jiliac could respond, Teroenza did. Settling deeper into his resting sling, the High Priest picked a pickled ruff-roach off a plate and sampled it. "Because," the t'landa Til said thoughtfully, "Durga will have trouble controlling Besadii. There are many in the kajidic who feel he is not fit to rule because of his birthmark. They say he is ill-marked, and thus ill-fated. Do away with Durga, and the kajidic may well unite much more strongly behind the new leader."

Jiliac inclined her head to Teroenza. "You reason like a Hutt, Priest," she said.

Teroenza was gratified. "Thank you, Your Excellency."

"No assault, no accident," Jabba muttered. "What, then?"

"I have a possible plan," Jiliac said. "A substance that Aruk can ingest. It has the advantage of being almost undetectable in the tissues. And while it is working, it slows and dulls the thinking processes, so that the victim makes poor decisions. For Aruk to make poor decisions is to our benefit."

"Agreed, Aunt," Jabba said. "But . . . poison? We

Hutts are extremely resistant to poisons. For one of us, even an old one like Aruk, to ingest enough poison to kill us would surely be noticed and remarked upon."

Jiliac shook her massive head, a mannerism she'd picked up from humans. "Not the way I am thinking of it, Nephew. This substance, when introduced into the body, gradually poisons the victim. It concentrates in the brain tissues of higher life-forms. Over a long period of ingestion, the victim becomes actually *addicted* to the poison, to the point where sudden cessation of the substance will cause withdrawal symptoms so severe, they will result in either death or such massive brain damage that Aruk will be of no further harm to any of us."

"And you can get supplies of this substance?" Teroenza asked excitedly.

"It is extremely expensive and rare," Jiliac said. "But . . . yes. I can procure sufficient quantities."

"But how do we get him to take it?" Jabba asked.

"Your Excellencies, I can manage that!" Teroenza was bouncing up and down in his sling, like a youngster in a game. "The nala-tree frogs! Surely they would work!"

"Explain, Priest," Jiliac commanded.

Teroenza went on to explain about the Besadii Lord's predilection for the nala-tree frogs. "Ever since he went home, two weeks ago, he has demanded an aquarium of live nala-tree frogs with every shipment of processed spice we send home to Nal Hutta!" The t'landa Til rubbed his tiny, almost delicate hands together excitedly.

"And how would we use them?"

"The nala-tree frogs are far from being higher life-forms. They have almost no brain to speak of. I doubt exposure to your poison would kill them."

"From what I know of this substance, that would be so," Jiliac said. "Continue, please."

"I could raise the nala-tree frogs in water to which I

have added your poison," Teroenza said. "From the time they are small wigglers, they would be swimming through water containing concentrations of your substance. The nala-tree frogs' tissues would be riddled with the poison— and Aruk will consume them greedily! As the months go by, I increase the concentration of the poison in the water, and Aruk gradually consumes more and more of the poison. Over time, he becomes addicted to it. Then, when he's thoroughly dependent on the substance—" He made a quick yanking-away gesture. "No more poison! Clean frogs!"

"And he will die in agony," Jiliac said. "Or suffer permanent brain damage. Either of which will serve our needs."

Jabba leaned forward. "I say we do it. Jiliac's scheme fits all our requirements."

"I will transmit the first of your payments," Jiliac said. "You must tell me where you want the credits sent."

Teroenza's bulging eyes took on a crafty gleam. "Rather than credits, I would mostly like items for my collection. That way I can hide the payments. When I need credits, I can sell off a piece, and no one will be the wiser."

"Very well," Jiliac said. "You must provide us a list of acceptable items. If we cannot find them, we shall deposit credits instead. But we will try for the pieces for the collection."

"Excellent," said Teroenza. "We have a deal."

"A toast," cried Jabba. "To our alliance, and to Aruk's end."

"A toast!" echoed Teroenza, raising an ornate cup. "My first use of my new wealth will be to place such a high bounty on Han Solo's head that every bounty hunter in the galaxy will be looking for him!"

"To the death of Aruk!" Jiliac said, raising her cup.

"The death of Aruk!" Jabba exclaimed.

Teroenza hesitated for barely an instant, then said, with great resolution, "The death of Aruk . . . and of Solo."

Together, they drank.

After Teroenza had left, to be spirited back to Ylesia aboard the *Dragon Pearl,* Jabba and Jiliac began planning their strategy. When Aruk was gone, they would gradually take over the Ylesian operation. One by one, they would eliminate key Besadii, until the decimated clan would fall into penury and obscurity.

The thought made them extremely cheerful.

Their good mood was broken, however, by Lobb Gerido, who appeared, wringing his hands. "Your Excellencies . . . one of your operatives on Regolith Prime has just forwarded a vid-cast to us. Most disturbing news from Imperial Center! The pilot has recorded it. If Your Excellencies will turn on your holo-projector . . ."

Concerned, Jiliac did so. The three-dimensional scene built before them, and the Hutts recognized their local Moff, Sarn Shild. This was obviously a formal press conference setting. Behind Shild, they could see the familiar skyline of Imperial Center, the planet that used to be called Coruscant.

"Citizens of the Inner and Outer Rim Territories," he said, his pale features beneath waxy dark hair set in grim lines, "our exalted and wise Emperor has been forced to put down yet another insurrection in Imperial space. Vicious rebels, using weapons that have been traced to our sector, attacked an Imperial emplacement on Rampa II, wounding and slaying a number of Imperial troops.

"The Emperor's reprisal has been immediate, and the rebels have been routed and captured. Many civilian lives were lost when the rebel butchers turned their weapons on innocent citizens. This outrage cannot be allowed to continue!

"Our Emperor has called upon all of his loyal sectors to

aid him in cutting off the trafficking in illegal weaponry. I am proud to say that I am responding to the Emperor's call in the most immediate and visceral terms. We all know that the source of much of the illegal gunrunning and drug trafficking emanates from Hutt space. To this end, I am calling on all citizens of our sector to support me as I shut down the Hutt scourge! It is my intention to wipe out the smuggling trade, and bring the Hutt crime lords to their knees!" Shild paused, as if suddenly recalling that Hutts did not *have* knees. "Um . . . figuratively speaking, of course."

He cleared his throat. "To reach this goal, I am authorized to utilize deadly force. The Hutts will learn that they cannot flout Imperial law with impunity." He raised a fist in a sweeping military gesture. "Law and order will prevail once more in our Territories!"

The holo faded out on Shild's ringing last words. Both Hutts looked at each other for a long moment.

"This is not good, Aunt," Jabba said, finally.

"Not good at all, Nephew," Jiliac agreed. She cursed softly. "How can Shild have found the courage to go against us?"

"Obviously, he is now more afraid of Palpatine than he is of us," Jabba said.

"We shall have to teach him his error," Jiliac said slowly. "We cannot allow Nal Hutta to be governed by the Emperor and his wretched minions."

"Indeed not," Jabba agreed.

Jiliac considered for a moment. "However, as a compromise . . ."

"Yes, Aunt?"

"Perhaps we can reason with Shild. Buy him off. Let him have Nar Shaddaa and the smugglers. We can always find more smugglers . . ."

Jabba licked his tongue over the edges of his lipless

mouth, as though he'd tasted something particularly sweet. "Aunt, I like the way you think."

"We must send Shild a message," Jiliac decided. "And gifts . . . expensive ones, so he will pay attention. You know how greedy he is. Surely he will . . . see reason."

"Surely," Jabba agreed. "But who will carry the message?"

Jiliac thought for a moment, then the corners of her huge, wide mouth turned up. "I know just the sentient . . ."

Chapter Nine:

Playthings for the Moff

Han Solo stood before Jiliac's dais, eyes wide. His mouth dropped open. "You want me to *what*?"

"Careful, Captain Solo," Jabba cautioned. "You must address the Lady Jiliac with respect."

Han ignored the Hutt Lord. "But . . . but . . ." he sputtered, "that's crazy! That's like asking me to point a gun at my own head and pull the trigger! We all heard Shild, how he was cracking down on smugglers. In case it's escaped your notice, Your Ladyship, *I'm* a smuggler"—he jerked his thumb at his own chest—"and if I walk into Sarn Shild's place to give him your gifts and your message, that'll be the last free walk I ever take! No! I ain't doing it!"

Inwardly he was a little surprised at his own temerity in

speaking to the powerful Hutt leaders in such a manner, but Jiliac's calm request had roused his temper. Just who did the Hutts think they were, anyhow?

"Captain Solo." Jiliac did not take umbrage at Han's words or tone. "Calm yourself. We will provide you with new clothing, the best of faked IDs, and one of our own courier vessels. No one will know you are Han Solo, smuggler. All they will know is that you are a diplomatic envoy from Nal Hutta, duly authorized and designated to deliver our message and our gifts."

Han took a deep breath. Under those circumstances, maybe . . .

"What is it worth to you, to get your message delivered?" he asked, finally.

"Ten thousand credits," Jiliac said, without batting an eye.

Han gasped. *That much! For just flying to Coruscant and back!*

He stared at the Hutt leaders for a moment, then turned to Chewbacca. "What do you think, pal?"

Chewie was plainly as torn as he was. The big Wookiee grumbled and rumbled, then finally commented that with that kind of money, they could start saving for a ship they could buy. But it was Han who'd be risking his skin, he added, so the final decision should be Han's.

The Corellian thought for another moment, then turned back to Jiliac and Jabba. "All right," he said. "I'll do it for ten thousand. All of it in advance."

Jabba began to protest, but Jiliac shushed him with a gesture. "Very well, Captain. Ten thousand in advance. When can you leave?"

"If you can get me the IDs and vessel today," Han said grimly, "we'll leave tomorrow morning."

"It shall be done," Jiliac said.

• • •

The Hutt leader was as good as her word. By the next morning, Han had received excellent faked IDs, identifying him as one Jobekk Jonn, official Hutt diplomatic envoy. The ship was a speedy little Corellian courier vessel named *Quicksilver*. Han was given a suit of clothing better than anything he'd ever even touched before—a tomuon-wool jacket and trousers, cut in the very latest style.

At Chewie's suggestion, Han cultivated a short beard during the time it took them to fly to Coruscant. When they docked at one of Coruscant's many spacedocks, he slicked his hair straight back from his brow, and was amazed at how different he looked. The spiffy gray suit made him look like a bureaucrat, completely erasing all traces of the smuggler.

"I feel naked without my blaster," Han grumbled. "But they restrict weapons here on Coruscant . . . I mean, Imperial Center. Besides . . . I guess diplomatic envoys don't wear guns."

Chewie commented sadly that Han no longer looked scruffy, in approved Wookiee fashion. Instead he appeared as sleek and polished as lapi-stone.

"Trust me, pal, I can't wait till I can turn back into myself," Han said.

Then, picking up his package of gifts, and the holocube message from Jiliac and the Grand Council of Nal Hutta, Han left *Quicksilver* and took a shuttle down to Imperial Center.

Being back in the Imperial capital city brought back a lot of memories, most of them unpleasant ones. Bria had left him on Coruscant. Here he'd been hunted across the rooftops by Garris Shrike. His court-martial had taken place in the headquarters of the Imperial Navy . . .

Han already had the address for the Moff. Shild maintained several residences on different worlds, but at the moment, he was in Imperial Center, attending conferences on law and order in the Empire.

Han reached the Moff's residence, a luxurious penthouse in one of the city's most elegant buildings. After going through multiple security checks, he handed his credentials to the majordomo, an elderly human male, and then sat down in the antechamber. Only a strong effort of will kept him from fidgeting.

After waiting for nearly forty-five minutes, the majordomo appeared. "My master can give you only a few minutes," he said. "He is departing this evening for Velga Prime."

Nice, Han thought. Velga Prime was the most opulent gambling planetoid in the known galaxy.

He followed the majordomo down a succession of carpeted hallways. Automatically, Han memorized the way, just in case things went sour and he had to make a quick escape.

Finally, the majordomo ushered him into an office bigger than Han's apartment back on Nar Shaddaa. "Master Jobekk Jonn, of Nal Hutta, Your Excellency," the old man intoned.

Moff Sarn Shild was a tall, pale, ascetic-seeming man with oiled black hair and a thin, pointy mustache. Slender to the point of emaciation, he had pale, cold-looking hands with elongated fingers.

He wore no jewelry except a black krayt dragon pearl in one earlobe. His suit was the same opalescent black as the jewel.

He gestured brusquely to a seat. "I'm afraid I must be brief, Jonn. I realize that the Hutts have been . . . generous to my administration in the past, but the Emperor has made his wishes clear. My hands are tied."

"Let's not be hasty, Your Excellency," Han said, watching his diction and grammar. Unconsciously, he slipped back into his speech patterns from when he'd been an Imperial officer. "I believe you will find the Hutt offerings and message I've brought to be of interest. May I?"

Shild nodded shortly. Han carefully placed the package on the table. "Please open it," he said.

"Very well," the Moff said. Carefully he opened the package, and from the way his eyes lit up, Han could tell that the Hutt Lords knew his tastes well.

A small silver pipe, encrusted with semiprecious gems. A miniaturized holo-projector so small it would fit into a human palm. A necklace made of gold and platinum wire, encrusted with golden corusca gems. "For your lady, sir," Han said smoothly.

"Yes, she will like this . . ." muttered the Moff. A line appeared between his brows as he quickly scanned the holocube's message, which he trigged to display by means of his retinal pattern.

"Look here, Jonn," he said when he'd finished reading it, "I wish that I could offer Nal Hutta more assurances, but as I told you before, I have no choice. The Emperor has called upon all Imperial worlds to tighten down on smuggling, gunrunning, and other illegal activities. My sector contains Hutt space, and unfortunately the Hutt reputation for dishonesty is so well known that I cannot possibly cover for them. I will, however, promise Nal Hutta no armed reprisals if they cooperate."

"Cooperate in what way?"

"Do their best to become loyal, law-abiding citizens of the Empire."

That'll be the day, Han thought. "What about Nar Shaddaa?" he asked, unable to help himself. Fear for himself and his friends made his mouth dry.

"I shall have to make an example of Nar Shaddaa," Shild said. "By the time I am finished with the Smuggler's Moon, it will no longer support the smuggling industry. Its inhabitants will be lucky if it can still support sentient life."

Han tried to conceal his shock. *What are we going to do?*

Shild shook his head. "And now, I'm afraid, I must depart. I regret that you had to travel so far for only a short interview, but I did warn your Hutt masters that I would be unable to . . . bend . . . over this issue."

Shild stood up, and automatically Han did also.

"Sarn?" came a voice from behind the door leading into the next room. Caught in the act of turning, Han froze. *That voice!*

"My dear, I am in here," called Shild. "I was just about to show the diplomatic envoy from Nal Hutta out."

The door opened, and a woman stood there, smiling. "Sarn, darling," she said, "we must hurry. The shuttle is waiting on the rooftop. Will you be much longer?"

Han turned his head, and their eyes met—for the first time in six years.

Bria Tharen. This time, there was no mistake. Bria stood there, dressed in a flowing silken gown that made her seem just as much of an ornament as anything else in Shild's palatial home. The low-cut gown was turquoise, the color of her eyes. She was stunningly beautiful.

As she stared back at Han, she blinked, and went a little pale. Her smile did not waver, though.

She's good, Han thought. He knew he'd betrayed his shock, but fortunately Shild wasn't looking at him. Han hastily pulled himself back together, composing his features into a polite, neutral mask.

Shild gestured at Bria. "Master Jobekk Jonn of Nal Hutta, my . . . niece . . . Bria."

Only Han's years of playing sabacc saved him. As Bria composedly held out her hand with a throaty, "It's a pleasure to meet you, Master Jonn," Han was able to take it and bow over it with a suave smile.

"The pleasure is all mine," he said. "Shild, you are a very lucky man, to have such a lovely . . . niece."

He saw a faint wave of color brighten her cheeks at his gibe. "You look familiar, sir," she said. "Haven't I seen you before?" Her voice was cool and disinterested.

Han knew she was baiting him. "Perhaps on WANTED posters," Han murmured, so quietly Shild couldn't hear.

Then bowing coldly over her hand once more, he let go of her—though all he wanted to do was grab her and bring her with him!—and bowed formally to Shild.

"Thank you for your time, Your Excellency."

Then, turning away, Han strode resolutely from the room.

Later that same night, much later, Bria Tharen lay in her small bunk aboard the Moff's yacht, muffling her sobs in her pillow. Every time she recalled the look in Han's eyes, she wanted to wail aloud.

It was only too obvious that he'd thought the worst— that she was Shild's concubine. Sobs shook her. That was what he was *supposed* to think, after all. That was what Sarn Shild *wanted* everyone to think.

In truth, the Moff's sexual preferences did not run to human females. Bria traveled with him as a lovely show object, to be displayed to Imperial officials, just as Shild would display any trophy.

She kept his home running smoothly, listened to him when he wanted someone to talk to, oversaw his household staff and office, and generally kept Moff Sarn Shild's life running smoothly.

But she had never shared his bed, which was the only thing that made this current assignment bearable.

And now . . . now Han had seen her, and thought the worst. Even all the information Bria had been able to funnel to the rebel movement back on Corellia couldn't ease the grief and shame she felt.

Her pillow was wet. Bria turned it over, and then lay there, staring into the darkness, as the Moff's yacht streaked through hyperspace.

"Han . . ." she whispered brokenly. *"Han . . ."*

Chapter Ten:
THE ADMIRAL'S ORDERS

On the way back to Nar Shaddaa, Chewbacca flew the Hutt courier ship *Quicksilver* competently, but his mind was not completely on his work. The Wookiee glanced over at his partner, the human to whom he'd sworn a life debt, and his blue eyes crinkled with concern. Han was slumped in the copilot's seat, scowling blackly at the star-lined void of hyperspace. He'd been like this for days now, ever since he'd boarded *Quicksilver* following his mission to the Moff's residence on Coruscant. He rarely spoke, and when he did, all he did was complain and make sarcastic comments.

And he complained about everything—the food, the speed of the little courier ship, Chewie's piloting, the tedium of space travel, the greed of the Hutts . . . any subject the Wookiee had tried to introduce, Han had had a great many negative things to say about it.

For the first time since he'd met the Corellian, Chewbacca actually wondered whether there might be circumstances under which renouncing a life debt was the honorable thing to do. More honorable, say, than murdering the person to whom one owed the life debt . . .

"This thing moves like a thousand-year-old Hutt," Han grumbled. "You'd think with the size of the engines, she'd be able to make some speed . . . think you could get her to go a little faster if I got out and pushed?"

Chewbacca restrained himself and commented that it wouldn't be too long now before they were back on Nar Shaddaa.

"Yeah, and it can't be too soon for me," Han said bitterly. He got up and paced nervously around the cramped cabin. When he turned abruptly, he whacked his head on a low stanchion and began cursing a blue streak.

When he finally began to repeat himself, Han growled, then threw himself back into the copilot's seat. "After we return the Hutts' little bucket of bolts to them, I guess we'll have to head for Smuggler's Run. If the *Br*—" he seemed to choke on the word, then amended, "if that blasted ship of ours will make it through the asteroid field."

Chewbacca asked why they'd be heading for Smuggler's Run. Wynni, he pointed out, would likely be at Smuggler's Run, and she was the last person he wanted to see. The Wookiee wasn't sure he could take much more of the way she was so free with her paws.

"Listen, pal"—Han's voice dripped sarcasm—"in case it ain't occurred to you, it's all over for Nar Shaddaa. Moff Sarn Shild has probably already ordered his fleet to assemble out near Teth. We're shakin' the dust of that miserable excuse for a moon off our feet for good."

What fleet? Chewbacca wanted to know.

"Oh, each Imperial Moff has his own discretionary 'peacekeeping' squadron," Han said, propping his boots on the console, not bothering to look before he plunked them down. Chewie was relieved to see that he missed the DECELERATE control. Sudden decelerations while in hyperspace were not a good idea. "No doubt Shild has one, too. His fleet's probably not the best, but it'll be more than enough for the mission."

Chewbacca was confused. Why wouldn't the Moff's fleet be the best available?

"Oh, it's just the way things go in the Imperial Navy. Since Hutt space is out here in the Rim, far from 'civilization'—that is, Coruscant—I'd bet Sarn Shild got stuck with all the older ships and weaponry, while all the newest, best stuff went to Rampa 1 and Rampa 2."

Rampa 1? Chewie asked. He'd thought only Rampa 2 had experienced an uprising.

"Yeah, well, when the citizens of Rampa 1 heard about what was going on, they rose up, too," Han said. "For all the good it's gonna do 'em."

Chewie commented that he hated the Empire that had enslaved him, and wished he could help bring it down.

Han snorted. "Hey, pal, don't hold your breath. Palpatine's got more weapons and starships than he knows what to do with. Any rebellion against the Empire is doomed."

The Wookiee pilot did not believe his partner's pronouncement, and said so. It made sense to him that at some point the Imperial worlds, tired of Palpatine's iron fist, would unite and rebel.

Han shook his head sourly. "Never happen, Chewie. And if it did, they'd be doomed. Just like Nar Shaddaa is doomed."

Chewie commented that it wasn't the Wookiee way to run away from a fight. Didn't Han want to fight back against the Imperial fleet? He was certain that the smugglers were much better pilots—and certainly better shots—than the Imperials. Maybe they could defeat the Imperial attack.

Han laughed out loud at the suggestion.

Annoyed, Chewie's lips skinned back from his teeth, and he snarled at his human partner.

Han sat up in a hurry, looking startled. Chewie rarely showed temper to the Corellian, and Wookiee anger was not something to be taken lightly. "Hey, no need to get sore about it! I can't help it if Nar Shaddaa doesn't stand a chance! It ain't *my* fault!"

The Wookiee growled, low in his throat.

"Okay, okay," Han soothed. "I'll definitely warn 'em, so they can get away. I'll talk to Mako about it, soon as we've reported in to Jiliac, okay?"

Chewbacca subsided, and went back to piloting. But the Wookiee was still thinking, still adding things up. He commented on Han's ill temper.

"Whaddaya mean, I've been hard to live with?" Han was indignant. "Nothin's wrong!"

Chewbacca's comment was short and to the point.

Han flushed. "Whaddaya mean, this has somethin' to do with a woman?" he demanded indignantly. "What makes you think that?"

Chewie reeled off a list of reasons, then put forth his best guess as to exactly *which* woman Han was upset about.

Han cursed, scowled, then, finally, slumped down and put his hands over his face. He rubbed his forehead and groaned aloud. "You're right, Chewie," he mumbled. "It was her. Bria. With *Sarn Shild.* I couldn't believe it. How could she?"

Chewbacca noted that appearances could sometimes be deceiving.

Han shook his head. "Not this time," he said miserably. "She called him 'Sarn darling.' "

The Wookiee wondered whether Bria might be married to the Moff.

Han sighed. "Nope. It wasn't that . . . formal . . . a relationship. Chewie, I can't believe she'd do that! It's so . . . cheap!"

Chewbacca tried to be comforting, reminding Han that sometimes sentients had to do things they didn't particularly like because they were necessary. Maybe there were extenuating circumstances in Bria's case, too.

Han tried to smile. "Thanks, pal. I wish I could say I thought you were right. But . . ." He shook his head, and subsided into silence.

It was a very silent flight back to the landing platform on Nar Shaddaa.

Han and Chewie reported to Jiliac and Jabba the moment they returned to Nar Shaddaa. The Hutts were not pleased to hear that Sarn Shild was no longer in their pay. "We shall have to do some investigating about this fleet and the situation," Jiliac said. "Come back in two hours, Captain Solo."

Han shrugged and agreed. He had his ten thousand credits, he'd checked his balance before he'd left Nar Shaddaa. So he was willing to do the Hutts' bidding for a little while longer. Besides, in two hours, he'd be able to find Mako and pass along the warning to the older smuggler.

Mako was even more upset than Jiliac and Jabba when he heard the situation. "Keep this quiet, Han," he said softly, staring out across the awnings and walkways of Nar Shaddaa. They were standing on his little balcony outside his ramshackle flat. "If the citizens get wind of this, there'll be mass panic. An Imp fleet ain't nothing to mess with."

"But with enough warning, maybe they could evacuate—" Han began, only to break off at Mako's quick headshake.

"Not a chance, kid. Too many of 'em don't have anywhere else to go. Take that Jarik Solo kid who's been riding with you and Chewie. He's a rat from the deep-down streets, born and 'raised'—not that anyone likely raised him—here on Nar Shaddaa. There's millions like him, Han. And if the Imps are out to teach Nar Shaddaa a lesson, then a whole lotta people are gonna die."

Han was considerably sobered by his talk with Mako. He hadn't thought of it in those terms before. He realized how lucky he and Chewbacca were, to be able to climb aboard their ship and fly away from the danger. He resolved that if it came to that, he'd take Jarik with him. He'd grown to like the youth.

But what about all the other sentients who wouldn't be able to get out? Nar Shaddaa had shields, but they wouldn't be able to stand for long against an Imperial bombardment. Han had a sudden, vivid vision of these crumbling towers in flames from Imperial turbolasers. People would be fleeing, filling the streets, screaming, cowering, clutching children against them. Rodians, Sullustans, Twi'leks, Wookiees, Gamorreans, Bothans, Chadra-Fans . . . and more. Not to mention humans. Lots of humans. The Corellian section was full of them . . .

Han reported back to Jiliac's audience chamber in a very troubled frame of mind.

The Hutt leader fixed him with a somber gaze. "What you have said is true. We checked our sources on Teth, and the Moff has indeed ordered his discretionary fleet to assemble there. Since some elements of the fleet have been out on patrol, it will take a week or possibly two for all the ships to converge on Teth, and then a minimum of several days to prepare for an assault on Nal Hutta. We are taking measures to ensure our safety on Nal Hutta."

But what about Nar Shaddaa? Han wondered. It was a pretty good bet that the self-centered Hutts would give the Smuggler's Moon barely a thought, in comparison to protecting their safety, and that of their homeworld.

"We have discovered that Shild's fleet is under the command of Admiral Winstel Greelanx. You used to be an Imperial officer, Captain. Do you know him?"

"No," Han said. "Never heard of him. But it's a big Navy."

"True," Jiliac said. "Our sources have assured us that Admiral Greelanx, while a competent officer, has, in the past, not been above furthering his own fortunes when the opportunity arises. He was in charge of several Imperial fleets doing customs patrol in the past, and we have confirmed that under the right circumstances he can be bribed."

Han nodded, not really surprised, much less shocked. The pay scale for an Imperial officer wasn't that good. He'd heard of more than one Imp officer on the take.

"With that in mind, we want you to go and see him, Captain," Jiliac continued. "We want you to negotiate with him on our behalf."

"Me?" The thought of just marching right into the middle of an Imperial fleet was not appealing. And offering a bribe to an Imperial officer carried the death penalty should he be caught. "But—"

"You are our best choice, Captain Solo," Jiliac said.

"But—"

"No buts, Han my boy," Jabba said, in those overly friendly tones he'd adopted recently. "You can handle this assignment better than anyone else. You were an Imperial officer. We will get you a uniform, forged orders, and a military ID. You can get in to speak with Greelanx, take him a small 'gift' from us. You speak his language, Han. You can talk to him in terms he will understand."

"Credits are what he'll understand," Han said. "Lots of them."

"We have been delegated to act on behalf of all Nal Hutta," Jiliac said. "Money is no object to ensuring the Admiral's . . . cooperation."

"But . . ." Han was thinking fast, "you can't expect him to not attack. The Moff would notice he hadn't fulfilled his orders. They'd court-martial him. And then they'd send an even bigger fleet to wipe us out!"

"And the next Admiral they appoint may not be amenable to our . . . persuasions," Jiliac said, nodding her massive head in agreement. "That is why we want Admiral Greelanx to stay in command. But there must be some way for us to ensure an Imperial defeat."

Han frowned. The entire thrust of his education at the Imperial Academy had been on ensuring *victory* for the Empire. "I don't know . . ." he said uncertainly.

"Couldn't we pay the Admiral to put his ships in the wrong positions, so they're not able to fire properly, or something of the kind?" Jiliac asked. "We Hutts are not military-minded sentients, Captain. What kinds of things would bring about the result we want? An Imperial defeat, without it being obvious that we paid Greelanx off."

"Well . . ." Han thought hard, "maybe he'll sell us his battle plan. With that in hand, we could create a defense that would put all of our ships in just the right spot to— maybe—defeat the Imperial fleet. Maybe. Especially if Greelanx had been paid to cut and run as soon as he could justify a withdrawal."

"Under what circumstances should we not attempt to engage the Imperial fleet?" Jiliac asked.

"If Shild's fleet has a Victory Star Destroyer or— worse—one of the Imperial Star Destroyers, forget it, Your

Excellency. But the Imps tend to assign older vessels to duty out here in the Rim. So maybe there's a chance."

Jabba was obviously impressed by Han's knowledge. "Another reason why you are the right person to undertake this mission, Han my boy. You will be able to assess the strength of the Moff's fleet, as few others could do."

Han looked over at Chewbacca. Even without asking the Wookiee, he could see that Chewie wanted to go for it—to do anything they could to help their adopted home. Han thought about Shug's spacebarn, and all the good times he'd had there with his friends. Sure, he'd had dreams of living a respectable life, of becoming a real "citizen"—but those dreams were in the past. He was a smuggler now, and probably a smuggler forever. He *liked* being a smuggler.

Thoughts of the towers of Nar Shaddaa in flames, of innocent sentients slaughtered, decided him. "All right. I'll get in to see Greelanx and talk to him."

"Emphasize that this is an offer no sentient in his right mind could refuse," Jiliac said. "We will pay well."

"I'll make sure he understands," Han said.

"When can you leave?" Jabba wanted to know. "Time is short."

"Get me the uniform and the ID and I'll leave tonight," Han said. "All I have to do is get a haircut . . ."

It felt very strange to be back in uniform again, Han decided as he walked casually along the permacrete of the Imperial base on Teth three days later. He tried not to fidget in his gray uniform with its blue and red lieutenant's insignia. Wearing the short-brimmed cap again felt odd, too. And he missed his old boots. These new boots weren't properly broken in, and were a shade too small. They pinched his toes.

The sentry at the gate had scanned his ID, then given

only a cursory glance at Han's orders before saluting and waving him through.

Han was watching for a special group of young officers. There should be shuttles going up to the Admiral's flagship, the Dreadnaught *Imperial Destiny,* throughout the afternoon, filled with officers and enlisted men reporting aboard after their last few hours of leave.

They'd be spending the next week preparing the big ship for its mission against the Hutt worlds. From what Han had been able to tell from passing the fleet while making their landing approach, Greelanx's force consisted of three Dreadnaughts—the *Imperial Destiny,* the *Pride of the Senate,* and the *Peacekeeper*—four bulk cruisers, plus nearly a score of customs and patrol ships, including some *Guardian*-class light cruisers and a couple of *Carrack*-class light cruisers. Lots of TIE fighters in the holds of the bigger ships, of course.

Certainly enough power to utterly destroy Nar Shaddaa, but it wasn't as bad as it could be. Han had seen no Star Destroyers, and it was a safe bet that if Greelanx's squadron included one, that would be his flagship.

As he walked along, Han noticed a milling group of young officers queuing up before an Imperial shuttle. *Here I go,* he thought, walking purposefully up to them, then falling in at the back of the line. Now that he was back in the uniform, his shoulders were automatically straighter, his steps more precise, his eyes forward.

The young officers filed aboard the ship, and took seats in the shuttle, strapping in. Han's seatmate gave him a pleasant nod. Han nodded back and smiled. The crew complement of a Dreadnaught was 16,204, so it was highly unlikely that anyone would realize for a long time that Lieutenant "Stevv Manosk" was an interloper.

The flight up to the Dreadnaught was uneventful. Han's

seatmate fell asleep. Han smiled. Too much shore leave, perhaps?

After they docked with the *Destiny*, Han filed off the ship, then headed for the nearest unoccupied datapad. The ship was big enough that nobody would be too surprised to see him call up a schematic showing what was located on each deck.

There we go . . . level four, section three . . .

Han quickly headed for the nearest turbolift. He boarded one, then was quickly shuffled into the back, as others crowded in on the next deck. Han was staring straight ahead when he suddenly realized to his horror that he *knew* the young officer standing near the door!

It was Tedris Bjalin, the young lieutenant who had, so systematically, stripped Han's uniform of rank during his court-martial.

Han surreptitiously eased himself as far to the right as he could, behind a taller man, crossing his fingers that Tedris wouldn't turn around. The lieutenant didn't, and he got off at the next floor.

Han breathed a long, quiet sigh of relief. *Of all the lousy coincidences, one of the few guys who could ID me!* Actually, it wasn't such an odd coincidence. Tedris was from the Outer Rim Territories. It wasn't too surprising that he'd be assigned out here, since he knew these spaceways. *I'll just have to make sure I stay out of his way . . .*

Once on level four, Han walked quickly along, looking for the corridor leading to section three. He found it, turned in, then walked down to the end. The highest-ranking officers always had offices with a viewport. One of the privileges of rank.

Han found the correct door, then hesitated, squared his shoulders, and felt in his pocket for the Hutt gift. It was a lovely (and quite valuable) man's ring, platinum, set with a large and flawless Bothan glitterstone.

The anterior office was occupied by a silver droid, who was sitting before a desk, entering data on a datapad. The droid looked up as Han entered. "May I help you, Lieutenant?"

"I need to see Admiral Greelanx," Han said.

"Do you have an appointment, Lieutenant?"

"No, not exactly," Han said. "But I know he'll want to see me. I have some . . . information . . . for him. You know what I mean?" He leered, then winked, deliberately attempting to overload the "inference" circuits in the droid's programming.

The silver droid's green eyes flashed slightly as the creature tried to interpret what Han was saying. Finally, it stirred. "Excuse me, Lieutenant, perhaps you should speak with the Admiral's aide."

"Sure," Han said, standing at ease.

The droid hastened into the next room, and Han could faintly hear it expostulating with someone inside. Finally, it came back out, followed by an extremely irritated-looking senior lieutenant. Han snapped to attention and saluted. "What's going on here, Lieutenant?" the man snapped.

"Sir, Lieutenant Stevv Manosk, requesting to see the admiral, sir!"

"State your business, Lieutenant," the man, whose name badge identified him as "Kern Fallon," ordered.

"Sir, I have a message for the admiral. It's a . . . personal . . . message, sir." Han was taking a calculated risk that Greelanx was as morally corrupt as many of the high-ranking Imperial officers he'd encountered. If the man took bribes, then there was a good chance that he was far from being an ascetic type where the ladies were concerned . . .

Fallon raised an eyebrow. "I beg your pardon, Lieutenant?"

Han sensed that he was being tested, and didn't change

expression. "Sir, she told me to give the message only to the admiral, sir."

"'She'?" Fallon's voice fell until he was whispering. "You mean Malessa?"

Han allowed his eyes to widen and gambled. "Sir, this message is from *Lady Greelanx!*" he said, in shocked tones. "Who is Malessa?"

If Malessa is Lady Greelanx's name, I'm done for, he thought.

But his luck held. Senior Lieutenant Fallon's eyes went wide. "Lady Greelanx, but of course! I meant her, I just . . . slip of the tongue, Malessa is *my* wife, I just . . . slip of the tongue, I assure you, I was just thinking of her . . . wait just a moment . . ."

Fallon bustled inside, and Han allowed himself a smug smile. *Pure sabacc,* he thought. It had been a fairly safe bet that good old Admiral Greelanx had a mistress or two on the side . . .

Moments later he was in the admiral's large inner office, with its tasteful furnishings and viewport that allowed the admiral to admire his squadron as they hung in orbit.

Greelanx was a stocky man of medium height, with thinning gray hair and a small, squarish mustache. He was standing behind his desk when Han entered, looking somewhat alarmed. "Lieutenant? You bring a message from my wife?"

Han took a deep breath and said, "Sir, what I have to convey can only be said in utter *privacy,* sir."

Greelanx studied him for a moment, then beckoned Han closer and slapped a control beneath his desk. "Privacy screen on, and jamming activated," he said. "Now, tell me what this is all about."

Han held out the ring. "Admiral, I bring you a gift from the Hutt Lords of Nal Hutta. They want to deal."

Greelanx's eyes lit up at the sight of the valuable piece of jewelry, but he did not touch it. "I see," he said. "I can't say I'm surprised, either. The slugs don't want to have their comfortable, crime-ridden lives disturbed, eh?"

Han nodded. "That's about the size of it, Admiral. And they are willing to pay well for the privilege. We're talking all the Lords of Nal Hutta, here. They are prepared to be very generous."

Greelanx finally allowed himself to pick up the ring and examine it, then he slipped it onto his finger. It fitted perfectly. "Suits you very well, sir," Han said.

"Yes, it does," Greelanx agreed. He toyed with the ring, sliding it back and forth thoughtfully. "I must admit, I find the Hutt offer . . . tempting," he said, finally. "Especially since I plan to retire next year. It would be nice to have a chance to . . . augment . . . my pension."

"I quite agree, sir."

"But my orders are clear, and I cannot go against them," Greelanx said, slipping the ring off and holding it out toward Han. "I'm afraid we cannot do business, young man."

Han tensed, but made himself stay calm. He could tell Greelanx was really tempted. "Sir, what are your orders?" he asked. "Perhaps we can think of something that will benefit us both, and yet leave you free of any charge of wrongdoing."

Greelanx laughed bitterly, a short, bitten-off laugh. "Hardly, young man. My orders are to enter the Hutt system, execute order Base Delta Zero upon the Smuggler's Moon, Nar Shaddaa, and then blockade Nal Hutta and Nar Hekka until the Hutts agree to allow full customs inspections and a complete military presence on their worlds. The Moff doesn't want to cripple the Hutts too badly, but he wants Nar Shaddaa reduced to rubble."

Han swallowed, his mouth dry. Base Delta Zero was an order that called for the decimation of a world—all life, all vessels, all systems—even droids were to be captured or destroyed. His worse nightmare come true.

"Admiral . . . have you completed your battle plan?" Han asked.

"My staff has been working on it," Greelanx said. "And I am reviewing it now. Why?"

"The Hutts would like to purchase the detailed plan, sir," Han said. "Name your price."

Greelanx was obviously intrigued by Han's statement. "Buy the battle plan?" he said, his voice expressing surprise. "What good will that do you?"

"Give us a fighting chance, perhaps, sir," Han said.

"Us?" the admiral looked sharply at Han. "You're one of them? A smuggler?"

"Yes, sir."

Greelanx shrugged. "I'm surprised," he admitted. "You wear the uniform well."

"Thank you, sir," Han said, and he meant it.

Greelanx paced slowly around the office, obviously thinking, tossing the ring up and then catching it. Finally, he came to stand before Han again. "You're saying that your Hutt employers will pay me what I ask for my battle plan," he said.

"Yes, sir," Han said. "For that, and for taking the first reasonable, strategically justifiable opportunity to withdraw your squadron. We'll take care of the rest."

"Hmmmmmm . . ." Greelanx thought some more, then, finally, as if making a decision, he slipped the ring back on his finger. "Very well, young man, we have a deal," he said. "I want my payment in gems . . . small, easy to dispose of, and not terribly traceable. I shall make you a list of the types and weights I wish."

"Fine, sir," Han said. "You do that."

"Sit down, over there." Greelanx pointed to a couch

across his office. "I'll finish reviewing the battle plan, and then you can have it."

Han nodded, and went to sit down, as told. He was a little surprised that it had been that easy. He wondered if he should be suspicious of Greelanx, but the man seemed genuinely motivated by greed. But there was something else going on, too . . . something Han couldn't put his finger on . . .

Greelanx worked for nearly two hours, then, finally, stood up and beckoned Han into the privacy field again. "I have it," he said. "Nothing terribly inspired, standard Imperial tactics, but eminently workable. We should be able to cut any smuggler fleet to ribbons, I'm afraid."

"That's our concern," Han said. "You just stick to this, Admiral"—he indicated the battle plan—"and when you can justifiably withdraw your squadron, you do it. I'll be back to pay you."

"You are a pilot, are you not?" Greelanx asked.

"You bet I am, sir," Han said. He grinned at the older man. "You're going to wish you had me on your side."

The admiral chuckled. "Cocky, aren't you? But the best pilots always are. Very well, then, I'll leave a shuttle for you at these coordinates." He added a line to the sheet of flimsy containing the battle plan. "Wear that uniform. All the docking codes you'll need will be in the navicomputer. I'll expect you one week to the day and hour after the attack. Is that understood?"

Han nodded. "Yes, sir, I understand. I'll be back, count on it. The Hutts are only too aware of their danger. They'll pay off, no complaints."

At least none you'll hear, he added silently.

"Very well. That concludes our business," Greelanx said. "Although, young man, I believe you are overly optimistic about your chances against my squadron."

Han nodded. "Noted, Admiral. But all we want is a fighting chance."

"You'll get it," Greelanx said. "But your people had better be prepared to defend themselves. My attack will be genuine."

Han saluted. "Yes, sir."

Then he executed a perfect about-face, and strode from the room.

Chapter Eleven:

BATTLE STATIONS?

The corners of Aruk the Hutt's wide, lipless mouth turned down as he squinted his protuberant eyes at the shipping report displayed on his datapad. He used to relish going over all the facts and figures . . . the quarterly, semi-annual, and annual reports, the Ylesian profit statements, the prospectuses for new companies, his net worth statement, and all the other reports on the vast and varied financial enterprises of Besadii kajidic . . . but lately, it was becoming more and more of a chore to concentrate on them.

Abstractedly, Aruk reached for another of the nala-tree frogs that Teroenza shipped him from Ylesia. The t'landa

Til had been faithful to his promise to provide only the biggest, tastiest, freshest frogs to his Hutt overlord.

Aruk's hand closed around the nala-tree frog. The terrified creature squirmed wildly in the Hutt Lord's grip. Opening his mouth, Aruk tossed the wriggling morsel in, then rolled it around on his tongue, savoring its frenzied struggles for a long minute or two before finally swallowing the thing whole.

Delicious . . . Aruk thought with a contented sigh.

He frowned again at the datapad. These reports could wait. Perhaps he'd take a nap, though he knew he really shouldn't. His physician and the med droids had both insisted that he get more exercise. Every day that he didn't get off his sled and wriggle around under his own power, they complained and lectured. Every time he ate rich food, or smoked his hookah, they fussed, insisting that he was endangering his cardiovascular system. Aruk knew they were right, that his circulation was sluggish, he could tell because the greenish patches on his leather hide had darkened.

But he was old, blast it, and at his age, he should be allowed to do just as he liked—which included smoking, eating what he wanted, and *not* exercising. And . . . *not* reading incomprehensible financial reports.

Aruk resolved to turn the financial report over to Durga. Time the youngster began taking some of the load off his parent's shoulders.

The aging Hutt Lord took another nala-tree frog to savor, then, with a sigh, he closed his bulbous eyes for a delightful afternoon nap . . .

"All right, you sentients, settle down!" roared Mako Spince. His amplified voice resounded off the walls of the large auditorium at The Chance Castle where Han had first seen Xaverri perform. The hotel-casino had generously donated the space, when Mako had called a meeting of representatives from every enclave, both humanoid and nonhumanoid, on Nar Shaddaa. "I said, settle *down*!"

Slowly the crowd quieted. Mako waited until he had their full attention, then he said, "Okay, guys. I'm no politician, so I don't know how to make a speech. The best I can do is just tell you the facts as we know 'em. Okay?"

The crowd indicated their approval of Mako's words with a muted buzz of applause. In the front of the crowd, a Gotal yelled, "Go on, Mako!"

"Okay." Mako held up his right hand, and used his left to tick off points on his fingers as he spoke. "Fact number one. Fellow sentients and inhabitants of Nar Shaddaa . . . we are in a world of trouble. Within a week, a squadron of Imperial vessels is going to be dispatched from Teth, sent by our own beloved Moff, Sarn Shild. This squadron has orders to *wipe us out*. Not give us a bloody nose, or destroy some of our ships. I mean they're going to do their best to see that no more smuggling happens out of Nar Shaddaa—ever. The place will be a smoking ruin."

A murmur of fear ran through the auditorium as the assembled smugglers tried to assimilate Mako's words.

"Fact number two," Mako went on, "we're on our own for this one, folks. The Hutts have just spent a bundle of credits installing brand-new planetary defense shields so they can hide behind 'em on Nal Hutta, while the Imp fleet uses up their ammo on *us*. The Hutts have, by report, hired a small fleet of mercs to come in and help defend them, but their primary strategy is just to let the Imps have Nar Shaddaa, and hope that'll satisfy 'em."

Boos, hisses, and catcalls of all kinds filled the space, drowning Mako out. The smugglers howled their rage, their threats, their anger at the Hutts. It was nearly five minutes before Mako could make himself heard again.

"Yeah, yeah! It makes me mad, too, friends, but what can you do? They're *Hutts,* so whaddaya expect, folks? But anyway that's the point. Whatever we do about this, it's our call. The slugs ain't gonna help us out."

Grumbling, the crowd subsided.

"Okay, fact three. We ain't exactly helpless, fellow sentients. We have it on good authority that the Imp squadron doesn't include anything with super-heavy firepower. No Star Destroyers. That's good news for us. That means we can fight back!"

Mutters of consternation swelled, mingled with yells of determination: "Yeah! We'll fight! We'll kick their butts! We wanna fight! Those Imps can't shoot for sour trig-berries! We ain't running from a bunch of Imps! We'll make 'em sorry they attacked us!"

Mako grinned. "Hey, fellow sentients, my thoughts exactly. I intend to fight this fleet, and if it's just me out there in my one ship, so be it. *Nobody* is wiping me out without a fight! Nobody!"

This time, the cheers from the crowd were deafening. "Yeah! Mako! You lead us, Mako! Yeah, we'll fight!"

Mako motioned for quiet. "All right, those who want to fight, raise their hands, or paws or tentacles or whatever you got. Those who don't wanna fight—I suggest you take your belongings and your families and head out *right now.* It's gonna get dicey around here, real soon."

Han, who was watching from the wings of the stage, was surprised to see that the vast majority of the assembled beings stayed. Only a couple of dozen sentients got up and left.

Mako waited until they were out of the way before he started in again. "Okay, folks. First thing we need is for everyone with some battle experience to come on down here to the front. I'm not talkin' about winging a pirate who got too close, I'm talkin' real combat experience in space, specially against the Imperials. C'mon down here."

Over the next several minutes about forty sentients, most of them humanoid, made their way down front. "Okay, guys," Mako said. "The first thing we need here in planning a counteroffensive is a leader. Anyone wanna volunteer?"

One of the humanoids, a Bothan, pointed up at the senior smuggler. "You, Mako! You be our leader!" he shouted.

The crowd reacted enthusiastically to this suggestion, and soon a swelling chant was heard. "Ma-ko! Ma-ko! *Mako!!* MA-KO!"

The chanting went on, gaining in volume, until Han wanted to put his hands over his ears. Mako waved his arms, and silence descended. "Okay! Okay!" he said, his teeth flashing in a wide grin. "I'm real flattered, folks. And I swear to you that I'll do my best for you. I swear it!"

Thunderous cheers erupted again.

"Okay, one more thing, then I'm gonna dismiss you for now," Mako said. "I want you to meet my right-hand man, folks. A lot of you know him as a smuggler with a cranky ship and a big, furry sidekick. Han Solo, c'mon out here!"

Han walked out. He and Mako had basically figured that the senior smuggler would get tapped to lead the Nar Shaddaa forces. Things were going just as the two of them had figured they would.

More thunderous cheers, and a chant of "Ma-ko! Han! Mako! Han!" sprang up.

Han waved at the crowd, feeling his cheeks grow warm. He'd never before had thousands of people cheering just for *him* before. When he'd been Xaverri's assistant, he'd shared the spotlight, but it wasn't the same as this. Hearing all these people applauding him was a weird—but pleasant—experience.

"Okay, folks," Mako said, waving again for quiet. "I'm gonna ask my combat veterans down there"—he indicated the little crowd—"to stay in close touch and check in here at The Chance Castle each morning. We'll post notice of meetings or drills outside the auditorium, okay? Now let's have a round of applause for our brave volunteers here!"

Cheers resounded. It was obvious that the crowd of sentients felt tremendously better, just knowing they were going to *do* something, instead of tamely waiting to be slaughtered.

Once the main crowd had left, Mako addressed the combat veterans. "Okay, Han and me are gonna put together a plan for our defense over the next day or so, and then we'll brief you on it, and begin battle drills. By the time those Imps get here, everyone is going to know just what to do, and that's a promise. If you folks know any other sentients with combat experience, bring 'em along to the briefing. Got that?"

The veterans all indicated that they did. "Good," Mako said. "Over the next couple of days, get your ships in prime fighting condition. Shields fully charged, armor reinforced, all lasers charged . . . you know the drill. We need all our ships working at full capacity. So let's get started, right?"

"Right!" they shouted.

After Mako dismissed the combat veterans, he and Han headed for one of the meeting rooms in the back of the casino, where they were joined by the rest of the smuggler "High Command"—as Mako and Han had jokingly dubbed their group. Chewbacca, Roa, Shug Ninx, Salla Zend, Lando Calrissian, Rik Duel, and Sinewy Ana Blue made up Mako's elite group of experienced smugglers.

Mako and Han didn't plan to tell anyone but the High Command that they were in possession of the Imperial battle plan. They figured that might make the smugglers overconfident, and that would be disastrous for their side. Also, some smugglers would sell their grandmothers for enough credits, and they couldn't afford a security leak.

As Han sat beside him, Mako called up a holographic schematic on his datapad, and projected it above the table-top. All those present leaned forward to study the plan.

"Look here." Mako used a laser pointer to indicate the small, holographic representations of the ships in question. "We've got the Imp capital ships coming out of hyperspace *here,* and advancing on Nar Shaddaa. And sixteen skirmish line ships, *Guardian*-class Customs light cruisers, they'll be coming out of hyperspace in a shell formation to surround Nar Shaddaa. Then we've got two recon line vessels, that'll be these *Carrack*-class cruisers, one on each side . . . here and here. Everyone got that?"

"Got it," Rik Duel said.

"And then, back here in a wedge formation, are the three Dreadnaughts and the four bulk cruisers . . . the heavy stuff. Remember that these Dreadnaughts each carry twelve TIE fighters, and the *Carrack*-class light cruisers each carry four recon TIEs. That's at least forty-four TIEs we're going to have to deal with."

The members of Mako's "High Command" looked at each other with worried expressions. "Smuggler's Run is beginning to look better and better," Sinewy Ana Blue said. "The Imps would never be crazy enough to send a fleet into an asteroid field."

Han was quick to reassure them. "Hey, we can handle these TIEs," he insisted. "No shielding, don't forget. They're fast little suckers, true, but even a brush with a quad or turbolaser beam and . . ." He opened both hands and mouthed "boom."

Mako nodded. "Han used to fly TIE fighters in combat situations, and while I was in the Academy I trained in them. The only reason we're still here is that we're not still doing it. TIE fighter pilots are really, really good . . . but that doesn't keep most of 'em from winding up really, really dead."

"Okay," Lando spoke up, "so we know what the Imperial force is, and how they're going to approach us. How do we fight back against them, using freighters and a few one-man fighters like the one Roa's been building?"

Everyone turned to look at the senior smuggler. "Yeah, I've almost finished work on her," Roa said. "She's gonna be a sweet little ship to handle."

"What are you naming her?" Blue asked, with an impish grin.

Roa grinned back at her. "The *Lwyll*, of course," he replied.

Roa and his lady love, Lwyll, had been an on-again, off-again item on Nar Shaddaa for over ten years. Everyone knew Lwyll. The lovely blond woman was one of the few people on the Smuggler's Moon who lived a completely legitimate life, earning an honest credit for an honest day's work. Roa had been after her for years to come and live with him, but Lwyll would never do it. She saw him, but she saw other men, too, and Roa was wounded whenever she did it.

Still, he'd never been able to bring himself to take the ultimate plunge and ask her to marry him. Han and the other smugglers had teased Roa about his indecision. All his friends could tell that Lwyll was the best thing that had ever happened to Roa.

"You're planning to fly *Lwyll* against the TIEs?" Mako asked. "What does the real Lwyll have to say about that?"

Roa sighed, and then gave his friends a rueful grin. "Believe me, she had plenty to say. You guys aren't going to believe this . . . but last night I up and asked Lwyll to marry me."

General murmurs of surprise ran around the table.

"Don't keep us in suspense," Blue cried, "what did she say?"

"She said 'no,'" Roa said. The senior smuggler's broad, open features sagged. "She said she didn't want to wind up a widow."

"Can't blame her for that," Lando said. None of the smugglers in the room was married, and it was no accident. Living on the edge as they did, it was impossible for them to maintain anything approaching a normal family life.

Chewbacca turned to Han and spoke earnestly. The Corellian translated for those who didn't understand Wookiee. "Roa, Chewie says that if you were a Wookiee, it'd be time for you to settle down. He thinks Lwyll is too good to lose. He likes her."

Roa grinned. "He's right. She's too good to lose. That's why this battle is my last stand as a smuggler, guys. If I live through it, I'm gonna quit this life and go straight."

Everyone was amazed to hear this from the senior smuggler, knowing how much Roa loved the life he'd chosen. "Yep, I'm gonna do it," Roa insisted. "And Lwyll says if I do, she'll be my wife."

"Well . . . congratulations!" Lando said. "That's great news. You're getting one wonderful woman, Roa."

All the smugglers echoed the young gambler's sentiments.

"I know it," Roa agreed. "So . . . all I gotta do is make it through this battle . . ."

"Speaking of which, we ought to get back to it," Mako said. "And figure out a way to beat these Imps."

"We have one big advantage," Roa said. "The element of surprise."

Mako stared at him. "We know when they're coming, so there's no element of surprise there. But . . . *they're* invading *us*. How are we supposed to surprise them?"

Roa smiled genially and waved a hand at the ceiling. "Think, my friends, think! What's up there?"

"A shield that needs fixing a lot," Mako said grimly.

"Past that," Roa said.

"Traffic buoys," Han said.

"Farther," Roa said.

Han thought for a moment, then a slow smile crept over his face. Salla laughed. "I get it! Space junk! Dozens . . . hundreds . . . of junked spaceships and parts of space-ships."

Roa was nodding at the tall lady smuggler. "Right. So much space junk in that ring around Nar Shaddaa that ships could hide behind it, or beneath it, or in its shadow—and then pop out and catch the Imp fleet by surprise."

Chewie voiced a loud "Hrrrrnnnnnnn!"

Now it was Mako's turn to nod excitedly. "I think you got something there, Roa," he said. "And it might work. Especially if we staged a couple of ships frantically running for cover—freighters, they'll think they're civs—and got the Imps to chase 'em until they're right where we want them, then"—he punched the air—"wham! We pop out of cover and clobber them!"

Excitedly the senior smuggler keyed the operation Roa had described into the datapad. The "High Command" watched as the ring of debris around Nar Shaddaa swam into view. As the Imperial skirmish ships zoomed in in pursuit of two small freighters, converging on the rightmost hemisphere (if one were facing Nal Hutta), suddenly a multitude of assorted freighters and other ships zipped out of concealment in the debris ring and zeroed in on the Imperial ships, lasers flashing.

"Okay, that should enable us to take care of a good percentage of those skirmish ships," Han said. "But what do we do about the recon vessels, and that wedge of capital-class ships . . . the Dreadnaughts and bulk cruisers?"

A gloomy silence fell. Finally Mako spoke up. "I know the Hutts are hiring a merc force—probably pirates—to defend Nal Hutta. The slugs don't give a hoot about Nar Shaddaa, not in comparison to their own precious hides, but if that merc captain has any smarts, he'll recognize that we could add significantly to his firepower. Maybe we can get him, whoever he is, to take part in the battle. It's worth a try, at least."

Lando was staring morosely at the creeping holographic image of the bulk cruisers and Dreadnaughts advancing on Nar Shaddaa. "Those pirates are apt to have superior fire-power, right?"

Mako nodded. "Right. They'll probably have some captured Imp vessels that they've modified. Maybe even some heavy weaponry like proton torpedoes. But their ammo would be limited. It's hard to just *buy* proton torpedoes to arm pirated Imp vessels. The Imps kinda frown on having their own ships used against 'em."

He said this last so dryly that a chuckle ran around the table.

Han was studying the wedge of capital-class ships. "All of these ships have forward-firing main guns," he said. "Too bad we can't hit them with a flank attack. But we just don't have the ships to do it, if the main part of our fleet will still be engaging those skirmish ships and the TIEs."

"Maybe that's where we can convince the mercs to help us," Mako said thoughtfully. "If they attacked on the Imp flank, they'd stand a decent chance of crippling one of those big ships, and that would be a ship they could commandeer after the battle. They'd love that!"

"Yeah . . . provided we could create some kind of diversion so the pirates could flank them," Han said.

Rik Duel stroked his short, elegant beard while he thought. "What we need is another fleet to come at them in a head-on run," he said.

"But we don't have enough ships to divide our forces that much," Roa said. "If we do, we're likely to lose everything."

"If we don't, we're likely to lose Nar Shaddaa," Lando pointed out. "I'm no ex-Imp officer like Han here is, but it seems to me that we've got to do whatever it takes to keep these big ships from turning and blasting away at our moon's shields. They're old, and it wouldn't take too many salvos to disable them. Then they'd level the place."

"Lando's right," Shug Ninx said. "We need something to keep those big ships occupied so the mercs—or whoever—can make a flank attack. Maybe we can . . . I don't know . . . divert their attention somehow."

"Well, a formation of ships coming at them head-on would certainly get their attention," Salla said. "Question is, where do we get them? We're going to have our hands full over here"—she pointed into the holographic display—"fighting these skirmish ships and TIEs."

Han had been staring into the holographic display, thinking how *real* the minuscule fleet appeared, down to the tiny TIE fighters. *Too bad,* he thought, *we can't project a hologram at the Imps and make them believe they're under attack* . . .

The idea suddenly coalesced in his brain. "That's it!" he shouted. "That could work!"

Conversation around the table ceased, and everyone stared at the Corellian. Han grinned at his friends excitedly. "Hey, I think I may know somebody who can provide us with that head-on attack force. We can use them as a diversion, for long enough to distract those heavy cruisers!"

Chewbacca had obviously followed Han's thinking. The Wookiee banged his fist on the table and roared his approval.

The remainder of the group, however, stared at Han,

confused, apparently completely in the dark. "Huh?" Lando said. "Who? What?"

Han ignored his friend. Leaping to his feet, he gestured at Mako. "I've gotta put in a call—does the manager here have a comm unit?"

The manager of The Chance Castle was only too happy to allow Han to use his unit. All of the big casinos knew that a major Imperial raid would be *very* bad for business . . .

Chapter Twelve:
Dreams and Nightmares

B ria Tharen stood beside Sarn Shild on the observation platform of the space station orbiting the planet Teth. The observation platform was enclosed mostly by force fields, so there was nothing visible between them and the surrounding vacuum. Bria could look straight ahead, to her left, her right, and overhead, and see nothing but naked space or the massive, turning shape of the planet. The young woman repressed a shiver as she thought of the cold, airless blackness scant meters away.

Despite her unease, the brilliant, adoring smile on her face never wavered. When she'd taken this assignment, Bria had already been a fairly good actress, able to conceal her true feelings automatically.

But by now, she thought grimly, *I probably deserve an award. Too bad there isn't an "Undercover Agent of the Year" trophy* . . .

The thought was so ridiculous that it made her smile genuine, for a brief second. Moff Shild put an arm around her and squeezed her shoulders, pointing. "Look, my dear! Here they come!"

The small contingent of VIPs on the observation platform began applauding as the Imperial fleet hove into view.

Bria smiled and clapped as the skirmish ships, the recon vessels, the bulk cruisers, and the Dreadnaughts glided slowly toward the reviewing platform. TIE fighters swooped and darted around the bigger ships like small insects poised to feed off a herd of grazers.

Shild was grinning ecstatically as he beheld his squadron. He gave Bria's shoulders another hug, and she kept herself from shrinking away by an effort of will. "Today marks the beginning of a new era of law and order in the Outer Rim, my dear!" he said, in his "political" voice. Then he added, in a conspiratorial whisper, "And the beginning of a new life for us, Bria!"

Bria looked up at the Moff inquiringly. "Really, Sarn? How so?"

He kept his voice low, but it was still intense, still forceful. "Once my fleet has wiped out Nar Shaddaa, and brought the Hutts to their . . . well, brought them to heel, my power in this sector will be unquestioned. And when I tap into the wealth of the Hutts—the lesser clans and Desilijic, at least—I will be able to afford to augment my military forces until I can take on much greater foes than a mob of thieving smugglers."

Why does he always sound like he's making a campaign speech? Bria wondered. Aloud she said, "Desilijic? Why not Besadii, too?"

"In a private communiqué, the Emperor made it clear

that Besadii is to remain unmolested," Shild said. "They're useful to him, providing the Empire with trained slaves. Besadii must continue to prosper."

Bria filed this information away as something to relay to Rion as soon as she could. *Palpatine even has his fingers in Hutt internal politics? Is there anything the Emperor doesn't try to turn to his personal advantage?*

Aloud she said, "Oh, well, that makes sense."

"Yes, the Emperor is a canny fellow," Shild said, still speaking in that almost whisper. "But . . . perhaps . . . not canny enough."

Bria was puzzled. "What do you mean, Sarn?"

He smiled, his "public" smile, but there was something in his eyes that made Bria uneasy. "I fear that between the growing rebellions on the innermost worlds and the internal political squabblings in the highest echelons, our beloved Emperor has overextended himself. He is losing his grip in the Outer Rim Territories. The Imperial forces are spread so thin in these sectors that a strong leader with a powerful military force to back him could simply . . . secede . . . from the Empire."

Bria looked at him, her eyes wide with shock. He was talking sedition! Didn't he realize that?

Shild mistook her look for amazed appreciation. He beamed at her. "Oh, don't think I haven't thought of it, my dear. There's no reason that the Outer Rim Territories couldn't become another Corporate Sector, with no ties or allegiance to the Empire. If I had sufficient military might, I could lead the Outer Rim to independence and prosperity—it would be glorious!"

Bria had to clench her teeth to keep her jaw from dropping. *What in the name of Xendor's Minions has gotten into him? I always knew Sarn was arrogant, but he sounds like a madman!*

Was it possible that the Moff had fallen under some kind

of . . . influence? Bria knew there were some telepathic species of aliens, but she'd never heard of any that could do anything like this. Maybe Shild had simply gone crazy. That was one possible explanation.

But the light in Shild's dark eyes was not that of a madman, it was the light of a man with a mission.

"And after leading the Outer Rim Territories to glory, my dear"—he gave her another one-armed hug—"it's possible that I should turn my concentration . . . well, shall we say, toward more *populated* areas of the galaxy. There are unhappy worlds, here in the Empire, worlds that are looking for new leadership. *I* could provide that leadership."

I can't believe I'm hearing this! He's talking about challenging the Emperor!

Bria was terrified to even stand here and listen to Shild. Palpatine had ears everywhere. Surely the Emperor would discover Shild's outrageous ambition, and eliminate him as casually as she might slap a stinging insect.

The Imperial fleet was moving magnificently past them now, passing in review. Shild dropped his arm from around Bria, stepped forward to stand on the very edge of the platform, looking slim and elegant in his Moff's uniform. He saluted his troops as they glided past him.

Bria stood back, near the entrance, feeling that coldness, that near panic grow, until it was everything she could do not to leave, to just run away and abandon Shild to face the consequences of his own egotistical ambition.

I'll find out just what he's planning, if I can, she promised herself, *and then I'll go.*

Bria stared at Shild, realizing she was now regarding him the same way she would a man who had contracted a terrible incurable disease. A walking dead man. She found she was actually sorry that Shild had contracted this "disease," this craving for power. The Moff had always treated her well, and her assignment could have been far worse.

For a wild moment she considered trying to talk some sense into Shild, but she quickly abandoned the thought. The Moff knew she was intelligent, and he valued that, but he had sufficient masculine arrogance that he'd never listen to a woman he was using as a front to disguise his sexual peccadilloes.

The fleet was nearly past the reviewing stand now. In minutes, as soon as they'd cleared Teth's gravity well, they'd jump to hyperspace on the first leg of the long journey to the Y'Toub system. On the Outer Rim, systems tended to be spread farther apart than they were in the more crowded central portions of the galaxy.

Bria found herself, as she often did, thinking of Han. Surely he was no longer on Nar Shaddaa. He'd gone back to his Hutt masters, delivered Shild's warning, then taken off. Han was good at self-preservation. He wouldn't try anything crazy like trying to *fight* the Imperial squadron, would he?

Would he?

Bria's mouth was terribly dry. She licked her lips, forced herself to swallow, then drifted back through the massive door to the magnificent reception inside, in search of a cup of stim-tea.

As she sipped it, Bria tried again and again to convince herself that Han was long gone from Nar Shaddaa, safe from Admiral Greelanx and his troops.

But, in her heart of hearts, she didn't believe it. Bria had a sudden vivid memory of the Corellian that time they were about to be boarded by slavers, remembered Han drawing his blaster and squaring his jaw . . . remembered him vowing, "They're not getting me without a fight!"

The odds against them had been approximately forty to three . . .

Bria's hands were shaking so badly she had to put the cup down on the table. She closed her eyes, fighting for control. *What if he tries to fight? What if they kill him? I would probably never know* . . .

And that was the most terrible thought of all . . .

Captain Soontir Fel stood on the bridge of the Dreadnaught *Pride of the Senate,* preparing to follow his commander into hyperspace. In his gray uniform, with decorations and rank insignia providing touches of color, Fel was an impressive sight that inspired confidence in those under his command.

One of the youngest people ever to receive a captain's commission in the Imperial Navy, Fel was a tall, muscular man, broad-shouldered and exceptionally strong. Black hair, dark eyes, and rugged, almost handsome features made him look as though he'd just stepped out of an Imperial Navy recruiting holo-poster.

Fel was a good, conscientious officer, well liked by his men. He had a special camaraderie with his TIE fighter pilots. Soontir Fel had once been a TIE fighter pilot himself, and his exploits and accomplishments were almost legendary.

In a way, Fel wished he could be back down there in the TIE fighter squad room right now, relaxing, joking, and sipping cups of stim-tea with the others. Fel was unhappy with his current assignment.

For one thing, this Dreadnaught was a clunky old wagon, especially compared to the new Imperial Star Destroyers. Fel would have given a great deal to be able to command one of *those* ships!

But he was determined to do his best by the *Pride;* he just hoped he'd get the chance. Fel had studied Admiral Greelanx's battle plan, and he was not impressed. Oh, it was by the book, all right, but Fel thought the battle plan was too inflexible, too dependent on several assumptions that Fel perceived as either shaky or outright erroneous.

In the first place, Greelanx was certain that the smugglers were nothing but a disorganized rabble, who couldn't possibly mount a coordinated attack. Soontir Fel had commanded Customs patrol ships (as had Greelanx), and he knew for a fact that many of these smuggler pilots were the equal of any Imperial pilot ever graduated. They had fast reflexes, were excellent shots, and possessed a reckless courage that made them dangerous customers in a fight.

They were tough and independent, but *if* the smugglers found someone to lead them wisely, Fel thought that they might well put together a defense to be reckoned with.

Secondly, Greelanx believed that since the smugglers could not possibly pose a threat to this force, there was no point in attempting surprise. The admiral's plan called for their squadron to emerge from hyperspace well within range of Nar Shaddaa's sensors.

Fel thought that assumption amounted to overconfidence, pure and simple. And overconfidence was frequently a disaster in combat.

The worst problem, as far as Fel was concerned, was implementing order Base Delta Zero on Nar Shaddaa.

Fel knew that last wasn't Greelanx's fault. The Sector Moff had issued that order. But in the admiral's place, Fel would have at least tried to get Sarn Shild to modify that instruction. The Emperor's directive had been to shut down the smuggling operations out of Nar Shaddaa and other smuggler nests, especially the gunrunners. The directive hadn't included anything about razing the entire moon. Fel had had considerable combat experience, and he knew that sentients of most species would fight like cornered Corellian vrelts when it came to protecting their homes and families.

There were millions of sentients on Nar Shaddaa, many of whom were only peripherally involved with the smuggling business. Elderly sentients, children . . . Soontir Fel grimaced.

This would be his first Imperial-ordered massacre. He'd been lucky to avoid such an order for this long, the way things were going.

Fel would carry out his orders, but he wasn't happy about them. He knew images of the flaming buildings would haunt him, as he gave each order to fire. And afterward . . . they'd have to send down shuttles and ground troops to mop up, and he, Fel, being a conscientious commander, would have to oversee that operation.

Visions of smoking rubble strewn with blackened corpses filled his mind, and Fel took a deep breath. *Stop it,* he ordered himself sternly. *There's nothing you can do about it. Tormenting yourself over it serves no purpose . . .*

As Fel watched, the *Imperial Destiny* suddenly accelerated strongly, then vanished from sight as it engaged its hyperdrive. *Peacekeeper* followed.

Fel was relieved to have something to do, anything to distract him from his thoughts. He glanced over at his navigator. "Course laid in, Commander?"

"Yes, Captain."

"Very well. Commander Rosk, prepare to make the jump to lightspeed, on my order."

"Yes, sir."

Fell watched the coordinates flash by on the navigational boards, then said, "Engage hyperdrive."

"Yes, sir."

Fel watched as the stars suddenly elongated, and there was, for the first time, a sensation of terrible velocity aboard the big ship.

The mission to wipe out Nar Shaddaa was under way.

. . . .

Admiral Winstel Greelanx stood on the bridge of his own Dreadnaught, watching the star trails of hyperspace. The admiral had his own concerns about this mission, very different concerns from those felt by his captains, Reldo Dovlis and Soontir Fel.

Greelanx was aware that Fel did not think much of his planned strategy. Dovlis was a less imaginative, older officer, content to follow orders without question, so Greelanx expected no problems with him. Fel, on the other hand . . . there could be problems there.

Greelanx sighed. If only this mission was as cut and dried as it appeared on the surface! Go to Nar Shaddaa, wipe out the wretched smugglers, and then blockade the Y'Toub system. But it was far from being that simple.

Less than a full day after Moff Shild had called him into his office on Teth to give Greelanx his marching orders, the admiral had received a message in the most secret Imperial code, sent "eyes only" under the tightest security to Greelanx's personal comlink.

The secrecy code on this message had been so restrictive that the admiral hadn't even dared to have it decoded by one of his staff, even his top administrative aide or secretarial droid. No, he'd laboriously sat down with a code key and translated the entire thing by himself, writing it out by hand onto a sheet of flimsy.

As directed, the admiral had kept no copies of the message, destroying the flimsy as soon as he was finished reading it through.

The admiral had checked and rechecked the codes, thinking there *had* to be some mistake. But they all checked out. This message came from the very highest echelons of Imperial Intelligence. Excomm was the branch of

Imperial security that was answerable only to the Emperor himself, or to his top-ranking aide, Lord Vader.

Greelanx had never received such a message before in his career—and he had served over thirty years in the Navy.

He had memorized the message, and that was easy, for it had been short. The message had read:

Admiral Winstel Greelanx, eyes only, destroy after reading. Regarding Nar Shaddaa/Nal Hutta engagement.

You are advised for the good of your Empire to engage the enemy and suffer a strategic defeat. Minimize Imperial losses, and withdraw in good order.

Repeat: you are to LOSE, Admiral. Do not attempt to confirm these orders. Do not discuss them with anyone. If you fail to comply, no excuses will be accepted.

Do NOT fail.

What did it all mean? Greelanx wondered. Someone very high up wanted Sarn Shild's foray against the Hutts to fail. Who? And why?

Greelanx was not a particularly imaginative or intelligent man, but he was smart enough to realize that if he told Sarn Shild about those orders, he would sound like a madman. He had no proof that he had received them. The encoded message had been "time-sensitive"—impossible to copy, except manually, and designed to vanish within minutes after being downloaded.

And then had come the Hutt bribe. What a supreme irony, under the circumstances! A chance to increase his retirement nest egg by a thousandfold or more. Even if he hadn't gotten those secret orders, Greelanx would have found the Hutt offer difficult to reject.

Could the two things be related somehow? he wondered. Or was it just an incredible coincidence?

Greelanx had no way to tell.

The admiral was edgy and nervous about the entire venture. Schemes ran through his head, only to be discarded as too risky. Should he try to contact the High Command? Tell the Moff? Take the *Imperial Destiny* to some remote location, then abscond in an Imperial shuttle?

That last option seemed the most likely to ensure his continued existence. He could go to the Corporate Sector, perhaps. Somewhere far, far away.

But if he did that, Greelanx had soon realized, his family would pay for his escape. His son and daughter, his wife. Perhaps even his two mistresses.

Greelanx was not particularly fond of his wife, but he wished her no harm. And he loved his children, who were grown and married. He had a grandchild on the way.

No, the admiral decided, he could not risk them. If he'd kept the flimsy and showed it to the Moff, Greelanx knew that he'd have signed his and their death warrants. The Imperial security forces were swift and ruthless. Greelanx and his family could run to the ends of the universe, and the storm troopers would still hunt them down.

All he could do was obey, and hope for the best.

As he stood on the bridge of his ship, Admiral Winstel Greelanx thought of the young smuggler who had brought the Hutt offer. An offer he hadn't been able to refuse. Had the young man sensed there was more going on than Greelanx was telling?

He'd seemed like an intelligent young fellow. Greelanx would have been willing to bet he'd worn an Imperial uniform before. Why had he left the service to become an outlaw?

The admiral hated to think that young smuggler might be one of the sentients he'd have to kill in order to make his attack on Nar Shaddaa appear legitimate.

Greelanx watched the star trails, thinking . . . and worrying. *How did I get myself into this?* he wondered. *And how in the name of all that's sacred do I get myself out of it?*

Durga the Hutt was working in his office when a servitor droid rolled rapidly in. "Sir! Sir! The Lord Aruk has been taken ill! Please come!"

The young Hutt Lord abandoned his datapad and wriggled quickly after the droid, down endless corridors in the huge Besadii enclave. He found his parent lying limp, eyes rolled back in his head, sprawled across his repulsor sled. Aruk's personal physician, a Hutt named Grodo, was working over the unconscious Besadii leader, assisted by two med droids.

"What happened?" Durga demanded breathlessly as he undulated up to them, his tail pushing him along in long, swift glides. "Is he going to be all right?"

"We don't know yet, sir," the physician said brusquely. He was working hard over the unconscious Hutt, giving him a jab with an injector, then administering oxygen. A circulatory pump stim-unit was adhered to Aruk's midsection, automatically sending mild jolts into the massive body to keep Aruk's heartbeat regular.

Aruk's green-slimed tongue lolled limply out of his mouth. The sight terrified Durga. The young Hutt forced himself to halt several meters away, not wishing to get in the way. "He was talking to his scribe, giving an order about some work, when suddenly, as the droid reported, he just slumped over."

"What do you think caused this?" Durga said. "Should I summon security, have them seal off the palace?"

"No, sir," Grodo said. "This is the result of some kind of brain seizure, I suspect due to poor circulation. You know I have been warning your parent about—"

"Yes, yes, I remember," Durga said. In his anxiety, he grabbed the edge of a low inlaid table, and only realized he'd been twisting it when the heavy wood splintered in his hands.

Minutes later Aruk suddenly blinked, stirred, and then slowly raised himself, looking very puzzled. "What?" he croaked, his deep voice raw. "What happened?"

"You collapsed, Lord," Grodo said. "Some type of brain seizure. Caused by lack of oxygen to the brain, I suspect."

"Caused by poor circulation, no doubt," Aruk grunted. "Well . . . I feel fine, now. Except that my head is pounding."

"I can administer something mild for the pain, Lord," the physician said, triggering his injector.

Moments later Aruk sighed with relief. "Much better."

"Lord Aruk," the physician said sternly, "I want you to promise me that you will take better care of yourself. Let this episode be a warning to you."

Aruk grumbled deep in his massive chest. "At my age, I should be able to do—"

"Please, Father!" Durga blurted. "Listen to Grodo! You must mend your ways!"

The Besadii Lord grunted, then sighed. "Very well. I promise to exercise for at least half an hour each day. And I will give up smoking my hookah."

"And the rich food!" cried the physician triumphantly, seizing the moment.

"Very well," Aruk growled. "All except my favorite nala-tree frogs. I will *not* give them up."

"I believe we can allow Your Excellency one treat,"

Grodo said, now prepared to be magnanimous in light of his win. "If you give up all other rich foods, you may have a sensible amount of nala-tree frogs each day."

Durga was so relieved to see Aruk recovering that he glided right up to his parent and placed his small hand on that massive neck. "You must take care of yourself, Father. I will exercise with you. It will be more enjoyable that way."

Aruk's wide mouth turned up as he regarded his offspring. "Very well, my child. I promise I will take better care of myself."

"Besadii needs you," Durga said. "You are our greatest leader, Father!"

Aruk grumbled a bit more under his breath, but Durga could tell that he was pleased by his offspring's concern.

The young Hutt Lord left his parent to the care of the physician and his med-droid assistants, and went back to his office, badly shaken.

For a moment he'd thought that Aruk was dying, and that he would wind up trying to run Besadii all by himself. Durga had received a frightening insight—he wasn't ready.

Especially with this crisis coming, he thought. *The Imperial fleet may be on its way to attack Nar Shaddaa* . . .

Aruk had told his offspring not to worry, that the Imperials would not harm Besadii, or Ylesia. "We supply them with slaves," the elderly Hutt said reassuringly. "The Empire needs its slaves. Therefore they need Besadii."

Durga devoutly hoped that his parent was right about that . . .

Chapter Thirteen:
Making Magic

Han, Chewbacca, and Salla Zend stood together on the windswept landing platform, watching *Phantasm*'s ramp extrude from the ship. Moments later a figure with long black hair appeared and started down the ramp. Spotting Han, she waved.

"That's her, c'mon!" Han told Salla. Chewie was already loping forward, growling a friendly greeting.

"Solo!" the newcomer cried. "Chewbacca!"

"Xaverri!" Han called back, jogging toward her. It was so good to see her again!

When they reached each other, he grabbed her shoulders, but she flung her arms around him and hugged him, hard. Han hugged her back, but he carefully kissed her forehead, rather than her mouth. After Xaverri greeted Chewie with a big hug and a Wookiee head-rub, she turned back to Han and Salla. "Xaverri, I want you to meet Salla Zend," Han said as the two women stood regarding each other. "Xaverri, this is Salla, smuggler and expert mechanic."

"Hi, pleased to meet you!" Salla said, sticking out her hand.

"My pleasure," Xaverri said, shaking hands. "Any friend of Solo's is a friend of mine."

Han was vastly uncomfortable. *I've never had two girlfriends meet each other before,* he thought. The Corellian wondered whether Xaverri would want to take up their relationship where they'd left off, months before. Salla, he knew, would likely take a dim view of that.

But, hey, she doesn't own me, he thought defensively. *It's not like we're married or anything.*

Still, he was careful to walk beside Salla as he picked up Xaverri's bag and they started across the permacrete of the landing field together.

Later, over flatbread and traladon-cheese appetizers at Han's favorite Corellian eatery, he explained his plan to Xaverri.

When he'd finished, she regarded him searchingly. "Let me get this straight. You want me to create a holo-illusion of a whole bunch of smuggler vessels coming straight at these Imperial *Capital*-class ships. You want the illusion to be real enough, and last long enough, to cause the Imp vessels to be fooled into turning to fire on the fake fleet. Have I got it right?"

"That's it," Han said. As she'd detailed the plan, he'd realized just what he was asking. Xaverri had never created anything on this scale before. Probably no one had.

Xaverri shook her head, her long black hair sliding over her shoulders. "You don't ask much, do you, Solo?"

"Hey," Han said, trying to grin, "think of it as a challenge. Your greatest illusion ever!"

"Any holo-illusion requires projectors," Xaverri said. "What can we use for them?"

"I was thinking we could get all the tri-dee projectors from the casinos," Han said. "You know, the ones that they use to project shows onto the screens in the gambling areas, so people can watch the shows while they lose their shirts."

Xaverri frowned. "Maybe," she said. "But even if we could create the image of the fleet, the Imp sensors would tell them right away it was an illusion. They'd ignore it."

"Maybe we could jam their sensors?" Salla suggested. "After all, we can jam transmissions going out. Isn't there some way to jam what's going in?"

The magician was looking at the smugglers with her eyes wide. "You know something," she said, "I think I'm getting an idea . . ."

Han leaned forward. "Yeah? What?"

She sipped her drink, thinking, then replied, "I think we may be able to use the traffic-control buoys to send false data to the Imps. So they'll *see* the holo-illusion, at the same time as their sensors pick up data that tells them what they're seeing is real!"

Salla was excited. "Great! That sounds perfect!"

Xaverri smiled at her. "But I'll need help building all this. Slicers to help reprogram the traffic-control buoys, techs to build the projectors for the illusion. Do you know any good slicers and techs?"

Salla grinned back and impulsively reached out a hand. The two women clasped hands over the table. "You bet I do, Xaverri," the tall smuggler said. "Shug and I will help."

Chewbacca let out a loud, emphatic roar that caused a passing wait droid to drop a food tray and scuttle back into the kitchen.

"Chewie says, include him in, too," Han supplied the translation with a grin. "Xaverri . . . I know you probably gave up a fancy booking to come here and help us. I want you to know I—*we*—all appreciate it."

"Hey, Solo, it's a chance to hurt the Imperials," the magician said. "How could I refuse?"

When Han and Chewie arrived for the promised big briefing of their combat pilots, they found most of the smuggler pilots and crews assembled in the auditorium of The Chance Castle. Mako was already onstage, exchanging jokes and jibes with his audience. When he saw Han and Chewie, the senior smuggler rapped his knuckles on the rostrum to get his audience's attention.

"Okay, all of you, listen up!" he shouted.

Silence descended. "Listen good, you spacebums," Mako said, the pride and affection in his voice as he regarded his troops taking away any possible sting from his words. "'Cause your lives, and the lives of those you're flyin' with, may be at stake here."

Mako paused, surveying them all, seeing that he did, indeed, have their full attention.

"Here's how we're gonna pull this little trick off. We can't be sure when the Imps are going to attack, but we've got a pretty good idea of the battle plan they'll follow. That's 'cause the Imperial Navy has standard battle plans for just about any situation, and they're trained to follow them, no matter what. Old Han here used to be an Imp officer, and he'll back me up on this. Right, Han?"

Han walked out onto the stage and nodded exaggeratedly. "Mako's right!" he shouted, because his voice wasn't amplified the way Mako's was. The senior smuggler motioned to the Corellian to come over and share the podium. Han did so.

"So, the standard plan for this kind of operation has them rendezvous and deploy fairly far out. If we're lucky, we'll pick them up on our sensors. If not, we may have to scramble to get to our ships. Everyone prepared to do that?"

All the smugglers agreed, with a shout, that they were prepared.

"Good," Han said. "So they're gonna deploy, maybe fix any last-minute problems. Then the Imps should make a microjump through hyperspace, so they'll arrive pretty close to the far side of Nar Shaddaa, but well out of weapons range. By that time, we'll be in our ships and launched. Each ship is gonna go to its hiding place among the debris, or lose itself in regular space traffic. A couple of smaller fighters, like Roa in his *Lwyll*, are gonna do recon. The bigger ships will fly false transponder codes, and the fighters will be either in cargo bays of the big freighters or clamped on to their hulls. The rest of us will just be innocent little spacers, and properly panicked when the Imps zoom into view. Right, gang?"

"Yeah! Right!" they yelled, loving the idea of getting the drop on the arrogant Imperial Navy.

Mako took over again. "Okay, at that point the Imps will send in their pickets for a quick look around."

One of the captains in the front row waved a taloned paw. "What's a picket, Mako?"

Han and Mako looked at each other and sighed.

"Sorry," Mako said. "Pickets are the bigger recon ships and their recon TIE fighters, okay? We expect there will probably be two bigger recon ships, probably *Carrack*-class light cruisers. Each can carry four recon TIE fighters. Taken together, they're called the pickets. Okay?"

"Okay!" yelled the smuggler.

Mako grinned evilly. "Now, the Imps aren't expecting us

to put up any kind of organized resistance, and we don't want to disappoint them, do we, fellow sentients?"

"No!" shouted the smugglers.

"Okay, then. We want to keep the Imps where *we* want them, right?"

"Right!"

"Okay, then. To do that, we've got to show them exactly what they expect to see. That way we can predict what they'll do, because they'll follow those Imp guidelines I told you about. When the Imp Admiral sends in his recon ships and then the skirmish vessels, which will follow a few minutes behind the recon ships, he'll be expecting us to think that this is *the* big attack.

"He's going to sit back with his big *Capital*-class ships in their nice little regulation wedge, and he'll expect this disorganized band of bozos to come out fighting with everything we've got, since we're not smart enough to hold back. That Admiral is figuring we'll take the recon pickets—the *Carrack*-class vessels—and the skirmish ships—most likely customs corvettes—to make up his whole attack force."

"We'll show 'em we're not dumb!" yelled a smuggler from the back.

"That's right, we're gonna show 'em. What we're gonna do is make it look like we've thrown everything we have against the first Imp ships to cruise up to Nar Shaddaa. That'll be those recon ships and, approaching more slowly, the skirmish ships. Look here, and we'll show you."

Mako nodded at Han, and he took up the narrative, while Mako used a holographic image and pointer on the large tri-dee screen to illustrate the battle plan for their troops.

"All right," Han said, "as you can see from Mako's diagram, we're gonna split up our ships into two groups, the First Strike Element and the Main Strike Element. The First Strike Element will be all the small ships without exceptionally heavy armament, plus a couple of the merc captains with those modified Customs patrol ships. So, listen up. I'm going to read the ship and captain names of the First Strike Element, while Mako puts your names up on the display."

Han read off the list. "Okay, then. Before we're through, you people will know where you have to go, and what you have to do, and when you have to do it. What we're here for today, as we said, is to show you what part you're going to play in the Big Picture."

Mako handed Han the pointer, and then took over. "Okay, now for the Main Strike Element. That's gonna be all our big ships, plus the freighters with heavy weapons, and the starfighter squadrons. We've got six Y-wings, some Cloak-shape fighters, and assorted types of Z-95 Headhunters. Here's the list."

As Mako read off the list of the Main Strike Element, Han kept augmenting the holographic display. Soon the huge tri-dee screen in the casino auditorium looked like an elaborate pattern of different colored lines and squiggles, interspersed with three-dimensional representations of ships.

"Okay, so now you people know which Strike Element you belong to. Anyone not know?"

Several newcomers raised their hands, or paws, or tentacles, and were hastily assigned to one or the other element. Mako then went on: "The First Element will attack first, just like it sounds. Stay in the pairs we've assigned you to, please! Two ships can cover each other and are more than twice as effective as two single ships!"

Han leaned close to the podium. "And, everyone . . . watch out for the turbolasers on the Imp cruisers. They can blast you out of space with one shot. Keep your ships dodging whenever you're in range of the bigger Imp vessels. Got that?"

"Yeah!" the pilots shouted.

Mako resumed. "Remember, fellow smugglers, that mixed in with these bigger Imp recon and skirmish ships will be dozens of TIE fighters. They're fast, real fast, and they have okay lasers, but they're fragile. One good hit, and they're blown to pieces. They're too fast for a lock-on, so you'll have to shoot by eye. Take your time and lead your targets. Since most of your freighters have some weapon that can shoot behind you, use that one to keep the TIEs off you while you hit the picket ships. You with me?"

"Yeah!" the crowd yelled. "Kill those TIEs!"

"Okay, so this is still early in the battle. We're gonna hit the recon pickets with what they're going to *think* is everything we've got. With luck, we'll drive off a couple of these Imperial picket ships, kill some recon TIEs, maybe even disable one of the *Carrack*-class ships, though even Lando wouldn't bet on our chances to do *that*."

Mako paused for the general laugh this remark occasioned. Someone yelled at the young gambler, "Hey, Lando, what odds are you giving?"

Han took over again. "Somewhere in here the Imp commander will commit his lighter skirmish vessels, order them to increase to full speed and attack, 'cause he's thinking that he's seen all we've got, and now he's going in for the kill. He'll most likely hold the big cruisers back for now, saving them, planning to bring them in when he goes to strafe Nar Shaddaa. When the pickets, then the skirmish vessels, engage you, it's critically important for everyone to *stay in your assigned position!* Here's where you get your chance to hit them hard from one side to overload a shield. Then you or your partner can score some damage and then both of you get out! Those of you with missiles or torpedoes can really hurt these light Customs corvettes."

Han gave his troops a long, serious look. "Guys, by now it'll be pretty confused up there; civilian ships caught up in this'll be trying to run, and all of our lighter stuff except the fighters will be mixing it up with the Imps. Don't lose track of what's going on! Stay in position! Stay focused! Be sure to keep someone on your ship listening to the comm for instructions, in case we have to move you off your assigned positions. You got that?"

"Yeah, we got it!" came a few voices. Han put on a very shocked face and cupped his ear.

"Hey, am I gettin' old and going deaf, or what? I asked if you guys *got that*?"

"Yeah! We GOT it!" they yelled, much more forcefully.

"That's better," Mako said, taking over again. "Okay, let's move on. Frankly, fellow sentients, we're expecting you to clean up on the Imp picket and skirmish ships; we'll have the advantage of numbers and this is our home ground. We're expecting to kill at least half of them, which is gonna surprise the blazes out of that Imp Admiral. But when he gets over being shocked and upset—and has gained a little more respect for us—"

Mako paused dramatically, and the hall was filled with shouts of "Oh, *yeah*!" and "We'll teach him some *respect*!"

"We sure will!" Han yelled, then stood back to let Mako continue.

"Okay, but this Imp Admiral ain't gonna stand there with his jaw dropped for very long, I hate to tell you. No, what he's gonna do is think, 'How DARE they?' and he'll send in his heavy *Capital*-class ships. We can expect at least two or three big bulk cruisers, with maybe a Dreadnaught or two to help. These big boys will have thicker shields and armor, and more and bigger guns. Frankly, fellow sentients, we've only got a handful of ships that are even capable of challenging 'em, let alone hurting them."

A considerably sobered silence fell over their audience. Han had worried that at this point they might lose them, but nobody got up and left, much to his relief.

"But," Mako said, "here's the trick. If we can really hurt even one or two of those heavies, the Imps will almost certainly withdraw, since they won't be able to complete their job, and it's standard Imperial doctrine to cut your losses and run if you can't win."

"So how *do* we hurt them, Mako?" yelled a human smuggler.

"Good question. We've worked out a strategy that we think will do the trick. Listen closely, guys. When those big guys come at us, we'll pretend to give way. I'll pass the word over the comm to fall back between Nar Shaddaa and Nal Hutta. But by Doellin's halter, don't everyone turn in formation and zoom away the instant the Imp cruisers attack! No, we've got to make this look good, or the Imps'll get suspicious!"

"So what *do* we do?" yelled one wag—a Bothan. "Hang around and invite them over for a drink?"

Mako glared at his heckler. "Get serious, clown. What we're tellin' you to do is to fall back, but do it like it was your own idea, not following orders. Turn tail and run like terror-stricken rabble, that's just fine. We *want* them to chase you. Got that?"

"Yeah!" they yelled.

"Hey," yelled the wag, "we can fake bein' scared, specially if we *are!*"

Laughter followed.

"Okay, good," Mako said, "right around *here*"—he used the pointer to indicate a point in space close to Nar Shaddaa, on a straight line between the moon and the planet—"we're going to have our own big ships waiting. And we have a little surprise for our Imperial friends." He turned and gestured into the wings of the stage. "Xaverri, please step out here."

Xaverri came out onto the stage, dressed in a pilot's coverall. Her black hair was braided tightly to her head, and she wore little makeup. Han had suggested she wear her stage magician's costume for this part of the presentation, but she had demurred. "No, Han. If they're going to trust me and what I can do, I want to seem like one of them."

"Pilots and crews . . . I want to introduce you to Xaverri. She's the person who's going to win this battle for us. Some of you already know her. For those of you who don't know her, let me tell you that she's the best in the galaxy at what she does. What she does is make illusions. Xaverri?"

With a graceful wave of her hand, Xaverri suddenly made the lights in the auditorium flicker, then, without warning, the air was filled with Kayven whistlers. The trick was part of her act, but even Han, who was expecting it, had trouble not ducking when one of the vicious flying creatures swooped directly at his head.

The audience of smugglers yelled and ducked, then when Xaverri made the whistlers disappear with a second wave of her hand, they broke into spontaneous applause.

Mako led the crowd in clapping and stomping his feet in appreciation. Xaverri stood there, smiling serenely, but not taking a bow.

"She's good, guys," Mako said. "And just for us, Xaverri is going to create her masterpiece. When we've got the big Imp ships *here,* where we want them"—he pointed to the spot again—"Xaverri is going to create the illusion that a really big fleet is coming at the Imps from the direction of Nal Hutta. Then, when the Imp ships turn to fire their forward guns at this phantom fleet, that's when we'll hit 'em in the flank and from the rear with everything we've got!"

Cheering broke out from the crowd.

Han stepped forward when the noise died down. "Just to let you know, Captain Renthal and her big ships will be waiting with Mako and the Main Strike Element. Captain Renthal"—he turned and extended a hand to her where she sat in the front row, a big, squarish woman with pale skin and close-cropped red-and-gold-striped hair—"please stand up."

The smugglers clapped for her, too, which was surprising, because some of them had undoubtedly run afoul of *Renthal's Fist* or other ships in her pirate fleet.

"Captain Renthal, your big ships will have to clear the path for your Y-wings, and our fighters and strike ships. Any of the smaller Imp cruisers between our force and the flanks of those *Capital*-class ships will be your target. Your heavy turbolasers and proton torpedoes must knock them out. We can't make a run on heavy cruisers if we're having to dodge fire from too many directions at once," Mako said, for the benefit of the audience. He and Han had already gone over every part of the battle plan with Renthal many times.

Drea Renthal nodded. "I'll do my part," she said, in a clear, strong alto. "I was hired to keep the Imps from getting near Nal Hutta. After seeing your battle plan, I agree that this is the best way to accomplish that." She turned to face the smugglers. "So you can count on me and my fleet to fight with you all the way!"

More cheers. Renthal pumped her fist in the air, and the crowd went wild.

"Okay," Han continued when the noise had died down a bit, "the fighters without missiles or torpedoes will serve as escorts. You guys have *got* to keep those TIEs off us while we make our run." The Corellian waved at the remainder of the smugglers. "The rest of us will go in and target one or two of the heavy cruisers. When the time comes, Mako will give you your orders. We'll have to get in as close as we can to their rear and then let them have it with a concentrated volley right into the engines. Don't hold back, let them have every bit of firepower you've got!"

Cheers broke out again from the crowd. Obviously, the realization that they'd have help from Xaverri's illusion, and a well-armed pirate fleet, had lifted the smugglers' spirits.

"Okay, fellow sentients," Mako said, "one more thing. If what we're tryin' for here works, you *clear out fast!* Those cruisers make a pretty big explosion. You don't want to get caught in it, right?"

"Right!" they roared.

"And . . ." Mako finished up, "if this doesn't work . . ." He shrugged. "Well, we'll just have to keep trying. It's not like *we* can just give up and go away."

The crowd regarded him, alert but sobered by his final words.

Han stepped back up to the podium. "Okay," he said. "That's the plan. We'll go over it until you've got it down pat. Any questions?"

To Han's amazement, over the next several days, Xaverri and Salla became the best of friends. He and Mako were busy staging repeated battle drills for their pilots and crews on the Nar Shaddaa defense squadron, so he didn't have much time to hang out at Shug's spacebarn, but every time he did go there, he found Salla and Xaverri working together on creating the illusionist's "masterpiece."

"It'll only be good for about a two- or three-minute distraction, Solo," Xaverri warned. "They're going to see these ships swooping at them, real close, and they're going to see data that corresponds to their visual sightings appear on their instrument panels. But I want these ships to appear *close*, so their reaction will be to turn all their vessels to bring their forward guns into play. That makes them vulnerable to your flank attack."

Xaverri took a sip from a cup of stim-tea Han had brewed for Shug, Salla, Chewie, Jarik, and the other technician volunteers who were working on making Xaverri's illusion a "reality." "*But* these ships are going to appear such a threat because they're going to be *close*. Within a couple of minutes, when the Imps realize that none of them has been hit by the blasts they're seeing emanate from those ships, they'll realize it's a fake."

Han nodded. "A minute or three is all we can ask for, Xaverri. We'll be really grateful for that diversion. We've contacted the pirate captain the Hutts hired. Drea Renthal. Her flagship, *Renthal's Fist*, is gonna be hiding 'behind' Nar Shaddaa—that is, on the Nal Hutta side of the moon—along with the rest of her fleet. When those *Capital*-class ships come swinging around the moon, then turn to face your illusionary fleet, she and Mako are going to hit them hard."

Jarik Solo wiped tiredly at his dirty face with an even filthier hand. "Han, what's the strength of that merc fleet? Are they gonna be much help?"

Han nodded. "Yeah, Jarik. *Renthal's Fist* is a Corellian corvette. She's heavily modified, and heavily armed. Even has proton torpedo launchers in the front. Only problem is, they don't have many torpedoes. Renthal can't afford to miss."

"How many other ships?" Xaverri wanted to know.

"Renthal also has a bulk freighter, *Golden Dreams*, that's been converted to carry fighters. SoroSuub medium transport. Big ship. Not much shielding, though. She'll launch her Z-95 Headhunters, then hang back, letting *Renthal's Fist* carry the attack. Then there's the *Too Late Now* and the *Minestra*. *Too Late Now* is a captured Imp patrol craft. Renthal replaced one of the laser turrets with an ion cannon, so hopefully she can knock out some of those bulk cruisers. *Minestra* is a Rendili Stardrive light corvette. Nice ship, modified so she has concussion missiles and ion cannons to go with her laser turrets."

"That sounds like a pretty good force to me," Xaverri said. "Of course, I barely know the difference between an ion cannon and a concussion missile."

"When I first started smuggling, I barely did, too," Salla said with a laugh. "But when the Imp patrols start *shooting* at you with 'em, you find yourself getting real knowledgeable real fast."

The two women smiled at each other. Han still couldn't get over how quickly they'd become friends. To tell the truth, he was a bit jealous. In many ways, Salla and Xaverri seemed closer to each other than either woman had ever been to *him*. He wondered whether they'd ever talked to each other about him. Compared notes, maybe?

The thought made his face redden. Jarik provided a welcome distraction. "Hey, Han . . . can I talk to you a minute?"

Han gulped the last of his stim-tea and stood up. "Sure, Jarik. Want to go into Shug's office so we can be out of the way?"

"Yeah," the youth said. "If we try to talk here, someone will run over us with an anti-grav lifter or something!"

The spacebarn was a hive of activity. Everywhere smugglers were fixing up their ships, in some cases modifying them, trying to squeeze extra speed out of their engines, or adding an extra quad laser or missile launcher.

Han and Jarik walked by Salla's *Rimrunner,* and waved to Shug when he raised his face shield to wipe his sweating face. Han stopped to cup his hands around his mouth and shouted up at the master mechanic. "Looks good, Shug! You and Salla are sure gonna give those Imps a rude surprise!"

Whenever they weren't working on helping Xaverri create her master illusion, Salla and Shug, with Rik Duel's help, had been modifying *Rimrunner,* installing a pair of camouflaged concussion missile launchers in the stern. Salla's smuggling ship was a CorelliSpace *Gymsnor-4*-class light freighter and, like virtually every smuggling ship in the business, was heavily modified. The ship looked rather like a flying wing or—if you wanted to be insulting and gain a punch in the nose from Salla—a mynock. *Rimrunner* was a fast, agile ship, and Salla was an excellent pilot. Han was counting heavily on her during the coming battle.

He knew that Salla would be in a much better position to do serious damage to the Imperial ships than *he* would. The *Bria* was a decent little ship, but nowhere near as fast as the *Millennium Falcon* or the *Rimrunner.* She was more lightly armed, too.

When Han and Jarik reached Shug's office, they had to clear several odds and ends of greasy equipment off the chairs before they could sit down. Once they were comfortable, Han sighed. "Glad you wanted to have a talk, kid. This is the first time I've sat down all day, seems like. Organizing this battle has kept me and Mako hopping."

"Yeah, I've been busy, too," Jarik said. "When I wasn't busy helping the Lady Xaverri, I've been helping Chewie with the *Bria,* or Shug with the *Rimrunner.*"

"Shug tells me you're gettin' to be a pretty good mechanic, Jarik," Han said. "And you're becoming a decent pilot and gunner. I'm going to be glad to have you flying with me as a gunner. Chewie's good, but two gunners are more than twice as good as one."

"Han . . . that's . . . that's what I wanted to talk to you about." Jarik's handsome young features were shadowed. "I . . . I've never been in a battle before." He swallowed. "Last night, I fell asleep while I was cleaning carbon scoring off the *Bria,* and I . . . I had this dream. Nightmare, really."

"Yeah? What about?"

"I dreamed we were fighting the Imperials, and"—he swallowed—"Han . . . we got blown up. I had a TIE in my sights, and I . . . I froze. I didn't shoot. And then I saw the streak of green from the laser blast coming straight at me, and there was nothing I could *do*. I dreamed that I . . . died."

Jarik's face worked. He shivered. "Han . . . I'm scared. I don't know if I've got what it takes. What if I mess up, and get us all killed, the way I did in my dream?"

"Jarik," Han said, "if you *weren't* scared, I'd be worried about you. The first time I went into real combat, as a TIE pilot, I was so scared I nearly upchucked in my helmet. Fortunately, I was already strapped in my cockpit, in vacuum, so I knew that if I did that, I'd choke and die. So I managed to hold it back. Then someone shot at me, and without even thinkin' about it, I found myself shootin' back. The training just . . . took over."

"Really?" Jarik looked as though he didn't know whether to find Han's story reassuring or not. "But, Han . . . everyone says you're brave. It's the first thing they say about you—'He's got courage!' Nobody ever told me I had courage. What if I'm a coward? How can I risk letting you all down?"

Han gave the youth a long, measuring look. "Jarik, you're facin' something that we all have to face. We're not citizens here on Nar Shaddaa. We live outside the law, and that's dangerous, by definition. Cowards don't make it here on Nar Shaddaa. They get eaten alive."

"Well, yeah, I can handle myself with a vibroblade or in a fistfight," Jarik allowed. "But that's not the same thing as just being blown to atoms. Boom, and you're history."

"Kid, I've watched you, and I can only tell you that I think you've got what it takes. Yeah, people *do* freeze sometimes in battle. But that's why Mako and I have been gettin' everyone out in their ships for all these battle drills."

Han shrugged. "We did the same thing when I was with the Imps. You drill and you drill, and the reason for that is that *anyone* can freeze when faced with real combat. Even combat vets. But if you know the drill cold, chances are that even if your *brain* freezes, your hands and body *won't*. They'll go on autopilot, keep on doing what you've been drilled to do, even though your mind ain't giving 'em instructions for a few seconds.

"But then, if you've drilled well, and know your stuff cold—and, kid, you *know* your stuff, I've watched you—then your brain is gonna click back in. The fear will still be there, but you'll be able to work past it, around it. It won't slow you down anymore. You'll just keep on doing what you gotta do. And you'll be all right."

Jarik wet his lips. "But . . . what if I don't? Maybe you should get another gunner, Han. I'd rather die than let you down."

"If you want me to, I will, kid," Han said. "But I'd rather have you. I know you, we work well together. We've drilled together. But it's your decision. Just let me know, okay?"

The youth nodded. "Thanks. I'll . . . think . . . about it."

Han gave him a pat on the shoulder as he walked by. "Get some sleep, kid. We're all gettin' a little worn down."

Jarik gave the Corellian a wan smile. "Okay, Han."

Lando Calrissian hated getting dirty, but he was growing accustomed to it. Readying the *Millennium Falcon* for serious combat was a grimy, greasy job, but somebody had to do it. Last week, Shug had helped him find and install a "new" gun turret on the *Falcon's* starboard side, aft of the cockpit, just above the boarding ramp. But there was still a lot to do. Han, Chewie, and Salla would have helped him, he knew that, but they were tied up either helping Xaverri prepare her holo-illusion, or fixing up their own ships.

Lando gathered that Xaverri and Han were a thing of the past. As he used a hydrospanner to tighten up the bolts on the new quad laser mounting, the young gambler found himself thinking about Xaverri. She was certainly a very fine woman, intelligent, attractive, sharp dresser, good sense of humor—all qualities Lando found irresistible. He wondered whether she'd have any interest in taking up with him where she and the Corellian had left off. It was obvious that she liked rogues and scoundrels, or she'd never have had a relationship with the Corellian.

Maybe I should try growing a mustache, Lando thought. *Might give me a . . . rakish . . . air.* The corners of the gambler's mouth curved upward. Perhaps Xaverri would be interested in traveling with him, when this was all over.

Lando was considering going back to the Oseon system. He had a couple of moneymaking schemes he wanted to try. And he needed to sharpen his already considerable sabacc skills. There was a big high-stakes sabacc championship scheduled to be played on Bespin's Cloud City in about six months. Lando very much wanted to play in that championship. But he'd need to raise a considerable stake to qualify, and the easiest, quickest way to do that was to head back for the Oseon. Things were looser there . . .

And it would be very agreeable, Lando decided, to have a lovely lady traveling companion.

Only problem was . . . was Xaverri still in love with Han? And how would Han feel about having his former girlfriend take up with his best buddy?

Well, Lando amended, his best *human* buddy. Han's best friend was indubitably Chewbacca . . .

Immersed in fantasies of himself and Xaverri wining and dining in the finest resorts of the Oseon system, Lando managed to whack the knuckles of his other hand with the

hydrospanner. Cursing, he started to suck the injured dig-
its, but his hand was so dirty, he desisted.

"Master?" Vuffi Raa said, emerging from beneath the
Falcon's belly. The little droid carried various tools in each
of his five-armed, tentacle-digited limbs. Its single red eye
stared up at Lando. "Master, what happened?"

Still wishing he could suck his injured knuckle, Lando
gritted, "Vuffi Raa, how many times have I told you not to
call me 'Master'!"

"Five hundred and sixty-two times, Master," replied the
little droid promptly.

Lando snarled. "I just whacked my knuckle, that's all,
you little junkheap. I'll be all right. Let's get back to work.
We have to have the *Falcon* spaceworthy by tonight. Mako's
calling for another drill."

"Very well," Vuffi Raa said.

"Hey, Vuffi Raa?" Lando called.

Already on his way back under the ship, the little droid
paused. "Yes, Master?"

Lando let the title slide this time. "Are you sure you're
going to be okay piloting the *Falcon* during this battle?"

"It will strain my circuitry, Master, because, as you
know, I am programmed not to cause harm to living—
especially sentient—beings. However, since you will be the
one doing the shooting, I believe I can manage to fly. Just
don't order me to ram another vessel. Then I will be unable
to comply."

"I should hope not!" Lando exclaimed. "All right, little
vacuum cleaner, back to work."

"Yes, Master."

Han and Mako had told almost no one the actual time
that Greelanx was planning to attack. Some of the smuggler
"High Command" knew that Han and Mako knew the tim-

ing of the operation, but they accepted the two ex-Imperials' decision that it would be better for most of the smugglers not to know.

Lando, Shug, Salla, Rik Duel, Blue, and Jarik . . . all of them were aware that one of the times they went out on a drill, it would wind up being the real thing. The other smugglers did not know.

Han and Mako had to be careful in drilling their troops. They didn't want the smugglers to get bored and lax, which might happen if they drilled too much. On the other hand, they knew that their smuggler squadron would need lots of practice. The key to having a fighting chance to defeat the Imperial fleet was for the smugglers to stick with the battle plan Mako and Han had devised.

The smugglers of Nar Shaddaa were all rugged individualists, unused to doing anything as part of a large, orchestrated group. "It's like tryin' to herd vro-cats," Han told Xaverri wearily. "They keep thinkin' they know better, and they want to question every blasted decision we make. What a pain in the rear!"

"Yes, but the last time you called a formation drill," Xaverri pointed out, trying to encourage him, "they got into position and made their runs in one-third of the time it took them to do it the first time."

"Yeah," Han agreed with a noticeable lack of enthusiasm. He sighed. "But it's giving me gray hairs, honey."

She grinned, and pretended to inspect his scalp. His hair was still very short from his visit to Admiral Greelanx. "Nope," she announced, after a minute, "I don't see any."

He grinned back at her tiredly. "Well, I got gray hairs growin' internally, then."

She patted his hand. "Don't worry, Solo. We'll get through this."

"I hope so," he said. "And, Xaverri, honey?"

"Yes?"

"I want to thank you for comin' here to help us. Without you, we wouldn't have a chance."

She gave him a roguish smile. "I wouldn't have missed it for anything. Just meeting Salla has made it all worthwhile."

"Yeah, I noticed that you two have gotten real chummy," Han said warily. "So . . . what *do* you two talk about while you're laughin' and workin' together, anyhow?"

She chuckled. "You egotistical spacebum, Solo! You think we're talking about *you,* don't you?"

Han shook his head. "Me? Of course not!"

"Oh, yes, you do!" She laughed at his discomfiture. "Admit it, Solo!"

Han steadfastly refused to admit it. But inwardly he was wondering when this was all over, if he'd be able to take up with Salla where they'd left off. He'd seen Lando eyeing both Xaverri and Salla, and he knew Calrissian wouldn't hesitate to move in on her if he thought Salla was looking around.

Did Salla really care about him? The way Xaverri and Bria had? He didn't know. They never talked about that kind of thing. They had fun, good times, and they worked well together. Any discussion of inner feelings or a future together had never come up, by, Han suspected, mutual consent.

How did *he* feel about Salla, anyway?

Han wasn't sure. Most of the time he was too busy to give the subject any consideration. He knew for a fact that he wasn't ready to do what Roa was doing . . .

As he was sitting there in Shug's spacebarn, Chewie came over to him and growled a reminder. Han looked up. "Oh! The briefing? I lost track of time!"

Quickly he and the Wookiee hastened back to The Chance Castle to the auditorium. Time for another run-through, so they could make sure each smuggler understood his, her, or its role in their strategy . . .

Two hours later Han caught up with Shug Ninx as the smugglers filed out of the auditorium. The half-blood was walking with Salla Zend. When Han caught up with them, Salla grabbed Han's arm and squeezed it, then gave him a kiss on the cheek. "You were great," she said. "You're always great, Han. I swear, you're a natural leader."

The Corellian grinned, a little abashed. "Who, me?"

They walked out, and Shug said, "When's the next drill?"

"Don't know," Han lied. "Mako will call this one. Is the *Rimrunner* ready? The holo-projectors in place? The traffic buoys ready?"

"Ready," Shug confirmed. "I tell you, Han, when this is all over, if I'm not dead, I'm going to sleep for a week."

Salla punched her friend's arm. "Don't talk like that, it's bad luck!"

"Did you find a rear gunner?" Han asked.

"Yeah, Rik volunteered to handle those rear missile launchers," Salla said. "He says he's a good gunner."

"He's right," Han said. "But . . . don't leave him alone in your ship, loan him money, or give him the security access codes to *anything* you value, okay?"

Salla grinned. "Yeah, we've been warned about him. Light-fingered even with his own kind, right?"

"That's putting it mildly," Han said. "Did I tell you we've got some good news?"

"No, what?"

"Mako had been planning to command the resistance from *Renthal's Fist*. But a couple of days ago we realized we'd got lucky. Guess who got so wrapped up in motherhood that she forgot to send a pilot to bring her yacht back to Nal Hutta? And guess whose calls to her favorite pilots have somehow failed to go through, because communications between Nal Hutta and Nar Shaddaa are so over-loaded these days?"

Salla began to grin. "You mean the *Dragon Pearl* is still here?"

"Yeah. And unlike her nephew, Jabba, Jiliac's conscientious about keeping her combat-ready. She's got six Head-hunters, and we've checked 'em out. All in prime working order. We've got pilots for 'em, too. Plus a gunnery crew for Mako, and we talked Blue into piloting. Her ship is too slow to help us out much, but she's a good pilot, too good to be wasted. That way Mako can concentrate on his tactical screens, keepin' track of everything."

Shug whistled softly. "That yacht will be a big help. Not too great on armor, but nice weaponry and good shields."

"But if it gets shot up, Jiliac is going to have somebody's hide for a wall decoration . . ." Salla mused. "I guess we have to take the chance, though. We need every bit of firepower we have."

"Well, we're keepin' it quiet about who is actually gonna be aboard *Dragon Pearl*," Han said. "And if Mako has to take a nice long vacation on Smuggler's Run while Jiliac gets over it, he says he's prepared to do that." He grinned. "Blue promised him she'd make his stay . . . interesting."

Shug shook his head, and Salla snorted. "I'll just bet she will!"

Clad in a pilot's pressurized flight suit, Roa stood on the permacrete of the landing pad, looking down at the beautiful blond woman who stood before him, tears in her eyes. "Take it easy, Lwyll," he said. "Don't worry. I'll be careful."

"Please . . ." she said, clutching his forearms with her hands, "please come back to me, Roa. Life wouldn't be worth much without you."

"I promise I'll come back," the older smuggler vowed.

"The *Lwyll* is a good ship. She'll take care of me, just like *you* would. That's why I named her that."

He leaned over and gave her a kiss. "Besides, this is just another drill, honey. You've come out here and kissed me good-bye eight times now, and I've always been back within half an hour or so. This is just like that."

She nodded, but a tear broke loose and slid down her cheek. "I love you, Roa."

"And I love you, Lwyll. I'm coming back, honey. I'm going to go straight. And we're going to get married. You'll see. It'll be all right."

She nodded. "Okay. You'd better go."

"Right. Don't want to be late for the drill!"

Grinning, Roa hoisted his stocky form up into the cockpit of the *Lwyll*, a modified *Redthorn*-class scoutship, fast and maneuverable, but lightly armed with only forward-firing triple lasers. The little ship looked like a needle-pointed cylinder, with a stubby delta wing. Almost as fast as a TIE fighter, the *Lwyll* possessed an overwhelming advantage in a dogfight—she had shields.

Roa looked down at his bride-to-be, standing on the permacrete, waving to him, and he grinned down at her, then gave her a thumbs-up sign.

Then he checked his instruments, strapped himself in, and put on his helmet. In order to achieve maximum speed and power to his weaponry, he'd elected to forgo diverting power to life support.

Easing forward on the throttle, then activating the belly thrusters, he sent his little ship climbing, climbing, up and away. Glancing down, he tried to make out Lwyll's bright head, but she was lost in the distance.

Quickly Roa headed out for his assigned coordinates. He was one of the few pilots who was not assigned to fly with a partner. His assignment was to use the *Lwyll*'s fast speed to reconnoiter the movements of the Imperial fleet. He had a special channel that allowed him to report back to Mako.

As the atmosphere thinned around him, and the sky changed from blue-gray to cobalt, then to black, speckled with stars, Roa relaxed. He'd always loved to fly, and the *Lwyll* was a joy to handle, quick and responsive.

Roa headed for his assigned coordinates, swooping past the limb of Nar Shaddaa, and reached them in only a few minutes' flight time. As he approached his station, he anticipated hearing his headphones come to life with Mako's message that he'd heard so often before: "All ships, return to base. This was a drill. All ships return to base after completing your drill . . ."

Seconds later, as expected, the aging smuggler heard Mako's voice: "Attention. Attention. All you spacebums, listen up. This is it. The Imps have appeared on our sensors. This is it. This is not a drill. Repeat, *not* a drill. This is the real thing, kiddies. Prepare to engage the enemy."

Roa's eyes widened. *Huh? Not a drill?*

As Mako's voice faded from his hearing, Roa stared, taut with fear, as the Imperial vessels popped out of hyperspace . . .

Chapter Fourteen:

The Battle of Nar Shaddaa

The first thing Admiral Winstel Greelanx saw when *Imperial Destiny* emerged from its hyperspace microjump was a small scoutship turning tail and racing frantically away from him. The Admiral smiled dryly. *I expect I'll see a lot of that today . . .*

The thought depressed him. It was going to be very difficult to manage to lose to this disorganized rabble. How in the galaxy was he going to manage it?

"Sir, the squadron has emerged from hyperspace," his second-in-command, Commander Jelon, informed him.

Habit took over, and Greelanx found himself issuing orders automatically. "Order the squadron to deploy."

Greelanx knew what was happening, and did not bother

to watch. The seven *Capital*-class ships arranged themselves into Greelanx's stipulated fighting wedge—with the *Destiny* as the point of the wedge. Then came two bulk cruisers, *Arrestor* and *Liquidator*, followed by the *Peacekeeper* and *Pride of the Senate*. The last two bulk cruisers, *Enforcer* and *Inexorable*, brought up the rear. The Dreadnaughts launched their TIE fighters, which moved to surround the wedge.

The two recon *Carrack*-class ships, *Vigilance* and *Outpost*, moved out in front of the squadron and launched their recon TIE fighters. The sixteen skirmish ships, *Guardian*-class Customs corvettes, were already in their shell-torus formation, ready to block any escape from the Smuggler's Moon.

It all happened quickly and smoothly, without a hitch. Greelanx had drilled his commanders well on every point of his battle plan.

"Admiral, sir, the squadron has been deployed as ordered," announced Jelon, scant minutes later.

"Very well. Order the squadron to proceed as planned."

"Yes, Admiral."

The squadron moved forward at the specified speeds, with the pickets advancing on Nar Shaddaa at flank speed, the skirmish line advancing at cruising speed, and the capital ships advancing at flank speed.

Greelanx stared through the viewport of the bridge, then checked the long-range scanners, seeing that the moon Nar Shaddaa was surrounded by hundreds, perhaps thousands, of pieces of debris. He wouldn't be able to take his *Capital*-class ships through that sargasso, especially if the smugglers put up any resistance. When they reached the moon's vicinity, he'd have to order them to alter their straight-on approach to swing wide of the floating debris.

Greelanx stood with his hands behind him, seeing the minuscule dot on the tactical "repeater" display that represented that tiny, panic-stricken vessel he'd first seen. As the little scoutship approached the floating debris, two other small ships, freighters at a guess, joined it in its panicked flight.

The admiral sighed. His battle plan called for the entire engagement to be over in less than fifteen minutes. He had better get busy, figuring out how he was going to manage to lose . . .

For the first minute or so, it was all Roa could do not to panic and flee into hyperspace. The sight of the Imperial squadron emerging from hyperspace had rattled him badly. Even though he'd known, intellectually, that the Imperial squadron was going to contain dozens of ships, some of them so huge they dwarfed any ship he'd ever flown, that hadn't prepared him for nearly flying right down their throats.

Almost without knowing he'd done it, Roa found himself turned around and heading back for Nar Shaddaa at top speed. He forced himself to take several deep breaths, and fought back the fear. The drill came back to him as the *Lwyll* streaked along. *Report in. I have to report contact. I'm a scoutship, remember?*

He activated his comm on the special coded frequency they'd rigged. "Defender Central, this is *Lwyll*. Come in, Central."

Mako's voice in his helmet. "We read you, *Lwyll*. Have you spotted them?"

"Affirmative, Central." Roa checked his sensors and rear tactical display. "They are deployed, and advancing."

"Good, that's what we want, remember. Just keep leading them in. Cut your speed a little, if you can do it without giving yourself away, Roa. I'm sending *Elegant Interlude* and *Star Traveler* out to help you lead at least one of those pickets to where we want it."

"I read you, Central."

Roa slowed down a bit, making sure to do it gradually. He was startled at how quickly the *Carrack*-class vessels were approaching. *Fast ships!* He was glad Mako had assigned the two ships he had to help out. Both were speedy vessels, and Danith Jalay and Renna Strego were experienced captains.

He took a deep breath. The fear was still there, deep down somewhere, but it no longer threatened his thinking processes.

Settling deep into his seat, Roa concentrated on the task at hand.

On the bridge of the *Dragon Pearl*, Mako Spince watched the sensors and tactical readouts, hardly daring to blink. The *Pearl* was too large to actually hide amid the floating hulks and debris, the way some of the smaller vessels could, but he'd ordered Blue to position her so that the *Carrack*-class ships wouldn't spot her until they had the Imp vessels where they wanted them.

Mako saw that one *Carrack*-class ship, the *Outpost*, had altered course to approach the other side of Nar Shaddaa, while the *Vigilance* continued toward the ambush. That made sense, since Greelanx couldn't know where the smugglers would engage him. Once the smuggler attack began, the *Outpost* would probably just wait there, rather than engaging, ready to report on and possibly engage any smuggler ships attempting to escape the Imperial attack.

The other *Carrack*-class, the one whose ship ID broadcast identified her as the *Vigilance*, continued to move toward his position.

Almost there, Mako thought, wiping his sweating palms on his trousers. *Almost . . .*

Falan Iniro was a Corellian, and his friends frequently told him he was hotheaded and impulsive. Iniro would counter this criticism by pointing out that his quickness to act was usually a virtue, often giving him the jump on the sweetest deal, the finest cargo, the best sabacc hand.

Now, aboard his modified *YT-1210*-class light freighter, the *Take That!*, Iniro chafed at the waiting. *Blast it,* he thought, *what's going on?*

It was frustrating, having to hide here in the shadow of a wrecked freighter, grappled to its side by a magnetic claw. Iniro checked his instruments again, and this time, something caught his attention. Something really *big* was moving toward them. Close, really close.

It has to be one of them, Iniro thought. He wished for a moment that he'd installed new sensors, modern ones with better ID capability. Aloud he said to his gunner, a Rodian named Gadaf, "Hey, Gadaf, I got something on the sensors. Get ready to shoot."

"Okay, Captain," the Rodian said. "Standing by."

Some of the other smugglers had commented that they thought the *Take That!* was too lightly armed to go against an Imperial ship, but Falan Iniro was convinced that his piloting skills—which were considerable—would more than make up for the fact that he had only a single laser, mounted in a turret on the top of the ship.

"I just wish . . ." the Rodian's voice reached him, sounding wistful.

"You wish what?"

"That we'd had time to calibrate the sights on this laser, boss. I keep having to compensate for it. It's firing consistently to the right."

Iniro was not sympathetic. "That's easy to compensate for, Gadaf. I score hits with that laser all the time."

"Yes, I know, boss," the Rodian said. "I don't do too bad, either."

"Huh . . ." Irritated, Iniro fidgeted. *When are we going to get our blasted orders?*

The something big—whatever it was—had moved almost past the *Take That!* on Iniro's sensors.

Come on, come on! What are you—

Iniro's body went rigid as he heard a voice in his headphones. Mako Spince's voice, garbled by distance and intervening space debris, but still recognizable. "First Strike Element, this is Defender Central. Prepare to—"

Iniro let out a whoop, and realized that he hadn't quite caught that last word. "Engage," wasn't it? He was pretty sure.

For a moment he thought of keying his comm and asking, "Say again, Central," but he didn't. The other guys would laugh at him, and he'd get left behind as they attacked!

"Let's go!" he yelled, and disengaged his magnetic grapple.

Swooping out from behind the hunk of space junk, Iniro saw that there were two other ships with him. Only two? Where in the name of Xendor's Minions were the others?

Iniro didn't have time to wonder, because almost immediately he found himself under attack. Some kind of TIE fighter.

A blast struck his forward shield. Iniro compensated, and felt the ship shudder as Gadaf shot at the TIE. Clean miss, too far to the left.

Overcompensated, the fool!! Iniro thought. He sent the *Take That!* into a sweeping turn, pouring on all the power he could. "Get him, Gadaf!" he yelled.

A red bolt streaked out, barely missed the twisting, turning TIE.

Iniro swore, and gave chase. It wasn't easy, here in this junkyard of space debris. He was constantly having to flip his vessel up on her side, or resort to other, even more drastic maneuvers, to avoid crashing into something.

"Clear shot . . . coming!" yelled Iniro. "Be . . . ready!"

As he had promised, the next instant the TIE fighter and the *Take That!* were in a straight line with nothing in between them. Another red bolt tore through vacuum, and this time it impaled the recon TIE fighter dead center!

For a moment the explosion flared out, yellow, then white, expanding, expanding . . .

Then the TIE was gone, and there were only sparkles of blazing debris and ash drifting in vacuum . . .

But before Iniro could celebrate his victory, his eye was caught by his tactical display. The something *big* was closing on him! In a second it would be right on top of him!

Captain Iniro twisted frantically in his pilot's seat, slapping his controls, trying desperately to evade, trying to see it. He caught just a glimpse out of the corner of his eye. *Minions of Xendor, it's so—*

Falan Iniro never had time to complete the thought. The *Carrack*-class light cruiser's heavy turbolasers engulfed the little freighter in a wash of green fire, utterly obliterating the *Take That!* in less time than it takes for a human eyeblink.

Ten seconds later not even spacedust remained.

Within seconds of following Falan Iniro's *Take That!* out of hiding, Niev Jaub knew that he'd made a terrible mistake. The little Sullustan was flying his small light freighter (modified, of course), the *Bnef Nlle,* and when he'd seen the *Take That!* blast out of hiding, he'd assumed he'd missed Mako's order, and followed the other vessel. The moment he was out in the "open," Jaub noted that only one other ship was with them. They'd obviously jumped the gun and the attack hadn't started yet.

For a moment Jaub considered trying to swoop back and hide again, but it was too late. A green blast from a TIE fighter nearly singed his whiskers. Jaub sent his small freighter (which rather resembled one of the shelled reptiles of his homeworld) skittering to his right in an evasive maneuver.

Unlike most of the defenders of Nar Shaddaa, Jaub was an honest trader, who happened to do business on the Smuggler's Moon, delivering exotic foodstuffs to the once-elegant hotel-casinos. There was a sizable Sullustan enclave on Nar Shaddaa, and the little sentient had kin and friends living there. So, when Mako's call for help had gone out, Jaub had figured it was his responsibility to respond. He couldn't let his friends and family be injured, and not try to help them!

Now what? he wondered, firing at a TIE fighter. *I can't compete with these pilots! I've never even fired my weapons before, except in target practice!*

But there was no turning back now. The *Carrack*-class light cruiser had entered the fray. Jaub's already huge eyes went even wider as he saw the *Take That!* impaled in a green burst of turbolaser fire.

Sickened, he watched as the Corellian's ship was vaporized.

If Jaub had thought he could outrun any of these ships, he might have tried. But he knew better. All he could try to do, he figured, was to stay alive and maybe get in a lucky shot. Mako was bound to order the real attack any second now!

Jaub zigged again as a TIE roared by him, seemingly out

of nowhere. The evasive maneuver brought him within range of the *Carrick*-class ship's turbolasers. The Sullustan pilot squeaked in utter terror as the barest edge of green licked past his vessel.

I'm all right, he didn't hit me, he didn't hit me, he didn't . . . oh, gods . . . he hit me . . . the Sullustan thought.

His power indicators were dropping. That blast had barely brushed him, but it must have wiped out his stern shields and disabled his engines. The *Bnef Nlle* was still hurtling along, still in the grip of inertia, but his engines were dead.

Jaub tested his maneuvering thrusters and realized they still functioned. He couldn't brake, or speed up, but he *could* turn his vessel.

He looked around, saw that two TIEs were bearing down on him from the rear. In seconds, they'd catch him and blast him into atoms.

The *Carrack*-class ship was obviously content not to have to waste its heavy turbolasers on the likes of one small, crippled freighter. The big Imperial ship was sailing serenely along, parallel to and a little behind Jaub's flight path.

Seconds . . . I've got only seconds. Make them count, Jaub thought. He didn't think of himself as particularly brave, but Sullustans were known to be a practical species.

Jaub sent his ship rolling over, using his maneuvering thrusters hard, deliberately sending the *Bnef Nlle* into an uncontrollable spin. Stars and space debris revolved in his viewport, making his stomach flip over.

"Bnef nlle, everyone!" he screamed as he hurtled toward the flank of the *Carrack*-class ship.

"Bnef nlle" meant "good luck" in Sullustan.

At first Jaub thought he wasn't going to make it, that the *Carrack*-class vessel was going too fast—but then he had one final second to realize that he was, indeed, going to impact against the big vessel's port shields.

Joy filled him, and then there was nothing but fire . . .

"Blasted, stupid *fools*! Why didn't they wait for my order?" Mako shouted as he stared into his tactical screen. *Why did they jump the gun?*

Maybe they'd misunderstood him. Mako had said, "Prepare to evade," and just as he finished speaking, those three impetuous freighters went streaking out of cover. Mako had stared at the screen, cursing steadily in many languages, as he watched two of the errant ships get blown up.

At least that second guy, whoever he was, had made his exit count for something. And even the fool that had started the whole mess had nailed a recon TIE.

Now the third vessel was streaking back toward him, with a TIE fighter in hot pursuit. "Great!" Mako yelled. "Just lead 'em right to where we're hiding! If you live through this, I'm gonna personally hunt you down and *strangle* you!"

"Mako, he's gonna buy it if we don't do something," Blue said tensely.

"I oughta let the fool pay for his mistake," Mako growled, but a last check on his tactical screens convinced him that the *Carrack*-class vessel was far enough into the debris to be unable to turn quickly and get out of range. *Close enough,* Mako thought.

"All right," he said to Blue and the gunnery crew, "let's go save his worthless hide!"

Snapping on his comm, Mako said, "All right, commence attack! First Strike Element, attack now, boys and girls! Get those TIEs, and I'll move in on that *Carrack*-class. Be prepared to back me up! We're gonna nail that sucker!"

Blue was taking the *Dragon Pearl* out of hiding now, and the racing freighter saw them and swung toward them, like a child running to hide behind mama's skirts. Blue gave a tense order to the gunnery crew, and the Hutt yacht's six powerful turbolasers sent green blasts of destruction to impale the TIE fighter.

The TIE blew up spectacularly. "Waste of power," Mako grunted. "Stupid ships don't even have shields."

The *Pearl* was now moving toward the *Carrack*-class ship, which was only then realizing it was being challenged. "Blue, launch those Headhunters!" Mako yelled.

"Already did it two minutes ago!" she shouted back. "Quit tellin' me my job!"

The *Vigilance* swung toward the yacht, and the two vessels engaged.

The *Carrack*-class, of course, had the advantage in the fight. It was armored much more heavily than the yacht, had better shielding, and more weaponry. It was also faster, but not by much.

However, Mako's crew had two major advantages over the *Vigilance*. Blue was used to maneuvering through Nar Shaddaa's debris, while the *Carrack*-class vessel's pilot was not. The Hutt yacht was also smaller, thus far more agile.

Blue pressed that advantage for all she was worth, darting in to shoot, then straining every rivet in the big ship to evade the returning fire.

After being flung to the deck when the artificial gravity shorted out for a second from a hit, Mako got smart and strapped himself into his seat. He saw bursts of color reflected against the viewport from laser fire and turbolaser fire reflecting off shields, but he couldn't see the *Vigilance* from his command center.

He had been worried that *Vigilance* might be one of the new, refitted models that were equipped with tractor beams, but apparently it was not.

The Hutt yacht shuddered with the blasts, over and over. "We're losing the starboard shielding," Blue said tersely. "Another hit there, and—"

WHAM!

The *Pearl* lurched horribly, like a wounded animal dragged down by a predator's claws. Blue swore. "Fire! Hit 'em again!"

Jiliac's yacht shuddered as the turbolasers fired again, then again.

Mako was dying to get up and see for himself what was happening, but the ship was pitching so violently that it would have been dangerous. All he needed was a broken arm—or neck.

WHAM-WHAM!

"Blast," Blue said. "We've lost three turbolaser mounts."

WHAM!

"Make that four."

"Blue, what in blazes is going *on*?" Mako yelled over the next volley. "Are we hurtin' them at all?"

"Yeah," she grunted. "We're hurtin' 'em. Fire, boys! Again!"

Unable to stand the suspense any longer, Mako unsnapped his harness and staggered across the heaving deck to see what was going on.

"His port shields are weakening," Blue told him. "Our starboard shields are gone." She maneuvered the Hutt yacht so the relatively intact bow shielding was pointing toward the *Vigilance*.

"Engines are sluggish," Mako said, feeling the ship strain to move.

"Tell me about it," Blue snapped.

The *Pearl* fired again, then again, and then—

Mako let out a whoop of glee as he saw, instead of the splash of turbolaser fire against a shield, a big charred mark appear on the *Carrack*-class ship's armored hide. "His port shields are down!"

"So are our starboard ones," Blue snarled.

"But, baby, we've *got* him now! Disengage!"

Mako raced back to his comm center. "All right, listen up! *Too Late Now! Minestra!* Defense Central calling. Come in, over!"

Mako was addressing two of the merc vessels that he knew had been assigned to these coordinates. *Too Late Now* was a captured and modified Imperial patrol craft, and *Minestra* was a captured Imperial light corvette. Both vessels now sported the "blazing claw" insignia that marked them as pirates.

"*Minestra*, we read you, Mako," said a voice.

"*Too Late Now*, likewise."

"Listen up, guys, good news! We just took down *Vigilance*'s port shields!"

"We're already moving in to finish him off," said the voice of *Minestra*'s captain. "Mako, we saw the pounding you took. You'd better get out of here before more Imps show up."

"We're only too happy to," Blue said, and with painful slowness, the *Dragon Pearl* limped away. Mako glanced at her diagnostic sensors, and cursed. *No starboard shields, sublight engines crippled, hull damage, and we're leakin' some atmosphere. Jiliac's gonna be right irritated 'bout this . . .*

The two pirate ships had arrived by now, and they and the freighters were ganging up on the injured *Vigilance*, drawing in like scavengers toward a staggering prey. Mako saw the *Carrick*-class ship take hit after hit, until finally the armor couldn't take any more, and a huge hole was blasted in her port side. The smugglers targeted her engines, then her bridge, and within minutes, she was drifting helpless in space. Lifepods launched from the *Carrack* as some of the crew began abandoning ship.

Mako grinned. "You did good, guys! Okay, my ship's out of it, at least until we do some damage control, so I'm heading for Illusion Point ahead of schedule. You guys stick it out. Those skirmish ships should be arrivin' any minute!"

Admiral Greelanx stared at Commander Jelon, taken aback by his subordinate's report. "You say that the *Vigilance* is out of the battle? Captain Eldon is dead?"

"Yes, Admiral. I regret to say it, sir."

"What about his TIEs?"

"All destroyed, sir."

Greelanx was too disciplined to swear aloud, but he did so mentally. "Order the skirmish ships to full speed. Order two squadrons of TIEs to accompany them. Instruct them to engage the enemy at will."

"Yes, sir!"

For a moment Greelanx considered bringing the other *Carrack*-class, the *Outpost*, into combat, but he decided against it. The *Outpost* might be needed for mopping up, later. He didn't want to risk his only remaining recon vessel.

We'll show these wretched criminals, Greelanx thought angrily, completely forgetting, for the moment, that he was supposed to lose this battle . . .

Captain Soontir Fel stared at Admiral Greelanx's tiny holo-figure as it seemingly stood perched atop the *Pride of the Senate*'s comm board, feeling as though someone had punched him in the stomach. "Eldon is dead?"

Greelanx nodded shortly. "Unfortunately, yes."

"I see, sir. Permission to speak, Admiral?"

"Go ahead." Greelanx was anything but welcoming.

"Perhaps we should take these smugglers a bit more
. . . seriously . . . sir? They apparently *are* capable of
mounting a coordinated attack, as opposed to simply shooting at random."

"Your comment is noted, Fel. Greelanx out."

The tiny holo-figure popped out of existence.

Soontir Fel stood for a moment, head bowed. Captain
Darv Eldon had been one of his classmates in the Academy. They had been close friends for nearly ten years. His
death was like a vibroblade wound.

Fel swallowed, then straightened his shoulders. He
would have time to grieve later. Right now, it was his duty
to kill as many of these smugglers as he could . . .

At first, Han Solo found it very strange to shoot at TIE
fighters, rather than fly them. As soon as Mako had ordered
in the First Strike Element, Han, with Chewie and Jarik in
the *Bria*'s wing-mounted gun turrets, had gone after and
engaged several TIEs. He'd nailed two, so far, and was
cruising through the debris, looking around for more.

The *Bria* had one weakened rear shield, which put her
engines in possible jeopardy should she take another big hit
there, but was otherwise undamaged, due largely to Han's
flying expertise.

Han was one of the few smugglers who was flying without a partner. Mako wanted him free to keep watch over
the fleet, to go where he was needed without encum-
brances. Han recognized that Mako's decision was a testa-
ment to his own flying skill and was pleased.

Han glanced over at the left gun turret on the *Bria*'s
wing, and saw Jarik in the movable seat, headset in place.
So far, the kid hadn't done well. He'd been overeager, nervous, and had managed to miss everything he'd aimed at.

Han was beginning to think he shouldn't have encouraged him to come along for the ride.

Chewbacca had done considerably better, hitting one TIE fighter and sending it wheeling away. Seconds later it had crashed into a large piece of debris and exploded.

Han himself had gotten another TIE with his bow-mounted twin lasers.

Mako's voice came over his headphones. "Listen up! Those skirmish ships are arrivin' and engaging at will! Everyone stay sharp!"

Han had just decided to go hunting for one of the skirmish ships, when suddenly a TIE fighter swooped toward them, lasers blasting.

"Chewie, Jarik!" Han yelled. "Look sharp!" Automatically he evaded the blasts, and triggered a shot with his bow guns.

A clean miss. Han swore.

Another TIE was swooping toward them, eager to catch the *Bria* in a crossfire. Han snapped off a shot at it as he sent his ship swooping away, and saw the TIE wobble. He'd hit it!

The other TIE came in again, and this time Chewbacca was right there, firing, firing—

A sudden Wookiee howl of rage and frustration echoed in Han's headphones. *He's been hit!* was Han's first thought, and his breath caught in his chest, but when he looked to his right, he saw Chewie bouncing up and down in his movable seat, roaring, cursing, and waving his long, hairy arms, obviously furious—but unhurt.

What's got into him? Han wondered, then he looked again, and saw what had happened.

The *Bria*'s gun-control yoke, wires dangling, was clutched in Chewie's paw-hands. In his enthusiasm to nail the TIE, Chewbacca had forgotten to ration his great

Wookiee strength; he'd ripped the control yoke clean out of the gun mount!

Now it was Han's turn to swear. "Chewie, you big furry oaf! Look what you did!"

Chewbacca snarled in Han's headphones that he was only too aware of what he'd done. Han had never heard his hairy friend use language like that before.

Whump! A shot from the TIE had impacted on the *Bria*'s amidships shield.

Hey, Solo! Concentrate on your flying, or you're gonna be dead! Han shook his head, realizing that from now on, he'd have to consider his right side as crippled, and shield it as best he could.

He spoke into his headset. "Jarik, listen up, kid! Chewie broke off the blasted gun yoke in the right turret! It's all up to *you* to nail these TIEs!"

Jarik's voice was faint and shaky. "Mmmm . . . me?"

"Yeah, you! Now look sharp! He's comin' in again!"

Jarik crouched in his movable seat in the left gun turret, frozen with terror. *My worst nightmare come true! I'm going to kill us all!*

He forced himself to straighten up and swiveled, looking for the TIE. The targeting grid hung before him. Would he be able to zero in on anything? He didn't know. He'd failed miserably, so far.

Where is it, where is—

Suddenly he saw it. There it was, coming in a looping path from overhead that would allow it to flip over and then get off a shot at the *Bria*'s bow.

I can't do it . . . what if I can't do it? Jarik's mind screamed, but somehow his hands were moving, and then his body was following suit as he swiveled in his seat. There was the targeting grid, there was the TIE and suddenly—

—the two images were one.

Without conscious volition, Jarik's thumb squeezed the firing trigger.

A red beam shot out, catching the TIE in the middle of its small body.

In magnificent silence, the TIE blew up.

Jarik sat there, staring in shock. *Did I do that?*

Han's voice in his ears. "Great shootin', kid! Let's go do it again!"

Did I do that? I did! I did it! I can do it!

Jarik "Solo" grinned, felt a wave of satisfaction and pride. "Okay, Han!"

Jarik checked the charges on his gun, then, as the *Bria* swooped off, began searching their surroundings for more targets . . .

Aboard the *Rimrunner,* Salla Zend checked her position, then glanced quickly out of her viewport to make sure her flying partner was in correct position. Because the *Rimrunner* equaled the *Millennium Falcon* in speed, she'd been paired with Lando and his odd little droid pilot.

Salla had to hand it to Vuffi Raa. She's never before heard of a droid that could pilot, but she gathered that Vuffi Raa was some special type of droid, from some completely different part of the galaxy. Obviously not your everyday astromech. From the moment they'd deployed, Vuffi Raa not only had kept formation with her, the droid had occasionally outflown her!

She spoke into her headset. "Any of those skirmish ships on your sensors, Vuffi?"

"Nothing so far, Lady Salla," the little droid replied. "And my name is Vuffi Raa, please."

"No problem, Vuffi Raa," she replied. "So what does that name mean, anyhow?"

"In the language of those who programmed me, it is a number, Lady Salla."

"Huh." Salla was doing a visual inspection as she flew through the debris. No skirmish vessels so far, but her sensors showed a large group of vessels moving through the "cloud" of debris surrounding Nar Shaddaa. It was only a matter of time. "Lando, stay sharp with your guns. I see Imp slugs everywhere."

"Right, Salla," Lando said.

"Rik, Shug? We could have incoming any second. You guys ready?"

"Ready, Salla," Shug replied.

"We are ready, pretty lady," Rik Duel said, in a manner that he fondly imagined to be charming.

Salla grimaced and rolled her eyes. "Can it, Rik. Stay sharp. This is no time to get cute."

"Hey, Salla, I can't help it if I've got eyes!" Rik said, in mock-injured tones. "That jerk Solo doesn't appreciate you, you know. You deserve better than that Corellian creep. You are one fine woman, and he—"

"Stow the chatter, Rik," Salla snapped, tiring of the banter. "And rein in your hormones. Your routine is getting real old."

"But, Salla—" he protested, sounding very, very injured, "I fell for you the moment I—"

"Lady Salla!" Vuffi Raa broke in. "Incoming!"

Salla checked her sensors and ship ID codes. An Imperial Customs *Guardian*-class light cruiser, the *Lianna Guard*! She altered her flight path to challenge the newcomer head-on, and was impressed to see how quickly Vuffi Raa followed her lead.

Seconds later the *Lianna Guard* came zipping toward them, firing its laser cannons. Salla took a minor hit, but the shields deflected it. The Imp vessel was fast, and as maneu-

verable as the freighters—matter of fact, the ship was a
Customs patrol ship, designed to stop smugglers cold.

Shug took a shot with his quad lasers, but scored a clean
miss as the Imp pilot evaded. *He's really good!* Salla
thought. *But we'll get him. He's outnumbered.*

She'd been so occupied with engaging the *Lianna
Guard* that Salla failed to notice three slug blips on her
sensors, all coming in incredibly fast. Vuffi Raa squeaked,
"Lady Salla! TIE fighters!"

Salla took a hit in her bow, but the shields handled it.
Shug was shooting steadily now, and so was Lando. One
TIE was hit, and promptly exploded. Salla couldn't tell who
had made the kill.

Evasive! Salla flipped *Rimrunner* up on her side, but
took a hit anyway. Her shields took the brunt of it, but the
freighter shuddered violently.

"Get those TIEs!" she yelled.

"I'm *trying*!" came both Lando's and Shug's voices at
the same time.

Salla swore grimly. *Where's the* Lianna *Guard?* She'd
lost track of the *Guardian*-class ship in the melee.

BAM!

Rimrunner shuddered again. Salla struggled to hold her
bucking ship, narrowly missed crashing into a huge piece of
space debris. They'd been hit in the flank, and her shields
were weakened back there. From the strength of the blast,
it must have been the patrol ship, not a TIE.

"AWriiiiight!" Lando shouted in her headset, and she
saw another TIE wiped out.

Two to two. Much better odds!

Okay, now . . . where was the *Lianna Guard*? On
Lando's tail? No! Coming up directly behind her!

Lando said urgently, "Evasive, Salla!"

"Not on your life!" she bellowed. "This is what I've been
waiting for! Rik, blast your worthless hide, *get him*!"

Captain Lodrel of the Imperial ship *Lianna Guard* smiled grimly as his ship streaked toward the mynock-shaped freighter's stern. *I've got you!* he thought smugly, and opened his mouth to give the order to destroy the helpless vessel.

But before he could speak, Lodrel noticed something strange about the rear of the CorelliSpace ship. Two camouflaged gun ports had just slid open in the ship's stern!

Instead of shouting "Fire!" Lodrel screamed, "Evasive!"

But two concussion missiles were already streaking toward him. *Hey! That's not fair!* Lodrel thought indignantly.

It was his *last* thought . . .

"Yahoooooooo!" shouted Salla as she saw the patrol ship blown to atoms on her rear sensors. "We got him! Sweet shooting, Rik!"

"Does that mean you'll kiss me when we get back to base?" he demanded in her headset.

"Not a chance," Salla said cheerfully. "But I'll buy you a drink!"

"Congratulations, Lady Salla," Vuffi Raa said, in his prissy, overly refined tones.

"Great going, Salla!" Lando shouted. "In all the excitement, I totally forgot about those missile launchers. Shug, you are the best!"

"Yeah, Shug, we all owe you," Salla agreed.

"That was fun," Shug said, chuckling. "Want to do it again?"

"Sure!" Salla and Lando chorused.

. . .

Mako Spince heaved a sigh of relief when the crippled *Dragon Pearl* managed to reach Illusion Point, and the relative protection offered by the bigger ships in Drea Renthal's mercenary fleet. He checked his sensors, all the while listening to his ships report in.

The smugglers were doing well against the Imp skirmish vessels. They were taking losses, though, ships they couldn't afford to lose. Mako frowned as he checked ship after ship. *I'm losing a lot of friends today,* he thought sadly. *Too many good ships and people gone . . .*

He ran a status check. Almost twenty-five percent of his smuggler vessels . . . gone. Even if they won this battle, the smuggling operations out of Nar Shaddaa were going to be affected for a long, long time.

But the Imps had probably lost half their TIE fighters, and nearly fifty percent of their skirmish ships.

The big question is, Mako thought, *when is Greelanx gonna move in with his capital ships?* The big ships were approaching steadily, but were still out of range.

Mako glanced nervously at his sensors, saw two skirmish vessels converge on a smuggler ship. *Oh, no!*

A panicked voice erupted in Mako's headset. "Defender Central! Can you get me some help? I'm crippled, and—"

The voice scaled up into an agonized scream, and abruptly stopped. Mako watched as the blip on his sensors winked out. He cursed softly, helplessly.

"Commander Jelon," Admiral Greelanx said, "order the remainder of the TIEs to deploy and engage at will."

"Yes, sir."

The big Imperial ships were now within five hundred kilometers of the Nar Shaddaa debris shell. Greelanx took a sip of stim-tea, then checked their sensors again. He could see the remaining twelve TIE fighters streaking toward the battle.

"Commander, instruct the capital wedge to assume an external-approach orbital pass. We're going to avoid that debris."

"Yes, sir."

"And order the wedge to accelerate to full speed. We are starting our attack."

"Yes, sir!"

Greelanx checked the status of his squadron again. He was impressed by the smugglers' tenacity. He'd expected them to break and run before now. But they were still fighting, and doing significant damage to his skirmish vessels.

Still, losing wasn't going to be easy. The smugglers were fighting bravely, granted, but those little freighters were no match for his capital ships. Greelanx sighed. It was possible that he'd have to order one of his ships to do something that would be guaranteed to cause its destruction.

The admiral swallowed another sip of tea, feeling as though a fist were closing around his throat. He'd sent troops to their deaths before, many times, but never *on purpose*. He wasn't sure he could do it . . .

But what choice did he have?

They're making their move! Accelerating to attack speed! Mako realized as he stared into his sensors. He keyed his comm to a special, private frequency. "Han, Mako here. You read me?"

"Yeah, Mako," came the voice of his friend, garbled but understandable. "I read you. What's happening?"

"Greelanx is starting his move with his capital ships. I'm going to order the retreat. Do me a favor, pal?"

"Sure."

"You and Chewie play rear guard during the retreat. Hang back and ride herd on those spacebums, okay? Keep 'em on track, Han. Don't let 'em go too slow, but keep on their tails about goin' too fast. We want those Imps following right on their heels."

"Will do," Han said. "How're we doing?"

"Overall, not bad. But we've lost some friends."

"I know. I've seen wreckage," Han agreed, sounding bleak.

"Mako out."

Mako keyed in another special frequency. "Captain Renthal?"

"Renthal here."

"I'm going to order the retreat now. Be ready."

"We are ready. I'll recall *Minestra*."

"What about *Too Late Now*?"

"She's gone."

"Oh . . ."

"Renthal out."

Mako keyed his general frequency. "Boys and girls, this is Defender Central. You done good, fellow spacebums. Now it's time to leave the party. All vessels, retreat along assigned vector. Remember your drills. Repeat, you are to retreat along your assigned vector, starting now. Defender Central out."

Xaverri stood in a cordoned-off section in Shug Ninx's spacebarn, intent on the tactical display she was receiving, transmitted by *Dragon Pearl*. She watched as the smugglers turned tail and raced away from the oncoming Imperial capital ships and remaining skirmish vessels. Her friends were fleeing in what seemed to be a panicked rout, but was, in actuality, a carefully coordinated and rehearsed withdrawal under fire. Mako and Han had drilled and drilled them in just how far they should stay ahead of the Imperial vessels—tantalizingly within weapons range, so the "stragglers" would have to take evasive maneuvers to avoid being blasted if the Imperials got lucky.

The magician licked her lips in anticipation, thinking that this was her big chance, the chance to wipe out more Imps at one time than she'd probably ever get again.

That's right, she thought, watching the wedge move closer and closer to the Illusion Point coordinates. *That's right, come along, chase them, yes, chase them right into the trap* . . .

Poised like a hunting Togorian, she stared fiercely into the tactical display until her eyes burned and she was forced to blink.

When her vision cleared, there they were! The entire capital wedge was right in the middle of the IP coordinates!

Xaverri grinned, a predatory smile that had nothing pleasant about it. She activated her comm, spoke on a special frequency. "Mako, Xaverri here."

"This is Mako. Xaverri, I read you."

"Activating illusion . . . *now,*" she said, and broke contact. Then, slowly, deliberately, she pressed the big red button on her console, the one marked, DON'T TOUCH UNLESS YOU'RE XAVERRI!

"Now you die," she whispered.

Imperial Destiny rounded the limb of Nar Shaddaa, swinging wide as ordered, in order to avoid the floating debris surrounding the Smuggler's Moon. As it did so, Admiral Greelanx could finally see Nal Hutta, large even at a distance of over 123,000 kilometers. His flagship was leading the charge against the fleeing smugglers, his capital ships moving in perfect formation, with his remaining TIE fighters and skirmish ships flanking the wedge.

Greelanx stood on his bridge, watching them close on their prey, seeing the red and green trails of Imperial lasers and turbolasers blasting at the motley assortment of freighters, wondering once again how he was going to manage to stage a realistic defeat and retreat.

The smugglers had fought hard, Greelanx had to admit that, but the sight of his big ships had obviously terrified them, frightened them so badly that any fighting spirit they'd had was gone.

Now they were running like Corellian vrelts before a pack of canoids.

"Admiral Greelanx, sir!" the sensor operator spoke up urgently. "Sir, I'm getting something, but where did it— We've got incoming, sir!"

Greelanx took a quick glance at the sensors, then turned to look out the viewport. His eyes widened.

Coming straight at them from the direction of Nal Hutta were hundreds of smuggler ships of assorted sizes—including several Corellian corvettes! *Mercenaries,* Greelanx thought. *The smugglers don't have anything that large!*

"Where did they come from?" Jelon demanded of the sensor operator. "Why weren't you tracking them?"

"Sir, they must've just launched from Nal Hutta! Sir, I was concentrating on tracking the smuggler fleet, as ordered, Commander!"

Greelanx frowned. His instincts, honed after decades in the Imperial Navy, made him wonder if this could be some kind of a trick.

"Full sensor scan!" he snapped.

"Yes, sir!"

Moments later the sensor operator displayed the results of his check. Greelanx studied it. *The Hutts must have held these mercenaries in reserve, then launched them in desperation,* he decided.

Greelanx cleared his throat. "Commander Jelon, instruct

the wedge and our fighters to execute a one-hundred-and-ten-degree turn, Y axis, and engage the newcomers. When they have completed their maneuver, they may fire at will!"

Mako Spince let out a yell of triumph as he watched the phantom fleet appear, and saw the Imperial ships begin their turn. "*Yes!* They're fallin' for it!" He keyed his comm. "Captain Renthal!"

"I see it," she said tersely. "I didn't believe it would work until now, but I gotta admit . . . I'm attacking, full speed!"

"Go get 'em!"

As Mako had requested, Han Solo had stayed back, behind the other smugglers, as they wove their way out of the debris during the retreat. Once past the limb of Nar Shaddaa, Han had ordered them to swing wide, and get out of the debris. That way Greelanx would have a clear view of the fleeing smugglers, and would continue his pursuit, straight into their trap.

When Han finally emerged from the shell of debris, he found himself actually trailing the Imperial fleet. He could see them ahead of him, and considered trying to loop around them at top speed, so he could take part in the attack that was planned at the IP coordinates.

Ahead of him, he spotted a pair of vessels on his sensors, and was surprised when he checked their vessel IDs and found that the wayward pair was Salla and Lando in *Rimrunner* and the *Falcon*.

Han wondered if one of them had taken a bad hit and needed help. Activating his comm, he said, "Defender Central, this is Han. Come in, Mako."

Mako's voice was clearer, now that Han was out of the

debris field. "Mako here, Han. The Imps have almost reached the IP point."

"I've got Salla and Lando on my sensors, and we're all behind the Imp fleet, Mako."

"Yeah, I asked 'em to take it easy, figuring you might need some help if you ran into any stray skirmish vessels," Mako said.

"Okay, so they're all right?"

"Far as I know."

"Patch me through to them, will you?"

"Sure."

In order to keep the frequencies as clear as possible, all communications had been routed through Mako, except for designated pairs like Lando and Salla. Moments later Han heard Lando's voice. "Han, old buddy!"

"Lando, I'm behind you, wondering how to get past the Imp fleet so I can get back into the action."

"Salla and I were just wondering the same thing. I don't want to miss out on the chance to score some more hits on those Imp skirmish ships. Salla and I got quite a few of them," Lando said proudly.

"Three *Guardian*-class light cruisers," Salla interjected.

"Hey, congratulations!"

"Master." Vuffi Raa's precise tones were unmistakable. "Would you like me to swing us around so we can fly back to the action with Captain Solo?"

"Yeah, Vuffi Raa, why don't you do that? Oh, and . . . don't call me master."

"Yes, Master."

Han was now close enough to his friends that he could see them in the distance as they peeled off and swooped back to join him. Han chuckled. "Where in the galaxy did you pick up that droid, Lando?"

"Long story."

Moments later the three vessels were flying together.

Han was fiercely glad to find out his friends were okay. It felt good, all of them flying together, united against the Imperials.

Han keyed his comm again. "So, guys, how are we gonna get past the fleet, back to the IP?"

Suddenly Chewie, who had abandoned his useless gun turret and come up to serve as copilot and to man the *Bria*'s bow guns, growled urgently and gestured at the sensors.

Han looked, and saw the wedge of pursuing capital ships slow, then begin to execute a ponderous turn, all the while remaining in perfect formation.

"Go, Xaverri!" he shouted, then he keyed his comm.

"Hey, Lando, Salla! Check your forward sensors!"

The Imperial ships were just out of visual range by now. Han found himself wishing fiercely that he could catch up to them, do some more damage.

"They can see it!" Lando said. "Why can't we?"

"Because we're behind it," Han said. "It all has to do with the angle of the light rays. Complicated, but trust me. The Imps are seeing a big fleet comin' straight at them!"

The Imperial fleet continued to execute their turn. *I hate being stuck back here, out of the action!* Han thought.

Suddenly, seeing the direction in which the fleet was turning, Han had an idea. He keyed his comm. "Lando, Salla! We're close enough to the wedge to be able to do a two-second hyperspace microjump right into the middle of the illusion. If we alter our approach vector slightly just before the jump, we'll wind up on the right approach path to come roaring in with those phantoms, firin'! Let's give Xaverri's fleet some real teeth!"

"Han!" Salla protested. "We're right in the middle of a gravity well, in case you haven't noticed!"

"We're close enough to where the two bodies balance

each other out," Han insisted. "We can do it, guys! C'mon! Follow me!"

He altered his flight vector slightly, and was pleased to note that *Rimrunner* and the *Falcon* followed him.

"Okay, we're all set!" Han said tensely. "Now for the microjump!"

"Hey, Han, that illusion is only going to be good for another couple of minutes!" Lando protested. "We can't possibly get a course out of the navicomputers in time!"

"I got it covered," Han said. "You just order that fancy little droid of yours to compute our microjump and put the three of us right in the forefront of that fleet. He can dump the figures into our navicomputers over the comm. Can't you, Vuffi Raa?"

"I am a class two droid, of course I can make such an elementary calculation," Vuffi Raa said, sounding affronted at having his abilities questioned. "But, Captain Solo, I must point out that what you are suggesting presents a considerable risk." From the way the little droid spoke, Han could picture it wringing its tentacles at the very idea.

"Lando, c'mon! Order him to *do* it!"

Han could hear Lando sigh even over the comm. "All right, you crazy Corellian. Vuffi Raa, you mechanical mastermind, do what Han says!"

Moments later Vuffi Raa said, in a subdued voice, "Course laid in."

"Punch it!" Han yelled, suiting his actions to his words. The stars striated around him for a brief second, then he found himself racing straight at the Imperial fleet!

He glanced from one side to the other, saw that Lando and Salla were still in formation with him. And, behind them and to either side of them, stretched Xaverri's illusion. Han could see it now, and even though he'd been prepared for something *big*, he was impressed.

"All right!" he yelled. "Thanks, Vuffi Raa!"

As the phantom fleet drew nearer the Imperial wedge, the big capital ships began blasting away. Han realized immediately that there was a huge advantage to being part of an illusion. With this many ships to shoot at, chances were pretty good that none of the three solid vessels would be targeted.

Nevertheless, he prepared quickly for evasive. "Jarik, you ready, kid?" he called.

"Ready, Han!"

"Chewie, you ready with those twin lasers?"

"Hrrrrrrmnnnnnnnn!"

Han chose a target—the leftmost Dreadnaught, which was the one closest to him. "I'm going after that Dreadnaught dead ahead," he said over the comm. He glanced at the vessel ID. "The *Peacekeeper*."

"We'll stay with you," Lando said. "We can cover each other."

"Great!" Han was having the time of his life. "Ain't this fun, guys?"

"Han, what are you planning to do?" Salla inquired apprehensively.

"Oh, I just thought I might zip by the *Peacekeeper*'s bridge and wave at the captain," Han said with cheery good humor. "Just a friendly little visit . . ."

"Han!" Salla protested. "I'd rather we all lived through this!"

"Crazy Corellian . . ." Lando muttered.

"Hey," Han said. "What are you worryin' about? It's me!"

Captain Reldo Dovlis, in command of the Imperial Dreadnaught *Peacekeeper,* shook his head in disgust. "Cease fire!" he snapped. "It's not real. It can't be. Our shots haven't taken out a single ship. And none of their shots have done us the slightest bit of harm. We're just wasting our fire and our time."

His sensor operator looked up. "Sensors still indicate that what we are seeing is real, sir."

"Sensors are lying, then," Dovlis snarled. He studied the tactical array, and saw a number of ships heading for *Peacekeeper*'s stern, coming fast. "Vessels approaching from the rear," he said. "Turn to bring our forward turbolaser battery to bear on them. Lock in weapons. Prepare to fire on my order."

Slowly the big ship began to swing around. Dovlis kept a sharp watch on the approaching vessels, and was relieved to see that he'd have time to fire several salvos at them. From the size of them, that ought to—

His pilot gave a strangled yelp, and the *Peacekeeper* shuddered. Red laser fire spattered against *Peacekeeper*'s forward shield.

A bare second later a ship swooped by, so close to the bridge viewscreen that even Dovlis yelled and ducked. The ship, a small, battered SoroSuub freighter, executed a perfect inside loop and came back for a second run.

They're not all phantoms! Dovlis realized. "Turn back!" he shouted. "Fire on that ship!"

Peacekeeper began turning back again. Now Dovlis could see the smuggler fleet again, and he gasped at how close they were.

Two more beat-up freighters strafed the *Peacekeeper*.

"Target those vessels!" the Captain ordered. "Fire!"

Mako Spince's crew had managed to jury-rig some repairs to the *Dragon Pearl*, so the Hutt yacht now had partial starboard shielding, and her hull leaks had been sealed. Her sublight speeds were still impaired, but Mako was willing to risk taking her back into battle. Captain Renthal had assigned a Y-wing fighter to accompany him, and the swift, powerful little ship now cruised beside him, prepared to keep incoming off his weakened starboard side.

Scanning the tactical and sensor arrays, Mako saw that he was now in range of his target, the Imperial bulk cruiser *Liquidator*. The ship was still pointing its stern toward the oncoming smuggler and pirate vessels, still vulnerable to attack.

"Mako," Blue said, "we're within firing range."

Mako nodded at the beautiful smuggler pilot. "Great! I'm going to let the Y-wing have first pass, then we'll get in our licks. Instruct the gunnery crew to target his left rear deflector, right over his engine room. We want to hit him in the same place as the Y-wing."

"Right," Blue muttered, and relayed the order.

Mako was grateful to have that Y-wing to help cover his starboard side. The swift, modern little fighter was not only equipped with lasers, but with proton torpedoes, which were bound to come in real handy.

He keyed his comm, spoke to the pirate gunner aboard the Y-wing. "Mako here. You ready?"

"We're ready!"

"Go for it!"

Mako watched the Y-wing on his sensors. The little ship made its run, slamming four proton torpedoes into the designated target before sheering off. "Okay, Mako," the gunner said, circling back to join the yacht, "shields are either down or barely holding. Your turn!"

"My pleasure!"

Mako turned to Blue and gave her a nod. She increased speed to maximum (which still wasn't very good) and headed for the *Liquidator*, turbolasers blasting away.

With their first blast, Mako knew the bulk cruiser's shields were already down. The *Pearl*'s gunners pummeled their target repeatedly with the two remaining turbolasers, before the cumbersome Imperial vessel could turn to bring her heavy forward guns to bear.

Moments later the Imperial ship's right flank, and the engine room beneath it, was a blown-out wreck. The *Liquidator* spun slowly in space, helpless, leaking atmosphere.

Captain Drea Renthal leaned forward excitedly in her command seat. *Finally! A little action of my own!* Guiding her ships throughout the battle had been challenging, but not like *this*. Now she was flying her own vessel, and she was going in for the kill.

Her target was another of the big bulk cruisers, the *Arrestor*. These ships were outdated, clumsy, and not heavily shielded enough. By comparison with *Arrestor*, *Renthal's Fist* was a heavily armed, sleek engine of destruction. In addition to its two twin turbolasers in top and bottom turrets her Corellian corvette had four twin laser turrets on the sides for shooting fighters, and a pair of capital-ship proton torpedo launchers in the front, beneath her bridge.

Her supply of proton torpedoes was limited, as Han had predicted. Renthal had only four. They were *extremely* hard to come by.

But as she closed in on *Arrestor*, Renthal was determined to make every one of them count.

As she neared firing range, she spoke to her gunnery crew. "Prepare to launch torpedo one and two. Target her stern. I'd love to get a reactor overload going!"

"Yes, sir!"

Renthal smiled. She liked being called "sir."

As *Renthal's Fist* swooped by, she shouted, "Fire!"

Her ship lurched slightly, once, twice, as the proton torpedoes went streaking out in a blaze of blue fire.

The first torpedo took out the cruiser's shields. The second bored into the hull and caused damage.

"Fire turbolasers!" Renthal ordered, coming around for another pass.

The *Arrestor* was lurching now with the impacts. The turbolasers bored ever deeper into her vitals, seeking her heart—the reactor that powered her engines.

Renthal was never quite sure what warned her. Instinct, perhaps, developed after twenty years of fighting. She turned her ship sharply, and accelerated away at top speed.

Behind her, *Arrestor* exploded as thoroughly as any fragile TIE fighter.

Renthal smiled seraphically. *My, that was fun!*

Mako cheered as he watched five of Renthal's Y-wings strafe the Dreadnaught *Peacekeeper*'s stern, targeting its vulnerable engine area, volleying it with proton torpedo salvos.

The Dreadnaughts were a lot tougher targets than the clumsy bulk cruisers, but he thought they might have a chance to kill this one.

Apparently Han, Salla, and Lando had pulled some typically harebrained stunt to keep the *Peacekeeper* occupied until the Y-wings could move in. Mako could make out their blips, following the Y-wings, waiting for those proton torpedoes to deal with the shields before wasting shots on the big vessel.

Mako found himself doing some mental figuring as the Y-wings strafed the Imperial Dreadnaught. *Two salvos of two torpedoes each, from five Y-wings . . . that equals twenty torpedo hits!*

It sounded like a lot, but Mako had trained aboard an Imperial Dreadnaught, and knew how tough the old ships were.

There goes the first salvo . . . ten torpedoes . . . ten hits . . .

Mako did some rough calculations, figured that the *Peacekeeper*'s stern shields ought to be in real trouble by now.

As the Y-wings swooped by on their second pass, blackened holes began appearing in the Dreadnaught's starboard flank, where its massive engines were.

Now that the shields were down, other smugglers were attacking the Dreadnaught's stern with abandon. The Imp Captain tried to turn his ship so he could fire on them, Mako could tell, but the ship was already sluggish, unresponsive.

And then, suddenly, there was a bright flare on the starboard side, and then the light from the *Peacekeeper*'s engines went out.

Mako whistled softly. *I think he's in trouble* . . .

"Sir, the starboard reactor overloaded! The safeties shut it down!" Reldo Dovlis's second-in-command reported. "No engine power remaining, sir!"

Dovlis looked around, feeling desperate. Without engines, he couldn't escape. The smuggler ships were too small to do him much damage quickly, but over time they could cut his ship to ribbons, starting from the unprotected starboard stern, and working their way up, toward the bridge, destroying shields piece by piece, boring into his ship with their little lasers . . .

"We've got to restart those engines, or we've had it," Dovlis said, knowing he spoke the truth. "Override the failsafe. We need power!"

"But, Captain—" The young man's face was ashen with fear. Dovlis didn't blame him. Reactors weren't something to mess around with. But what other alternative did he have? All the other Imperial vessels were engaged—it was unlikely that an appeal to Greelanx would bring help quickly enough.

Dovlis was counting on the fact that the override on the reactor was designed to trip long before there was actual danger of an explosion.

He fixed his subordinate with a steely gaze. "I gave you an order, Commander."

"Yes, sir!"

If only we can fire the engines for long enough to get closer to the other ships! Dovlis thought. Drifting, the *Peacekeeper* would tend to be pulled in by Nar Shaddaa's gravity.

Dovlis heard his ship's engines fire, strain, and his heart ached at what he was having to do to her. But all their lives were at stake.

Peacekeeper strained, lurched, then crept slowly forward—

—and then shuddered in agony as her starboard engine exploded. The port engine was still firing, however, and the unequal thrust sent the Dreadnaught into a dizzying spin!

"Engines off!" shouted Dovlis, but found that the Commander had already anticipated his order. *Peacekeeper* spun now in silence, whirling over and over.

The artificial gravity was still functioning because of the emergency power cells. But they weren't enough to power the ship's maneuvering thrusters. They had no way to pull out of this spin. Firing the port engines again would only make them spin harder, faster.

Reldo Dovlis watched in utter terror as the stars whirled by, then the surface of Nar Shaddaa, hazy because of the moon's planetary shield, then the stars, then the moon . . .

Do something! his mind screamed. *We're being drawn by the moon's gravity! In about a minute, we're going to hit Nar Shaddaa's energy shield!*

And what an explosion *that* would be!

Stars . . . moon . . . stars . . . moon . . .

Whirling in a dizzying spin, whirling, spinning, utterly powerless to stop . . .

Stars . . . moon . . . stars . . . moon . . . stars . . . moon very close now . . .

Dovlis strove for dignity. He was, after all, an Imperial officer. "Can anyone think of anything that might help?" he asked, keeping his voice steady and calm.

His bridge crew looked at him silently. The law of gravity was, in this case, as cruel and inexorable as any of those imposed by the Emperor.

Stars . . . moon . . . stars . . . moon   so   close now . . .

Stars . . . moon . . .

And then there was only the moon, clutching them to her, dragging them into her shield.

And then there was nothing at all . . .

One of the smugglers who had darted in to take shots at the dying *Peacekeeper* was Roa, who was feeling pretty cocky. Lately he'd been wondering if he wasn't getting old, losing his edge, but today he'd engaged in two dogfights with TIE fighters, and come out victorious.

Hey, I've still got it! he thought, sending the *Lwyll* darting after the spinning Dreadnaught. Just for the thrill of it, he sent the *Lwyll* hurtling beneath the plummeting Imp, pulling out steeply, feeling the gee forces grip him, so strong was the pull—

—and then the *Peacekeeper* hit Nar Shaddaa's shield.

Even climbing as he was, the shock wave threw Roa forward. He smashed into his control yoke with bruising force. Parts of his instrument panel shattered, sending shards of glassine to impale his arms and chest like tiny daggers.

As the big ship exploded, it wiped out a section of the planetary shield, and flaming debris was sucked through, down into the upper atmosphere.

And so was Roa.

The concussion shock wave had stunned him, and he struggled to regain full consciousness. It wasn't easy. Waves of blackness rolled over him like a night sea.

But Roa was a fighter. He didn't give up his struggle to open his eyes, to blink, to raise his head.

Seconds later he was able to focus again, and realized where he was and what he was doing. He was falling like a stone, down and down, hurtling through Nar Shaddaa's grimy atmosphere.

Roa blinked. There was something in his eyes. Blood? Most likely.

He shook his head, and pain stabbed. Trying to move brought agony. His instrument panel was a mess, but some parts were still lit and functioning. His flight suit was no longer vacuum-proof, but he wasn't in a vacuum any longer . . .

Forcing himself to move, to take control, Roa grabbed the controls and began to wrestle the little scout craft down through the atmosphere, using every bit of skill he had to achieve a soft landing.

Or even a hard landing.

Any kind of landing!

The *Lwyll* tried valiantly to respond to his commands. He brought her nose up, got air beneath her wings. His headlong fall slowed.

Roa began testing his braking and maneuvering thrusters, and they responded sluggishly. He was still falling, but now it was a relatively controlled fall.

Beneath him, he could see a landing platform. Using his maneuvering thrusters, he managed to edge the *Lwyll* over, until he was certain he'd land on it, as opposed to tumbling over the side, down into the abyss between buildings . . .

The permacrete was rushing up at him, fast . . .

Too fast!

Roa fought gravity as he would have fought a human opponent in a wrestling match, using every bit of skill he possessed.

As the permacrete hurtled up at him, Roa braced himself . . .

He never remembered the moment of impact.

How much later did he blink, swim back to consciousness? Seconds? Minutes? Hours?

Roa didn't know and didn't care. He hurt in a hundred places, but a more visceral fear than any he'd ever known drove him to full consciousness.

The smell of burning. The *Lwyll* was burning. Any moment now, she might explode, and all his struggle to land her would be for nothing . . .

Ignoring the stabbing glassine shards that still impaled him, Roa reached up and stabbed the control that would pop his cockpit. Clumsily he unsnapped his flight harness. He managed to pull himself up, out of his seat, then half fell over the side. He kicked weakly, trying to get the strength to draw his legs over.

Suddenly hands grabbed him, lifted him. Voices babbled in his ears, faint because of the helmet.

He was being lifted, carried.

He heard steps on the permacrete. They were hurrying, running steps. He was being shaken, jounced, almost as badly as when the explosion had hit him.

Roa raised his head slightly, looked back at the *Lwyll*, just in time to see his beloved little ship blow up.

But I'm alive, he thought foggily. *I'm alive, and I still have the real Lwyll* . . .

And with that thought, he blacked out.

. . .

For a man who had been granted his wish, Admiral Winstel Greelanx was remarkably unhappy. The Admiral stared at his tactical screens, his sensors, saw the damage his squadron had taken, and was absolutely furious.

How dare those smugglers? How *dare* they?

One Dreadnaught utterly destroyed. A *Carrack*-class cruiser fit only for salvage. One bulk cruiser a helpless cripple, another that was now part of the debris and spacedust floating around Nar Shaddaa . . .

Greelanx fought back the urge to rally his troops and continue the battle. He still had a formidable force, especially against these smugglers. There was a decent chance, perhaps more than fifty-fifty, that he would be able to achieve victory and implement his orders.

But he couldn't do that. He had been looking for a way to justify withdrawal, and now it had been handed to him.

He turned to Commander Jelon. "Order our ships to fall back in an orderly fashion. When they have disengaged, order them to rendezvous at our hyperspace rally coordinates."

Jelon stared at his commanding officer in open surprise. "Retreat, sir?"

"Yes, retreat," Greelanx said harshly. "We cannot achieve our directive here in the Y'Toub system. Approved tactical wisdom dictates an orderly retreat, while we still have some control over the situation."

Usually Greelanx would no more justify his orders to a subordinate than he would step out an airlock without a spacesuit, but in his mind he was composing his official report, trying those phrases on for size.

Jelon snapped to attention and saluted formally. "Yes, sir!"

. . .

Retreat? thought Captain Soontir Fel in blank astonishment. *Retreat? We can still win!*

It wouldn't be easy, but it was do-able. Fel was sure of it. He simply couldn't believe that Greelanx had so little backbone.

"Retreat in orderly fashion," Commander Jelon repeated. "Those are the admiral's orders."

Fel outranked Jelon, and that gave him the courage to speak his mind more bluntly than he would have dared to the admiral. "But there are still unrecalled TIEs out there. We can't abandon them!"

"The admiral is expecting the squadron to make the jump to hyperspace at the rally coordinates within the time he specified," Jelon said stiffly.

Fel's mouth tightened. "Fel out," he said curtly, and the tiny holographic image of Jelon vanished.

Soontir Fel turned to his second-in-command. "Broadcast an emergency recall to all TIE fighters to rendezvous with the *Pride.* I will take as many as I can, until the docking bays and shuttle bays are full. At the same time, we will disengage and withdraw, Commander Toniv."

"What speed, sir?"

"One-quarter speed, Commander."

"One-quarter speed, sir?"

"You heard me."

"Yes, sir!"

Fel had ordered such a ridiculously low speed in order to give as many TIEs as possible the chance to get aboard his vessel. Technically, he was obeying his orders—Greelanx had neglected to specify a speed—but he was disobeying them in spirit.

Frankly, at the moment, Soontir Fel could have cared

less about his orders. He wasn't going to abandon those
TIE pilots!

Five minutes later his docking bays were full of the regulation twelve TIE fighters, and his shuttle bay contained
another three. Sensors didn't indicate any other TIEs out
there to be picked up, so Fel ordered *Pride* up to full speed
to catch up to the rest of the squadron.

A minute later the tiny holographic image of Admiral
Greelanx materialized on his comm board. "Captain Fel!"

Fel had no trouble staying cool. He was still too angry to
be apprehensive. "Yes, Admiral?"

"You deliberately disobeyed my order!"

"I retrieved our fighters, Admiral. And their pilots. I
considered that . . . important."

Greelanx's little image bristled. "Captain, this decision
on your part could wind up costing you your command. I
shall make a full report."

Fel swallowed, but his gaze did not waver. "And I shall,
of course, make *my* full report," he said. "As per regula-
tions, I intend to offer all the facts of the battle as I ob-
served it."

Greelanx stared at Fel for a long moment. Neither gaze
wavered.

Finally, the admiral nodded. "As you wish, Captain."

The tiny image vanished. Soontir Fel dropped into a
seat, resisting the urge to hold his head in his hands. Were
the lives of those TIE pilots worth a career?

It was entirely possible that he was about to find out.

Soontir Fel sighed. Life could be very complicated, at
times. But then a thought occurred to him, and it cheered
him considerably . . .

*At least I didn't have to execute Base Delta Zero . . .
that's worth something, too . . .*

Chapter Fifteen:
Leave-takings

Twenty-four hours after Han and Chewie had brought the *Bria* safely back to Nar Shaddaa, undamaged save for the gun mount and a weakened stern shield over her engine housing, Han and Xaverri stood together on the windswept landing platform beside *The Phantasm*'s landing ramp. Salla and Chewie had accompanied them most of the way, but had discreetly fallen back, to allow them to say a private farewell.

Now Han looked at Xaverri, who had once more assumed her colorful, stylish clothes, and shook his head. "I hate good-byes," he said miserably. "I can never think of anything to say, and this is worse than usual. How can I find words to thank you, Xaverri? Your illusion saved us. Without you, we wouldn't have been able to do it."

She smiled at him, her dark eyes full of affection. "Hey, Solo . . . I wouldn't have missed it for all the credits in the galaxy. I just wish I'd been on the bridge of a few of those Imperial ships to see their reaction."

Han laughed. "They had to have been surprised, that's for sure." Impulsively he reached out and took her hands, then found himself hugging her fiercely. "I'm gonna miss you," he said, his voice muffled by her hair. "Just when I thought I'd gotten used to living without you, here I have to do it all over again. It ain't fair, Xaverri."

When he pulled back a bit, she reached up and kissed him firmly on the mouth. "Don't worry," she said with a smile, "Salla won't mind. She's a classy lady."

"She is," he agreed. "We think a lot alike."

Xaverri nodded. "I hope you two are happy, Solo. You take care of each other, okay?"

Han nodded. "You, too."

"I will, Solo. Don't forget me . . ."

"Never," he said, his throat tight. "I could never forget you, Xaverri."

Xaverri pulled away, and he let her go. She ran up the ramp, into her ship, and did not look back . . .

Three days after the Battle of Nar Shaddaa (as it was coming to be known), Han, Chewie, Salla, and Lando attended Roa's wedding. The aging smuggler was nearly healed, thanks to a prolonged dunk in a bacta tank, and Lwyll looked radiant in an elegant gown.

It was generally known that the four smugglers had been instrumental in turning the tide of battle in Nar Shaddaa's favor. Han and his friends were the toast of the party. They wandered around, sipping drinks, scarfing appetizers, shaking hands, and being congratulated by all and sundry.

Lando came up to Roa, threw an arm around the smuggler's shoulders, and said, "I understand that getting out of the smuggling business is one of the conditions to this wedding, Roa."

"That's right."

"Well, you're going to need honest employment, then. Would you like to work for me?"

"Doing what?"

Lando laughed. "Don't look so suspicious! Managing my used spaceship lot. I'm going on an extended trip back to the Centrality, and I need someone reliable to look after the business."

Roa looked very thoughtful. "Well . . . sure! I think I'd like that. Thanks, Lando. So . . . why are you heading out? Got something planned?"

"Vuffi Raa and I are heading back to the Centrality because I've got a hunch I could make a quick fortune running cargo to those backward planets. And"—Lando smiled and stroked his fledgling mustache—"if that doesn't work, there are always the casinos in the Oseon system. It'll do me good to polish up my sabacc game. When you don't play, you get rusty. The games here on Nar Shaddaa are pretty small, credit-ante. I need some real high-stakes action to get ready for the real action."

Han, who had been wandering past, stopped when he heard Lando's speech. "Sabacc game? Real action? What's going on? Whose sabacc game needs polish?"

Lando laughed. "Mine does. If I can raise the stake, I'm going to get myself into the big sabacc game that's being held on Bespin in six months. Ante's ten thousand credits."

"Ten thousand credits!" Han whistled softly. "That's a big game, all right."

Lando smiled at his friend. "Hey, you're a pretty decent

sabacc player, Han. You ought to consider getting together your own stake."

Han shook his head. "No way!"

"Why not?"

"Too rich for my blood!" Han said. "If I could manage to scrounge up ten thousand credits, I'd put it toward a ship of my own."

"Yeah, but you might win enough to buy one," Lando pointed out.

"I'm not that lucky," Han said.

"Oh, c'mon, Han," Lando urged, "you could raise the credits." He looked over at Chewbacca. "Chewie would loan 'em to you, wouldn't you, Chewbacca? He's your best friend, right?"

Chewbacca gave an eloquent growl, then shook his head emphatically.

Han laughed. "Not a good enough friend to risk ten thousand credits, Lando!"

Durga the Hutt crouched beside his parent's repulsor sled, grief-stricken, watching the med droids and Grodo, the Hutt physician, work desperately to save Aruk. But even he could tell that their efforts were doomed to failure.

Aruk had collapsed minutes ago, gasping in pain, retching, moaning, then jerking in frenzied spasms. Durga had never felt so helpless as he watched his parent struggle for life and breath.

Aruk the Hutt had always been strong, strong and stubborn. It took him four hours to die, four agonizing, pain-filled hours. Durga crouched by him the entire time, hoping that his parent would regain consciousness, but Aruk never did.

It was a relief when the Besadii Lord's straining heart finally gave up the struggle, but even though he was glad that his parent was free of the terrible pain, Durga was devastated. He had lost his best friend, as well as his parent.

He clutched Aruk's limp hand, seeing the rivulets of green slobber running out the slack, dead mouth, and knew, without knowing how he knew, that this death was murder.

Who had done this?

Who else but Desilijic stood to profit by Aruk's death?

For days Durga was too devastated to function, barely eating, dragging himself around like a lost spirit. He refused to let his parent's body be interred. Even though the physician's tests on the contents of Aruk's stomach indicated that there was no poison, that the Hutt Lord had died of natural causes, Durga was convinced that there had been foul play. He had Aruk's massive corpse frozen, and resolved to hire a team of forensic specialists from Imperial Center to perform a thorough autopsy as soon as things settled down.

The Besadii kajidic was in an uproar. Two factions emerged, the pro-Durga and the anti-Durga faction. Durga took steps to consolidate his power. He contacted an infamous crime syndicate, Black Sun, that was owned and commanded by the powerful prince Xizor, and explained to the prince how their organizations might prove beneficial to each other . . .

Over the next three weeks, three powerful Besadii Lords died—two in shuttle crashes, one by drowning when his river barge struck an uncharted rock and sank.

After that, the anti-Durga faction became far less vocal.

While he waited for the forensic specialists to arrive from Imperial Center, Durga made a list of possible suspects. Surely there would be some clue, somewhere, as to who had done this—and *how*.

Durga resolved to start with the financial records. As a

Hutt, he understood finances, and profit. He would check the finances of every member of Desilijic, then go on to Besadii, then the other clans. He would look for a pattern. There was always a pattern to finances, if one knew how to see it . . .

Slowly, day by day, the young Hutt Lord found the strength to carry on without his parent.

Someone is going to pay for this, he vowed every morning when he looked at Aruk's holo hanging on the wall in his chamber. *And they will pay dearly . . .*

Chapter Sixteen:

The Payoff

This time around, the snooty administrative aide waved Han into Admiral Greelanx's private sanctum without question. It was obvious to Han that his arrival was eagerly awaited. The Corellian smiled grimly as he walked in. He supposed he'd be glad to see someone who was going to give him a fortune, too . . .

The admiral was standing by the viewport, staring out moodily. He turned as Han came in, nodded, but did not smile. "Did you bring them?" he asked.

"Yes, sir, they're all here, exactly as specified," Han said. Carefully he pushed items away from the center of Greelanx's desk and then emptied the small pouch he carried into the cleared spot.

Greelanx stared down at the sparkling fortune in assorted untraceable gems, and his eyes lit up. "The Hutts are true to their word," he said. "But you won't mind if I—" He gestured with a magnifier.

"Go right ahead," Han said.

The admiral spent the next few minutes examining several of the largest, most beautiful gems—Gallinorean rainbow gems, corusca stones, and Krayt dragon pearls of various sizes and hues. "I assume you found your shuttle at the rendezvous point," the admiral said, "since you are here exactly on time."

"Yes, sir, everything was just like you said it would be, Admiral."

Greelanx glanced up, still holding the magnifier up to his face. His right eye was enormous, as seen through the lens. "How are you planning to get off my ship?" he asked, as if only mildly curious.

Han shrugged. "I have a partner who will pick me up."

"Very well. Young man, these stones are exactly as specified. Please tell your Hutt masters that I am satisfied."

Han nodded, but said, "They aren't my masters. I just work for them."

"Whatever," Greelanx said. He hesitated, then said, "I didn't believe you could do it, you know. Even with the battle plan."

"I know," Han said. "But it was that or die. We were fighting for our lives. You were fighting for credits. Makes a big difference."

"That holo-illusion was a brilliant tactical stroke."

Han smiled and executed a slight bow. "Thank you."

Greelanx seemed taken aback. "You did it?"

"No, I had an expert do it. But it was my idea."

"Ah." The admiral seemed to consider for a moment, then said, with a trace of wistfulness, "You despise me, don't you, young man?"

Han stared at him in surprise. "Not at all. I do lots of things I'm not tickled about for credits."

"But there are some things you will not do."

Han considered. "Yeah, that's true."

"Well, I—"

Greelanx broke off as the door suddenly opened, and his aide stood there, eyes wide and frightened. "Admiral! Sir!"

"What is it?" Greelanx was annoyed.

"Sir, I was just advised by the docking-bay crew . . . *he* has just landed. An unscheduled inspection, apparently. *He* is on his way to speak with you at this moment!"

Greelanx took a deep breath, then waved the man out. "I suppose I should have anticipated this, under the circumstances," he muttered, racing over to the wall. Behind a Certificate of Merit, there was a wall lockup unit. Greelanx stood for a moment, letting the unit scan his retinas. The door swung open. The admiral grabbed a double handful of jewels, raced over, dumped them in, then came back and brushed the last of the gems into his palm, dumped them, too.

While all this was going on, Han was standing there, totally bemused by the admiral's actions.

"What's going on?" he asked.

"No time," Greelanx said, shutting the lockup. "Here, you'll have to wait in here. You can't let him see you. If he did—" The admiral bit his lip, yanked open the other door, the one leading to his secretary's office. The room was vacant, dark. "In here. Don't make a sound. Not a sound, understand?"

"No," Han said, totally confused. "I don't."

Greelanx did not bother to reply. Grabbing Han's arm, he shoved him into the office, then shut the door.

Han stood there in the dark office, wondering what in blazes was going on. Who was *he*? It sounded like Greelanx was expecting some kind of monster out of a kid's adventure tri-dee!

Half-tempted to storm back out and just say "good riddance," Han tiptoed over to the door. The doorseal, he discovered, hadn't quite caught. He was able to hear Greelanx moving around, and then came some small thumps and rustles.

Putting his desk back to rights, Han realized.

Then came a squeak, as Greelanx sat back down in his luxurious lizard-hide chair. Han could almost picture him, being elaborately casual.

The doorseal to the outer office hissed. Han heard a heavy, measured tread and the whisper of something that might have been fabric. Was the newcomer wearing long robes? A cloak?

Then came another sound that the Corellian recognized—loud, stentorian breathing, respirations that were artificially stimulated because the wearer was unable to breathe on his own. A respirator mask . . . the visitor was wearing a respirator mask.

Somehow the sounds of those loud, hissing breaths was ominous. Han swallowed and didn't make a sound.

Greelanx said, in a deliberately bright, pleasant tone that was supposed to sound casual, but instead sounded terrified, "Lord, what an unexpected pleasure! The Outer Rim is honored by your presence. I gather you wish to conduct an inspection. You must understand that we have just recently been engaged in battle, so—"

"Greelanx," said a deep, mechanically enhanced voice that made Han's skin crawl, "you are as stupid as you are greedy. Did you imagine that the High Command would remain unaware of your treachery?"

Now Greelanx made no attempt to hide his fear. "Lord, please! You don't understand, I was ord—" His voice broke off in a choked cry. Han's eyes widened, and he wouldn't have opened that door into Greelanx's office for all the dragon pearls in the galaxy.

Silence, except for that loud, harsh breathing. Silence, for many seconds. Then . . . a heavy *thump* as something landed on the thick carpet. The voice said, "Ah, but I understand perfectly, Admiral."

The heavy footsteps came again, passed the door where Han was hiding, did not pause. Then came the sound of the doorseal activating.

Silence.

Han waited a good five minutes before he dared to unseal the door and peer out. He wasn't particularly surprised to find Greelanx sprawled on the carpet. He checked for a pulse, found none, which also wasn't surprising.

What *was* surprising was that there wasn't a mark on the body. When Han hadn't heard a blaster, he'd assumed the visitor had used a vibroblade. An expert assassin could use one to kill with little blood, and no struggle.

But Greelanx didn't have a mark on him . . .

Han stood there, looking down at the admiral's dead features, which were frozen in a look of utter terror. He shivered. *Who was that guy?*

Han walked over to the wall, took a cursory glance at the lockup, but it was as he'd expected—a good unit, retinally activated. And even if he were to dig Greelanx's eyeball out of its socket—a grisly task, all right—the admiral had already been dead too long. The retinal patterns wouldn't work right.

I'm gettin' outta here . . . Han decided. He walked back, stepped over Greelanx's outflung hand, and then stopped when something his toe had kicked rolled across the carpet.

Han stooped, grabbed it exultantly. A Krayt dragon pearl! Small, but it seemed, to the naked eye, flawless. Opalescent black. A valuable color.

Sealing the jewel in an inside pocket, Han hurried out.

Ten minutes later he'd finished making his preparations for his escape. He stood by the hatch on the lifepod deck, hastily finishing a rewiring job on the pod-ejection controls. Then he pressed a button, and the lifepod hatch hissed open softly.

He froze as he heard a step, then a familiar voice. "Stop right there, Han. Turn around . . . slowly."

Han did so, and found, as he'd expected from the voice, his old friend Tedris Bjalin.

The man stood there, holding a blaster aimed at Han. "What are you doing here? I saw you in the corridor, saw you go into the admiral's office. Why were you talking to the admiral? What's going on?"

They're going to think I murdered Greelanx, Han realized. *They'll shoot me first and ask questions later!*

"Hey, Tedris, take it easy," he said, smiling crookedly. He took a slow, careful step forward. "You know you couldn't shoot your old pal."

"Stop it right there, Solo," Bjalin said, but his hand wasn't quite steady on the blaster's grip. They had, after all, been close friends. "What are you doing wearing that uniform? Who are you—"

"Hey, pal, you got questions, let's go somewhere and talk about this," Han said. "I can answer every—"

Breaking off in midword, Han flung himself at Tedris, using a *very* dirty Corellian street-fighting trick. Bjalin went down, then lay on the deck, wheezing for breath, his eyes accusing. Han stooped down, appropriated his old friend's blaster.

He went down on one knee beside his friend. "Listen to me, Tedris," he said softly. "You're not gonna die, though you won't be real comfy for a while. I want you to know something. *I didn't do it.* Okay? Just remember that, later on. And you know something, Tedris? You're too nice a guy to stay in this lousy, massacre-happy Imperial Navy. Take my advice and get out while you can."

With that, Han stunned Tedris, then stepped over his friend's unconscious form. Hastily he dragged Bjalin into one of the other lifepods, making sure the hatch wasn't fastened, so there was no way he could accidentally be ejected.

Then he ducked through the hatch of the lifepod he'd rewired. Moments later he was ejected into space. He'd rigged the lifepod so it would look like an accidental ejection. Not surprising, under the circumstances. After all, the *Destiny* had just been through a battle . . .

He worried for a while that the Imps might retrieve his pod, but they did not. Han figured that Greelanx's murder was occupying everyone's attention.

Chewie picked him up an hour later, as he drifted, still puzzling over what had happened to Greelanx.

The Wookiee scooped Han's stolen lifepod into the *Bria*'s cargo bay, whining and growling that they had to get out of here, fast, there were recon TIE fighters prowling around.

Han agreed. Hastily he and Chewie headed for the bridge. They were halfway there when they heard the *WHUMP!* Seconds later another followed, this one so strong it knocked both of them to the deck.

"Chewie, we're under fire!" Han yelled. "Get to the gun mount!"

Han hastily slipped into the pilot's seat, saw two recon TIEs circling back for a second pass—and then he saw the blinking red light on his control board. "Chewie! Reactor overload! They hit us right in that weak shield! We've gotta abandon ship!"

Leaping up, he ran to the gun turret, then grabbed the Wookiee and began dragging him out. Chewbacca shook his head, arguing, but Han screamed, "Run, you big oaf! This ship is gonna *blow*!"

When they reached the cargo deck again, the Wookiee was hesitant about crawling into the Imperial lifepod, but Han insisted. "Don't you get it, Chewie? The *Bria* is finished! This is our only chance! Now get inside and put on this respirator mask!"

Once Chewie was safely inside, Han hastily donned a spacesuit, then opened the cargo-bay doors wide.

WHUMP! WHUMP-WHUMP!

Give up, Han thought at the TIEs as he attached an anti-grav unit to the lifepod, then floated it over to the cargo door. *We're doomed anyhow . . .* Tapping on the viewport, he gestured out what he planned. Chewie, now wearing the respirator, nodded.

Then, in one smooth motion, Han slid the pod toward the opening, just as Chewie popped the hatch and yanked him inside.

The entire sequence took maybe six seconds. Not enough time for explosive decompression to rupture tough Wookiee hide. A second later the hatch was closed and dogged, and atmosphere was again filling the pod.

The pod had barely cleared the cargo-bay doors when the *Bria* blew up.

The concussion knocked the little lifepod spinning. Han braced himself, half expecting one of the TIEs to attack them, but as he'd hoped, their escape was covered by the explosion.

The lifepod was very, very cramped. Han managed to get his helmet off, then he and Chewie just crouched there, almost in each other's arms, and stared at each other, then back at the flaming debris that had been their ship.

"Lando isn't gonna like this," Han said ruefully. The *Bria* had been a cranky, temperamental ship, but he'd kind of gotten used to her.

Chewie growled softly in Wookiee. Han looked at him and shrugged. "What do we do now? Your guess is as good as mine, pal. This is an inhabited system, so the lifepod controls ought to soft-land us somewhere near where we can get a transport . . ."

Chewie whined. "Oh, you mean what will we do for a *ship*?" Han sighed. "That's a real good question, pal . . ."

He's dead, Teroenza thought in disbelief, looking at the message from Nal Hutta. *It worked. I can't believe Aruk's really gone!*

For just a moment he felt a tiny prickle of guilt, but it was swiftly drowned in excitement. With Aruk out of the way, and Desilijic's credits pouring in, nothing could stop him from taking over complete control of the entire Ylesian operation. Durga was back on Nal Hutta, with his hands full trying to control Besadii. Kibbick was, as everyone knew, an idiot.

Teroenza pictured his collection, and then pictured it as it would be soon. He would build a separate building to house it!

And he would bring his mate here. No more lonely days and nights. They would slosh in the mud wallows together, rich beyond their wildest dreams . . .

Teroenza spent several minutes putting on a suitably lugubrious expression, then the t'landa Til went off to find Kibbick, and inform him that his uncle was dead . . .

Moff Sarn Shild sat alone in his palatial home on Teth, wondering just what had gone wrong. The attack on Nal Hutta had obviously been a huge mistake. Greelanx—Greelanx had failed, and now the admiral was dead under suspicious circumstances.

Shild was alone in his house, save for the droids. All his living servants were gone, he knew not where. Bria . . . she was gone, too, had disappeared days ago.

She hadn't even said good-bye . . .

Yesterday, the Emperor had summoned Shild back to Imperial Center, to face a board of inquiry about the ill-fated attack on the Y'Toub system. Palpatine's message had made it clear that the Emperor was *most* displeased.

Shild sat alone, struggling to comprehend it all. Scant days ago, he'd been on top of the galaxy. Now he couldn't even remember *why* he'd done the things he'd done. It was almost as though he'd been possessed by an alien entity.

Shild stared down at his ornate desk. Before him lay a blaster, side by side with a vial of poison. Shild took a deep breath. He had no illusions anymore. Traveling to Imperial Center would only prolong the inevitable.

Anything would be better than facing Palpatine's wrath.

But which should he use, the blaster or the poison?

Shild considered for a while, but couldn't make up his mind. Finally, in desperation, he fell back on a childhood memory. Moving his finger from one means of death (and escape) to the other, he began to chant aloud: "Wonga, winga, cingee wooze . . . which of these do I choose?"

Epilogue

I t was strange, being back on Corellia after all these years
away, Han thought, six months later. The streets were
both familiar and strange, comforting and threatening.
Bad things had happened to him on his homeworld, lots of
bad things . . .

But maybe, just maybe, his luck was about to change. As
he walked down the street, Han patted his pocket, which
held the little dragon pearl, and a small gold statuette with
ruby eyes. It was a palador, an extinct Corellian animal.
Years ago, Han had cached the statuette, which he'd stolen
from Teroenza's collection, in a safe place on his
homeworld.

Now he planned to fence both the statuette and the

dragon pearl. He figured that, together, they were worth about ten thousand credits. The big sabacc game on Bespin would be held in ten days . . .

Han was relieved to find that Galidon Okanor's shop was still there. Okanor paid top dollar, though, like all fences, he liked to haggle.

Ten thousand credits, Han thought. *Never thought I'd be desperate enough to risk it all on one high-stakes sabacc game . . . especially if I'm playing against a sharpie like Lando . . .*

But he *had* to have a ship of his own. And he could think of no other way to get the credits to buy one.

Han paused outside Okanor's door to take a deep breath. *Here goes nothing . . .*

Then, clutching his hopes and dreams in a sweaty hand, he opened the door and walked in . . .

ABOUT THE AUTHOR

Ann C. Crispin is the bestselling author of more than sixteen books, including four *Star Trek* novels and her original *StarBridge* science fiction series.

Her first appearance in the *Star Wars* universe came when her friend Kevin Anderson asked her to write two short stories for the *Star Wars* anthologies, *Tales from the Mos Eisley Cantina* and *Tales from Jabba's Palace.*

Ann has been a full-time writer since 1983 and currently serves as Eastern Regional Director of the Science Fiction and Fantasy Writers of America. She is a frequent guest at science fiction conventions, where she often teaches writing workshops.

She lives in Maryland with her son, Jason, five cats, a German shepherd, two Appaloosas, and Michael Capobianco, a writer of hard sf. In her spare time (what's that?) she enjoys horseback riding, sailing, camping, and reading books she didn't write.

Her forthcoming works include the seventh novel in her *StarBridge* series, *Voices of Chaos* (co-authored with Ru Emerson), and *The Exiles of Boq'urain,* a fantasy trilogy from Avon Books.

The World of
STAR WARS Novels

In May 1991, *Star Wars* caused a sensation in the publishing industry
with the Bantam release of Timothy Zahn's novel *Heir to the Empire*.
For the first time, Lucasfilm Ltd. had authorized new novels that
continued the famous story told in George Lucas's three block-buster
motion pictures: *Star Wars*, *The Empire Strikes Back*, and *Return of
the Jedi*. Reader reaction was immediate and tumultuous: *Heir*
reached No. 1 on the *New York Times* bestseller list and demonstrated
that *Star Wars* lovers were eager for exciting new stories set in this
universe, written by leading science fiction authors who shared their
passion. Since then, each Bantam *Star Wars* novel has been an instant
national bestseller.

Luasfilm and Bantam decided that future novels in the series would
be interconnected: that is, events in one novel would have
consequences in the others. You might say that each Bantam Star
Wars novel, enjoyable on its own, is also part of a much larger tale.

Here is a special look at Bantam's *Star Wars* books, along with
excerpts from the more recent novels. Each one is available now
wherever Bantam Books are sold.

The Han Solo Trilogy:
THE PARADISE SNARE
THE HUTT GAMBIT
and coming soon
REBEL DAWN
by A. C. Crispin
Setting: Before *Star Wars: A New Hope*

*What was Han Solo like before we met him in the first STAR WARS
movie? This trilogy answers that tantalizing question, filling in lots of
historical lore about our favorite swashbuckling hero and thrilling us
with adventures of the brash young pilot that we never knew he'd
experienced. As the trilogy begins, the young Han makes a life-
changing decision: to escape from the clutches of Garris Shrike, head
of the trading "clan" who has brutalized Han while taking advantage
of his piloting abilities. Here's a tense early scene from* The Paradise
Snare *featuring Han, Shrike, and Dewlanna, a Wookiee who is Han's
only friend in this horrible situation:*

"I've had it with you, Solo. I've been lenient with you so far, because you're a blasted good swoop pilot and all that prize money came in handy, but my patience is ended." Shrike ceremoniously pushed up the sleeves of his bedizened uniform, then balled his hands into fists. The galley's artificial lighting made the blood-jewel ring glitter dull silver. "Let's see what a few days of fighting off Devaronian blood-poisoning does for your attitude—along with maybe a few broken bones. I'm doing this for your own good, boy. Someday you'll thank me."

Han gulped with terror as Shrike started toward him. He'd lashed out at the trader captain once before, two years ago, when he'd been feeling cocky after winning the gladitorial Free-For-All on Jubilar—and had been instantly sorry. The speed and strength of Garris's returning blow had snapped his head back and split both lips so thoroughly that Dewlanna had had to feed him mush for a week until they healed.

With a snarl, Dewlanna stepped forward. Shrike's hand dropped to his blaster. "You stay out of this, old Wookiee," he snapped in a voice nearly as harsh as Dewlanna's. "Your cooking isn't *that* good."

Han had already grabbed his friend's furry arm and was forcibly holding her back. "Dewlanna, no!"

She shook off his hold as easily as she would have waved off an annoying insect and roared at Shrike. The captain drew his blaster, and chaos erupted.

"Noooo!" Han screamed, and leaped forward, his foot lashing out in an old street-fighting technique. His instep impacted solidly with Shrike's breastbone. The captain's breath went out in a great *houf!* and he went over backward. Han hit the deck and rolled. A tingler bolt sizzled past his ear.

"Larrad!" wheezed the captain as Dewlanna started toward him.

Shrike's brother drew his blaster and pointed it at the Wookiee. "Stop, Dewlanna!"

His words had no more effect than Han's. Dewlanna's blood was up—she was in full Wookiee battle rage. With a roar that deafened the combatants, she grabbed Larrad's wrist and yanked, spinning him around and snapping him in a terrible parody of a child's "snap the whip" game. Han heard a *crunch,* mixed with several *pops* as tendons and ligaments gave way. Larrad Shrike shrieked, a high, shrill noise that carried such pain that the Corellian youth's arm ached in sympathy.

Grabbing the blaster from his belt, Han snapped off a shot at the Elomin who was leaping forward, tingler ready and aimed at Dewlanna's midsection. Brafid howled, dropping his weapon. Han was amazed that he'd managed to hit him, but he didn't have long to wonder about the accuracy of his aim.

Shrike was staggering to his feet, blaster in hand, aimed squarely at Han's head. "Larrad?" he yelled at the writhing heap of agony that was his brother. Larrad did not reply.

Shrike cocked the blaster and stepped even closer to Han. "Stop it, Dewlanna!" the captain snarled at the Wookiee. "Or your buddy Solo dies!"

Han dropped his blaster and put his hands up in a gesture of surrender.

Dewlanna stopped in her tracks, growling softly.

Shrike leveled the blaster, and his finger tightened on the trigger. Pure malevolent hatred was etched upon his features, and then he smiled, pale blue eyes glittering with ruthless joy. "For insubordination and striking your captain," he announced, "I sentence you to death, Solo. May you rot in all the hells there ever were."

SHADOWS OF THE EMPIRE
by Steve Perry
Setting: Between *The Empire Strikes Back*
and *Return of the Jedi*

Here is a very special STAR WARS story dealing with Black Sun, a galaxy-spanning criminal organization that is masterminded by one of the most interesting villains in the STAR WARS universe: Xizor, dark prince of the Falleen. Xizor's chief rival for the favor of Emperor Palpatine is none other than Darth Vader himself—alive and well, and a major character in this story, since it is set during the events of the STAR WARS film trilogy.

In the opening prologue, we revisit a familiar scene from The Empire Strikes Back, *and are introduced to our marvelous new bad guy:*

He looks like a walking corpse, Xizor thought. *Like a mummified body dead a thousand years. Amazing he is still alive, much less the most powerful man in the galaxy. He isn't even that old; it is more as if something is slowly eating him.*

Xizor stood four meters away from the Emperor, watching as the man who had long ago been Senator Palpatine moved to stand in the holocam field. He imagined he could smell the decay in the Emperor's worn body. Likely that was just some trick of the recycled air, run through dozens of filters to ensure that there was no chance of any poison gas being introduced into it. Filtered the life out of it, perhaps, giving it that dead smell.

The viewer on the other end of the holo-link would see a close-up of the Emperor's head and shoulders, of an age-ravaged face shrouded in the cowl of his dark zeyd-cloth robe. The man on the other end of the transmission, light-years away, would not see Xizor, though Xizor would be able to see him. It was a measure of the Emperor's trust that Xizor was allowed to be here while the conversation took place.

The man on the other end of the transmission—if he could still be called that—

The air swirled inside the Imperial chamber in front of the Emperor, coalesced, and blossomed into the image of a figure down on one knee. A caped humanoid biped dressed in jet black, face hidden under a full helmet and breathing mask:

Darth Vader.

Vader spoke: ''What is thy bidding, my master?''

If Xizor could have hurled a power bolt through time and space to strike Vader dead, he would have done it without blinking. Wishful thinking: Vader was too powerful to attack directly.

''There is a great disturbance in the Force,'' the Emperor said.

''I have felt it,'' Vader said.

''We have a new enemy. Luke Skywalker.''

Skywalker? That had been Vader's name, a long time ago. Who was this person with the same name, someone so powerful as to be worth a conversation between the Emperor and his most loathsome creation? More importantly, why had Xizor's agents not uncovered this before now? Xizor's ire was instant—but cold. No sign of his surprise or anger would show on his imperturbable features. The Falleen did not allow their emotions to burst forth as did many of the inferior species; no, the Falleen ancestry was not fur but scales, not mammalian but reptilian. Not wild but coolly calculating. Such was much better. Much safer.

''Yes, my master,'' Vader continued.

''He could destroy us,'' the Emperor said.

Xizor's attention was riveted upon the Emperor and the holographic image of Vader kneeling on the deck of a ship far away. Here was interesting news indeed. Something the Emperor perceived as a danger to himself? Something the Emperor feared?

''He's just a boy,'' Vader said. ''Obi-Wan can no longer help him.''

Obi-Wan. That name Xizor knew. He was among the last of the Jedi Knights, a general. But he'd been dead for decades, hadn't he?

Apparently Xizor's information was wrong if Obi-Wan had been helping someone who was still a boy. His agents were going to be sorry.

Even as Xizor took in the distant image of Vader and the nearness of the Emperor, even as he was aware of the luxury of the Emperor's private and protected chamber at the core of the giant pyramidal palace, he was also able to make a mental note to himself: Somebody's head would roll for the failure to make him aware of all this. Knowledge was power; lack of knowledge was weakness. This was something he could not permit.

The Emperor continued. "The Force is strong with him. The son of Skywalker must not become a Jedi."

Son of Skywalker?

Vader's son! Amazing!

"If he could be turned he would become a powerful ally," Vader said.

There was something in Vader's voice when he said this, something Xizor could not quite put his finger on. Longing? Worry?

Hope?

"Yes . . . yes. He would be a great asset," the Emperor said. "Can it be done?"

There was the briefest of pauses. "He will join us or die, master."

Xizor felt the smile, though he did not allow it to show any more than he had allowed his anger play. Ah. Vader wanted Skywalker alive, *that* was what had been in his tone. Yes, he had said that the boy would join them or die, but this latter part was obviously meant only to placate the Emperor. Vader had no intention of killing Skywalker, his own son; that was obvious to one as skilled in reading voices as was Xizor. He had not gotten to be the Dark Prince, Underlord of Black Sun, the largest criminal organization in the galaxy, merely on his formidable good looks. Xizor didn't truly understand the Force that sustained the Emperor and made him and Vader so powerful, save to know that it certainly worked somehow. But he did know that it was something the extinct Jedi had supposedly mastered. And now, apparently, this new player had tapped into it. Vader wanted Skywalker alive, had practically promised the Emperor that he would deliver him alive—and converted.

This was most interesting.

Most interesting indeed.

The Emperor finished his communication and turned back to face him. "Now, where were we, Prince Xizor?"

The Dark Prince smiled. He would attend to the business at hand, but he would not forget the name of Luke Skywalker.

THE TRUCE AT BAKURA by Kathy Tyers
Setting: Immediately after *Return of the Jedi*

The day after his climactic battle with Emperor Palpatine and the sacrifice of his father, Darth Vader, who died saving his life, Luke Skywalker helps recover an Imperial drone ship bearing a startling message intended for the Emperor. It is a distress signal from the far-off Imperial outpost of Bakura, which is under attack by an alien invasion force, the Ssi-ruuk. Leia sees a rescue mission as an opportunity to achieve a diplomatic victory for the Rebel Alliance, even if it means fighting alongside former Imperials. But Luke receives a vision from Obi-Wan Kenobi revealing that the stakes are even higher: the invasion at Bakura threatens everything the Rebels have won at such great cost.

STAR WARS: X-WING
by Michael A. Stackpole
ROGUE SQUADRON
WEDGE'S GAMBLE
THE KRYTOS TRAP
THE BACTA WAR
Setting: Three years
after *Return of the Jedi*

Inspired by X-wing, the bestselling computer game from LucasArts Entertainment Co., this exciting series chronicles the further adventures of the most feared and fearless fighting force in the galaxy. A new generation of X-wing pilots, led by Commander Wedge Antilles, is combating the remnants of the Empire still left after the events of the STAR WARS movies. Here are novels full of explosive space action, nonstop adventure, and the special brand of wonder known as STAR WARS.

In this very early scene, young Corellian pilot Corran Horn faces a tough challenge fast enough to get his heart pounding—and this is only a simulation! [P.S.: "Whistler" is Corran's R2 astromech droid]:

The Corellian brought his proton torpedo targeting program up and locked on to the TIE. It tried to break the lock, but turbolaser fire from the *Korolev* boxed it in. Corran's heads-up display went red and he triggered the torpedo. "Scratch one eyeball."

The missile shot straight in at the fighter, but the pilot broke hard to port and away, causing the missile to overshoot the target. *Nice flying!* Corran brought his X-wing over and started down to loop in behind the TIE, but as he did so, the TIE vanished from his forward screen and reappeared in his aft arc. Yanking the stick hard to the right and pulling it back, Corran wrestled the X-wing up and to starboard, then inverted and rolled out to the left.

A laser shot jolted a tremor through the simulator's couch. *Lucky thing I had all shields aft!* Corran reinforced them with energy from his lasers, then evened them out fore and aft. Jinking the fighter right and left, he avoided laser shots coming in from behind, but they all came in far closer than he liked.

He knew Jace had been in the bomber, and Jace was the only pilot in the unit who could have stayed with him. *Except for our leader.* Corran smiled broadly. *Coming to see how good I really am, Commander Antilles? Let me give you a clinic.* "Make sure you're in there solid, Whistler, because we're going for a little ride."

Corran refused to let the R2's moan slow him down. A snap-roll brought the X-wing up on its port wing. Pulling back on the stick yanked the fighter's nose up away from the original line of flight. The TIE stayed with him, then tightened up on the arc to close distance. Corran then rolled another ninety degrees and continued the turn into a dive. Throttling back, Corran hung in the dive for three seconds, then hauled back hard on the stick and cruised up into the TIE fighter's aft.

The X-wing's laser fire missed wide to the right as the TIE cut to the left. Corran kicked his speed up to full and broke with the TIE. He let the X-wing rise above the plane of the break, then put the fighter through a twisting roll that ate up enough time to bring him again into the TIE's rear. The TIE snapped to the right and Corran looped out left.

He watched the tracking display as the distance between them grew to be a kilometer and a half, then slowed. *Fine, you want to go nose to nose? I've got shields and you don't.* If Commander Antilles wanted to commit virtual suicide, Corran was happy to oblige him. He tugged the stick back to his sternum and rolled out in an inversion loop. *Coming at you!*

The two starfighters closed swiftly. Corran centered his foe in the crosshairs and waited for a dead shot. Without shields the TIE fighter would die with one burst, and Corran wanted the kill to be clean. His HUD flicked green as the TIE juked in and out of the center, then locked green as they closed.

The TIE started firing at maximum range and scored hits. At that distance the lasers did no real damage against the shields, prompting Corran to wonder why Wedge was wasting the energy. Then, as the HUD's green color started to flicker, realization dawned. *The bright bursts on the shields are a distraction to my targeting! I better kill him now!*

Corran tightened down on the trigger button, sending red laser needles stabbing out at the closing TIE fighter. He couldn't tell if he had hit anything. Lights flashed in the cockpit and Whistler started screeching furiously. Corran's main monitor went black, his shields were down, and his weapons controls were dead.

The pilot looked left and right. "Where is he, Whistler?"

The monitor in front of him flickered to life and a diagnostic report began to scroll by. Bloodred bordered the damage reports. "Scanners, out; lasers, out; shields, out; engine, out! I'm a wallowing Hutt just hanging here in space."

THE COURTSHIP OF PRINCESS LEIA
by Dave Wolverton
Setting: Four yars after *Return of the Jedi*

One of the most intersting developments in Bantam's STAR WARS novels is that in their storyline, Han Solo and Princess Leia start a family. This tale reveals how the couple originally got together. Wishing to strengthen the fledgling New Republic by bringing in powerful allies, Leia opens talks with the Hapes consortium of more than sixty worlds. But the consortium is ruled by the Queen Mother, who, to Han's dismay, wants Leia to marry her son, Prince Isolder. Before this action-packed story is over, Luke will join forces with Isolder against a group of Force-trained "witches" and face a deadly foe.

HEIR TO THE EMPIRE
DARK FORCE RISING
THE LAST COMMAND
by Timothy Zahn
Setting: Five years after *Return of the Jedi*

This No. 1 bestselling trilogy introduces two legendary forces of evil into the STAR WARS literary pantheon. Grand Admiral Thrawn has taken control of the Imperial fleet in the years since the destruction of the Death Star, and the mysterious Joruus C'baoth is a fearsome Jedi Master who has been seduced by the dark side. Han and Leia have now been married for about a year, and as the story begins, she is pregnant with twins. Thrawn's plan is to crush the Rebellion and resurrect the Empire's New Order with C'baoth's help—and in return, the Dark Master will get Han and Leia's Jedi children to mold as he wishes. For as readers of this magnificent trilogy will see, Luke Skywalker is not the last of the old Jedi. He is the first of the new.

The Jedi Academy Trilogy:
JEDI SEARCH
DARK APPRENTICE
CHAMPIONS OF THE FORCE
by Kevin J. Anderson
Setting: Seven years after *Return of the Jedi*

In order to assure the continuation of the Jedi Knights, Luke Skywalker has decided to start a training facility: a Jedi Academy. He will gather Force-sensitive students who show potential as prospective Jedi and serve as their mentor, as Jedi Masters Obi-Wan Kenobi and Yoda did for him. Han and Leia's twins are now toddlers, and there is a third Jedi child: the infant Anakin, named after Luke and Leia's father. In this trilogy, we discover the existence of a powerful Imperial doomsday weapon, the horrifying Sun Crusher—which will soon become the centerpiece of a titanic struggle between Luke Skywalker and his most brilliant Jedi Academy student, who is delving dangerously into the dark side.

CHILDREN OF THE JEDI
by Barbara Hambly
Setting: Eight years after *Return of the Jedi*

The STAR WARS characters face a menace from the glory days of the Empire when a thirty-year-old automated Imperial Dreadnaught comes to life and begins its grim mission: to gather forces and annihilate a long-forgotten stronghold of Jedi children. When Luke is whisked onboard, he begins to communicate with the brave Jedi Knight who paralyzed the ship decades ago, and gave her life in the process. Now she is part of the vessel, existing in its artificial intelligence core, and guiding Luke through one of the most unusual adventures he has ever had.

DARKSABER by Kevin J. Anderson
Setting: Immediately thereafter

Not long after Children of the Jedi, *Luke and Han learn that evil Hutts are building a reconstruction of the original Death Star—and that the Empire is still alive, in the form of Daala, who has joined forces with Pellaeon, former second in command to the feared Grand Admiral Thrawn. In this early scene, Luke has returned to the home of Obi-Wan Kenobi on Tatooine to try and consult a long-gone mentor:*

He stood anxious and alone, feeling like a prodigal son outside the ramshackle, collapsed hut that had once been the home of Obi-Wan Kenobi.

Luke swallowed and stepped forward, his footsteps crunching in the silence. He had not been here in many years. The door had fallen off its hinges; part of the clay front wall had fallen in. Boulders and crumbled adobe jammed the entrance. A pair of small, screeching desert rodents snapped at him and fled for cover; Luke ignored them.

Gingerly, he ducked low and stepped into the home of his first mentor.

Luke stood in the middle of the room breathing deeply, turning around, trying to sense the presence he desperately needed to see. This was the place where Obi-Wan Kenobi had told Luke of the Force. Here, the old man had first given Luke his lightsaber and hinted at the truth about his father, "from a certain point of view," dispelling the diversionary story that Uncle Owen had told, at the same time planting seeds of his own deceptions.

"Ben," he said and closed his eyes, calling out with his mind as well as his voice. He tried to penetrate the invisible walls of the Force and reach to the luminous being of Obi-Wan Kenobi who had visited him numerous times, before saying he could never speak with Luke again.

"Ben, I need you," Luke said. Circumstances had changed. He could think of no other way past the obstacles he faced. Obi-Wan had to answer. It wouldn't take long, but it could give him the key he needed with all his heart.

Luke paused and listened and sensed—

But felt nothing. If he could not summon Obi-Wan's spirit here in the empty dwelling where the old man had lived in exile for so many years, Luke didn't believe he could find his former teacher ever again.

He echoed the words Leia had used more than a decade earlier, beseeching him, "Help me, Obi-Wan Kenobi," Luke whispered, "you're my only hope."

THE CRYSTAL STAR
by Vonda N. McIntyre
Setting: Ten years after *Return of the Jedi*

Leia's three children have been kidnapped. That horrible fact is made worse by Leia's realization that she can no longer sense her children through the Force! While she, Artoo-Detoo, and Chewbacca trail the kidnappers, Luke and Han discover a planet that is suffering strange quantum effects from a nearby star. Slowly freezing into a perfect crystal and disrupting the Force, the star is blunting Luke's power and crippling the Millennium Falcon. *These strands converge in an apocalyptic threat not only to the fate of the New Republic, but to the universe itself.*

The Black Fleet Crisis
BEFORE THE STORM
SHIELD OF LIES
TYRANT'S TEST
by Michael P. Kube-McDowell
Setting: Twelve years after *Return of the Jedi*

Long after setting up the hard-won New Republic, yesterday's Rebels have become today's administrators and diplomats. But the peace is not to last for long. A restless Luke must journey to his mother's homeworld in a desperate quest to find her people; Lando seizes a mysterious spacecraft with unimaginable weapons of destruction; and waiting in the wings is an horrific battle fleet under the control of a ruthless leader bent on a genocidal war.

Here is an opening scene from Before the Storm:

In the pristine silence of space, the Fifth Battle Group of the New Republic Defense Fleet blossomed over the planet Bessimir like a beautiful, deadly flower.

The formation of capital ships sprang into view with startling suddenness, trailing fire-white wakes of twisted space and bristling with weapons. Angular Star Destroyers guarded fat-hulled fleet carriers, while the assault cruisers, their mirror finishes gleaming, took the point.

A halo of smaller ships appeared at the same time. The fighters among them quickly deployed in a spherical defensive screen. As the Star Destroyers firmed up their formation, their flight decks quickly spawned scores of additional fighters.

At the same time, the carriers and cruisers began to disgorge the bombers, transports, and gunboats they had ferried to the battle. There was no reason to risk the loss of one fully loaded—a lesson the Republic had learned in pain. At Orinda, the commander of the fleet carrier *Endurance* had kept his pilots waiting in the launch bays, to protect the smaller craft from Imperial fire as long as possible. They were still there when *Endurance* took the brunt of a Super Star Destroyer attack and vanished in a ball of metal fire.

Before long more than two hundred warships, large and small, were bearing down on Bessimir and its twin moons. But the terrible, restless power of the armada could be heard and felt only by the ships' crews. The silence of the approach was broken only on the fleet comm channels, which had crackled to life in the first moments with encoded bursts of noise and cryptic ship-to-ship chatter.

At the center of the formation of great vessels was the flagship of the Fifth Battle Group, the fleet carrier *Intrepid*. She was so new from the yards at Hakassi that her corridors still reeked of sealing compound and cleaning solvent. Her huge realspace thruster engines still sang with the high-pitched squeal that the engine crews called "the baby's cry."

It would take more than a year for the mingled scents of the crew to displace the chemical smells from the first impressions of visitors. But after a hundred more hours under way, her engines' vibrations would drop two octaves, to the reassuring thrum of a seasoned thruster bank.

On *Intrepid*'s bridge, a tall Dornean in general's uniform paced along an arc of command stations equipped with large monitors. His eye-folds were swollen and fanned by an unconscious Dornean defensive reflex, and his leathery face was flushed purple by concern. Before the deployment was even a minute old, Etahn A'baht's first command had been bloodied.

The fleet tender *Ahazi* had overshot its jump, coming out of hyperspace too close to Bessimir and too late for its crew to recover from the error. Etahn A'baht watched the bright flare of light in the upper atmosphere from *Intrepid*'s forward viewstation, knowing that it meant six young men were dead.

THE NEW REBELLION
by Kristine Kathryn Rusch
Setting: Thirteen years after *Return of the Jedi*

Victorious though the New Republic may be, there is still no end to the threats to its continuing existence—this novel explores the price of keeping the peace. First, somewhere in the galaxy, millions suddenly perish in a blinding instant of pain. Then, as Leia prepares to address the Senate on Coruscant, a horrifying event changes the governmental equation in a flash.

Here is that latter calamity, in an early scene from The New Rebellion:

An explosion rocked the Chamber, flinging Leia into the air. She flew backward and slammed onto a desk, her entire body shuddering with the power of her hit. Blood and shrapnel rained around her. Smoke and dust rose, filling the room with a grainy darkness. She could hear nothing. With a shaking hand, she touched the side of her face. Warmth stained her cheeks and her earlobes. The ringing would start soon. The explosion was loud enough to affect her eardrums.

Emergency glow panels seared the gloom. She could feel rather than hear pieces of the crystal ceiling fall to the ground. A guard had landed beside her, his head tilted at an unnatural angle. She grabbed his blaster. She had to get out. She wasn't certain if the attack had come from within or from without. Wherever it had come from, she had to make certain no other bombs would go off.

The force of the explosion had affected her balance. She crawled over bodies, some still moving, as she made her way to the stairs. The slightest movement made her dizzy and nauseous, but she ignored the feelings. She had to.

A face loomed before hers. Streaked with dirt and blood, helmet askew, she recognized him as one of the guards who had been with her since Alderaan. *Your Highness*, he mouthed, and she couldn't read the rest. She shook her head at him, gasping at the increased dizziness, and kept going.

Finally she reached the stairs. She used the remains of a desk to get to her feet. Her gown was soaked in blood, sticky, and clinging to her legs. She held the blaster in front of her, wishing that she could hear. If she could hear, she could defend herself.

A hand reached out of the rubble beside her. She whirled, faced it, watched as Meido pulled himself out. His slender features were covered with dirt, but he appeared unharmed. He saw her blaster and cringed. She nodded once to acknowledge him, and kept moving. The guard was flanking her.

More rubble dropped from the ceiling. She crouched, hands over her head to protect herself. Small pebbles pelted her, and the floor shivered as large chunks of tile fell. Dust rose, choking her. She coughed, feeling it, but not able to hear it. Within an instant, the Hall had gone from a place of ceremonial comfort to a place of death.

The image of the death's-head mask rose in front of her again, this time from memory. She had known this was going to happen. Somewhere, from some part of her Force-sensitive brain, she had seen this. Luke said that Jedi were sometimes able to see the future. But she had never completed her training. She wasn't a Jedi.

But she was close enough.

The Corellian Trilogy:
AMBUSH AT CORELLIA
ASSAULT AT SELONIA
SHOWDOWN AT CENTERPOINT
by Roger MacBride Allen
Setting: Fourteen years after *Return of the Jedi*

This trilogy takes us to Corellia, Han Solo's homeworld, which Han has not visited in quite some time. A trade summit brings Han, Leia, and the children—now developing their own clear personalities and instinctively learning more about their innate skills in the Force—into the middle of a situation that most closely resembles a burning fuse. The Corellian system is on the brink of civil war, there are New Republic intelligence agents on a mysterious mission which even Han does not understand, and worst of all, a fanatical rebel leader has his hands on a superweapon of unimaginable power—and just wait until you find out who that leader is!

Here is an early scene from Ambush *that gives you a wonderful look at the growing Solo children (the twins are Jacen and Jaina, and their little brother is Anakin):*

Anakin plugged the board into the innards of the droid and pressed a button. The droid's black, boxy body shuddered awake, it drew in its wheels to stand up a bit taller, its status lights lit, and it made a sort of triple beep. "That's good," he said, and pushed the button again. The droid's status lights went out, and its body slumped down again. Anakin picked up the next piece, a motivation actuator. He frowned at it as he turned it over in his hands. He shook his head. "That's *not* good," he announced.

"What's not good?" Jaina asked.

"This thing," Anakin said, handing her the actuator. "Can't you *tell*? The insides part is all melty."

Jaina and Jacen exchanged a look. "The outside looks okay," Jaina said, giving the part to her brother. "How can he tell what the *inside* of it looks like? It's sealed shut when they make it."

Anakin, still sitting on the floor, took the device from his brother and frowned at it again. He turned it over and over in his hands, and then held it over his head and looked at it as if he were holding it up to the light. "There," he said, pointing a chubby finger at one point on the unmarked surface. "In there is the bad part." He rearranged himself to sit cross-legged, put the actuator in his lap, and put his right index finger over the "bad" part. "Fix," he said. "Fix." The dark brown outer case of the actuator seemed to glow for a second with an odd blue-red light, but then the glow sputtered out and Anakin pulled his finger away quickly and stuck it in his mouth, as if he had burned it on something.

"Better now?" Jaina asked.

"*Some* better," Anakin said, pulling his finger out of his mouth. "Not *all* better." He took the actuator in his hand and stood up. He opened the access panel on the broken droid and plugged in the actuator. He closed the door and looked expectantly at his older brother and sister.

"Done?" Jaina asked.

"Done," Anakin agreed. "But *I'm* not going to push the button." He backed well away from the droid, sat down on the floor, and folded his arms.

Jacen looked at his sister.

"Not me," she said. "This was your idea."

Jacen stepped forward to the droid, reached out to push the power button from as far away as he could, and then stepped hurriedly back.

Once again, the droid shuddered awake, rattling a bit this time as it did so. It pulled its wheels in, lit its panel lights, and made the same triple beep. But then its holocam eye viewlens wobbled back and forth, and its panel lights dimmed and flared. It rolled backward just a bit, and then recovered itself.

"Good morning, young mistress and masters," it said. "How may I surge you?"

Well, one word wrong, but so what? Jacen grinned and clapped his hands and rubbed them together eagerly. "Good day, droid," he said. They had done it! But what to ask for first? "First tidy up this room," he said. A simple task, and one that ought to serve as a good test of what this droid could do.

Suddenly the droid's overhead access door blew off and there was a flash of light from its interior. A thin plume of smoke drifted out of the droid. Its panel lights flared again, and then the work arm sagged downward. The droid's body, softened by heat, sagged in on itself and drooped to the floor. The floor and walls and ceiling of the playroom were supposed to be fireproof, but nonetheless the floor under the droid darkened a bit, and the ceiling turned black. The ventilators kicked on high automatically, and drew the smoke out of the room. After a moment they shut themselves off, and the room was silent.

The three children stood, every bit as frozen to the spot as the droid was, absolutely stunned. It was Anakin who recovered first. He walked cautiously toward the droid and looked at it carefully, being sure not to get too close or touch it. "*Really* melty now," he announced, and then wandered off to the other side of the room to play with his blocks.

The twins looked at the droid, and then at each other.

"We're dead," Jacen announced, surveying the wreckage.